P9-DNU-332

DISCOVER

READ

EXPLORE

LEARN

NEW HANOVER COUNTY
PUBLIC LIBRARY

If found, please return to:
201 Chestnut St.
Wilmington, NC 28401
(910) 798-6300
http://www.nhclibrary.org

COME WITH ME

Also by Helen Schulman

This Beautiful Life

A Day at the Beach

P.S.

The Revisionist

Out of Time

Not a Free Show

Wanting a Child

(coedited with Jill Bialosky)

COME WITH ME

A NOVEL

HELEN SCHULMAN

**NEW HANOVER COUNTY
PUBLIC LIBRARY
201 CHESTNUT STREET
WILMINGTON, NC 28401**

HARPER

An Imprint of HarperCollins*Publishers*

This is a work of fiction. Names, characters, places, and incidents are products of the author's imagination or are used fictitiously and are not to be construed as real. Any resemblance to actual events, locales, organizations, or persons, living or dead, is entirely coincidental.

COME WITH ME. Copyright © 2018 by Helen Schulman. All rights reserved. Printed in the United States of America. No part of this book may be used or reproduced in any manner whatsoever without written permission except in the case of brief quotations embodied in critical articles and reviews. For information, address HarperCollins Publishers, 195 Broadway, New York, NY 10007.

HarperCollins books may be purchased for educational, business, or sales promotional use. For information, please email the Special Markets Department at SPsales@harpercollins.com.

Brenda Shaughnessy, excerpt from "Drift" from *Human Dark with Sugar*. Copyright © 2008 by Brenda Shaughnessy. Reprinted with the permission of The Permissions Company, Inc., on behalf of Copper Canyon Press, www.coppercanyonpress.org.

FIRST EDITION

Designed by Bonni Leon-Berman

Library of Congress Cataloging-in-Publication Data

Schulman, Helen.
Come with me : a novel / Helen Schulman.
p. cm.
ISBN 978-0-06-245913-8
1. Fiction—Family life. 2. Fiction—Psychological.
PS3569.C5385 C66 2018
813'.54—dc23   2018043839

18 19 20 21 22 LSC 10 9 8 7 6 5 4 3 2 1

To Sloan Harris,
cherished reader, partner in crime

I'll go anywhere to leave you but come with me.
All the cities are like you anyway.

—BRENDA SHAUGHNESSY, "DRIFT"

COME WITH ME

I'M GAME," SHE SAID. "I'M IN."

She pushed her sunglasses up onto the top of her head. The super-bendy photochromic lenses were constructed out of something called NXT, which had been invented by the army. Designed for battle, this pair was also great for trail running, deflecting slingshotting branches from scratching her eyes out, and mitigating the rapid-fire one-two shock of shadow and blazing sunshine during high-intensity sprints in the woods. Now she was using the sunnies as a headband; they pulled the escaping wet wisps of her ponytail off her forehead and behind her ears. Still, she rewrapped and twisted the whole sweaty, tangled, mess up into a bun so it was high off her neck, and sat the glasses on top again, too. A little plastic crown.

"What do you want to know?" he said. He was tapping on his smartphone. His feet, in Adidas flip-flops, were tapping along with his fingers.

"When I was your age, I wanted to eat the world," she said. "Love, heartbreak, I wanted to feel it all."

He didn't look up. Why should he? He wasn't a feelings kind of guy. He was forever young, at least at that moment, so this was boring and he wasn't listening anyway. She sounded like someone's Aunt Sadie; she wouldn't listen to herself. "Then for a long time, I didn't want to feel any of it. But now I am at a point."

They were meeting on campus. Tresidder Union. She'd insisted. She didn't want to have this conversation at the office. It was 11:00 a.m., on a Saturday, spring quarter, most of the coders probably had already stumbled their way out of the dining halls and onto their bikes and then off their bikes and into work. Sometimes some of them didn't even bother returning to the dorms on Friday nights, they slept in the office on the couches, arm wrestling over the hammock, the beanbag chairs.

She pulled her shorts down farther on her legs. The flesh of her thighs was sticking to the metal lattice of her seat and she could feel it puffing like Play-Doh through the grille. The morning was growing warm. Good thing she'd already finished her workout. They sat outside on the deck of the student union at a round white table with three red wiry chairs surrounding it, leaving one empty; now he was using it as a footrest. These oddly floral configurations dotted the cement terrace in a utilitarian, but somewhat attractive manner. Very Marimekko. Most of the seats were already occupied, the sun was bright and the air was dry. Kids on their computers, their iPhones. Profs on their computers, their iPhones. Some older guys, nerdy in bike helmets, with short-sleeved button-down shirts and even pocket protectors, were reading actual newspapers. At the base of the steps, a young Korean mother was sharing her muffin with her toddler twin girls. So cute, they each wore matching hickory striped overalls, and pigtails, although the one in the red T-shirt had one plait that went north and the other south, like a cockeyed weather vane.

She remembered those days—there never was enough muffin to go around, there was never much left over for her. She was thinner then.

They'd met at the Starbucks inside. "First Starbucks on any campus anywhere," he'd bragged for the ninety thousandth time while they stood in line. As if she didn't already know this, everyone who lived in the area knew this, she'd been living here far longer than he had. He ordered; she paid. He was drinking a Teavana Shaken Iced Passion Tango™ Tea Lemonade. She had a Clover-brewed coffee; those were invented by a bunch of caffeine-craving graduates. Product-design majors, she figured. Single-cup coffeemakers. They cost a zillion dollars. She had hers with milk. Her husband called that "Regular, no sugar," which in some way was how she might describe herself. Regular, no sugar.

When the Clover machines were introduced at the first campus Starbucks on any campus anywhere a few years earlier, well, you would have thought those boys actually found God.

"What does the TM stand for?" she wondered out loud. "Transcendental Meditation?"

"Trademark," he said.

"You said you had all this info on me," she said.

"I said, 'the Cloud has all this info on you.' But it doesn't matter; it's out there. We have it. It has it. Everyone has it. But I know how to use it."

"To find out," she said.

"To make money," he said. "I need to know if you'll care enough for your eyeballs to get sticky."

"So how do we begin?" she said. "You said, 'infinite chances, infinite universes.' How do you tease the important stuff out?"

He nodded. For the first time that morning, he looked, well, serious. Less spectrumy and more engaged. Like he didn't live on planet Pluto, but right there where she lived, like he lived somewhere on Earth beside her.

"I'll take care of the algorithms," he said. "You take care of the questions."

She sighed. This was the easy part. She thought about it almost every day. She'd had a therapist once who said the best thing for her to do was to sweep the obsessive thoughts away. For the past twenty-three years, she had been sweeping.

"What would have happened if she'd lived?"

He looked at her Petite Vanilla Bean Scone. He'd already eaten his Ham & Cheese Savory Foldover. She guessed he was still hungry.

She pushed her pastry toward him. He took a bite. Then, with food in his mouth, a chalky paste, he said, "That's all?"

"There are no other questions," she said.

There were crumbs on his chin and a whitish spume in the corners of his lips. As if he were foaming at the mouth! She swallowed the urge to pantomime dabbing her own mouth with a napkin or just reaching out and dabbing his. But she wasn't *his* mother.

"Oh, you'll have more," he said.

Which was true. More questions were soon to follow.

PART ONE

I T WAS A COOL BLUE morning. Later, at dawn, which was coming
too fast—Amy wasn't ready yet to face the day—sunlight would
layer the sky into swaths of paler blues, grays, pinks. But not now.
Now the whole world, or at least her ludicrously perfect patch of it,
was encased in a clear inky gel, an atmospheric snow globe, seemingly flawless. Amy had just been awakened by a tactile hallucina-
tion, sensing her phone vibrating minutes before the alarm actually
was set to go off. She'd grabbed it from her nightstand, saving Dan
that juddering hand-buzzery sound—a gag that came daily, like Uncle
God's worn-out prank. These days, her nights comprised marathon
hours of lacy sleep, in and out of dreams so wild and disturbing, the
interruption by her own inner alarm clock could be viewed less as
a textbook case of conditioning—Pavlov's wake-up call—and more
accurately as an act of self-preservation.

She moved Dan's open laptop carefully off his belly, closed it, and
set it down onto the cream-colored cut-pile carpeting on her side of
the bed. Dan must have fallen asleep while updating his LinkedIn
file. Back in the day, when he first started out in newspapers (ha-ha),
he often conked out while writing on yellow legal pads, and Amy
had had to pry the pens out of his hand. The attic still held several
ink-stained coverlets documenting that period. Time capsules. So last
century.

Quietly, she slipped on a pair of running tights and exited their
bedroom. If she tiptoed down the stairs and kept Squidward, their
psychotic Vizsla, from barking, if she put on the sneakers she'd left
to air outside the back door, she could hit the ground running. She'd
circle around the faculty ghetto, following the campus blue lights like
bread crumbs, then up into the hills. She'd head for the Dish, an old

radio telescope that probably sort of functioned, sitting close to the top of one of the highest local gradients. If she was in luck as she ran, she'd see the fog lift and the light of day do the lifting. On a clear morning, the view was all the way to San Francisco.

Amy didn't have time to do the whole seven-mile loop today. Thing One and Thing Two, as they referred to the little boys—they were idents—had to be hauled out of bed by six thirty if any of the stuff that needed to happen before they went to school was to occur: the corralling of homework, clothes, tooth brushing, deodorizing poor little Theo (Thing Two), who on top of the rest of his issues appeared to be showing signs of way-early puberty, while Miles, his exact replica, had not a solitary hair where it counted, nor a single one of Theo's hurdles. Amy poked a nose in their room before shutting the door carefully: no signs of life in the trundle beds, same mop of carroty curls exploding like a burst of fireworks on each pillow—always a surprise. Both she and Dan had dark hair, although recently Dan's was shot through with silver, as though he'd stuck his finger in a light socket and it had been electrified. (She supposed in a way, he had.) Then she moved down the hall to check on Jack.

In her oldest boy's room, Lily was the only one up, still lounging in bed, her loose blond ponytail fanned out seraphically against her flowered pillowcase, blue eyes so bright they startled, black mascara melting prettily beneath her lashes, daisy-eyed. Jack's girlfriend. She and Amy waved to each other via Skype, Jack's laptop permanently open on his desk, angled toward his bottom bunk. Lily lived in Texas now, although she was a constant presence in Amy's household—she'd moved two years ago, two weeks after the kids began dating—and slept under a fluffy pink duvet, surrounded by stuffed animals, a photo of a calla lily framed above her bed. It was a Mapplethorpe; Jack had found the print online; he had it sent to

Lily for her sixteenth birthday. Their whole relationship, it seemed, was conducted over devices, although apparently not *all* of it.

Amy gently covered up her sleeping son's bare chest with his quilt out of some weird sense of propriety, even though she knew Lily had seen it all before. They'd had sex. Cindy, Lily's mother, had told Amy as much in an email after Lily had visited last summer. God knows what the kids did together over the Internet.

Now Amy posed her phone's clock in front of Jack's webcam. It was two hours later in Texas and she didn't want Lily to be late for school. For this, she was rewarded with a sweet smile.

Downstairs, Squidward was sleeping in his crate in the kitchen. Amy dug his chow out in fistfuls so he wouldn't hear the kibble hit the metallic bowl. Asleep, the animal was magnificent, a deep glossy auburn; as he doggy-snored, his muscled belly shimmered like sunset on a lake she'd never seen—maybe in Maine or Vermont? Gently she unbolted the crate and shoved the tin bowl inside. He opened a wild eye—he had two settings, it seemed, on and off—and then began to scarf down his breakfast. Quickly, she refilled his water bowl, set it down, and then unlocked her back door. Still blue outside. She could smell the eucalyptus. She pulled yesterday's socks out of her sneakers, which were a little wet with dew, sat down on her back step, and put them on. In five, four, three, two, one, Squidward dashed out past her, jet-propelled and ready for his morning run. They paid a Stanford track star to take him out for an hour at midday. It was a delicate matter right now, keeping the kid on payroll: Dan was around; they needed to think about money. But the last thing she wanted was to further rock his confidence.

She obediently fell into step behind Squidward, and they turned left, running toward the elementary school. She would escort the twins there later that morning. Empty, with its retro playground—

slides and tire swings and little habit-trails—no one could guess the tortures that awaited poor Theo inside.

Amy had a lone real friend at work, the CFO, Naresh; his wife, a venture capitalist, was one of their angel investors. Naresh and Nancy put their kids in the local Waldorf School, which was vehemently anti-tech; perhaps without the distraction of computers and video games Theo could learn to read there, too, though Naresh said even in the fifth grade the kids spent all day knitting and digging for worms in the dirt. Thirty-something grand a year to live like a sharecropper's child in Appalachia. Dan would have a seizure.

A half-mile in and Amy caught her stride, clearing away the cobwebs in her hips and knees as they became oiled by synovial fluid, and then the onset of that weird divine heat that spread across her sacrum like Tiger Balm. It was one of those subtle bodily shifts that signaled the difference from starting a run to *running* (the way falling in love that first time had transformed the impatience of waiting-for-life-to-begin into the exhilaration of actually living*),* her breath even and deep. Soon she would enter a different plane. No more monkey mind.

Amy hadn't started running with any seriousness until the twins were thrown out of preschool. (Theo had hit another kid in the head with a piece of iron pipe that was part of a construction "work." "Iron pipe? In a classroom of two-year-olds?" Amy had asked. "What is this, *West Side Story*?" Apparently not. *Montessori*.) So during the premorning hours while Dan still slept, Amy had begun, like now, sometimes wearing a headlamp, to navigate the darkness, before the babies woke. While running she could pretend she was unencumbered again, working her way up the corporate ladder with discipline and drive, eager to get a head start at her desk, blowing through a bunch of calories now so she could go crazy later, on the free bar snacks at happy hour.

Or if it had been a rough night—Theo was a somnambulist, one time he'd sleepwalked into Jack's room, pulled down his pull-up, and peed on the older boy as he'd been innocently dreaming in his bed; and with all the caterwauling that ensued, Amy was surprised none of the neighbors had called the police—she'd take a post-breakfast run, pretending to be a smug little Earth Mother now while she ran, her hair in braids, wearing tie-dyed capris, pushing the twins around the Palo Alto high school track in a double-baby jogger, each munching beneficently on a rice cake smeared with cashew butter. If they napped after a couple of miles, she'd park the jogger by the football dugout and tackle the stadium steps while they slept, fantasizing about joining an ashram in India as she ran up up up into the sky. Midday Amy switched roles in her mind's backstage: she might transform into a French au pair, outsourcing the boys to a children's museum art class or the library story hour and ignore them, hanging out in the back of the room, listening to Youssoupha and Daft Punk on her iPhone. In the afternoons, more often than not, she'd turn into a mixologist when it was five o'clock absolutely anywhere, finding the time to fix herself a fancy cocktail, when there were days where there wasn't even time to shower it seemed, but still she was able to muddle mint and slice cucumbers on a mandolin, blasting music, the Things safely eating Cheerios off the ground in the rubber room she'd constructed out of gym mats on the floors and the walls in the dining area.

She'd confessed all this to Dan *after* she'd gone back to work, while taking a large frozen organic pizza out of the microwave, Jack's postdinner snack, and Dan had said, his long arms snaking around her middle, his lips pressed against her neck: "If you'd only told me earlier, we could have brought the au pair with us into the bedroom." He could be funny, Dan. But not that time.

Running made everything better. It was a vacation from her

life. What lengthy list of crap could she *not* think about for the next hour? It was what sex did—now only birthday and anniversary weekends away, or when the kids were at sleepovers at some other hapless mother's house—filling her with liquid light. The skin on her arms prickled beneath the morning chill, and also the fascia on her right shin. The body was so fantastically surprising sometimes. Stretch a hamstring while lying on her back and feel the music shoot up and out of her spine and through her cranium. Craziness. The furnace of her sacrum was working its hot magic now.

Then she saw him. At the school.

Fuck no, thought Amy.

In shorts, Tevas, and a hoodie—such pretension, he'd have to lose the hoodie; a yesteryear cliché—he was sitting on a swing. Waiting for her.

"Amy," said Donny.

Under the playground lights, he looked just like her old roommate from college, Lauren—except for the hairy legs—wiry and short, blond, a ferrety handsomeish face, which made sense because he was Lauren's son. When he'd come to Stanford three years before, to be nice Amy had invited him over for a welcome brunch and to do laundry, although the machines in the dorm were newer than hers—Donny pointed this out—and Energy Star–qualified. Plus, he sent his out to a campus Fluff and Fold. Now he was her boss.

"What are you doing up?" said Amy, jogging in place, uselessly, her heart rate already coming down. Usually Donny trailed in a good couple of hours after her at work. Donny was a sleep camel, often up all night, drinking Mountain Dew Kickstart and writing code, being smart, acting dumb—catching up sometimes with eighteen-hour naps on the weekends. Once in a while he stayed awake to actually do his schoolwork.

"I stalked you via Find My Friends," said Donny. "I thought I could use the exercise."

He stood and started pumping his knees, his feet slopping in the Tevas. Hard to tell if he was joking or not.

Squidward was nowhere in sight.

"The dog," said Amy, weakly.

"He'll boomerang," said Donny. "I think maybe I'm thirsty." Apparently this was a self-revelation. "You could buy me some green juice or a Philtered Soul."

She looked at her phone. 5:23 a.m. Philz Coffee wasn't open. Nothing was open.

"Or we could have breakfast at home," said Donny.

The first three months of the start-up they'd worked out of Donny's room in the "Entrepreneurs' Dorm," but that hadn't lasted long. Thank God, really, because it smelled like a dorm room, and there was always pee on the toilet seat, just like in the twins' bathroom at her house. (Except for Tuesdays. Tuesdays the suite lavatories were cleaned by Facilities, and Amy could actually sit down.) Since the Things were officially school-aged (another argument for public school—they couldn't be expelled), Amy had gone back to work part-time. In the beginning, she had been commuting three days a week up to the City at her real part-time job, working in PR/ crisis management, hoping for employment at Google, where she fantasized about dropping off the dry cleaning on campus, eating in a cafeteria, putting in endless hours, never seeing her family. But some dreams weren't meant to be. So, when the start-up moved into an office, she'd stayed on the Peninsula to work full-time with them.

Donny and his roommate, Adnan, had been pivoting around

several ideas at once when they came up with Invisible E-nk. With Invisible E-nk, emails and texts were timed to disappear after they were read straight through once and therefore the messages were both unsaveable and unforwardable, even with a screenshot. Now it was possible to have cybersex without a career-ending trail! No potential sex offender status when flirting with your underage crush! Invisible E-nk had raised enough seed money for the office off California Avenue. But, of course, there was Snapchat. So, the stakes were higher, and/or it was all really fucking stupid. The E-nkers could beat Snapchat at the same game with their superior coding and bespoke blah-blah or give up and try another option. "We are exploring all the possibilities," Adnan told the film studies students who were trailing him for a senior thesis documentary project.

One thing Amy learned in her brief tenure at a start-up was that failure was endemic to the enterprise; the businesses that succeeded in the Valley were bouncy and regenerative. "Investors like to see you roll with the punches," wise-man Adnan said before the cameras. When he'd uttered that phrase, he had done a long soft aikido roll to illustrate the point. (Naturally he was a black belt.) "As long as the computer science is good—and these kids are the best"—Adnan pointed to Kenneth Cheng, seventeen, their youngest employee, still in braces, playing Candy Crush on his cell phone—"and the ideas keep coming, one of the objectives is bound to be a hit and stick."

Hit and stick: like a wide-shouldered, small-hipped, broad-chested puberty-delayed female Russian gymnast doing a triple vault over a horse, or the ramen noodles Donny twirled and tossed up to the linoleum tiles on the ceiling when he was bored—his only hobby.

i.e., as the E-nkers called themselves, was located on a side street, in the back of a small suite, on the second floor, up a flight of outdoor stairs. (Make Actual Memories was another moniker they'd toyed with, but it sounded too much like "Ma'am," the least sexy word in the English language; Amy had put her foot down. And for a while, Donny had been partial to "As If (IRL)," *in real life,* which as logos go was far too noisy. Some cute but artsy girl in Donny's "Failure and the American Writer" class had lent him a Raymond Carver book he'd never read, but it gave him a taste for longish titles. Amy had been surprised to hear that he'd even bothered to take a lit course, but he was looking for ideas, Donny said. He *had* the technology. He thought maybe some writers somewhere could supply him with conceptual objectives for what to do with it.)

It took Amy forever to realize that it was the sitar music that wafted up the staircase from the yoga studio on the ground floor that made her so often crave Indian food at lunch. Some of the student programmers she worked with took class midday as a stress dump, and when they returned, the middle-school stink in the office intensified. Very few techies appeared to use adequate toxic-chemical deodorant; no one—not Amy, not her running buddies from the comp sci department—seemed to know exactly why, writ in the cool bible of High Domes, it was Tom's Natural Deodorant or nada.

The company office was in a very good location. For Amy, walkable. She lived over in College Terrace, once a modest community of young faculty and grad student housing, now the home of $2.5 million teardowns and people like Amy and Dan, who were still holding on by their fingernails. Theirs was a two-story vanilla box on Cornell Street, Dan's alma mater, parallel to Columbia, ironically Amy's first choice back in the day, though she'd never gotten off the waitlist. She'd stayed in state, and gone to Cal. The i.e. office was just across the main thoroughfare, El Camino, and off California Avenue with its casual restaurants and coffee houses and Geek Fitness store. Fleeces and sweats and fuzzy boots, Asian street food, veggie burgers, and guacamole. "What's not to like?" said Dan. But Donny, an Eeyore and a classicist, had wanted a garage.

Even this morning's stroll was a borrowed Steve Jobsian tic—go for a walk with a coworker or competitor, coax what you want out of him. Donny was an avid student of tech stardom. Oh, he'd just pretended he stalked Amy for free breakfast and some family time, but sure as the sun doth shine he was picking her brain for something. Lauren had warned Amy when Donny had first hired her: "He always has an ulterior motive, even if he himself doesn't know yet what it is." He'd inhaled the Isaacson biography as a kid. Donny and Adnan had each seen the film *The Social Network* at least a dozen times on Netflix when they were still in middle school. Ironically, the movie, which Dan, the over-the-hill, out-of-work editor-of-content, had interpreted as a cautionary tale about loneliness and assholicism, had become a generational call to arms. It was what the Watergate film *All the President's Men* had meant to Dan, when some teacher screened it in sixth grade, and set into motion his life's course.

After interrupting Amy's run, and then eating the last of the twins' Puffins with rice milk at her breakfast bar, Donny checked his Twitter feed patiently as he waited for her while she scrambled: getting the Things up and dressed, cajoling Dan into walking them to school, breaking Jack's directive—"Don't talk, Mom, text"—by bellowing at him *to get the lead out!* Squidward arrived panting at the back door just as she and Donny finally were leaving the house, a dead rat in his open, salivating mouth. A love gift. Today's first. But the frightened dog took off again when Amy lost it and shrieked at him.

After the rat grave was dug—Amy dug it, in the side yard by the manzanitas, while Donny drank the remains of Jack's peanut butter/honey/yogurt/banana smoothie, "a sandwich in a glass,"

Jack liked to say—Amy and Donny walked to work. Already, she was pretty much exhausted. A couple of blocks down El Camino, Donny picked a persimmon off a tree, and Amy almost scolded, but so much low-hanging fruit lay rotting wasted in the yard and on the sidewalk, she figured it would be hard to call this stealing. More like an act of salvation. As Dan would say, "a mitzvah." Better Donny slurped the deep orange pudding away from the satiny skin and stained his T-shirt than let the persimmon continue growing solely to molder away in organic compost.

Even after hoovering all that breakfast food, Donny was still hungry. When he'd spat out the seeds—three long, smooth metallic hard hearts, lifted, it seemed, straight out of the rib cage of a Giacometti— he asked if she remembered his grandma. "A sweet woman," Amy murmured. At the end, Lauren's mother's hair had been so white it appeared blue; it glowed eerily in the casket like a nimbus cloud, but Amy left that detail out.

After crossing over to California Avenue, they stopped at Printer's Ink, once a bookstore/café; now only the lattes survived. Amy wasn't ready to brave the rock 'n' roll depths of Philz Coffee, and Donny hadn't even whined about it. Instead, he thumbed quietly through a copy of *The Daily* while she paid. She handed him his soy mochaccino and he looked up from his paper. His hazel eyes were round. Usually they were hooded, like a lizard's.

"The problem with out here is that someone is already working on anything you can imagine," he said, "so to fucking break stuff we need to stay ahead of the unimaginable all the time."

He sighed loudly. He was one world-weary kid.

Amy patted his shoulder. She wanted to slug him. She felt sorry for him and he annoyed her, both. The Donny Paradox. It was a tie at times, between him and her darling impossible-to-mother little Theo, as to who might be the bigger chore.

.　.　.

"Must save Blossom," muttered Theo, "must save Blossom." It was lunch recess at Escondido Elementary School, he and his best friend, Blossom Hernandez, were in the thick of a freeze tag game, and she was frozen and he was King of the Playground—although he was a sovereign without an army, with Blossom cruelly held prisoner in need of rescue in the schoolyard, and his twin brother, Miles, trading Magic cards by the picnic tables, and therefore useless to him.

Theo looked over at Miles, steadily working Thomas Hannahan, one Nike'd foot up on a redwood stump, cards laid bare across a table. He was not "twinning"; Miles almost never twinned, never felt Theo's ache in his own ear when it was time for antibiotics but Theo was too oddly numb to notice until his eardrum burst and the goo dripped out; Miles was never startled awake at night when Theo was lost in the time-warping labyrinth of one of his hideous dreams and in dire need of someone to rouse him; and right now Miles didn't sense how much Theo wanted Miles by his side, to prevail in freeze tag, sure, but also to calm him down. Instead Miles coolly continued to do his own thing, always at home in the home of himself, immune to the heat rays Theo sent from his identical brown eyes.

Theo also played Magic: The Gathering, and frequently he and Miles played together; Miles liked winning, which he did often; what Theo liked was that the game had so much awesome replayability. With skill and imagination, the very same cards could produce totally different outcomes, which Theo thought was cool.

If Miles was on Theo's team in freeze tag and not at the picnic table, *he* would be King of the Playground, because Miles could run faster, and could jump far and leap and stuff—he could make his body do what he wanted, plus most kids liked him, or were scared of him in the way kids are scared of kids other kids like. Theo's power was that he could go from zero to ten in a nanosecond, and also he didn't mind bodily harm; he kind of craved being thrown in the dirt with a thousand second-graders piling up on top of him. He liked to wrestle and he liked to be pounded.

Blossom needed rescuing and rescuing Blossom was Theo's pleasure—he heard his mom say that whenever Blossom came over. "It's my pleasure to have her here," his mom said over and over to Blossom's mom, whose name was Begonia, like the plant, and she let him call her that, not Mrs. Hernandez, the way his mom had introduced her. Begonia had said, "Call me Begonia, sweetheart. Blossom is my little flower, so I named her after me," when Begonia came to pick her up that first time. As soon as his mom said having Blossom in the house was her pleasure, Theo could tell his mom really meant it, because (a) Blossom was a girl and Mom only had boys, and (b) Blossom was his mom's kind of kid, full of heart, Mom said, just like Theo.

"Theo!" screamed Blossom. "Help!!!!!" Her reddish-brown curls flew around so much they seemed more mane than hair, and he couldn't see her eyes or cheeks, just her little flat nose sometimes, sort of. She was frozen in the worst spot to be frozen in, inside a tire swing, Maximus, that jerkass bully, spinning her cruelly in one direction. Maximus sometimes played Magic: the Gathering, too, and even liked to call himself Greven il-Vec, the Gathering wizard. *"I will flay the skin from your flesh and the flesh from your bones and scrape your bones dry. And still you will not have suffered enough,"* Maximus screamed, quoting Greven's flavor text on the Oracle Hatred's card. Then he cackled maniacally as the chain untwisted rapidly in the other direction, spinning poor Blossom now like a top magic UFO gyroscope, the kind with music and LED lights.

"I'm gonna throw up! Theo, help!"

Blossom's shrieks hurt his ears. He could feel them like pointy needles inside his teeth and at the bottom of his feet, so he wanted to run screaming to the other side of the schoolyard, but he knew Blossom, and she threw up a lot. Begonia always sent her with two plastic bags to throw up in when they went on class trips on the school bus, one for the way there and one for the way back. Those were the only times Theo didn't want to be near her. They liked all the same things, baseball and trains and running games, and neither of them could read, but his fear of the stench of her potential throw-up kept him sitting up ahead in the bus with his brother as a buddy. That was a good thing about Miles; he knew Theo needed the wind on his face to settle down, so he always let him have the open window. He knew it from experience, not twinning. If the bus window wouldn't open, Miles would agreeably slap Theo's cheeks for him until he could sit still.

Maximus was a bully, big for his age, with black hair and blue eyes, he was "Silicon Valley royalty," Theo heard his mom whisper to his dad once. Maximus liked to torture Blossom; he made fun of her red hair and red skin. He called Theo *Ronald,* for Ronald McDonald, on account of his hair, only who cared? But he called Blossom *Tomato* and *Tomatillo*, even though everyone knew tomatillos were green, on account of hers. That made her so mad, sometimes she would chase him all over the playground and then end up with a time-out.

Maximus loved getting under Blossom's skin and driving her crazy, he teased her mercilessly over the fact that she couldn't read. In class during "**D**rop **E**verything **A**nd **R**ead" Ms. Hiraga would go around the circle and have each kid tackle a small section from *The Lion, the Witch and the Wardrobe,* although she recited the bulk of it herself out loud.

That very morning, she'd asked Blossom to read from the page: "'Well, sir, if things are real, they're there all the time.' 'Are they?' said the Professor; and Peter did not quite know what to say."

Blossom got as far as the word *things* and said: "Tings."

"See this letter, Blossom?" Ms. Hiraga pointed to the letter *T* up on the whiteboard, using her patient voice, and Blossom nodded. "The letter *T* can have a hard sound, like *tah*," she said, "like in *toy* or *treat* or *turtle*."

Blossom smiled because who didn't like toys or treats or turtles? And who didn't like Ms. Hiraga, who was so very beautiful and taught so sweetly?

Then Ms. Hiraga added the letter *H* to the *T* and said, "But if you add an *H* to a *T* the sound gets softer, *thuh,* like in *th*eater or *th*row or *th*ought. So, can you try and sound out this word one more time?" And she pointed to the word *thing* again.

Blossom smiled too wide and her eyes got shiny and then she'd said, "Tah hing?"

Ms. Hiraga shook her head softly, and said: "It's *th*ing, Blossom. We can work on the sound some more together later." She called on someone else to continue.

"Retard," said Maximus in a whisper, so Ms. Hiraga couldn't hear. He liked it when Blossom or Theo couldn't find the answer. And he liked the way Begonia said good-bye to Blossom every morning, while blowing her kisses, "Adios, Mami."

"You got kids already, *Mami*?" he said every day like it was a new and funny joke.

Maximus was a big fucker, and Blossom's head was now drooping, like her neck was a wilting stalk and all those red curls were falling petals, which meant the throw-up was coming, so Theo charged at him ninety-five miles an hour. Theo's head went straight into Maximus's pelvis, and that's how Maximus ended up in the

Urgent Care center and his mother threatened to sue at first, and Theo himself saw stars. Maximus's pelvis might even have given Theo's head a concussion. It definitely had knocked the wind out of him. Eventually Mrs. Maximus—that's what his dad called her—calmed down over the phone when the doctors pronounced everything fine at Urgent Care, and Theo ended up on a bench outside the principal's office, and Theo's dad ended up behind the door inside.

"Sometimes I don't know how to be your dad," Theo's dad said as they held hands walking home together, subsequent to Theo being suspended for the rest of the day. But when they were in the hallway, after Theo and the principal, Ms. Zhang, had talked and then Dad and Ms. Zhang had talked, when Ms. Zhang's office door had opened and both adults had stepped outside to talk with Theo again, Dad had said: "Ms. Zhang and I both agree you've had enough excitement for one day. We're going to go home now, Theo," which sounded like something someone who knew how to be a dad might say. It was confusing.

Ms. Zhang had said, "Remember what we spoke about in my office, Theo, you need to stop and breathe when your engine overheats like that." She held up a paper STOP sign she had conveniently taken out of her office with her when she was walking his dad out. "Take this home with you and practice with your father. When he holds up the sign I want you to take deep belly breaths and count to ten. The deep belly breaths will cool down your engine. If it is too hard to stand still while you're breathing, I want you to jump ten times, with great big juicy knee bends, can you do that?"

Theo nodded. He took a great big jump and landed in a great big juicy knee bend.

"Good, Theo," she said, but she was looking at Theo's dad when she said this.

Theo was crying at this point. He didn't mean to hurt Maximus, just dominate and obliterate him. He hadn't wanted to send him to the hospital or anything; he never even thought that far.

"I know you didn't mean to hurt Maximus," said Ms. Zhang, "but if you run into anyone full steam you will hurt them. You know that, right, Theo?"

Theo just stared at her. Did he know it or not? Sometimes he felt pain and sometimes he didn't.

"Theo," said Dad.

He looked at Dad then, what did he want?

"Tell Ms. Zhang you know not to run full steam into other people."

"I know," said Theo.

"Okay then," Ms. Zhang said. "Because you also could have really hurt yourself, Theo."

She spoke to his dad again like Theo was and wasn't there. "I'm going to arrange for more O.T. for Theo, to help him keep regulated. I'm also going to consult with our learning specialist . . . Maybe lunch recess is too stimulating for him."

She'd turned her gaze to Theo. She was a petite woman with short black shiny hair and she wore tightly buttoned suits with pants or skirts that made her seem even smaller, and she wasn't that much taller than he was, so their eyes sort of kind of met: "Your dad and I were talking and we might arrange for some quiet time for you, Theo, instead. Library or a lunch club."

Theo was a lunch recess kid, not a lunch club kid. What did quiet time mean for a kid like Theo?

"Check in with your wife and let me know if next Thursday works," said Ms. Zhang. She pressed a pink sticky note into Dad's hand. "Maximus's home number. Julie and Chris Powell. Perhaps Theo can make an apology himself."

His dad had nodded. Then he'd started to say something. Then he'd stopped.

Ms. Zhang raised an eyebrow.

"That kid has been bullying my son and his friend all year," Dad said, running a hand through his thick gray hair. "You'd think in this community . . . With the losses that we've had . . . Everyone talks about the pressure on the high school students. And rightly so. Because we're in the middle of an epidemic . . . But what about the pressure on these little kids? You know, when does that kind of self-esteem problem start? I know Theo. He was looking out for Blossom."

"Ramming his head into Max's pelvis didn't help Blossom, Mr. Messinger," said Ms. Zhang in a principal's voice. And then more quietly, "Are you suggesting that you are worried about self-harm? I don't see that myself, but we could arrange for Theo to talk with someone."

"No," said Dad. "Absolutely not. I just think it's unhealthy for him to be treated this way."

"As long as you're not concerned."

"I'm not," said Dad.

Ms. Zhang nodded her head. "Okay then. Right now we're discussing how Theo treated Maximus. I assure you I will be speaking with Maximus's parents later about how Maximus treats Theo."

His dad was tall and handsome, and usually people didn't speak to him that way, even lately, when he bent over more, and his tummy curved out. But though Ms. Zhang was kind, she also meant business. (Theo was mind-quoting his mother, that's what she often said.)

"Theo had several other choices, including the best one, speaking with a lunch recess monitor."

Even Theo knew it was time to go home then. They said their

good-byes politely, and he and his dad walked out of the building and into the yard and then down the back path and out of
the school gate in front of SCRA, the faculty and staff sports club
where the Stanford kids who lived on campus got to swim after
school and he and Miles did not.

Jack had had swim team meets there before he joined the water
polo team at Paly. Theo and Miles had gone sometimes with their
mom to cheer Jack on. Jack didn't want them to come, now that
he was in high school, but sometimes he let Mom just so she could
video the meet for Lily. Dad had usually been at work. Now he
mostly stayed at home. It was funny, like now, when Dad was the
one to show up. He'd not been the one before.

"I wish you could teach me how to be your father," Dad said
again as they crossed the parking lot and headed for Stanford Avenue. They were only a few blocks away from home.

Theo was quiet. He didn't know that dads needed teaching
to be dads. He pressed his cheek against his dad's hand as they
walked and his dad reached over and ruffled Theo's hair with his
other hand, the one with the gold ring and the watch his mom had
bought his dad a long time ago, when he turned forty.

.   .   .

After they'd finally arrived at i.e., Donny spent all his time in the
back office he shared with Adnan, pretty much ignoring Amy, as
usual. It was hard to figure out what he'd wanted from her that
morning, something was percolating, or maybe he just missed his
mommy . . . And Amy was the next best thing. Who knew, who
cared? Amy needed energy to start this next round of her day. Out
front, in the open workspace, where she sat, she had her own desk.
"Age before beauty," she'd said when she'd claimed it, and nobody

had laughed or told her what a rocking body she had for her age, even though in her own humble opinion she still looked pretty good. Didn't they know she needed to hear it?

Naresh had his own desk, too, and he was twirling endlessly in his ergonomic chair as he talked on the phone, like he was on the autism spectrum—although Amy didn't think he was. Maybe it was a sensory-integration issue with Naresh. Theo had those; when he was small they'd had to brush him all over his body with a little soft corn silk brush in order to calm him down. There were probably a ton of sensory issues in their office—hence the massage chair in the corner, the extra earbuds in the supply closet, and the stacks of chewing gum in the pantry.

Around one o'clock burritos wrapped in foil were tossed like fat silver zeppelins between the couches. At two o'clock, Twizzlers were eaten. Someone made an Izzy's Bagels run at four; Donny always ordered the same thing, a chocolate chip bagel with jalapeño cream cheese, and he never barfed. He had bragged about this at their last party (which just meant staying later at work than usual on a Friday, with beer), and then again today.

"I've never barfed in my whole life," bragged Donny, chomping on his bagel.

Adnan hooted. He said, "And I've never farted."

Donny just returned to his office.

"Tell us another one, Don-Key," Adnan called after him. Then Adnan went mountain biking.

Some of the staff, sick of coding, searched out the likelihood of Donny's nonbarfing online and then unsatisfied, still arguing his veracity, posted the debate on Quora.

Donny and Adnan's private office lay behind a one-way mirror: a joke from all the years when psychologists had observed Donny as a little kid. Esmeralda Sanchez—a rarity on staff, a female and a freshman—pretended to stick her finger down her throat and made gagging motions while staring at her own reflection, seemingly forgetting that Donny could be monitoring her every move.

Amy herself had slipped up often enough, glimpsing the back hem of her skirt to see if the Scotch tape still held or fluffing her hair in the glass, forgetting he was back there. The man behind the curtain.

The beauty of Invisible E-nk was that it was conceptually iterative and flexible. In production terms, it lent itself to elegance—they were using Pylon and Comet for the back end and Ubuntu Linux for its operating system. Amazon Elastic Compute Cloud would host the servers—this was all vintage Naresh. And unlike Snapchat, it truly left no Internet shadow. The coders were working simultaneously on Invisible Pix and now, Inaudible Voicemail, both of which would exist solely as mobile apps but could be easily adapted to AirPods and neural lace when the technology became available, "because computers are so ten years ago," Adnan drawled, "and phones are fucking clunky," making fun of himself and nearly everyone else on the planet.

All these services needed government clearance and tracking ability without raising privacy issues—so they outsourced legal.

Most of Amy's day was spent planting items in the Valley blogs, refining ideas for a company website (which proved difficult because the general concept was so constantly fluctuating, but necessary still if she were ever going to create intrinsic SEO). She also was attempting to drum up some dead-tree interest in the business sections of the remaining papers. She hounded the folks at *Help a Reporter Out* and Techcrunch.com, fingers crossed, hoping to enter the company into their databases. Billboards were her newest pet project. Traffic was awful these days. Road rage was mitigated by off-road entertainment. What if she had some doofy visuals of Donny and some of the upperclassmen with their youthful dad bods in their underwear up along the highway with just the company's tag underneath them? The goal was to get this company sold, right? She needed to increase their visibility. She had a meeting set up with Naresh and an outside advertising agency before she floated this one by Donny.

Part of Amy's campaign was ensuring that invisibility wasn't perceived as a code name for illegality, but rather as a means of discretion, although privacy as a concept seemed in and out of vogue these days—it was her job to track this, too. In one pitch she'd sent this morning she'd quoted Edward Snowden: *I don't want to live in a world where there's no privacy and therefore no room for intellectual exploration and creativity.* In fifty-three seconds, the editor at Tech-Crunch had shot back: "'*You already have zero privacy—get over it,*' Scott McNealy, 1999!!!"

They had lived together so long, Amy sounded in her own head like Dan, but wasn't the exchange apples and oranges, like art and commerce? Not that Snowden was literally an artist, but sort of, as he was a whistleblower and/or a traitor and there was an art to all that tightrope walking. McNealy had founded Sun Microsystems in the early '80s, so wasn't he just an out-of-touch relic of the dot .com era? At sixty-something, McNealy represented realism, but maybe not his generation, who mostly seemed befuddled, and time after time reliably surprised by issues of confidentiality and discretion no matter how many times they'd previously faced them. (Carlos Danger? Amy Pascal? John Podesta?) Under-thirties didn't seem to give a shit about privacy; under-eighteens ironically did.

"Privacy as a concept is a whole lot like tattoos," Jack said recently. It was a Friday night a couple of months prior, just a few weeks after Lily's last visit. They were in the midst of what Jack called a "three way" over dinner, Lily Skyping in on Jack's computer, Amy picking their fertile zeitgeisty brains.

"Tell the truth to your old ma," said Amy. "Are we Invisible E-nkers just barking up the wrong tree?"

"Isn't Donny a genius?" Lily asked politely.

Sometimes she looked even prettier on the screen than the way Amy remembered her. Maybe every day her prettiness was increasing. As they spoke Lily rolled her long blond hair up into a twist, where it miraculously stayed, pin-less and perfect, resting in the nape of her swanlike neck. For a moment, Amy flashed back to her eldest brother's girlfriend from high school, Elodie. She'd had hair like that. The kind most white girls wanted.

Jack said, "Personally, I live on a flexitarian diet of Twitter and text, but I'm actively searching for the next best thing. What's cool about your start-up is how retro it is."

"What do you mean, baby?" asked Lily.

Lily called Amy's seventeen-year-old son baby. Right on the screen in front of her. Amy had ruled out the phone at the table, because if Jack was on the phone with Lily, even just texting, it didn't matter if he was there at the dinner table or not. He was away, away, with her, in cyber heaven; lovebirds in the cloud, up in their own little hot-air balloon. So, Amy said nothing but chewed at her salad. She'd bought some fresh goat cheese sprinkled with lavender at the Sunday California Avenue farmers' market about two weeks before and she'd forgotten about it. It had dried out quite a bit, so now she'd crumbled some on top of her greens, applied sea salt, and pronounced it feta.

Dan and the Things had eaten earlier. Their dishes were still in the sink to prove it. When she'd gotten home from work Amy had made a boy salad (iceberg lettuce, refried beans, sliced steak, shredded Pepper Jack, tortilla strips, and salsa fresca) and some grilled-cheese sandwiches for Jack—he'd had a team practice that evening. For herself, she'd tossed what was left in her crisper, all glorious fresh California produce, fresh at purchase at least, now freshly wilted but still better than anything she could have procured at the local Safeway. She also poured herself a small mason jar full of Chardonnay from Sonoma.

Seventeen hundred miles and just three states away, Lily picked at her yogurt and fruit. She was a bony thing. She sat cross-legged on a kitchen stool, her hip bones jutting out of the waistband of her short white shorts, her crop top revealing a sunken waistline. Amy found herself always encouraging Lily to eat.

"Lily, sweetie, I texted your mom with that link to the almond butter you liked so much when you were out here. I asked the guys at the stand if they did mail order and they do. Why don't you spread a little of what you have left on a piece of toast? For protein."

"Thanks, Amy, but I ate the most ginormous lunch. I have a food belly!" She puffed hers out as far as it could possibly go, which was not much.

"I think all the douches on Facebook are just a bunch of posers," said Jack, the only one still in the conversation. "They lie all the time, all that fake happy-image shit and bragging."

Lily said, "The most subversive thing you can do in eleventh grade in Dallas is *not* be on Facebook."

"So, subversive is still a good thing," said Amy, as a hybrid of a statement and a question. She took a sip of her white wine.

"Facebook's so old school. Herd mentality. Like ink," said Jack. "Now sleeve tats are prerecs for baristas, and tramp stamps for chicks that teach kindergarten."

"Interesting," said Amy. She forked up one of his cheesy crusts and took a bite. Then she started picking at his tortilla strips. When he was little, whenever she took Jack and his best friend, Kevin Choi, out for burgers after swimming, she'd say, "I'm going to teach you boys a trick about dating for when you're older; now act like you don't notice," and then she'd steal french fries off their plates. First the boys squealed in protest, but eventually they just rolled their eyes when she'd swoop in. Kevin was such a sweet kid; since both boys made the water polo team at Paly freshman year, whenever they were out celebrating a win, he'd push her the little cardboard carton of fries as soon as it hit the table, before even taking a single bite himself. Mission accomplished! Amy prided herself on a job well done in the mothering-of-sons department. But she'd never counted on a Lily, who seemed to live on air, contentedly.

That same weekend, Amy re-upped the conversation. Jack had actually deigned to go running with her, on a rainy day at Corte de Madera Creek, an hour's drive away, after she'd promised a strawberry pancake breakfast at the Farmhouse Local. They chose a single-file trail through velvety deep wilderness, fecund and foresty, dull emerald treetops and rust-colored tree trunks, some fancy footwork around the ruts and roots that *Runner's World* deemed good for strengthening the ankles, Jack taking the lead. There was something about the absence of eye contact, like when he was a little boy sitting in the backseat and they'd already dropped the other kids off after car pool, which was magic for communication. They were so gloriously alone then. She could get a wealth of info out of him, glancing at him surreptitiously in her rearview mirror. Those dreamy green eyes.

"The Internet should be very IRL," Jack said as they ran, his words flying back over his left shoulder on the wings of a thick, wet breeze. Redwood scent was sort of mossy; it flavored the air woody, verdant, like sweet rot plus mud. Also, there was a hint of pine. As she ran Amy inhaled so deeply she'd breathed Jack's words in, too, translating them with her exhalations, an exchange of carbon dioxide and meaning. Jack was saying that life online should be like life in life, she thought, one foot pounding the trail after another, which conceptually was both very radical and forward thinking, or she'd given birth to a poet or a Luddite. (If the Internet should be like life, then why bother with the Internet at all? It was a pain in the ass, sometimes.)

"Time in cyberspace should exist like it does on planet earth," Jack said. "Take the *space* out of it, and you'll finally have something new."

Finally? New? Wasn't it all new, too new for new words to capture how new it actually was? Isn't that what Donny had been saying in his own geeky way? And wasn't Jack really talking about something old, how it always had been before, just now mechanized through state-of-the-art instruments—a sort of time substantiation? Jack, Jack, Jack, she'd wanted to say, defying time seems to be a major point of the Internet—erasing its erosion and obfuscations, the fact that up until now everything had always ended.

But instead, she'd listened that Saturday morning in Corte Madera. Amy liked to hear Jack talk. She liked almost everything about Jack; she didn't even mind when his sweat flew back in her face. It mixed with the light mist of rain.

Amy thought about this now, in the office, not in a state of bliss, but in one of mild irritation. It was late afternoon already, she was tired, and Donny had just sent a link to some new article to the whole team. It was from the *Washington Post,* TECH TITANS DEFYING DEATH. Amy's eyes skimmed over the piece; those guys weren't discussing corporate failure, but were literally intent on curing human mortality. Hmmm, she thought, that's certainly ahead of the curve. Talk about "breaking stuff." She remembered explaining death to Jack when he was just a little kid. "Why hasn't anybody done anything about this?" he'd asked in outrage. Now, apparently, they had.

Donny could have just stood in the door to his private sanctum and told them all about the piece, but he'd messaged a link and a directive instead. One could argue, he'd delayed relaying the info, because it would have been more attention grabbing to have a person actually stand up and say "read this" than to add another post to everyone's endless beta channel. But by using Slack, Donny transmitted info that they could access again and again, the very evidence that by definition i.e. was designed to erase.

The article was about living forever, (a) by ingesting microscopic nanobots that continually repair the host organism; or (b) by downloading the human brain into a robot body. The article quoted V.C. Peter Thiel: "I believe that evolution is a true account of nature. But I think we should try to escape it or transcend it in our society." The shared article could indeed exist for eternity; even if it was deleted, it was infinitely recoverable. Having invented forever, these tech titans now thought they themselves could also live forever by using the tools of their trade, "on the most complicated piece of machinery in existence: the human body." That was also a quote. When she was in college and studied literature, it was male novelists who'd believed they could use their craft to achieve immortality. Updike, Mailer, Bellow. They'd behaved as if the written word could defy death, but clearly it, um, had not. They hadn't even survived the "Jack test": he'd never heard of any of them.

Most of the people quoted in the *Post*'s article were around Amy's age, mature enough to remember those dead old literary codgers, but also getting on enough for the idea of mortality to scare the living shit out of them. Strategically, middle-aged people were also Invisible's primary target. Maybe part of Donny's plan? Who knew? Who ever knew with Donny? For example, the service was perfect for someone who hoped to hook up with an ex-boyfriend from summer camp, but cared about not getting caught. Invisible Pix was for high school students "who acted like they were in junior high," said Adnan. And rapist athletes, Amy thought.

At around five o'clock Donny called Amy into his office, standing in his doorway, cream cheese crumbs still lodged in both corners of his mouth.

"Hey, Aim," he said.

She handed him a Kleenex as she walked in, and sat down in the chair across from his desk.

He tapped on his keyboard with one hand while swiping his lips with the back of the other, the one that held the tissue. The screen was tilted toward her.

Furrier.com.

"Whenever my grandma was pissed at my grandpa," Donny said, "she always used to say, 'I should have married the furrier.'"

Grandma. Twice in one day. Was he feeling homesick? She'd been sort of a recluse, Lauren's mother; a loner who'd loved to cook. There were two fully stocked freezers in her kitchen. One for dinners, one for desserts, although she hardly ever entertained guests—and her husband was diabetic. When Amy visited Lauren back east on school breaks, they'd get high in the backyard, come inside, and eat their way through the freezer burn.

"What would have happened if she had married him?" asked Donny.

"She'd have had at least one fur coat," said Amy.

"I mean what would have happened in the parallel universe?" said Donny. "The sliding doors. The alternative reality."

"You and I would not be sitting here," said Amy. "Your mother would never have been born." She sighed. She'd been up since 4:45 a.m. "You're not a sophomore anymore, Donny. You're a junior. You know that nobody knows the answers to that question."

Donny clicked on his Facebook page.

"Not true," said Donny. "There's an algorithm for anything. From now on in, it's all aggregation of information, plus math."

"Math can tell you what would happen if you altered history?" said Amy.

"Math plus info, sure. At least a fairly good approximation," said Donny slowly, as if she were intellectually challenged or deaf. "The universe *is* math, Amy." This was the way he talked to his own mother; she often heard them go at it on speakerphone.

"I'm good at math," added Donny.

Big effing deal, thought Amy. You and your perfect SATs. They're a dime a dozen around here. Plus, Lauren spilled: you had $350-an-hour test prep.

"Look," said Donny. "This part is easy. The odds that any of us are born are infinitesimal, right? And if we beat the odds once, then there are infinitesimal odds that yet again we could beat those odds twice and so on for infinity. You know, like snowflakes, none are the same except in a world of infinity where there are infinite chances for one to be exactly the same infinite times. You've got that much, right?"

Right, Amy nodded. She got that much.

"And at this point in time, we're all willing to *accept* that space is infinite because of, you know, physics, but in my gut I *know* it's infinite because it's essentially round. Even back in the day, Einstein thought you just have to go fast and far enough to come back to where you started."

"A circle," said Amy.

"Without edge," said Donny. "So if gazing into the distance is the same as looking at the past, I can also see alternate pasts, streaming alongside them, because there are infinite chances for these alternate pasts to have formed."

"Interesting," said Amy, biting at a cuticle. "You mean like a scallop shell? Like the past is fluted?"

"Remember the summer I went to MIT math camp?" Donny said.

Well, no, thought Amy, but she nodded in the affirmative. An affirmative nod often shortened a Donny story.

"My counselor there, he was way into parallel universes. Old news, but when I was eleven it made an impression. Multiverses. Where all that can be, is." He paused. "I want to monetize that."

"Okay, I'll bite," said Amy. Nothing wrong with making money.

"There is no reason to think that the Big Bang was unique, right? That would be arrogant. And you and Mom are always telling me not to be so arrogant. Plus, I never drank the Kool-Aid that wave functions collapse when measured. And if they don't collapse, all their values coexist but on different planes. The cosmos just keeps dividing into additional actualities, in each of which an atom or unit or a number is always in one of its multitudinous possible locations. Right?"

"Right," said Amy. Wrong? she thought, with a silent tee-hee. She had no idea what he was talking about.

He gave her a look, like, what's so funny?

"I thought you said it was a circle," said Amy, lamely.

"Without edge," said Donny, annoyed. "That's what makes it infinite. If there is infinite space, there are infinite Grandmas making infinitely different decisions, and therefore all these Grandmas lived infinitely different lives. In one she shacked up with the furrier."

"Sounds very *Twilight Zone* to me. Infinite Grandmas? A nightmare," said Amy. "No offense," she added. She loved that phrase. It was offensive in its essence. Use it and you could get away with saying anything and still leave a scorpion's sting. "Grandma was a very sweet woman," she murmured. Amy was enjoying herself.

"With math and info I can approximate what happened to all of them," said Donny. "We already do some of this 2.0. For example, if you'd taken that gig at MGM? When Dan was offered the job at the *San Jose Mercury* and you moved up here?"

One of those marriage crucibles. They had one child. Dan was at the *Hollywood Reporter*, but he'd been stuck. He wasn't into covering the movie industry. He'd been so full of fire back then; "Democracy is built on good reporting"—he said that all the time. "Local journalism is what keeps government in check." It was one of the reasons Amy had fallen in love with him; Dan was so intent on doing something meaningful and important with his life. She'd been so dazzled by him, and even after marriage she'd stayed dazzled. Permanently dazzled or so she'd thought. He was always the smartest person in the room. He wanted to change the world, and he wasn't afraid of taking action, again and again, picking hard, honest work over money. Sexy, tall, warm and caring, funny, kind, easy to talk to—he was *her guy*. His love had healed her. She wanted him happy.

So, she'd agreed to move, even though she'd wanted that job at MGM. She'd done what was best for him. It was a "girl" decision, one of the many she'd lived to regret. They bought the house in College Terrace; they kept waiting for the right time to have another baby. With the tech boom, everything kept getting more and more expensive. Finally, Dan got an editorial job at the *Chronicle*. It was a green light in the kid department, but then Amy couldn't get pregnant. That part had really sucked. She couldn't find a job at Lucas or Zoetrope or Pixar. She started working in PR. When she *finally* did get pregnant, after pretty much giving up, God laughed: twins. Dan was downsized; he wrote a column; he tried and failed to write a book; he freelance-edited for magazines; adjuncted, took a stab at custom publishing; blah blah blah and blah. And then nothing. And then now.

"I already know," Amy said. She googled sometimes, late at night, when she was miserable and couldn't sleep; she also gorged on real estate porn and knew what that MGM salary might have brought her. They could have bought a place in Venice and lived by the beach. The *Chronicle* was a shit paper anyway.

"They laid off the three women they hired for similar positions in 2009 and in 2010 and 2012."

"Hmmm, sexism. So, it was a wise choice," said Amy, "choosing love."

"See, you're already buying happiness," said Donny. "I'm making you happy. You've seen the road not taken, and you can congratulate yourself."

Amy broadcast a smile.

"I'm simplifying all this into terms you can understand. You understand that, right, Amy?"

"Yes, I do, Donny."

"Okay, so we establish that you made the right choice between MGM and Dan and that makes you happy and that happiness makes your eyeballs sticky. You'll keep coming back for more. You love the reinforcement. So will the advertisers dying to sell you face cream."

"I don't use face cream," said Amy.

"You should," said Donny. "Mom does."

Instinctively, Amy's hand reached up to the softening skin around her throat.

"Now we can know a lot of things—what Grandma and the furrier's children might have looked like. I have an algorithm for that. Easy peasy. We can estimate their offspring's interests and intelligence. What might have happened had she lived where he lived, which was, get this, Omaha, Nebraska. Her own career opportunities. Grandpa would never let her work. With the furrier, she could have modeled his fur coats. She could have been the queen of Omaha. We could even make a fair approximation of their sexual compatibility over time. Grandpa was a skunk and a hound dog. Anyone could have charted that disaster, even before they took their vows. But with what I'm working on now, the math of it, I can go even further into one of those alternate realities. I can create a virtual reality, so that you could be there then and be here now. What I'm proposing is Furrier.com. Our clients can ask: What would have happened if I'd taken that job? Who would I have met? What projects might I have worked on? How much money would I have now? All of life's regrets and little mysteries answered with more than some bullshit poetry and endless waxing about the road not taken. A scientific approximation. Using AI.

"If we want, we could go simple, attach visuals—a lady and her original nose now that she has her final chin, she'd know what her old age might have looked like without the face-lift. The stuff that wakes people up at night. Grandma's furrier. All in a boutique online website, maybe with fees, or a pay wall. Although it's a natural for luxury advertising—spas, makeovers, fitness getaways. And then for the masses another app, for those niggling second-guessing everyday questions. We could call it Furrierlight, or Summer Fur."

"Summer fur?" said Amy.

"Grandma had one," said Donny. "A silver sheared mink. We could use that app for stuff like: What if I'd turned down Middlefield instead of Alvarado? Would I have found a parking spot? Been hit by a drunk driver? Met a cute girl from French class when she was carrying groceries and offered her a ride? Or what if I'd gone to the seven-thirty showing of *The Avengers*? Who might I have run into buying popcorn? Sergey Brin?"

"Isn't that just Google married to Facebook plus Foursquare?" said Amy. "This is the kind of cocktail my best friend Lauren, your mother, drinks online all the time."

"It's a personalized crystal ball. And it's boomer focused, which means people who are used to spending money, unlike my friends who expect to amass stuff for free. Plus, it plays from Scarsdale to Peoria. It we're smart, if we're really daring, we could use AI to go VR and produce the whole nine yards in a three-hundred-sixty-degree Sensurround. We might have ourselves a unicorn."

"Talk about arrogant," said Amy. "A billion-dollar company? Right now, we're having trouble paying for all those free Cup-a-Soups. And what do you mean, Sensurround?"

"Like in surrounding someone with satisfying sensorial input," said Donny.

"Can you say that three times fast?"

She was purposely testing his patience, but Donny could perseverate endlessly, patient or not. "Remember those old-fashioned hair dryers? They looked like cones?"

"Yep," said Amy. "Your grandma had one. She bought it at a bankruptcy sale at a local salon."

"Exactly," said Donny. "I could blow your fucking mind sitting under one of those things. You'll grow eyes in the back of your head. Feel the wind blow. Smell the saltwater spray. I don't know, Amy, maybe we're a potential decacorn."

"That's unicorn shit," said Amy.

"It's business," said Donny, simply, as if that one little noun solved everything. "Do you want to know what happened to the guy who interviewed you at MGM? The one who was so hot?"

Fucking Lauren. Lauren and her big mouth. This is what happened when women didn't work. She had no life, Lauren.

"I'm bored, Donny," said Amy. "I've got a job to do."

To prove her point, she texted Dan in front of him: *did the dog ever come back? pizza or Mexican for dinner?*

To Donny she said, "I thought we had to imagine something new."

"Multiple universes?"

"You said they were old hat."

"Finding out what happened to you in another space and time, that isn't new? I didn't expect you to be so prosaic."

Donny stared through the glass. She followed his gaze. Naresh was digging something out of his ear. Slightly nauseated, she turned back around again. She looked at her phone.

Dan texted: *Thing Two got sent home from school today. It's okay. I took care of it.*

Amy texted back: *WHAAAAAT? Is he okay?*

Dan texted: *I just said it's okay.*

"What if?" said Donny.

Amy looked up at him.

"'What if I'd married the furrier?' Finding the answer to that question with accuracy, that's new. And if 'what-if' looks better than what-is, well, why not?"

"What are you proposing?"

"Well, Grandma's gone, but if she wasn't, maybe she'd still have a chance at love. Or at least the possibility would keep her coming back to us for more."

"Now who's prosaic?" said Amy, in the middle of texting *I'm allowed to be worried about my son.* "Sounds like a romance novel."

She put her phone down.

"You'd really use this thing to find out about a furrier? What about wars or global warming, cures for cancer, California's turning into a desert—we're drinking processed pee water!"

"Or," he said, spitballing, off in his own Donny orbit, "we can turn personalized alternative reality into a game, into a cyber-story with chapters, chapters you could augment, you could choose or mix and match. You can act on the information you receive in meat space or just mess around with it online."

What now, Theo? Amy worried about her son. Donny wasn't the only one who could choose to not listen.

"Music, visuals, avatars," said Donny. "You could even hook up with a partner. The furrier, for instance."

"Think that's called flirting. Can't picture Grandma doing that," said Amy.

"Grandma's dead," said Donny. "But you, if we're acquired by Google? We've spent the last few decades getting to know everything about you by what you do online, far more than your husband or your shrink or your BFF, my mother, ever did. Your shopping habits, your reading habits, your medical records, when you Dumpster dive for frenemies and old crushes, your political views, what you paid for your house—everything money. Of course, the porn . . .

"From that data alone we can predict your behavior. We know when you're stressed and when you're vulnerable. When the biopsy comes back. When you wonder what's a better way to go, fighting with chemo, or downing Xanax in a bathtub. C'mon, Amy, what messages in a bottle do you send out into cyberspace? We can factor in your secret secrets. All via algorithm, so you don't feel busted. The shrinks will go out of business, but who cares, really? That's the beauty of math. We could even do it behind your back. Like targeted advertising, although that seems so 2001." He paused.

"I don't think I'd want that," said Amy, slowly catching on.

"Well, your boss might. Your hubby. You know finding ways to lead you toward maximizing your potential."

"Donny, that sounds illegal and immoral and like outing and indoctrination."

He scratched his nose, stared into space.

"Well, what would you want to know?" said Donny.

He glazed. Or perhaps he was ruminating deeply. Profundities. Wise-man pretentious bullcrap.

"We have to think a bit outside the box here," said Donny. "Go rogue. Cater to the middle. Cleveland, Sacramento, Kansas fucking City."

As if he'd read her subconscious: "Do you want to see what your daughter would look like now? I could probably do that for you with a high degree of accuracy. I don't even think I need the DNA samples. Image-wise. You know, your hair, his aunt Elisabeth's tits."

A block of ice shattered somewhere in her cranium, sending cold spiky shards down her spine and through her shoulders, piercing the veins in her arms with its frigid needles.

A girl.

"Mom told me," said Donny. "About the miscarriage."

It was an abortion. Not even Lauren knew that much.

"No one knows," said Amy. "Dan doesn't. *He* doesn't."

"The Cloud knows," said Donny. "But I won't tell. You can trust me."

Trust Donny?

"They had fertility issues. His sperm's been tested. Unless he lied to her, Amy, they don't know."

Wow. What? What!

"He searches for you sometimes. He Google-images you."

She'd hoped, but she hadn't known. It was all so long ago. She could barely remember him. It was hard to picture his chin. When she tried to focus on it, it weakened, and began to slope down toward his throat. But was it true? Did he sometimes comb through cyberspace for her, at his desk at work, while eating his turkey sandwich and his take-out soup? Or was Donny just holding out a carrot?

"His wife is younger than you are. Want to see her? She's got a little chub. I think you could take her, maybe if you cared more. Face cream and all that."

She wouldn't fall down that rabbit hole.

"I don't want to take her. I love Dan. I haven't seen him in a million years. I actively don't think about him."

"He's a runner. You're a runner," said Donny. "I know Dan's got a gym membership, but Dan's a sitter. His wife throws pots. She's nutty for Pinterest." Donny rolled his eyes.

"That doesn't mean it would have worked."

"It didn't work," said Donny. "The question is, would it have worked if the kid had lived? Would you have married him or done it on your own? Gotten a divorce? Or would it work now? IRL or in cyberspace? I'm a little confused myself."

"Nothing works now," said Amy, rising. "Including me. Which is why I am now going back to my desk."

As she turned to go, she noticed her hands were shaking. Amy looked from her hands to the floor and said: "It's not nice to spy on people, Donny. Don't ever do it to me again."

"Invisible Spy?" said Donny, the permanently installed lightbulb above his head brightening and dimming. He looked at his phone. "Ugh, I have to take a French test."

That night when Amy walked home from work, it was already dark outside, there was a chill in the air, and a handful of stars were thrown scattershot across the sky. From the street, she could see lights on in every room in the front of her house, a little diorama of suburban life. Dan, her Dan, the one she'd built her life around, was a depressed, unemployed man, upstairs, lying with his computer on his belly on their bed. He never pulled the curtains. The

Things were in the family room playing PlayStation 4, rotting out their brains. She could tell at a glance that Thing One was torturing Thing Two and they were on the verge of a major brawl, just from the body language. Theo tended to fold in at the torso just before he exploded. Poor kid. A bad day.

She opened the mailbox, packed with junk and a padded manila envelope addressed to Jack—he was the only one who got snail mail anymore; Lily baked him brownies and sent him paperback books of poems. She had good taste: Rilke, Neruda, Keats. Whatever she sent, Jack read. "She's so amazing, Mom," Jack said, when she found him squirreled away in his room reading Dickinson. "Where does she find this stuff?" *Where did she find Dickinson?* Amy held her tongue. Their correspondence was so romantic. They were like the land that time forgot. The rest of the mail was mostly just catalogs and bills. She headed through the carport and walked around back, where all was blessedly dark and unilluminated, and entered the house through the kitchen. She put the mail down on the breakfast bar. God give me strength, thought Amy. There's so much left to do! But she wasn't ready.

Instead she veered into the laundry room, picking up the socks and tights she'd discarded that morning—no little elf had miraculously done the wash in her absence—and after stripping off her work slacks and blouse, slipped her running gear back on. She fished one of Jack's dirty T-shirts out of the laundry pile and pulled it on over her head. It smelled like him, like a crowded Metro in Paris in August where she and Dan had gone for a last hurrah just before he was born. It smelled like the human equivalent of skunk—it was a stink that woke her up. She tied her hair into a ponytail with the rubber band she always wore around her left wrist. Then she walked back outside and put on her sneakers where she'd left them on the steps. She did a little ballet stretch, using the handrail as a barre, and then bounced up and down on her toes some, listening to her ankles crack, trying to psych herself up.

It was a relief to be swallowed whole by the darkness, and to be alone that way, no kids, no husband, no job, no Donny, no dog, just Amy, a girl again, suspended in space, ready to take off. If her daughter had lived, Amy wondered, would they be friends now? Would she possibly be this lonely?

Her idyll was interrupted when Squidward erupted out of the solid wall of night and instantly loped right past her.

"Whoa," said Amy.

From down the block she saw the glow of Jack's phone. He and Lily walked the dog together, using FaceTime most school nights, or whenever both had too much homework to go out with flesh-and-blood friends on the weekends.

"Hey, Mom," said Jack. He was inarguably the best-looking person in their household, with his olive skin, green eyes, longish dirty blond surfer hair. Behind his back, Amy referred to him as "the lifeguard." She and Dan had made him.

"Is Lily joining us for dinner?" said Amy. "We can time our pizza delivery around hers."

"We had pizza yesterday."

"Then Mexican. I don't care. She likes that taco place at the mall near her apartment. . . . She could order a taco-free taco salad."

Jack gave a little salute and walked into the house.

"Our treat. But you be in charge of it," Amy called after him. "You can put her dinner on my credit card. Use Seamless."

The dog was a dark shadow waiting for her on the corner.

Maybe she should quit her job, Amy thought, although she needed her job. Maybe she should call up that bitch Lauren and ream her out. Maybe she could get one of those little nanobots to shoot a gamma ray into the recollection zone of her brain and obliterate the endlessly rolling arpeggio of grief and regret and mourning. Fuck you, Donny! It was the selective excising of memory that she craved. But it was too late. He'd awakened the beast inside her.

Amy took a step and then another. She would text Donny when she got home. She would meet him off campus, on campus, in the morning. Squidward's eyes glinted an unholy red as he galloped back to join her. Her lungs expanded with each stride. She could smell the eucalyptus, the gorgeous creature moving effortlessly by her side.

This is what I have instead of heroin, Amy thought.

So she ran.

.   .   .

If anyone ever asked, Dan would say he met Maryam online. That's where he spent most of his time, days like today anyway, at home, lying on his bed, laptop on his lap, fingertips to keyboard, indulging any random passing brain wave bothering to dress up as an idea—even the tiniest little hiccup of an inquiry. He tended to google a lot, when he wasn't actively job searching or reading his blogs and news sites or chatting with other out-of-work journos and publishers. One semisuicidal type he'd known who'd been a lifer at the *L.A. Times* had just posted "the future holds *blank*" on Twitter. Dan immediately filled in "TK," feeling clever. That spurred a whole twenty-five-minute data transfer at #shitouttaluck and then a couple of Facebook chats: What was the origin of the term "TK"? Who cared, except people like Dan and his underemployed cronies, still nerdy in an era where geeks reigned supreme?

He should have left already. Jack, his eldest boy, had ordered their dinner and texted Dan to pick it up, even though Jack had his driver's license. *I ordered it*, Jack texted. Dan had wanted to write back a rebuttal, *entitled brat*. But, in fact, he relished the opportunity to get out of the house. This time of evening had a perfect chill to it, and if he was lucky and it was an odd day pollution-wise, he would be able to smell wood smoke.

After all these years of writing and editing, Dan had momentarily forgotten what the letters TK stood for, a symptom of typical age-related memory loss, he supposed, but consoled himself as he strapped on his Chacos with the thought that the domino effect of dead neurons could probably be reversed—as posted on Digg.com at 2:00 a.m. that very morning, which came via an article in yesterday's *Guardian*. If he increased the blood flow to his brain by ingesting intense amounts of high-flavanol cocoa, which Dan could ostensibly obtain by drowning himself in buckets of hot chocolate or taking some as-yet-unproduced magic pill, he could obliterate a couple decades of neurological cell damage. He thought "a couple decades" instead of "a couple *of* decades" because the former had become an American standard in informal speech, and it was imperative that he keep up to compete, although his third grade teacher, Mrs. Rini, had done a hell of a job ingraining that rule into his thick skull.

"Unless we are referring to two people, as in 'the couple is getting a divorce,' *couple* requires the word *of* after it." (It had been the 1970s; all the couples actually *were* getting a divorce, including Dan's parents.)

At this age, only repeated acts of willful cognition could beat the old standards out of him.

He picked up his phone and his car keys and headed down the stairs, yelling as he went.

"Milo and Theo, no blood while I'm gone. Jack, keep an eye on them."

"'Live long and prosper, Dad,'" Jack said. They were both *Star*

Trek fans—the original series. "That means I'm in charge," Jack yelled to the Things from the doorway to his room, and then Jack firmly shut his door behind him.

"You can't check on them with the door closed," Dan muttered, but he did nothing to reverse his descent. He'd text Jack from the car, reminding him. Instead, lightning-thumbed Dan quickly searched for a definition, as he poked his head into the family room.

"'To come' is a printing and journalism reference," stated the polycephalic Wikipedia. Having that lost reserve of knowledge now actively restored into the language-recovery file located God knows where in his cerebellum (he'd have to look it up) was a miniblast of relief. God love the Internet! He knew "TK"; he'd always known it. Verbal amnesia had a beige elasticity to it, like a psychic ACE bandage. As he strained to find the words, Dan could feel it stretching gummily across his intelligence. But instead of worrying the panic—"What is TK? What is TK again?"—only to have it creep in later and unexpectedly through some neural cat-door, he now, with a visit to a search engine and a click of a return key, could instantly replace that painful, stretchy, mushroom-hued *lack* with a Technicolor waterfall.

Recollections, connotations, tumbled forth—a cover story particularly riddled with the proofreader's mark, TK, on the number of dead and injured when he was pushing copy on 9/11 (after the first wild-eyed projections, the count of the surviving injured plummeted to a crushing statistical insignificance). And he had an oddly visceral association that he assumed had to do with aging and forgetting in the first place: the lavender scent of Mrs. Rini's embroidered linen hankie, the whiter-than-white down on her sloping chin, the geometry of lines on the skin of her soft wrinkled cheek, which had been as frightening at the time as it was comforting.

The twins were playing PlayStation 4. Miles was sort of dashing in the screen's blue light. His red curls made him look like a boy in a Ralph Lauren ad—Waspy, a kid who would grow up to play rugby, maybe ride horses, someday own a humidor. On Theo, the same bright corona made him look like a sad and strange clown. His polo shirt fit less well than Miles's did. They were of matching weight and size, but Miles already had the swagger of a mini-man, straight shoulders and tapered waist, athletic somehow. Theo hunched and managed to look both gaunt and slightly paunchy, though he was by far the stronger of the two, powered at times by a lit gas jet of pure burning emotion; he was also sweeter. A lot of people could tell them apart, teachers, even some guests upon first meeting them, although they were identical. They wore the DNA differently.

"No blood," said Dan.

"Right, Dad," said Miles, without looking up from the screen.

Dan hesitated for a second. It was times like this, when the twins were getting along, that often turned catastrophic. If they were bickering or giving each other the cold shoulder, there would be momentary blasts of steam that relieved the pressure. If things were going well, a volcanic eruption might soon follow. And even though he'd let Theo have some "Theo time" where he "went into his imagination," for most of the afternoon, Dan bet he was still pretty wrecked from another damaging day at school.

He looked down at his phone.

Wikipedia again. "TK is used to signify that additional information will be added at a later date," although the page itself read: "This article has multiple issues."

"TK is one of a series of deliberate journalistic misspellings, like 'lede' for 'lead,' 'graf' for 'paragraph' and 'sked' for 'schedule,'" wrote two women who authored a useful blog called the Renegade Writer for those "embracing the freelance life." These purposeful spelling errors made them stand out on copy so that they would be deleted, fixed, or filled in before the article made it to the printers. Answers to his questions, large or small, gave Dan an instantaneous release of anxiety, sort of like taking a drag on a cigarette had done when he was a young reporter, the first inhale focusing the mind. Or the endorphin-induced chill in his veins that followed the sound of a source picking up the phone back when such a noise was still audible. Or even how jerking off had made him feel when he was young and horny.

"You're still here?" Miles looked over his shoulder at his father staring at his device. "Dan, you need rehab," he said, echoing his mother. He turned back to Call of Duty, Advanced Warfare, Exo-Survival. An Xmas present from Amy's psychotic brother, Michael, arriving via FedEx. They had not seen him in person for five or six years, thank God.

The problem with search engines was that they were more addictive than even smoking/beating off had been—after exhausting those two vices Dan had still wanted, eventually, to do something else. Not this depravity. Alone, on a sailboat, sitting out on deck, a laptop on his lap, the midnight-blue silvery water (like mercury, he dreamed, *like mercury*) taking him somewhere new, living online would have been a great way to spend retirement—but Dan was nowhere near ready for retirement. In fact, he never wanted to retire. He was just pushing fifty, he had a family, mouths to feed and all that. He had drive and hunger somewhere, like a phantom limb, agitating faintly away in his gut. He'd been an ambitious young man, he'd gotten drunk just looking at the constantly changing face of the churning, radiant world. He was simply interested in everything. But print had kicked the shit out of him. He felt so defeated and unemployable. So, he allowed himself these harmless hits of web vacations—but that wasn't how Dan met Maryam.

He'd met her at a bar. The same bar where he might run into her tonight. Just the thought of that, seeing her, not merely thinking about her, made him want to shout, but also curl into a ball in the back of his closet. He did neither but Snapchatted her. Then he exited the family room and walked to the front door. He picked a fleece up off the bench where all their jackets and shoes seemed to migrate. Was it his or Jack's? These days it was difficult to tell. Dark green. X-large. He pulled it over his head. He guessed it was his. He'd paid for it.

·   ·   ·

Jack picked up the envelope addressed to him from the breakfast bar when he entered the house, the lettering of his name, *Jack Messinger*, all curvy and round. Just seeing her handwriting gave him a hard-on.

"It's here," he said to Lily over FaceTime. "Now I got to get rid of my dad."

Conveniently, a text had come in from said parental—asking him to pick up the Mexican food. No fucking way. Jack had just placed their order, along with Lily's, he wasn't lifting another fucking finger. Plus, the timing was sweet. Dad might actually leave the house. Jack messaged his father back: *I ordered it.*

Not that Dad would have knocked or barged in, like his mom might. Dad pretty much stayed in his own room these days, unless he suddenly got all freaked out looking in the mirror at his gut and asked Jack to go with him to the gym, or to flip a Frisbee on campus and bond or something, or he'd cajole Jack into walking with him to California Ave for some fro-yo, Jack then being his excuse to pig out. It was his mom, most likely, who would be the one to burst in with the laundry folded or with a nag she was just dying to nag in person. But Mom was out running; she'd be gone for at least forty-five, maybe an hour, plus then she'd want to shower. A Thing might be stupid enough to come in without knocking, a Thing at loose ends or in the middle of a fight with another Thing, but not a Thing mentally handcuffed to the PlayStation 4, which was the same as a Thing heavily narcotized and in a straitjacket, strapped down onto a stretcher. Jack knew; he was young once, too. Still, he would lock his door, out of respect for Lily. It was the right thing to do.

"Baby, I can't wait to be alone with you," Lily said from the screen in his hand. His boner got bigger just listening to her voice. Somewhere between little girl and a purr. His dick had a life of its own; it was both inside and outside his body, its electric vibrato drowning whatever sensation every other appendage and organ could possibly muster. Each month, Lily sounded more southern. Word-honey oozed from her mouth.

He looked down at the screen. She'd turned her head, probably to pet the cat; it had been sitting sleepily on her bed next to her, like another one of her stuffed animals. Jack called it "the dead cat," even though it wasn't dead and its name was Coconut, but because it never seemed to move. It always magically appeared by Lily's side, silent and immobile, like a fluffy white bit of stuffed upholstery, and at the flat end of all that fur, it had a heart-shaped velvet-tipped leathery nose in its smashed-in face, both queenly and prizefighterish.

In the two years Jack and Lily had been going out, he'd given her a plush narwhal and an endangered snow leopard stuffie, which came as a gift with a donation to the World Wildlife Fund and had been suggested to him by his mother; also, a CVS teddy bear with Larry Astrichan's face pasted on it—he'd cut it out from a campus newspaper and used superglue. Astrichan was a middle-aged post-dad fanboy (his kid had already graduated high school a few years back) and the closest thing to a mascot that the Vikings had; he broke out into push-ups whenever Paly scored—which struck Lily as endearing and always made her laugh. Jack had given her the bear for their first Valentine's Day. Jack always made sure to catch Astrichan doing push-ups on his iPhone at football games because Lily thought Astrichan was so cute. Her own dad had walked out on her, so she was touched, she said, by "his cartoony loyalty and devotion."

Astrichan's kid was living in Philly now—Lily Facebook stalked them both, father and son. She was the only girl in the whole world who would Facebook-stalk Larry Astrichan, and it made Jack fall even more deeply in love with her. Someone else with a dad like hers might feel bitter. Someone else might think Astrichan too pathetic or dumb or mentally challenged to add up to anything more than a joke. Nobody else Jack had ever met would see the ineffable beauty of Astrichan, his enduring fatherly enthusiasms long after his active role as a parent was over, the way he threw his potbellied body full-throttle into the game in homage to a time when his appreciation and support were all that mattered, when the physical embodiment of his investment in li'l Lar (yes he named his offspring after himself) was enough to assuage the pain of any skin lost in the game. Astrichan's body was his testament; shaking it to his own rhythm was like a rapper barking out his love. Or so said Lily in her Lily way. "He's the sweetest," said Lily. No one in the world was as pure of heart as she was.

Jack took her with him wherever he'd go. She graced the routinized tedium of his days. He spent more time with Lily when she was away than when she visited. When she was in Palo Alto she had other friends to see. His mom wouldn't let her sleep in his room, even though they slept together by Skype every night. When she was in town, he couldn't go to the bathroom with her, or watch her put a tampon in; things she let him do by phone. In person, she was too embarrassed and uptight.

But when Lily was in Texas, she could be in her class and he could be in his class, and still their phones could be sitting in each other's lap, almost as if they were holding hands. Via her iPhone, he could perch on the light green toilet tank in her condo near the jar of pastel Gulf Coast sea glass petals Cindy, her mom, liked to collect, while Lily showered and washed her hair, and still watch the 49ers on TV with the Things and his dad in the redwood-paneled family room. He could be splitting a Mission-style burrito on one of the benches downtown on University Avenue with his buddy, Kevin Choi, on a Saturday afternoon while Lily was getting a pedicure with some girlfriends in Fort Worth. Just last weekend, she and the girls were squealing in disgust exactly the way he'd hoped they would when he caught Kevin shoving almost his whole burrito-half in his mouth at once on video and all that chunky guac squished out.

"Oh, Kevin, oh, sweetie, don't keep doing this to yourself," Lily had said, turning bright red as she giggled. "You can take little bites. We don't have to laugh. I'll still love you."

It made Jack feel like Lily was right there sitting next to him in the stadium to FaceTime when the ball was in play—they'd each high-five their respective screen with an index finger when Astrichan dropped down and gave 'em twenty.

Jack couldn't see Lily's face now, as he climbed the stairs to his room, as she was indeed bent over the cat, he could see that fluffy white dead tail, and just a sliver of the top of her ear, her blond hair so silky, that little pink half-moon sliced right through it, peeking out like a Japanese peach gummy candy just where she'd adorned it with the world's tiniest hoop. Lily's dad had sent it from Hong Kong four months prior at Christmas, although nobody knew why he was there. "A deal," he'd said. "That's his favorite word," said Lily.

Before Hong Kong the dad had lived in Hawaii and before that he'd said he lived in Detroit, but Lily and her mom, and even her dad's own mother, Grandma Rose, weren't exactly sure if he was telling the truth; he was a deadbeat and maybe a functioning alcoholic, and he'd long ago given up his landline and refused to give them his address, or anything like that. The earring was what Lily had asked for, filament thin like an angel's hair, with three tiny diamonds at the center of the hoop, almost like those bejeweled false eyelashes she'd bought at Dougherty's Pharmacy and worn to a disco-themed high school dance, but less coarse (she'd gone with a friend, a chill gay kid named Rex; Jack had checked him out when he'd visited over vacation). She'd wanted the earring for a septum pierce. Her yoga teacher Stefanie had one and it looked so delicate and so pretty, Lily said, but Jack said no. So, she'd pierced the crown of her ear instead; using the tiny hoop to decorate the rim, and sometimes in the right light the piece of jewelry looked just like one more shiny golden highlight on her shiny golden head.

Lily's dad hadn't sent her mom any money in a long, long time, which is why they'd moved to Dallas, where it was cheaper—a lot longer than before Jack and Lily had ever hooked up, although he'd seen her around. They were in the same grade but they'd never had a class together, and she walked across campus like she was floating, slow and with her feet barely touching the ground, so that anyone with eyes knew who she was. Both of Lily's parents were from Texas, and Grandma Rose still had the house Lily's father had grown up in, and Lily's mother had gotten a job through an old friend from high school, he knew the developer who had built the museum tower. The developer had sold it along with his consortium a few years back to the Dallas Police and Fire Pension System, which was working out all right—the job was; the tower not so much. Its glass skin reflected too much light on the museum below, wrecking some of the artwork inside. The new owners couldn't get rid of the luxury lofts, because people who loved art were the people who were supposed to buy them, and people who loved art didn't love the glare. Lily's mother said her old boss was sick over it. He treasured the museum, which was why he built his tower right next to it. He'd trusted the architect. Lily's mother was sick over it, too. She was still the "director of resident relations." Her job was to give the tenants what they wanted—wine tastings, speed dating, helping them plan events for their charitable foundations. Lily had sent him the link on the Towers website. It read: "It's Cindy's mission to make your dreams come true."

"It sounds like my mom's a prostitute," Lily said.

"She's doing her best to take care of you," Jack said. He was trying to be supportive. That's what good boyfriends did. They were "present" and "loving," even if they happened to be hundreds of miles away.

Imagine too much light wrecking anything, Jack thought. He was a fan of light. He liked illumination. Or was it the other way around, too much light, too much vision or clarity, being too much for anything or anyone to handle? At least Lily still had the earring from her father. She never took it off.

"Milo and Theo, no blood while I'm gone," Dad called out. He was descending the stairs right by Jack, but his head was in his phone and he didn't seem to see him. "Jack," he yelled, his voice way too loud for the lack of distance, "keep an eye on them."

"That means I'm in charge," Jack yelled back from the threshold of his room, startling his father. He firmly shut his door behind him. He locked it and put a chair under the doorknob, just in case.

Lily gazed up from the cat. Her smile, her mouth, the way her tongue sort of pressed a little bit out between her teeth, her lips; all of it knocked him out.

"Which ones did you put in there?" Jack said. It had been a long day, he probably needed a shower, but she didn't seem to mind the way he smelled, she kind of liked to cuddle up on his chest near his armpit even though she'd say: "pee-yew," and she wasn't exactly in the room anyway.

"The same ones I have on," said Lily.

She got that look, he could see it on the screen, where she was far away and right there at the same time, clouds in her irises, lips parted, the way she looked when they had sex.

No one else knows that look but me, Jack thought; and his dick swelled again with pride, so heavy and thick now it felt like it was bursting.

He sat down on the lower bunk of his bunk bed. He thought about Larry Astrichan, his bald head bobbing, his spare tire hitting the ground first when he dropped and gave twenty. Thinking about Larry Astrichan was always good when Jack wanted to control his erection. Kevin said he thought about grapefruit, but Jack thought that was sort of pervy and pretty effing weird. Kevin never had a girlfriend, anyway. Jack teased him about it sometimes, but Lily told him to stop.

He tore open the top of the manila envelope.

"How long did you wear them?" he said.

"Two days, like you told me," said Lily. And then she crinkled her nose. "Don't blame me if they're too stinky."

Inside wrapped in red tissue paper were a pair of tiger and lace thong panties with a pink ribbon threaded through the waistband and a matching push-up bra. Jack took just the paper to his face and breathed in. It smelled like her. Sweat and soap and pussy juice, musky and piscine and spicy, the faintest scent of pee. He buried himself in it.

"Stop," she said. "You're embarrassing me." When he looked up, she was indeed pink with embarrassment.

"I'm sorry," he said. "I'll slow down. It's just almost like having you here."

"Almost," she said.

"Better than almost," he said. "But not the same as real."

"Why?" she said.

"Because with the computer and the phone, I can see you from every angle."

She listened and set her teeth. The pink rising to purple on her cheeks. Then she said, "I guess you have it all figured out."

"I've been waiting all week," said Jack. He almost whispered it. "I think about you all the time. Come on, let's light the candles and turn the lights down."

"Why?" said Lily, kind of saucy now. "Because I'm shy?"

"Because you're fragile," said Jack, lighting the candles in his room and turning the lights down.

"I am *so* not fragile," said Lily. She lit a ring of votives on the surfaces surrounding her bed—bedposts, shelf, night table. "Look who's talking about being fragile. Look at your life and then look at mine," said Lily. "You have two parents. I only have my mom, and she's more of a teenager than I am." With a clicker, she turned her white candelabra chandelier with frosted flame-shaped lightbulbs down to a simmering glow.

Jack looked. At her silky blond hair and her pink ear tips and her stuffed animals and her white shorts with the tiger and lace thong panties snuggled secretly away inside and her sweatshirt-gray tank top with the matching bra's straps and her skinny arms, so thin above the wrist it wouldn't take much to snap one; her pink-and-orange bed.

"I'm not fragile in the least," said Lily.

"Okay, you're not," Jack said. "You're sweet. You're smart. You're gorgeous. Let's not talk about it now."

She still looked pissed. Her hair fell over one eye as she sorrowfully shook her head.

"Not now, or ever," Jack said. "Can you move your hair behind your ear so I can see your face?" He motioned with his hand. "Like this? Like the way I would touch you if I were there, the way I'd take that little strand of hair and I'd move it behind your ear."

Slowly Lily moved her hair behind her ear.

"Then I'd take my hand, and I'd press it against your chest, above the neckline of your shirt, flat like this," and he took off his T-shirt by pulling it up from the back of his shoulder blades and over his head, and then he laid his right palm flat across his bare chest. "And I'd feel your heart, and as I kept my hand on your chest your heartbeat would begin to race, can you do it, Lily? Put your hand on your chest. Can you feel it? And right now, there's a heat in your chest and there's a heat down there between your legs, and you want my hand there, put my hand there, Lily."

She put her hand down there, between her legs, her fingers with her sky-blue fingernails pressed flat like a little fan, in front of her white, white shorts.

"I'm putting my thigh there. You are sitting on my thigh, facing away, and I'm pressing up hard and you are pressing down. And you begin to rock, you rock against my thigh and it makes you feel so good. So fizzy inside, down there and up on your mound."

Lily turned pink. He didn't know if he was still embarrassing her or if it was because he was turning her on, but he wasn't about to risk it by stopping.

"Now I'm taking off your top, Lily. Take it off, take it off, sweetheart," and she took it off, sitting on the edge of her bed in her tiger-and-lace push-up bra, her hand pressing against her white shorts, rocking, and Jack spread the bra she'd sent him over his face. He could smell her underarms. He could smell her perfume and her deodorant. "I've got my head between your breasts, Lily, and I'm kissing you there, in between, and as I kiss you, you wrap your arm around my neck so your breasts squeeze against my face. Squeeze me, honey."

He didn't even have to look up then, he had the bra pushed up against his face, the cups so thick and padded you could push a pin through them and it wouldn't come out the other side.

"I'm reaching around behind your back and I'm unhooking your bra with my fingers, what a player, one handed! Go ahead now, take it off."

What was so amazing about Lily was when they did this, when they had phone sex, she just obeyed him. In real life, she sometimes talked. In real life, she'd say, "You're on my hair," or "Your face is too scratchy," or even something potentially dick-wilting, like "You're so cute" while pinching that extra inch that sat above his hips, even though water polo had made him strong, thin, and bony. But on the phone, it was like she was in a trance, like she'd do whatever he wanted.

While she was taking off her bra, he pulled down his jams and his dick was tent-poling his boxers. When she looked up, she gasped.

He loved that.

"Look at what you do to me," he said. He pulled his boxers up and away and then down.

"Okay, lie back now. Take off your shorts, too."

She did. Now he had her panties in his hand. He said, "Pull them down," and she did and kicked them off and he got a glimpse of her open pussy. "Pretend I'm going down on you. Use your fingers, they're my tongue," and Lily's hand went down. "Wait, get your phone," he said. She kind of rolled her eyes, but she did what he asked of her. "Put it down there, I want to watch my tongue on your pussy, put your fingers down there," and she did and he watched and he took her panties to his nose and mouth and he breathed and even licked them as he got up so close with such a clear view of her cunt. With his other hand he started to beat off.

"I'm making you come, Lily." She started to moan. He could hear her from the computer and from the phone. He could watch her fingers move around and around and around. Her back arched, he could tell by the way she lifted her butt and pussy up, for him, for him. Then he felt himself begin to peak, with the panties in his mouth now and his hand pulling hard and fast. Just as he rocketed, his dick pulsating, his jizz shooting out far over his bed, he whispered, "Lily, Lily, Lily.

"Come with me."

. . .

Before Dan ever laid eyes on Maryam, he had been aware of her, her Internet presence. He'd been reading Maryam's posts for a long time (he'd pictured her differently, less intense, not so crazily attractive) mostly on Fukushima.update, or Fukuleaks, or the *Japan Times* online. British nuclear watchdog websites. She was all over the net, covering "Fukushima Fog," her coinage, somewhat akin to "the Fog of War," which he'd looked up, the derivation, because why the hell not? It was originally a German term, *Nebel des Krieges,* and also the title of a documentary about Robert S. McNamara, the

S. for "Strange," his mother's maiden name. Dan had actually seen *The Fog of War* on a date night with his wife in 2003.

"Only you, Dan," Amy had said then, when he'd surprised her with the tickets. Not that she was wholly uninterested—they shared a leftist bent, sure; plus a love of history, a taste for documentary film—but come on. Even he, now in retrospect, had to admit the movie hardly qualified as a romantic evening, although it had indeed turned out that way. A long walk after, ice cream, stretching the precious time alone together. A bottle of red wine at home after they sent the babysitter on her way. The conversation never seemed to end in those days, except when it ended in bed. There had been nothing they hadn't talked about, except maybe sports. Amy was a good date; she'd go with him to see basketball games and yell as loudly as anyone; but it wasn't something she much liked to discuss. Statistics. Bad calls. Life got better for both of them when he finally had Jack to talk to; Jack loved that shit, too. Dan could go on and on. Amy was generous and indulgent. She was wonderful! She mostly listened then.

Their very first night out had been his choice as well, Luis Buñuel's *That Obscure Object of Desire*, at Theater 80 on St. Marks Place, in the brief period when they were both living in New York. Amy had had an internship at one of the women's magazines and Dan was writing freelance for the *Village Voice*. In the film, all that women want is money and all that men want is sex. After, Amy, so cute in her miniskirt and knee-high boots—her hair lustrous and still rolling all the way down to her waist—had thrust out her hand for a definitive evening-ending shake, making it clear she would not let him kiss her good night, that night or maybe ever.

Ha. Over the past twenty-something years Amy's lips and tongue had been on and in every available inch of Dan's body and vice versa.

Sure, he'd had to reel her in; she was so defended when he'd met her, but it was worth it. *A Love Supreme.* The John Coltrane Suite. They'd played the first movement at their wedding. The part where Coltrane chants the phrase, over and over again. The music, the poetry, gave some form of ecstatic shape to how he felt about her.

McNamara, the former U.S. secretary of defense, often referred to as an "architect" of the Vietnam War in the books and articles Dan liked to dig deep in, appeared in the film *The Fog of War* alternately denying his culpability and overcome by blistering self-recrimination. At one point, he'd admitted to complicity in mass murder during World War II, when as a boy-wonder strategist he had helped plan the annihilation of 100,000 civilians in Tokyo, using "conventional methods," aka incendiary bombs, which meant they burned to death. The confession stuck with Dan. Was McNamara so disassociated from typical human feeling that for him warfare felt like a chess game? Although clearly he'd been haunted by his own actions the rest of his life. And how could the Japanese, sixty-some-odd years after the dual atrocities of Hiroshima and Nagasaki, now find themselves in the bizarre position of self-radiating?

Dan would have to watch the film again to make sure he remembered it all correctly. There were a lot of things he remembered incorrectly. He had initially recollected the tattoo of a butterfly wing on Maryam's long left foot as covering the entire surface of her instep when, in reality, upon the privilege of seeing it a second time—one night sitting next to her when she had been wearing some attractive gold sandals—it was actually a much more delicate thing, its lacy edges kissing the pinky toe side, the two stained-glass wings in profile, energetically gathered together, as if the butterfly were readying to unfold and take flight.

In the film McNamara introduced his eleven rules of war. "In order to do good, you may have to engage in evil," which sounded like something Google might say *now,* and "Belief and seeing are often wrong," giving Dan the room to wonder which axiom was more valuable and which was more self-exculpatory.

Dan was probably ADD. That's what Amy said. Belief and seeing are often wrong. How his mind jumped around! Theo most likely had inherited his neurology. Amy had blurted that out, too, more than once actually, when she was tired and frustrated—which was pretty much all the time these days—then walked it back, because as angry as they got sometimes (they were married) she never truly wanted to hurt him. He'd always felt safe in the arms of her love.

"Coney Island brain," his mother had called it: whirring things, music, lights lighting up all over the place; it had been this way until he had found his life's work, writing and reporting (and then on the weekends, when he was supposed to rest, the whole amusement park jazz in his head would rev up again, unless he did something totally immersive, like pogoing in a mosh pit, or getting so fucked up he could no longer feel his legs, which got kind of hard of course once they'd had kids).

Now there was no job-related discipline around to gird him, no deadlines to narrow and deepen his focus, no coworkers to both impress and egg him on. He was going crazy not working. He felt worthless and he was going crazy. Belief and seeing are often wrong! Good thing for the lovers of out of sight, out of mind that radiation is colorless, odorless, tasteless, making it so easy to deny. Mrs. Rini had taught him that, too, in science class (which came directly after cursive), and he'd never forgotten to be terrified of radioactivity's invisibility, the inherent insidiousness, like an evil villain's superpower.

Ever since 2011, when the earthquake and tsunami hit Japan and the nuclear reactors at the Daiichi power plant had first flooded, then exploded, and *then* actively melted down, hard news, actual data on the results of these catastrophes, had been difficult to nail. The privately owned Tokyo Electric Power Company, which oversaw the plants—an embattled and, Dan thought, clueless firm since day one—had been less than forthcoming with information. Time and time again the Japanese government had proven itself to be an inept communicator. The Japanese lived in an official state of disavowal. The country's Government Secrets Act put reporters in danger of being jailed for revealing unsanctioned information. Dan was a freedom-of-the-press guy, *Je Suis Charlie*, a Twitter buddy of Glenn Greenwald's. He saw the GSA as Japan's Patriot Act. A dangerous, immoral abomination.

If he had a job, a real one, not, like the last two, in custom publishing—one, for God's sake, geared to producing a lifestyle mag for the owners of a specific brand of luxury car—Dan would have jumped into action at this kind of official taunt. "The Government Secrets Act." Fuck that.

Along with his fellow "people who tweet," he had from time to time—between expressing abject disgust *and* love for the New York Giants, and curating a gallery of Donald Trump's aerodynamics-defying hairstyles—bemoaned the lack of international coverage, which lulled the whole world into thinking things were actually under control *over there*. Or at least far away enough not to matter. He was busy worrying daily instead about, in no significantly apparent order: ISIS, Syria, the flood of refugees across Europe, Boko Haram, insane Republicans, income inequality, what to eat for dinner, the morality or potential deliciousness of foie gras and cinnamon French toast ice cream sandwiches, which Dan had just read about in an honest-to-goodness although lousy paper (the *Chronicle*, where Dan used to be employed) this very morning (and tweeted about it, good God, he was that desperate to connect).

Not working could flatten just about anyone's life. A person's dignity chewed up, extruded, and expulsed like a tasteless wad of gum, then poleaxed and crushed by throngs of inured stilettos, boots, and Crocs on a sidewalk in front of Neiman Marcus. Dan had joined the unemployed ranks of tennis moms, urban teens, ex–factory workers, midlevel managers, an army of newly minted PhDs, the undereducated, downsized, oversized, disabled, bored, and boneless nonworking Americans; he was now as ineffectual as the morbidly obese humans in that movie he'd tortured little boy Jack with, *Wall-E*. No wonder Dan, bitter and scared, clung to his iPhone the way "some cling to their religion and their guns." It was like an oxygen tank for his breath-starved mind.

He pulled into the parking lot next to the restaurant, sliding the old Volvo into one of ten empty spots. He put the transmission in park and then pulled his keys out of the ignition. It took him a moment to get out of the car. But he did. He unhooked his seat belt and stepped out into the evening. The air was so cool and glassy, the darkening sky so shiny and bright. Coming from the East, Dan never totally got over this nightly sensation of envelopment. He supposed it was akin to sliding a smooth leg into a classic silk stocking. Amy wore panty hose when she had to or simply went bare-legged. Maybe tonight he would ask Maryam what the real deal in fine hosiery actually felt like.

Dan walked down California Avenue. He walked past Avalon Yoga. Amy had made him take a sitting meditation class there a couple weeks ago to either rev him up or calm him down—it was hard to know what she was aiming for that day. If she wasn't ostentatiously holding her tongue, she was either complaining gently about his "lack of agency" or worrying aloud about his "anxiety and distraction." Whichever it was, her best friend, Lauren, had hit upon yoga and meditation as possible answers for him—a real original thinker, that Lauren. ("I need a job," Dan said in frustration when Amy wouldn't let up. "I know," Amy said. "But maybe this kind of mindfulness will help you approach the search from a fresh angle . . ." Which meant what, exactly? Teaching journalism at Jack's school? How much lower could he fall? Dan thought. Stock boy at Trader Joe's? And it infuriated him the way she let her sentences trail off in the manner of someone trying to be a good wife but sick and tired of carrying the bulk of the burden herself. Even her well-worn patience and innate kindness were an affront to him.)

At Avalon, he'd found middle-aged women with middle-aged haircuts, bowl-shaped and hitting them squarely at the chin, perversely highlighting that little hammock of skin below the jaw that started to appear around age forty. There was an ancient Japanese man and his handsome gray-haired son, both so lean and strong, the sinews on their calves were as impressively stringy as they were scary. Stanford girls with their sweatshirts and shorts and hairless legs, friendship bracelets tied around their ankles, ubiquitous ponytails. Dan was alone with his overheated gray matter, a dusky bubbling neural porridge. No Internet, no books, magazines, hell, no podcasts or Netflix, no streaming to help him cool off.

Apparently, that's what his own breath was for, or so sayethed the beautiful ageless dark-skinned female instructor in tunic and tights, with a long metallic-y braid snaking like liquid silver around her shoulder. "Take deep cleansing breaths," she'd said, or was it the idiot principal of Theo's school who had said this? Was he conflating again? Zhang. Dan had half expected her to walk into Mindful Meditation in a tight fleece pantsuit. The longer he sat, the more rabid his thinking felt. What could he say? Meditation didn't work for him. He survived on heedless cerebral infusions. In the yoga studio, he'd almost gone postal.

Dan left the circle before the hour was over. When he got back into his car, he simply shut all the windows and screamed. Then he drove to the gym and lifted weights for a while; at least the music kept him focused—Eminem, Macklemore, Kanye, a CrossFit play-list he'd downloaded while researching and then eschewing the discipline out of a wimpy brand of fear (he hated burpees). Now he looked in Avalon's window. He could see people in the back studio standing on their heads. Maybe he should try that instead. Flatten-ing his thoughts, thinking horizontally.

Fukushima was the kind of fucked-up crap that once got Dan out of bed in the morning, so now that he was living in bed, it would have been natural for him to post his own responses to Maryam's call for citizen scientists and citizen journalists at noon or at three in the morning, post or ante meridian, it sort of didn't matter anymore, but he hadn't bothered. Not until he met her. Once he met her, the story caught on fire. The obliterating wreckage from the one-two punch of the earthquake and the tsunami, the flooding that had shut down the electrical cooling systems, which were there to keep the radioactive spent rods from overheating in the six reactors, three of which *melted down,* the chaos of the forced evacuations—how about the scores who perished in the mass migrations, many of them elderly and infirm? How about the single patient left with-out food or care to die alone, abandoned in his hospital bed by the freaked-out medical staff? None of this even had anything to do with radiation poisoning. Panic and poor planning, more like it. And now the ghost towns still forbidden, all those displaced citi-zens, over 100,000, their anguish and desolation.

The Russians had eventually surrounded their own personal nu-clear disaster at Chernobyl in a tomb of cement. In contrast, the Daiichi spent rods, still leaking radiation, were in the long process of being moved individually to cooling ponds. It had taken over a year to remove four hundred tons of consumed fuel from the upper levels of Reactor 4. There were now three more reactors to go. The more difficult task of removing the actual cores was scheduled to commence in 2025. Dan could be a grandfather or dead in the ground by then. Japan had such a high level of seismicity, over 1,500 earthquakes estimated per year, he had to wonder: What if there was another accident or earthquake? Another tsunami with the reactors now stored at ground level?

Initially, Dan was more concerned with following the "official" spiel, the pure paucity of it, more interested in the theater, the Kabuki, Tepco's stance, posturing and withholding and their out-and-out lies. It took them two months to admit that the plant was in meltdown! Even now, years post facto, radiation continued to leak into the sea. Daily, three hundred tons of contaminated water poured into the Pacific, polluting Japan, entering the aquifer, poisoning the food chain, crossing the ocean, soon to be in his kids' milk, he was sure of it—the expensive local organic stuff that Amy insisted they drink, from Straus creamery, those beautiful fat cows up in Marin chewing on grass soaked with sea spray, sea spray with trace elements of the Fukushima nuclear disaster, dispersed across the Pacific now, leaching their way into his children's bones.

Even if some scientists pooh-poohed its dangers, Dan was concerned. "We live in a radioactive state," Dr. Angela Mayhews from the University of Texas–Houston pontificated in a podcast he'd downloaded from her website. "Our bodies learn to adjust to background radiation." Not that much radiation, Dan thought. After the attacks on the World Trade Center, the federal government, the EPA, Christie Todd Whitman, Rudy Giuliani all insisted the air was safe to breathe. Tell that to James Zadroga, if you possess a phone that reaches the dead, Dan railed internally, and to the thousands killed and still suffering from 9/11 disease.

Maryam wasn't the first person in cyberspace blogging and reporting on the nuclear disaster that Dan had followed, although she was one of the most interesting. But he hadn't reached out to any of them. Call him cyber-lazy; he'd met Maryam the old-fashioned way. At a bar.

Now he walked into Palo Alto Sol, ostensibly to pick up dinner. It was a Mexican family place right next door to Avalon Yoga—best green sauce north of the border. The doors were always open, as they offered simple wooden tables both inside and outside, the outside sometimes warmed by overhead heat lamps. Tonight was too balmy and soft for that. Donny, their foster child and Dan's wife's boss, had seen Zuckerberg at the restaurant several times. But Dan had seen only Zuck's wife, out with a gaggle of girlfriends, as he'd waited at the restaurant's bar to pick up dinner, and once alone with her baby in a Snugli—in New York she'd have required a bodyguard. Amy read somewhere that the Zuckerbergs had Palo Alto Sol cater their wedding dinner and that they'd opened an outpost at the Facebook campus. Those facts made both Amy and Dan feel okay, somehow, about feeding their children the same high-cholesterol grub as Valley gods and goddesses, often up to three times a week.

This was also the bar where Dan met Maryam a few months back, when he'd purposefully arrived early one night so that he had time for a margarita, up, with salt, and to dive into a bowl of chips, three salsas, while the cooks prepared his order. Jack, that human vacuum cleaner, always had the same thing, nachos, plus three enchiladas suizas, two chicken, one cheese. Thing One and Thing Two were taco al carbon fanatics, and Miles loved guacamole. Amy was the wild card—tortilla soup and salad if she was watching her weight, or cheese enchiladas with mole, if she was having an "I don't fucking care day," which bizarrely seemed to occur when she was most relaxed. Before a long run, she'd carbo-load.

When it was Dan's turn to pick up dinner, and it was his turn a lot these days, picking up dinner was a reason to venture out of the house. He'd make sure to arrive early so he could fill up on chips, sometimes a taco or two at the bar, and go home with his own salad, pretending to be good.

The night he met Maryam she had been sitting at the bar as well, surrounded by other Knight Fellows, fully holding court. Shmancy journalism scholars, all of them. International. Somewhere in the beginning middle of their careers—the sweet spot. Launched, surrounded by choice, nothing over and done yet. No custom publishing for that lot.

Dan was eager to eavesdrop. He was predisposed to the topic, and Maryam revealed herself to be a natural interlocutor, spouting not only facts but also big on narrative. "In a gentle way, you can shake the world," Maryam quoted Gandhi to her fellow fellows, about her monthlong photographic and video tour of the "exclusion zone," while Dan hovered nearby on his tall barstool.

She'd visited Japan in 2014; the country simply called to her. Alone, she'd walked the ghost towns and abandoned intersections in the Fukushima prefecture, still empty several years post-evacuation, without official recognition or even permission, in a sixty-pound radiation-proof suit and boots, accompanied only by her cameras and a Geiger counter.

"The beeping," she said, shaking her head so that her earrings chimed. "At first I thought I'd go mad. It was as if you could hear yourself cook," she said. "But it became a companion and a savior, reminding me of the dangers of where I was, so I didn't fall away into a dream. Which is easy when one is alone like that. The traffic signals, for instance, they still worked. I'd find myself waiting for the light to turn green, when of course there were no cars, no pedestrians, only once a tiny kitten crossing my path. I captured her on film. That sweet mewling thing."

"This is a crass question, I guess," said a skinny Indian guy, in a Facebook sweatshirt and cargo shorts, with black hair and what must have been prematuring silver temples because his forehead was still so ridiculously smooth, Dan thought. "But how do you go to the bathroom in one of those things? Is it kind of like astronauts?"

A couple of his fellow fellows laughed.

"Not that I know what astronauts do exactly," he added, and they laughed some more, especially the women, making him grin and blush. Exponentially increasing his geeky good looks.

"Don't laugh at poor Arvind," soothed Maryam. "It is a serious question. There were all these untrained workers at a cemetery that I was shooting. They were there ostensibly to decontaminate the area—which literally meant scraping the topsoil and gravestones and putting the outer layer of dirt and foliage into plastic garbage bags . . ."

"You're kidding me," said Arvind. "You mean like Glad bags?"

"You? Never, Arvind. No kidding," said Maryam, smiling at him. Clearly she liked Arvind, and/or she liked teasing him. Her tone made Dan feel unaccountably covetous; he wanted her to talk to him this way. "Yes, like Glad bags. I know, it is shocking. It is a shockingly lame response to a nuclear crisis. If that's what you're thinking, I agree with you! And then they just stacked all those garbage bags up on the side of the road and left them there . . . Full of highly radioactive material. Some of them wore hazmats, some had paper face masks and were not even wearing gloves. I believe they used Porta Potties.

"I wore adult diapers inside my suit," said Maryam. "Frankly, there were times I just peed down my leg."

Her audacity and frankness made Dan stand up. What should have felt off-putting was both beguiling in its honesty and all too real. As she spoke, he had entered the world of her story and gotten lost in it. So sensitive, his mother had always said. It was almost as if he could feel that steaming hot piss himself.

Maryam noticed him then; at least that's when she'd allowed him to realize that she was aware that he was listening. She gave him a quizzical stare. Ally or voyeur?

She leaned over the bar, asking Hector, the bartender, to please bring her another Modelo; and folded somewhat at the waist that way, her breasts pooling on the tiled surface; she was tall, Dan could see, perhaps taller than he was, and lithe, with amber glowing skin and dark luminous flowing hair. He'd always had a thing for Arab women. Maryam's fingers were long, and though she was fine-boned, her shoulders were broad. She wore gold dangling earrings that flirted with the bright lights of the liquor bottles—there were tiny bells on them, no wonder they'd chimed. She had a great ass. Was he objectifying? Sure. Why not? There was still privacy in his own mind, right? Pretty much anything he could come up with was sanctioned in there.

Beer in hand, she'd flipped around and sat back on her seat, finally, to take a sip, and when she did, Dan had said: "You're Maryam Ainsworth, aren't you?" She'd looked at him coolly then, iris and pupil the same enchanting velvety black, like who wants to know? But that changed, when he properly introduced himself and they started to talk. The group, which had protectively encircled her, allowed him entry then to, ahem, lean in.

He was a fragile ally at that point, that's what Maryam said, when they later reevaluated that initial meeting. "You were a fragile ally then and you are a fragile ally now, Dan," she said. "For all your best intentions, you've done nothing to earn my respect or trust."

Here, he remembered her giving him a little pat, but was that literal or figurative? Did he remember the pat, even if it never happened, because it was psychically accurate?

"You have to vote with your feet, Dan," said Maryam.

Dan had felt desperate at that moment to do anything to win Maryam over. But in actuality, he'd done nothing. Zip. He confused himself. He felt totally at sea. Like he had, at times when he was young, and more recently, increasingly, since he was jobless. For so long, because of work, love, family, Amy, Dan had been found. He'd forgotten what being lost felt like.

Maryam, unencumbered by marriage or family, financial responsibilities toward anyone but herself, wasn't lost and wasn't young, but she had the feeling of youth, her hair still black, her strong sculpted face held taut by the ferocity of her cheekbones; she didn't traverse a hamster wheel day to day; there was a floating free spirit element to her, even though she was physically the opposite of ethereal—she was no Ophelia, but Diana! The huntress. Cleopatra, the last pharaoh of Ptolemaic Egypt. She was, he saw almost immediately, as he tried to suss her out, infused by the glow of inner purpose. Her pursuits were saturated with meaning. It took her five minutes to tell him what was what, not boasting exactly, but immediately making certain he knew that her life didn't suck. She'd practically handed him her résumé, when he'd asked her gently where she was from, as she passed him the complimentary chips and dips Palo Alto Sol was so famous for; the server had just replenished the baskets and silver salsa bowls on the bar.

"I was born in London to a Palestinian mother and a British father," she'd said, like she was introducing a documentary about herself on PBS; he could hear the authority in her accent. "My mother, lonely and in exile, estranged from my father and befuddled by me, hanged herself when I was twelve. My father, a barrister, sent me off to Eton."

She continued in voice-over, turning the opening pages of her biography. "Eager to embrace my Arab heritage, I attended St. Joseph's University in Beirut, where I received degrees in law and journalism. From there I went to art school in Berlin, studying experimental media design."

Since then, she'd traveled the world, writing and filming, living everywhere, Paris, the West Bank, Southern California, where she'd had gender-affirmation surgery, before returning to Berlin. A stint in San Francisco and she fell in love with the Bay Area. Hence the Knight fellowship at Stanford.

Dan nodded his understanding when she delivered this monologue, obviously not for the first time; she'd sounded somewhat rehearsed.

He'd wondered. Now he was sure.

"I am a woman," said Maryam.

There was no room for doubt. Dan did not doubt her. He responded to her the way he'd always responded to a beautiful woman who fascinated him. It's just it had been such a long time since he'd been hit like that—he'd almost forgotten what it was like. And being that jacked up now, not just remembering it, but being it, made him feel animated and dynamic and like someone he'd gotten used to missing, but still recognized. Dan felt like Dan.

You learn something new about yourself every day, Dan thought. Although it was not true. He had not learned anything this elemental and complex at the same time, about himself, in a long time, if ever. He had not known before that he could be attracted to a woman who had once been a man.

"I was born a woman. The surgery released me from my cocoon."

That was when Maryam introduced him to her butterfly tattoo by a graceful pointing of her foot.

Dan wasn't much of a tattoo enthusiast, but he thought that this one, with its vivid blues, red, orange, and teal ink was striking, not corny, and fully suited her. It was regal and gorgeous, too.

When he'd queried, careful to control the excited, covetous wobble in his voice—because he envied her position at the university—she'd said her Knight fellowship was in experimental storytelling, immersive journalism, and interactive design. It reminded him of how Miles replied when asked what he wanted to be when he grew up: "a baseball player/VC/chocolatier." Maryam would use any tool available to tell a story.

"I came to Stanford to study the neurobiological effects of cyber-connectivity. But recently, every cell in my body has been crying for Japan." She paused, her eyes so dark it really was hard to discern the exact border of her pupils. "The people of Fukushima, they are not being seen. They have been so hurt, so abused. And no one cares really. I guess I am obsessed with invisibility," she said. "The pain of it."

After that, Dan was obsessed, too.

Tonight, she was sitting at the bar when he walked in. Of course, that is where she would be. He had Snapchatted her from his front hall.

I might be stopping by PAS Picking up dinner

Still, it seemed magical that he could ask and then receive.

Dan walked toward her and sat down next to her, his stool by her stool, bright as day. His family's meals had been ordered online. Maryam had already requested a drink for him. Hector had just made his margarita and it was sitting, sweating, an exciting proposition on the bar. Dan took a sip. Wow. The citrus was so alive on his tongue; it woke him up. He leaned both arms on the cool stone tiles on the counter.

"I've made my arrangements," said Maryam.

"I think you're insane," said Dan.

"You do?" she said, her whole face crinkling into a smile.

"Yes, I do," said Dan.

"I've been there before, you know," she said.

"I know," he said. "But suited up. You were suited up during the first shoot. And it was still fucking scary. If I'd known you then, I would never have let you go."

"Who knew you could be so macho?" Maryam said, slyly. Then to drive him nuts, "A nice Jewish boy like you?"

"Mar," said Dan, almost like he was begging her. Her ribbing was impossible.

"Four years has made a difference," said Maryam.

"It's your body," said Dan.

"Yes," said Maryam, "I am well aware of that. My body. My vehicle. My instrument."

"Sometimes you sound like a goddamn yoga instructor."

Maryam pursed her lips. She was wearing red lipstick, which he liked and she knew he liked.

"You roil inside, don't you, Dan."

Dan stopped and thought. It was true. He roiled and roiled. "Well, I know that," Dan said. "Nothing new. I think I've always roiled."

"Not like this," Maryam said. "Not to the point where you feel like you just might 'roil over' and die."

That was exactly how he felt. Maryam intuitively understood him. Why? Was it the quality of her observer status or more powerfully her ability to empathize? Or was it that he was in the presence now of someone who simply wasn't sick to death of him?

"Well, yes and no," said Dan, trying to cover up the sheer panic and joy of being recognized. "It's sort of what I do. Usually all that self-torture leads to something. Or once upon a time it did."

Her smile grew until it was a shit-eating grin.

"Why are you smiling like a fool?" said Dan.

"Because I know something you don't know." She smiled even wider.

"What?" said Dan. "Go on," he said. "I'm interested. It's been a long time since I've been the topic of anyone's conversation."

"When I go to Japan this time, you're coming, too," said Maryam. She sucked her margarita through her straw. "I'll shoot and you'll report. You can suit up if you want to be a pussy."

"I can't," said Dan.

"Why not?" said Maryam. "You're unemployed. Think of this as employment. Although I can't exactly pay you. Think of this as an investment in your career. Something will come of it; I can promise you. Something always does."

Dan did not know what to say. Some existent inside him heated up and melted, and flooded warmly throughout his arms and legs.

"I'm dying to work," said Dan.

"Of course you are. You're a storyteller, so you need to tell a story," said Maryam. "I tell you what, you really are going to die when I tell you this one. It's pretty fucking good."

"A good story?" Dan said.

"An excellent story," said Maryam.

"I love good stories," said Dan.

"Once upon a time," said Maryam, "there was a woman who fell in love with a man she met in Japan."

Back at the house, Dan parked in the carport and then he texted his eldest son: *Give me a hand downstairs.* Dan was capable of carrying two full bags of restaurant food, but he wanted to teach Jack responsibility. He also maybe didn't want to enter the house alone.

Jack, bare-chested, leaned out his window and shouted, "Okay, Dad, I'm coming down."

Propped against the car, with the smells of the Mexican food, tomatoes, chilies, melted cheese, grilled meat wafting up toward him, Dan took a moment to assess his life. There were more delicious things out there than what he had upstairs, in his room, on his bed, on his own, online.

The back door to the house opened and Jack came out, pulling a Yeezus T-shirt over his head.

"You take a shower?" Dan asked.

"Naw. No. Just whatever," Jack said. He picked up both bags of dinner and went back through the open door inside.

Dan followed him through the laundry room into the kitchen.

"Your mom home?" Dan said.

"*Sí, señor,*" Jack said. "She's in the shower." Then, after a brief pause, "Hogging the hot water, Dad."

"Okay, so let's set the table."

"The Things," Jack said.

"The Things can clear," Dan said.

"'I'm giving it all she's got, Captain,'" Jack deadpanned in a Scottish brogue, another *Star Trek* quote, as he carried the bags into the dining room. The glass doors overlooked the nighttime jungle of the yard. Not much to see in the dark but the shadow of leaves in the background, the furry bark of the redwoods, maybe. If they were lucky, a raccoon's yellowish eye shine.

Dan swept up yesterday's crumbs into his open hand. He walked back into the kitchen. He threw the crumbs into the sink. He opened a wooden cabinet and pulled out a stack of dishes.

"Silverware," Dan said.

"Sure," said Jack.

They passed each other coming and going. Dan walked out to the table and started distributing the mismatched plates, like a croupier.

Amy came in, her hair still wet from the shower. Makeup free and fresh-faced. She was wearing sweats and a faded Cal T-shirt. She looked like an undergraduate. An old undergraduate. She had the Mexican cloth napkins in her hands.

"Cloth?" Dan said.

"It'll feel festive," Amy said. She laid out six napkins. "I don't know. Whoo-hoo. It's Friday night."

"I don't know why you set a place for her," Dan said.

"Force of habit," Amy said. "She's a person."

"But she isn't here," Dan said.

"She is and she isn't," Amy said. "If she really wasn't here, believe me, you'd feel it."

She called out: "Miles and Theo, wash your hands and come to the table. Jack, is Lily all set up on her end? Come on, boys, you must be starving."

She finished with the napkins and wrapped her hair into a wet topknot.

Jack came in with the knives and forks and chopsticks. The Things loved chopsticks. Sometimes they even insisted on using them to eat cereal, shoveling the soggy flakes up like sodden leaves, drinking the milk down from the side of the bowl. Amy took two and used them to anchor her hair. Jack started emptying the food bags, reading the notations on the cardboard covers of the individual silver foil plates. He pulled out two wrapped burritos and set them in the corner. His phone began to vibrate in the front pocket of his jeans. He retrieved it.

"You're tickling me," he said to Lily.

"You're ignoring me," she said.

"Hi, Lily," Amy called out. "Jack, put down the phone, and put your computer on the table so we can all see her."

"Yes, boss," Jack said, and started off to his room.

"Give it to me." Amy motioned toward the phone. He handed it over as he walked back through the kitchen toward the stairs.

"Family dinner," said Amy, into the phone. "I want everyone at the table. You know what all the articles say. Your SAT scores will go up."

"Ha-ha," Lily said. "Amy, you're adorable."

Amy stared at the phone. "It's been a long time since anyone called me that," said Amy. Then she hollered, "Milo and Theo!"

Like two red clouds of prairie dust, the twins tumbled into the room.

"Sit," said Amy.

They sat opposite Jack's and Lily's seats. "Lily, I'm going to put you down now next to Jack," Amy said. "Do you have your meal there? All good?"

"All good," said Lily, and Amy set her down.

"We're going to have to get you one of those Beam robot things Donny told me about. They're like an iPad on top of a machine on wheels. We'd be able to see you on a screen, but you could navigate around the room on your own from home. So, let's just say you got sick of Jack, you could come sit closer next to me."

"You mean so I won't be trapped any longer?" said Lily. "Sometimes I feel like the little mermaid. Everyone has legs, but me."

"You have legs, Lily," Theo said. He turned to Amy. "She still has legs, right, Mom?"

"She still has legs," Amy said. "Everybody have what they need?" asked Amy.

"There's no water," said Miles.

"Then get water," said Amy. "Get some for everybody. I worked hard all day. I'm not getting up again."

Miles got up and went into the kitchen.

"Bring the Brita," said Dan, calling out after him. Then to no one, Dan said, "I'll get some glasses." He got up as Jack entered the room with his laptop open and he sat down.

Just then the back door opened.

"*Ni hao!*" a voice called from the kitchen.

"Kevin?" Amy asked Jack.

"No, it's another hungry rando Asian talking to us in Cantonese," Jack said.

Theo took the cardboard top off his tacos al carbon. Steam rose up and hit him in the face.

"That feels good," Theo said, luxuriating.

Kevin, well built and handsome, in blue Under Armour running shorts and a Stanford T-shirt, sweaty from a run, entered the dining room. "Family!" said Kevin. "You're already eating."

"Second son," said Amy. "Do you want to sit down?"

"Nope," said Kevin. "I was at the track and I gotta get home. Do you have my order?"

"Go out for a pass," said Jack. He stood up and winged one of the foil-clad burritos at Kevin as he jogged backward. Kevin caught it with ease. He tucked it under an arm and then Jack threw him the other one.

"Touchdown," said Kevin, catching it.

"Come on, cutie, sit for a sec," said Amy. "The least you can do is talk to me."

"Aw, that's so nice, but Mom's making dinner, and I'm late." He unwrapped a burrito and took a big bite. "You know how she gets."

"I do indeed," said Amy. "That's why she's so good at everything."

"Yup," said Kevin, still chewing. "Well, thanks, guys, enjoy your night." He gave a little wave and walked out through the kitchen.

The back door slammed shut.

Miles came back in with the Brita pitcher and set it on the table.

There were three containers of food in front of Jack now, and he opened all three. He liked to mix and match. He began to eat his nachos. They were fully loaded. Cheese, beans, meat, guac, pickled jalapeños, tomato salsa, sour cream.

"Wait," said Amy.

"No," said Jack.

"Jack," said Amy and Lily at the same time.

Everybody laughed.

"What's so funny?" asked Dan, coming in with the glasses on a tray.

Nothing. Nothing was really that funny. Just that everyone had forgotten to wait for Dan.

"Sit, Dan," Amy said. "Eat."

Dan tensed at the order, but he sat.

Dan sat down in his seat, and Amy opened a bag of chips and several containers of pico de gallo. She dipped a chip in the salsa and said: "God, would I love a beer."

Sighing, Dan got up to get it.

"Where's your mom tonight?" Amy asked Lily.

"She's out with her high school buddies. She's into reconnecting."

"Like dating?" asked Amy. "That's interesting."

"No," Lily said slowly. "I don't think so. I mean, I think they all just go as friends."

Dan came back with two sweating bottles of beer.

"Where's mine?" said Jack.

"Ha," said Amy. "Thanks, Dan." She took the cold bottle and

pressed it against her cheek and then her forehead. It felt so nice. "So, what's new, guys?" said Amy. "Anything special happen today?"

"Nope," said Jack, smiling down at his phone at Lily. Even though she was on Skype next to him, he also held her in his lap.

"Not me," said Lily, smiling back.

"Theo got sent home," said Miles.

"Let's not talk about that right now," said Amy, giving Theo's thigh a gentle caress. She didn't want to upset him.

Theo grabbed her hand and squeezed tightly. Amy squeezed tightly, too, but when she tried to let go, Theo wouldn't let her. It felt as if he were stopping the blood flow from her fingers to her wrist.

"Dan?" asked Amy. She was asking about his day, in her way.

He glared at her.

"Amy?" asked Dan, with a mocking edge in his voice. There was nothing new with him.

"No, just Donny, you know," said Amy, apologetically. She was sorry that she even asked.

They all kept eating, although Amy wasn't hungry any longer.

.   .   .

After her morning run, Amy met Donny up on campus. That was her pick. She hadn't wanted the office. On this, she and Donny agreed. The last thing either one of them needed was spies—you couldn't trust anyone with this stuff, he said, and Amy concurred. She categorized the whole operation as top secret classified.

"Let's just do it. We'll go back to my room," Donny said. "Adnan's training for the Deathride. He's *occupé*."

"Impressive, Donny," said Amy.

"My French?" said Donny. "I've been practicing!"

"The Deathride," said Amy.

One hundred and twenty-nine miles of biking, 1,500 feet of climbing, and five passes in the California Alps, Alpine County. Adnan had been boasting about it all semester.

Amy was glad Adnan was "*occupé*." The dorm was fine by her; after months of starting the start-up she was comfortable there. When she and Donny entered the guys' room, much was the same as it had been when she had last left it. Donny's bed was unmade. He was still sleeping in a sleeping bag on the two-hundred-dollar memory-foam mattress topper that Lauren had sent him with. There was a wet towel on Donny's desk chair, but Amy knew just where the hook was behind the door, so she hung it up. The scent of mildew and B.O. was familiar—she hoped it wouldn't linger on her fingers. At least that morning Donny had taken a shower. She hadn't. She'd gone straight to campus from running. Donny saged his room sometimes, so she preferred to concentrate on the aromatic herb's lingering spice—that girl he liked from his English class had told him that sageing a room could rid it of evil properties.

Adnan's side of the room was neat as a pin. Amy never understood how they could stand living and working together, but they did. The Odd Couple.

"You can sit at my desk," said Donny, even though Amy had already sat herself down there. He'd given her permission for something she'd automatically taken for granted. There must be a word for that, Amy thought. Or an analogy, like there used to be in the verbal SATs: Love is to marriage what attachment is to grief?

"I'm going to put headphones on you, and you can wear these little cardboard box goggles I got snail mail from the *New York Times*. They use them for VR," said Donny.

"You subscribe to the *New York Times*?" Amy was surprised.

"Lifelong bar mitzvah gift," said Donny. "That is if the paper outlives me, which I doubt. Part of my trust fund."

He pointed to the goggles. "Okay, put it on. It'll be better when I build my own instrument, but this will have to do for now."

Amy put on Donny's headphones and those weird little cardboard glasses. Donny leaned over her and typed.

"Also, maybe you should smoke some weed," Donny said.

"Why?" said Amy.

"Why not?" said Donny. He lit up the joint that was in the ashtray on his desk—even though it was a no-smoking dorm. He toked hard and then handed it to Amy.

Why the fuck not, Amy thought. This is already weird, why not make it weirder. She inhaled deeply and coughed. It had been a while. After her eyes stopped tearing, she inhaled again. This time the smoke went down more smoothly. She handed the joint back to Donny. He took another hit and pressed enter on the keyboard.

.   .   .

Amy ran.

She ran, and she ran, and she ran. She hadn't known that it was in her, that she even had the capacity to run this fast: she couldn't catch her breath. Her heart was beating up into her throat; it had already abandoned her itching, aching chest. Electric shocks were sparking throughout the space inside her rib cage where her heart was supposed to be: Was this cardiac arrest? The voltaic storm raging throughout her body was alarming. Her shoulders ached and her back burned, her lungs had sunken almost flat, they couldn't inflate fully enough or fast enough. It felt like she was drowning.

Amy was drowning as she ran. There was no air. She couldn't pull enough oxygen in. She was depleted. All the energy she had was spent in moving her legs forward, one after the other, her feet slapping against the pavement in those stupid flip-flops, all the strength with which she had been born was exhausted, it had leaked out the bottoms of her feet. She was fueled now only by fear.

She tripped, she tripped and she fell, but it felt instead as if she were flying. Like she fell up before she fell down. Air finally entering her lungs for the first time in forever: it buoyed her.

In the air, filled with air, floating above the sidewalk, Amy could see her little boy grinning up at her; he turned his face back to look. She must have screamed. He was all cheeks and golden-red curls; he was grinning because he thought that he was winning.

(She'd only put him down for one hot second to unfold the stroller and strap his twin brother in. Stupid, stupid. She should have secured him first. She wasn't thinking. Her mind had been on someone else.)

This was her punishment. He was grinning at her and running ahead of her straight into the street, so small still that the drivers of the cars whizzing by on El Camino could not possibly see his sturdy little body over their hoods and bumpers; he kept turning his head to smile the happiest smile she'd ever seen as he pulled farther and farther away from her. Was he thinking this was all a game? This is no game, Theo, she'd shouted when he'd first taken off, and then: Stop! Stop! Until there had not been enough air to run and to shout with at the same time.

There was a man up ahead. He was texting on his cell phone. Surely he would turn and stop the little boy, but the man's head was locked down, a swan-necked lamp, whatever light he possessed was fixed and shining onto his own keypad. Stop him! Amy had shouted when she could still shout, but the man didn't look up and Amy's shouts only made Theo charge ahead faster. Then, when she'd finally been running on pure adrenaline and the liquid smoke of her bones, her marrow vaporizing, burning herself out, she tripped and Theo burst out laughing.

Theo laughed as Amy flew through the air like she was a graduate of Clown College, and as she fell onto the sidewalk, scraping her palms, tearing her pants, the skin on her knees, blood welling where her teeth met her tongue and entered it, Theo ran laughing into the street and she could not reach him. The cars screeched and the man screamed, Oh, my God! He hit him! He hit him!

I am entering hell, thought Amy.

Amy ran.

She ran and she ran and she ran. She did not know it was in her to run this fast; she would do anything to get away from her brother Michael. He was chasing her. They were on a family picnic in Golden Gate Park. He was coming up from somewhere behind her, where she could not see him. She was running so hard trying to keep away that there was no time to waste to turn and look back.

Her parents were eating cheese and bread and vegetable slices—cucumbers and green pepper and carrots and celery sticks—her dad was drinking a beer; his eyes were closed. He seemed to like the feel of the sun on his face. His glasses were in his right hand, giving the bridge of his nose a rest; there was often a little red dent on it. Her mother in her ponytail and plaid shirt and Levi's had the newspaper spread out before her crossed legs, reading and talking out loud about what she read. Sometimes she took the glasses out of Amy's dad's hand and put them on herself to read the fine print.

Eric, Amy's older brother, was not even there. He was off at some dumb place, some concert or party or bedroom or parked car with his girlfriend, Elodie—Amy was nine years old, but she wasn't stupid. She knew about the flannel camp blanket he kept in the back of his van. Elodie had shiny blond hair that she wore in two braids that always unraveled; her hair was so silky it was practically fluid. Elodie wore cutoff shorts and Indian backless long-sleeve tops that tied under her shoulder blades with two narrow single strings. Tiny crystal beads hung across her clavicle and silver bracelets clattered from her wrists halfway up her slender, willowy arms.

This was long before Eric died in a rock climbing accident. He was probably wasted, but they never did an autopsy; her mother had not wanted to know. Her mother was a person who did not want to know a lot of things, except maybe what was in the newspaper. Eric was still in high school then. He was around, he still lived with them, but he'd already left her for Elodie.

What kind of pretentious bullshit French name is that? Michael said, her parents are from Pennsylvania, when Eric had introduced them. He'd said it out loud. Elodie had just good-naturedly rolled her big blue eyes; they were the color of a swimming pool in a magazine. My parents met on a bridge in Paris, she said. She had put out her delicate hand to shake, with her turquoise rings and silver bracelets, and her rose oil perfume on her little white wrist, the lacy blue veins looking like waxed organza ribbons tying her up like a gift. A gift Eric was now probably unwrapping somewhere on the Peninsula, Amy thought. There was no one in Golden Gate Park or on planet Earth who would bother to shield her from Michael.

No one cared about the things he did to her. When he was bored, for fun, he'd kick her so hard in the stomach when he babysat her and her parents went to the movies, that sometimes blood would come out of her vagina and stain her panties. She'd throw them away because they were evidence that the way he tortured her was real. Too painful for her parents. Too painful even for her.

Tag you're it, Michael had called as he started to chase her. I'll give you five four three two one, but Amy had already taken off out of a bolt of sheer unadulterated terror at the number four. Because she'd taken off, her mother would later say she'd agreed to play the game.

Now she was running.

Amy, wait up!

She ran as fast as she could, already mourning the lost sovereignty of her body, running over a hill when she tripped on a rock and she fell, sprawling flat on the cool wild lawn that hadn't been trimmed in forever. (Those budget cuts, her mother said later, when trying to ascertain whether Amy needed stitches below her chin or not.)

The grass was tall, so tall if Amy spread herself thin, thinner even than she already was—she was trying to disappear—then maybe Michael wouldn't be able to find her.

Her mouth was in the dirt. It tasted green. She could feel her chin bleeding into the grass, and she licked it. That fine iron taste of soil and blood and grass rolled on her tongue. The sun hit her bare legs below her cutoff shorts and it filtered through the back of her T-shirt. It felt so good on her arms, which smelled, even at this distance away from her nose, like bread. They were flattened in a cactus shape, surrounding her head.

She thought, God, let me die now, I'll believe in you if you just let me die now. The sun feels so good and Michael hasn't found me yet.

Amy ran.

She ran and she ran and she ran. She'd taken the subway to Fifty-Ninth Street and then jogged on the molten asphalt, heat steaming up to scald her bare legs. She entered the sultry, shabby park where it began, at its mouth, on Fifth Avenue, around the corner and across the street from the Plaza Hotel, where the horse carriages gathered, surrounded by flies and little haystacks of manure. She breathed that earthy odor in—it was moist and thick—and the stench of the sweat of the men sleeping on the wooden benches as she ran farther into the park, and then the sticky scent of stale cotton candy and honey-roasted peanuts fried in rancid oil, until she found a running lane next to one of the car arteries and hit her stride. There was so much on her mind! She needed to dump some stress! What was she doing in this crazy, polluted city, wasting her life on him?

He'd come home the night before after she'd already gone to bed and was curled up with the cat, LMNOP (they called her Elle), a little gray tabby, a runt, Amy's book opened near her face; she'd tried so hard to stay up reading. She saw double when she was that tired. She'd had to close one eye to see straight and lean the hardcover against the wall because she was too tired to hold it ajar, but then the other eye must have closed, too, because she woke up to the smell of another woman's vagina on his face when he climbed up into the loft bed, naked because of the heat, it was so hot up there, and leaned over to kiss her.

Sorry I'm late, he'd said. It was 3:00 a.m. They had a digital clock that glowed in the dark. It sat next to the little fan he'd brought home; he'd found it on Avenue A. He'd built a small shelf for her to put it on, plus her books, and his glass of water. He made gestures like this in the name of love; he brought her flowers during the day, and sometimes when he came home so late it was almost morning he brought her fresh cinnamon buns from the bakery on Second Avenue. She was pregnant. She was going to tell him. She was going to ask him: What should she do? What should we do? But what if he wanted to get married? Who could be married to him? He had no job, he wanted to be an actor, he read her poetry and talked politics and philosophy and strummed all day on his guitar—and he used his good looks to get over on everyone, even her. He was too pretty, and it was too late at night and it was too late anyway. This summer with him, following him to this hot urban place, living with him in this stupid overpriced dump, paying the rent when he went on auditions and was out every night, this was the last straw. The girl didn't matter and yes also she did. There were so many girls, girls she knew and didn't and to be fair she'd had her own boy on the side, off and on with him, too, during the torturous time they'd been together.

I'm so glad I'm not young, her mother had said on the phone. Amy was trying to do better. Trying to call home once a month, but by God that was too hard, maybe even harder than it was trying to stay with this guy.

When she woke up, he was still dead to the world. It was too early to fight and too hot for her to fall back asleep again. She'd made her way down the loft bed ladder carefully (she'd tumbled before), pulled on a pair of shorts and a T-shirt and her Pumas, and headed out to East Seventh Street. The punks were already up or maybe they'd never gone to bed. They were drinking their morning beers in their dog collars, some of the guys in leather vests. How could anyone wear leather on a morning hot like this one? They were already begging for money, so she gave them some. It wasn't worth getting spat on again, even though her boyfriend said that most of the kids on their corner were just taking a walk on the wild side and came from Great Neck, or were English majors at NYU. She stopped at the bodega and got a cup of coffee, with milk, no sugar, and a bagel with butter. She walked over to the 6 train, and took it uptown to the park.

It felt good to run, to sweat not just from heat, but also from exertion. It felt good to see trees and grass and dogs and little children in bathing suits in strollers and their tired parents heading to the sprinklers. Their neighborhood didn't have any of that. It had Indian food and cold sesame noodles thick with Skippy peanut butter and great old-man bars and a café with belly dancers and all the drugs anyone could want, although she was not sure she wanted any more. She ran up to Sixty-Fourth Street, outside the zoo. She imagined she could hear the sounds of the animals waking up. Maybe she would stop there on her way back. Maybe she would go into the penguin house and watch the birds in the cold water zip and zoom like swallows through an empty barn. That's what her thoughts felt like anyway, they zipped and zoomed. But first she'd run to the Sheep Meadow. There were always people there, sunbathing and playing Frisbee. She wondered if they slept there all night.

She decided to run across the mall. There were trees by the mall and probably it was shadier and maybe she wouldn't have to run on cement, maybe she could run on dirt. That's when she turned without looking and she heard a guy call: Heads up! He was on a bike and he whooshed right by her. She turned toward his voice, and as she stepped down she landed on her foot funny and her ankle gave. She heard it pop and she fell. She had no health insurance. She was here on an internship. She knew it was broken, even before she tried to stand up. They lived in a fourth-floor walkup. Their bed was a ladder's height off the ground. She knew she was fucked, even before a nice older couple stopped to see if she was okay. I'm a doctor, he said. He's the best, said his wife. Can he arrange for my abortion? Amy wanted to ask but didn't. He requested permission to touch her ankle.

She'd rubbed her forehead with her right hand and then ran it across her nose when she sniffled—she was trying not to cry, it hurt so much, even though the doctor was gentle—and she smelled the other girl's cunt on her fingers.

Your ankle is broken, said the doctor.

Yes, she said. I know. I could tell.

She'd known her ankle was broken before the rest of her hit the pavement, while she watched the biker whiz away. He was wearing a Walkman. He probably didn't even know that she fell.

This is no game, Theo, Amy shouted when he first took off, and then: Stop! Stop! Until there had not been enough air to run and to shout with at the same time. There was a man up ahead. He was texting on his cell phone. Stop him! Amy shouted when she could still shout, but the man didn't look up and Amy's shouts only made Theo smile more and run faster anyway. And then, when she'd finally been running on pure adrenaline fueled by fear, she tripped and Theo burst out laughing.

Theo burst out laughing when Amy tripped and fell, and that the man heard. He looked up as Theo ran by him and leaned over and picked the kid up by the collar of his shirt. Theo's little legs were still racing, like he was treading water, only he was stationary in the air. Now it was Amy's turn to laugh, but of course she couldn't; she was a bleeding, sobbing hot mess. She was crying tears of gratitude and relief as the man held him up and said: Lady, this belong to you?

Her mouth was in the dirt. The sun hit her bare legs below her cutoff shorts. It filtered through the back of her T-shirt. It felt so good on her arms, which smelled, even at this distance away from her nose, like bread.

Hey, Shorty, Eric said. Did you hurt yourself?

Amy looked up. Blood was streaming down her chin. She could feel it.

Oh, said Elodie. I'll go get your parents. She ran off down the hill, bracelets clattering.

I called after you, but you didn't stop, said Eric.

I didn't know you were here. I thought it was him. What are you doing here, anyway? asked Amy.

Eric took off his T-shirt. He was so skinny she could see his ribs against the dark fur of his chest hair. He was wearing some of Elodie's dumb love beads. We decided to get dim sum, he said. We thought you might want to come with. He kneeled next to her. Here, he said, press this against your chin.

Are you sure? she said. It'll wreck it.

I'm sure, said Eric.

Amy decided to run across the mall. There were trees there and probably it was shadier and maybe she wouldn't have to run on cement. Maybe she could run on dirt. That's when she turned without looking and she heard a guy call: Heads up! He was on a bike; he was whooshing right toward her. Amy froze. The heads-up made her freeze. The biker came to the world's shortest stop. Whoa! he said. Oh, my, said Amy. I'm sorry; I got in your way. That's okay, he said. He hopped back up on his bike and took off again. Over his shoulder he called out, Have a good day.

I'm trying, thought Amy.

Amy flew through the air like she was a graduate of Clown College. As she fell onto the sidewalk, Theo stopped running to laugh at her. He thought it was all a game. He was only a little boy. He walked over to her, where she lay flat and bleeding. She pushed herself up onto her bloody knees and palms. She spat the blood out that was pooling inside her mouth.

Theo said, Mama? Like he was scared.

Amy looked up, and sat on her heels. She opened her arms and Theo ran into her warm embrace.

Her mouth was in the dirt. It tasted green. She could feel her chin bleeding into the grass and she licked it. That fine iron taste of soil and blood and grass rolled on her tongue. The sun hit her bare legs below her cutoff shorts. It filtered through the back of her T-shirt. It felt so good on her arms that she thought, Please, God, let me die now. I'll believe in you if you just let me die now. The sun feels so good and Michael hasn't found me yet.

Found you, said Michael.

Heads up! A guy called.

She ran right straight into him.

He was on his bike and he fell off, and she fell down, and he and his bike fell down on top of her.

It took a moment. They were in a pretzel. But he untangled them. His leg from her leg, her arm from within the bike's wheel.

He stood the bike up and leaned it on its kickstand.

He said, Are you okay? I'm Dan, he said.

I'm pregnant, she said.

His eyes opened wider with a start. Then he looked at her arm. He said, Let's walk you to the first-aid station; I just passed it on my bike.

She started to laugh.

He said, Why are you laughing? He said, You must be in shock.

I'm sorry, Amy said, but I can't, I can't stop laughing.

He looked at her hard. He was awfully cute. A little older than she was, with dark brown hair. He looked concerned.

Okay, he said.

She nodded but she kept laughing. It all seemed so funny. The whole world was funny. So far this was the funniest part of the funniest day of her life.

He put one arm around her and the other around his bike. They started to walk. When she tripped a little on a stone, or from laughing, or because she was in shock as he said, life had shocked her, he held her tighter.

I got you, he said.

. . .

Amy pulled off her cardboard glasses. She felt like she was going to throw up.

"You look like you're going to hurl," said Donny.

At the suggestion, she began to heave and he got his wastepaper basket underneath her just in time.

"Eeww," said Donny.

"Sorry," said Amy. She wiped her mouth on the back of her hand. "Sorry," she said. "But not. How could you?"

"I think it will be better with the hair dryer," said Donny.

"What?" said Amy.

"You know, the hair dryer apparatus. I told you about it already. The cone."

"I don't care," said Amy. "None of that happened, except for some of it. All of it was wrong."

"What? What was wrong with it?" asked Donny.

"Are you kidding? Everything. Everything. How dare you show me something where Theo is hit by a car? That day, when I yelled, he stopped running and climbed into the stroller. That's all, that's all. Now how am I supposed to unsee the horror that I just saw?"

"I don't think it's a real bug in the algorithm," said Donny. "I'd term it a 'code smell.' I'm sure I can correct for it. All I have to do is stare at it for a couple of hours. It shouldn't be a problem."

"It *is* a problem, Donny. It's already in my head. I spend so much time running that shit out of my mind and there you are repopulating my brain with stuff I don't even have to worry about."

"Like Eric?" said Donny. "I have to admit I'm a little surprised you didn't ask me to multiverse Eric."

Amy closed her eyes. Her hands clenched into little fists. It was all she could do not to slug him.

"Do you know how many years and how much money I've spent on therapy to drive out the Eric fantasies? Eric died in Italy. It was a nightmare and he died and he is dead. Nothing else matters. I don't want to think about him maybe being alive anymore. It just hurts too fucking much."

It was hard for Amy to breathe then.

"Please, Donny. Please. Never again. Never again make me think of Eric not dead. I don't think I can take that." She took a deep conscious breath. "And . . . And that's not how I met Dan. I met him at a party in a loft on West Twelfth near the Meatpacking District. It was one great big space and the people who lived there lived in five different teepees. Plus, wasn't this whole stupid thing supposed to be about *my* choices? I thought this was about *me* choosing what to look at. About me choosing to find out what I want to know."

"The ride will be smoother when I build my own instrument," said Donny.

"Are you serious?" said Amy. "How could I ever trust you or it again? None of this ever happened anyway." She was crying now, for real.

Donny handed her the towel hanging on his closet door. She held it to her face. It still stank and it was still wet. She blew her nose in it, because she had to and for revenge.

"It happened in different multiverses," said Donny.

"Fuck different multiverses," said Amy.

"You say that now, but I can fine-tune, you know?"

"Donny," said Amy. "What the hell?"

"The hair dryer idea? The big cone? It will help it feel more real."

"Real I don't want," said Amy. "I wanted her."

"I'll get you her," said Donny. "I promise."

Amy was still crying. Donny put his hand on her shoulder. He wanted to comfort, maybe. But it was too late. Because of him, there was even more now to unlive, to pack away and forget. He was going to have to find himself another guinea pig. Amy and The Furrier were over.

PART TWO

D AN WAS JEALOUS.

Maryam had engaged with almost everyone they had encountered during their long flight across the silver-scaled skin of the Pacific, and almost to a person, they'd responded to her. This amazed Dan—not only the unfolding lengths of her billowing inquiries but also the ease with which strangers so readily disclosed to her. There was something about Maryam, her compassion, her intensity maybe, her focused attention on her subjects absolutely, that got them to confide. She was a natural-born interlocutor. Too bad she hadn't thought to shine her bright light on him.

Often Dan had been left out of these conversations, which made him feel lonely, of course, and a little relieved as well (he did not have her stamina). These seemingly antithetical sentiments led him to mull over the definition of "extrovert" that he carried around in his mind's back pocket (*someone who draws energy from the presence of others*), and his own forced introversion on their journey (*the state of being recharged by time alone*). He spent many hours quietly thinking these thoughts, plus others—could one be a good man and still forsake one's family? Was it selfish to feel this irresistible pull toward wildness and weightiness? Might there be a way to live more rapturously without resorting to the cheap thrills of hard drugs?—all while staring out the airplane window at the ocean's miraculously luminescent surface, as if it were tightly dressed undulating muscle instead of water, like sequins corseting a mermaid's tail. He'd never flown west from California before, straight into the sun.

Maryam chatted with the driver on the morning SuperShuttle from Stanford to the San Francisco airport. She was resplendent in a black tunic and leggings, cinnabar bangles clattering up her right arm when she gesticulated as she talked, Dan's favorite metallic sandals gracing her feet. She was far more elegant on this weekday morning than the other passengers in the van: the smattering of sweatshirt- and Polartec-wearing students, perhaps heading home for a long weekend? The California-casual women in loose sweaters and mom jeans, probably professors, Dan thought, their male counterparts in warm-up or golf jackets, everyone in running shoes. Both genders presumably jetting off to some think tank or conference to lecture on effective global governance or else to see the grandkids. The campus was lousy with Nobel Prize winners, also Pulitzer recipients and former political powerhouses, even war criminals; Condoleezza Rice, for example, a Hoover fellow. Dan saw her from time to time at the Palo Alto Creamery delicately eating her hash brown pie and two eggs, same as him. But whether they leaned left or right, these many unwitting models of "acting basic"—a millennial term for wearing practical, unobtrusive, supranormal clothing (Jack and Kevin used it)—disguised themselves as boring old people.

In the early 1990s, ironically, Dan had written a story on Yucca Mountain, a proposed geological repository for high-level nuclear waste located just about eighty miles outside Vegas. Twenty years later, the Department of Energy was still considering dumping about 150 million pounds of radioactive spent fuel there, material they otherwise did not know what to do with, even though the recommended location was close to a major city *and* geologically active. At the time, the DOE's complimentary bus tours of the site had proved bizarrely popular, and Dan's editor thought it might make a funny travel story. But the majority of those nuclear tourists turned out to be gray-haired retirees trying to stretch their Social Security payments (Dan was just a freelancer, there hadn't been a gray hair anywhere on his head back then; honestly, truly, he had really believed he was congenitally exempt from aging) and appeared to have taken the ride for the coffee, doughnuts, and free lunch. The others, he discovered, were nuclear watchdogs and reporters like himself. But it had been hard to tell one from the other. Most of the writers and the retirees on that bus had looked like the inhabitants of *this* van. Note to self, Dan remembered thinking—in his torn jeans and Ramones T-shirt he'd stuck out like a sore thumb—dress like everybody else. It was advice he'd taken to heart. On this very day, the day of his great escape, he was wearing the unobtrusive green fleece Jack had absconded with, or vice versa, and purposefully blended in. Dan didn't want anyone in the van to notice or remember him. Apparently, Maryam hadn't received the memo.

Parked in a single seat ahead of Dan and behind the driver, Maryam introduced herself warmly to the woman at the wheel. "We are the only two brown people on the bus," she said. The driver's name was Marisol Medina. "A full pleasure to meet you, Mrs. Medina," said Maryam.

Mrs. Medina was a mother of five: her eldest was a doctor, the next a physician's assistant influenced by his love and respect for his older brother; the middle son was a yoga teacher, her youngest boy still in high school; and her daughter, her only girl, was lost, lost to drugs, but Mrs. Medina prayed every day and night that her baby would find her way back home to her. Even though Maryam had eschewed the Christian faith she had been raised in by her father while facing the cruelties of her own youth, she remembered her mother's early teachings. The mother had been a lapsed Muslim herself, a lapsed person in every way, Maryam told Dan later. "Ommy spent much of her life lying on the couch willing herself to get up," but she had taught Maryam the Surah al-Asr, the 103rd Surah in the Quran, "We need each other," as a guiding principle.

(Ommy had called her only son Mika, which in Arabic meant "intelligent, beautiful, like God"; his father had called him Michael. She had named herself Maryam, because it sounded lovely, she said, and meant "bitter," which at that time in her life she was.) So, Maryam honored Mrs. Medina's needs and prayed with her.

"Where is home?" Maryam asked as soon as she deemed their shared moment of silence over, but when pressed, Mrs. Medina had demurred. She wasn't the type to call attention to herself or to complain, but Maryam drew it out of her, with kindheartedness and great skill, at least that is how it appeared to Dan, sitting directly behind her. (The van had a row of cushioned, blue-plush single seats behind the driver, an aisle, and then another row of three similar seats fused together on the right, like on an airplane. It was packed solid.) At times he tried to eavesdrop—he'd felt abandoned by Maryam when she'd plopped down in front solo—but mostly he found himself staring out the window at the rolling hills that surrounded 101 North, which looked a whole hell of a lot like Italy, with its scrubby greens and gold pitches and rises—he still thought this after some twenty years living out west, he was still comparing his adopted home to a place he had visited the summer of his sophomore year in college, the curse of youth, the indelible, lasting impressions of all those random firsts—wondering what the hell he was thinking, running away from home like a small child?

In a whisper, so soft it did not have the strength to fully carry itself rearward to Dan, Mrs. Medina told Maryam she commuted 120 miles every morning from Manteca to Palo Alto and back again at night, because it was the nearest affordable city. (Her *marido* was *discapacitado*, multiple sclerosis, he could not travel far and stayed local, working part-time in Medical Records at Kaiser Permanente.) Maryam, playing telephone between her companions, was sympathetic and outraged on her behalf—a two-and-a-half-hour commute dependent on traffic before Mrs. Medina even got behind the wheel of the van? She must live in a perpetual state of exhaustion. It wasn't safe or even healthy, Maryam surmised. SuperShuttle should help find Mrs. Medina and her family adequate housing.

Dan of course agreed—he was the original lefty in their dyad, a quasi–Red Diaper baby; his mother was always taking the train into the City or down to D.C., waving a banner and marching against something *bad,* while his dad stayed put in Jersey. Maryam's father was a Tory, as well as a rat bastard. She'd said as much, and Father Ainsworth probably would never bother to speak to a driver of a van anyway. But even Dan knew SuperShuttle couldn't do a lot for Mrs. Medina. The City of Palo Alto had to commit to building affordable homes. Stanford University with its $21.4 billion endowment, its eight thousand acres, 60 percent of it open even now, needed to model good citizenship with a little mixed-income lodging for both employees and the greater community. The state had to kick in. The tech industry was obscenely wealthy. (He'd recently read that Bill Gates's $90 billion fortune was .5 percent of the U.S. GDP.) There was still a federal government out there, no matter how frozen and hobbled by idiocy and partisanship and downright meanness; someone somewhere had to *care.*

Dan had edited a story, years ago now, about the homeless people who rode the number 22 bus from East San Jose to Palo Alto and back again all night, some unable to make rent even while working full-time jobs. One of the subjects of the article had referred to the bus as "Hotel 22," which stuck with Dan. He remembered the guy was a father with a school-age daughter. The girl did her homework on the bus, and they schlepped bedding and pillows in paper bags for the long ride each and every night. Had the original journo ever written a follow-up? Dan itched to google. He had to literally sit on his hands, which made his wrists hurt. But he'd purpose-fully turned off and packed his cell phone in his shoulder bag to keep himself from going online on automatic pilot. The thought of reading texts from Amy or the kids right now, all that whiny self-involved innocence, filled him with a shame so painful and deep he could feel its heft sink down into his balls. How would he possibly respond? Instead, with nowhere to cool his psychic jets, his mind ran here, there, and everywhere, although he tried to be supportive and nodded profusely whenever Maryam unbuckled her seat belt to turn to him for confirmation of the inherent righteousness of her outrage throughout the ride. Dan even wagged his finger playfully at her a couple of times, to make sure she buckled back in whenever she was returning to face-forward, tilting closer to Mrs. Medina's seat to yak, her lustrous blue-black hair a shiny curtain.

At the International Terminal, Maryam held court over sev-eral rounds of small-batch craft beers garnished with orange slices and some avocado-edamame hummus at the bar at Cat Cora with three Southeast Asian young male techies watching highlights of a Warriors game on an iPad. When Dan, left out again, expressed surprise at her knowledge about and passion for the game she'd replied, "You think there's no basketball in Britain, Dan, but you're thinking is often erroneous. I was a starter since First Form."

"I thought it was about as popular as snooker," Dan mumbled, already cranky, guilt-ridden over the injustice he was doing his wife by *lying* to her, and at that early point in the journey already hungry for Maryam's attention.

"Dan, you are about as popular as snooker," said Maryam, laugh-ing, "which by the way is *very* popular. In the UK and even more so in China." She gave him a big fat wink. The flutter of those black lashes sent a surprising thrill, like a tiny gust of wind, through the porthole of his pupils and down into the backs of Dan's knees.

Then she shared intimate knowledge of Steph Curry, the greatest shooter in NBA history, that she'd just coaxed out of the three skinny boys in T-shirts sitting next to them.

"Did you know his first name is really 'Wardell?' My friend Salik here told me." Maryam pointed at the skinniest boy with the wispiest beard who smiled then at the recognition.

"I'd call myself 'Steph," too," she said. "Did you know on his sneakers, the Curry One, the lace loop at the bottom of the tongue has '4:13' embossed on it? It's his favorite Bible verse: Philippians chapter four, verse thirteen. Salik told me that as well. Providentially, it just so happens to be a verse my father made me memorize as a child." She then recited it to the delight of the coders from Interactive Intelligence: "'I can do all this through Him who gives me strength.' Lovely, no?" said Maryam.

Know-it-all, Dan thought. Attention slut. Although he admired her accumulation of knowledge. She fed off facts the way he did. Intellectual detritivores, news-junkie arthropods, scandal-loving pill bugs, bottom-feeders, creepers, slugs. Her hunger, perhaps even larger than his. Her retaining capacity, clearly far superior.

After bidding the coders adieu, using the restroom, and joining the passenger queue, he and Maryam finally boarded their aircraft and took their seats. There, Maryam conversed with the Latino gay male flight attendant who home-based in San Carlos but loved this overseas junket, as he was both a self-proclaimed sushi and "kawaii" nut, which he explained to Maryam was a Japanese predilection for all things cute and beautiful. But she, of course, already knew. "I myself practice the art of amigurumi," said Maryam, nodding vigorously in agreement, and like some ersatz Mary Poppins, she pulled from her carry-on a half-completed small stuffed animal, which the flight attendant instantly admired, and that she proceeded to knit into being throughout the flight.

Next Maryam introduced herself to the young white college girl across the aisle and discovered that she was taking her junior year abroad in Kyoto, to study Japanese porcelain and pottery. After that Maryam bypassed poor Dan—who was stuck in the center seat—leaning over his belly to introduce herself to the older Japanese-American woman sitting by the window and offering her a lemon drop. (Which she took gratefully.)

Maryam—gregarious, spirited, heedless imbiber-of-life Maryam—continued to conduct this three-pronged conversation in a circuitous order throughout the first leg of their nineteen-hour series of flights, around and around, a narrative swirl, across the aisle, up to the flight attendant (who seemed to relish standing by her armrest), and traversing Dan's midsection to the impeccably dressed delicate gray-haired woman by the window. A Carvel cone of a story, Dan thought ridiculously, but that's how her multiple dialogues presented themselves in his head, in an everlasting, voluptuous, aerated soft-serve. She spoke with the budding ceramics historian about their destination—a small town called Tomioka, less than six miles from the crippled remains of the Fukushima Daiichi plant—as the area had been known for Amakusa stone used in pottery since the Edo period.

To the flight attendant, Jaime—she read his name aloud from the label pinned onto his jacket—Maryam elaborated on the purpose of their visit, to report on Yoshi Hibayashi, a middle-aged, fifth-generation rice farmer who had the highest levels of radiation in his body of anyone in Japan.

And to the woman by the window seat, who, as luck would have it, was an editor of cookbooks, Maryam discussed what she was most looking forward to eating along the way: "Oh, man, the Nishin-No-Sansyo-Zuke!"

"I like it, too," said the woman.

"What is it?" asked Dan.

"Dried herring pickled with sansho pepper leaves and soy sauce. Mama Mia," said Maryam. "That and the Kozuyu! Do you know Kozuyu, Dan? No? Really? You really don't?"

"No, I really fucking don't, Mar," Dan murmured.

"It's a clear soup," said the woman, gently butting in, as if to upend a potential marital squabble. "Filled with konnyaku jelly noodles."

"They are like little glassine eels," said Maryam.

"In Fukushima, they often eat soba with green onions as an implement instead of chopsticks," said the woman. "These are all traditional dishes of the prefecture; you cannot procure them in the same manner anywhere else in the world."

"I don't get it," Dan whispered in Maryam's ear. "We're eating the local produce?"

"We are. We are there for a short while."

"Aren't we worried about radiation?"

"The human body is very resilient when it comes to radiation." She was trying to reassure him. "We encounter background radiation all the time. There's point one microsieverts in a banana. It's the accumulation over time; it's the amount of the exposure; it's all the things no one yet knows that are so very worrisome. But would I insult my hosts by turning down their local bounty? The food they feed their children? The peaches? The Fukushima peaches?"

"Yes," said the woman to Dan's left, who clearly overheard them. "You've never tasted a true peach before you taste one of those. Although it is a little early in the season." And then, as an afterthought, "I wouldn't recommend the Fukushima beef. The cesium."

Maryam didn't sleep, she didn't nap; as far as Dan could tell, she didn't even rest her almond eyes. She was too excited!

Instead she engaged and she listened, on and on, through three airplane meals, the highlight being "Mos burgers," which the eager flight attendant explained were "the greatest hamburgers in all of Japan," but Dan thought they were blech, the spicy meat sauce on top of a pallid slice of airplane-cold tomato looking far too much like a skinned knee for his tastes.

While Maryam made friends, Dan searched for other forms of distraction. He'd forgotten to bring a book, and the movie choices— one of the Pirates of the Caribbean franchises, or some manga something—soon bored him. He turned to the stirring white noise of the airline's classical music in-flight system to bring him calm and ease. Opera. Knowing almost nothing about the genre made it simple; it allowed him space not to agonize and stew. He didn't have to care which recording of Mozart's "Dans un Bois Solitaire" was being proffered, he could take it in without chewing, letting it just melt, the way you might eat an oyster.

That kind of easy listening was conducive to thinking. So, Dan thought hard. Suppose he had read the tea leaves correctly and gotten out of the newspaper business back when the getting was good? Who else might he have become: a documentary film producer? An environmental activist? The founder of an NGO?

What would he have accomplished in his nearly fifty years if, boots on the ground, instead of choosing the pink suburbia of Palo Alto, he'd gone to Africa, Haiti, Appalachia, built schools and hospitals, did some tangible good?

More! What if he hadn't married, or had children? Would he be freer now to do the work that he was built for and so longed to perform? He had a friend from the *Mercury*. That guy never had a family and he went *on his own* to Iraq and then to Syria, without assignments, funneling back his stories after he'd first lived, then wrote them. He'd received grants, money from the Fund for Investigative Journalism, placed pieces in the *Atlantic* and the *New York*

Times Magazine, and ended up with a nice fat book deal; Dan had tortured himself by watching the dude on the *Today* show. With no overhead, no responsibilities, maybe Dan could have been a lot like him.

He looked up. Maryam and Jaime were now engaged in a merry exchange of some hard-core stats and sabermetrics—Maryam was a newly converted Stanford fan, and the flight attendant had grown up in the East Bay; they were having at Cardinal football.

Jaime said: "I've never gotten over it. Never! Kid blew past Barry Sanders's thirty-year-old record for all-purpose yards; how did Christian McCaffrey *not* win the Heisman?"

Maryam nodded vigorously in wide-eyed agreement, as if they hadn't been sitting on this stupid plane for goddamn fucking ever, and she wasn't going crazy like Dan was, but every interchange was fresh and new for her. It seemed her outlook didn't dampen.

Dan, on the other hand, was fading fast. He wasn't much of a sports guy and he was immune to fandom and by this time in their voyage he'd had the distinct sensation that his ears were bleeding, so much chatter coming from so many directions (is this how poor Theo felt in the lunchroom?)—they had just been served a juicy beef bowl, supplied in corporate collaboration with Yoshinoya, "Japan's most illustrious beef bowl restaurant chain," Maryam said. "Is that correct?" she asked the woman to Dan's left. Her newfound friend nodded in agreement.

Maryam sounded as if she were a victim of the dictates of an ad campaign. In fact, she sounded an awful lot like his twins, who always broke into hip-hop song and dance, reenacting a local Mack Mack Taco Bell commercial—"For cheese in the shell, go to Taco Bell"—whenever they pulled into one of the parking lots to pee. The lunch, which Maryam received with a little seat-dance of excitement, Dan thought looked a lot like something Amy fed

Squidward on his birthday (ground beef sautéed in Chef Boyardee tomato sauce; it's what Lauren's mother had fed *their* dogs on *their* birthdays), but Maryam and his seat companion clearly relished the dish.

I should just do it, Dan thought. Just go. Find and write my own stories. See what shit sticks. I'd only be making more money; I'm not making any now. Maybe my family would be better off without me. I'm a burden, anyway. I know I am.

"Dan," said Maryam. "Try this, freeze-dried natto! Fermented soybeans. Highly nutritious," she added.

She lifted her palm and Dan sniffed the greenish-gray pebbly snack that Jaime had just poured into her hand. It smelled like bad beer.

They both grinned down at him.

Dan stretched his lips in an effort to grin back. Then, using his thumb and forefinger as pincers, he tasted it.

It wasn't half-bad.

After they landed at Kansai International in Osaka Bay, and exchanged email addresses with all their new pals—Maryam first making sure that Dan's neighbor was properly escorted to her waiting wheelchair—Dan hissed at her in emulous awe as they exited the jet bridge: "You're way too nice to people."

Maryam stopped in her tracks and batted her long, long lashes. "Why, thank you. And I was afraid after the flight you were going to get cranky."

"I didn't mean it as a compliment," Dan said.

"Perhaps you only want me to be 'too nice' to you," she said.

Well, that was true. And rather embarrassing. So, Dan looked around the airport in an effort to get away from truth. He'd read about this place. Now he had a chance to show off some of his own arcane and useless knowledge.

"This airport is built on a man-made island," said Dan. "A bunch of mountains were excavated and plunked into the sea."

Maryam lit up. "You've done your homework. Good boy. Now, do you know how old it is?"

He desperately searched his memory; he wanted badly to impress her. "'87? '88? Someone, I forget who, twisted Renzo Piano's arm to design the aerodrome."

"I am a huge Piano fan," said Maryam as they began to walk. "'The serenity of his best buildings can almost make you believe we live in a civilized world.' Nicolai Ouroussoff—the former *Times* critic. He's married to that lovely painter Cecily Brown—her work is so excessive. I adore it. Her paintings possess a specific clotted beauty. It was initially considered a financial disaster—"

"Cecily Brown's work? Her paintings are worth millions."

Finally, Dan thought, he had her.

"No, not the paintings, dummy, the airport! But eventually it was pronounced the Civil Engineering Monument of the Millennium or some such rot, because it survived the Kobe earthquake. That was in '95. Just goes to show you how the fashions of the times do change. Now let's take the Wing Shuttle. I love the Wing Shuttle."

The Wing Shuttle turned out to be a sleek little train that took them across the terminal to the gate of their connecting flight in record time. Although, in retrospect, Maryam might have preferred the walk. "It would have equaled around two thousand strides," she said, and she was determined to make her daily quota of ten thousand on their journey.

She pouted fleetingly, and for a flash Dan saw the sad, vulnerable little boy buried somewhere in her skeleton.

That moment passed. He offered to take her camera bag off her shoulder, it looked so heavy. But she waved him aside. Grown-up Maryam was unbeatable and unstoppable, at least in any battle of verbiage; he couldn't imagine a more dominant force. She continued praising the airport's practicalities even after takeoff on the one-hour flight to Fukushima—how he longed for the SuperShuttle van now and its row of single seats—and then as they waited for both her bags to spin by at baggage claim.

"You pack like a girl," said Dan, who just had a carry-on.

"It was one of the first signs," said Maryam, laughter pealing. "That and I refused to stand up to wee."

From Fukushima Airport, it was a forty-minute bus ride (¥800) to Koriyama station, during which she continued to chat impressively, more about her life, did she have to be so goddamn fascinating?—Dan felt more useless and boring than ever, what could she ever see in him? But there was no time to ask this question, to grovel for her attention, Maryam on some manic traveler's high persisted, yip-yap-yapping, about her first lover as a woman and her final lover as a man (both the same guy, some South American professor/revolutionary/poet, a super hottie, a sexual adventurer, who had also been in the Olympics, Dan wasn't sure if he'd hallucinated the high jump or not), and upon arrival they'd had one very clear choice to make: take the high-speed Shinkansen train (¥2,920, fifteen minutes) or a forty-five-minute local train (¥820) to Fukushima station.

Dan knew what he wanted. The local, because every train car in Japan is a quiet car. He could not stand to be dazzled a second longer. Maryam had told him as much back at Palo Alto Sol when she'd first wheedled him into this misadventure; he'd wanted the local because she would then have to be silent for an extra half an hour. Since she was cheap, she'd agreed. Dan had never realized how cheap she was before—Yay! One mundane strike against her!—but maybe that's because they'd all, her friends, himself included, always lined up to buy her beers and dinners—so they took the less-expensive train. In Japan, every car *is* a quiet car, she'd been right about that, but she'd neglected to tell him they were also allowed to eat, albeit quietly, and eat she did, *kine ahora* ("don't tempt the devil," as his Yiddish-speaking grandma always said, spitting three times over her left shoulder). He'd look up at her dazedly every ten minutes or so: chips, chocolates, crackers, beef jerky, an eel-flavored dried-fish snack called "Me So Hungry," which Dan wouldn't touch for love or money, and ice cream, but who cared? As far as Dan was concerned, she could eat whatever she wanted, as long as she wasn't allowed to utter a single exuberant sound. As long as simply everything and anything didn't make her ridiculously happy. He wished the train would stall on the tracks for hours and the silence could last and last.

Intimacy breeds contempt, who said that? Aesop, as in fables, or Mark Twain? Or had it been his own weary-to-the-bone wife, Amy? Was the phrase really *familiarity* breeds contempt and Amy had augmented it to serve her own marital purposes when commenting on his morning fart, or on the way he smacked his lips when he ate cereal, or on the fact that he seemed incapable of (a) paying a bill on time, (b) putting his socks into the hamper, (c) making a non-corny joke, or (d) all of the above? Amy was now back in Palo Alto, ignorant of her own abandonment, left at home alone with three children and a job, three *boys,* thinking her husband had flown to Boston of all places, for an interview at the *Globe,* a paper that had offered buyouts and then layoffs three years running. Don't you ever google, Amy? Why did she simply trust him?

Dan had never done a thing like this before. He'd never run off to another country with another woman spending money they did not have for a story of dubious merit just because he was still alive and really wanted to. Perhaps he'd never really wanted to before. Who knew? Not Dan, who didn't recognize the palms of his own hands when he blearily stared at them during the train ride. Why was the lifeline on the left so strangely short? The one on the right was so ragged and so lengthy, it looked like an ultralong protracted painful fadeout tragically awaited him. At the time of his death, Dan's father was 98 percent demented, in a diaper, confined to a wheelchair, paralyzed by what his army of doctors thought was Parkinson's, but following his autopsy turned out to be plain old-fashioned arteriosclerosis. All that pastrami! The Parkinson's medication he did not need had made Dad hallucinate he was being eaten by bears. The value of his remaining 2 percent of cognition had made Dad agonizingly aware of the 98 percent of the intelligence that had forsaken him. Maybe for Dan a similar journey had already kicked off.

Who could blame him for wanting an adventure? His time on earth was rapidly diminishing. Even if said adventure cost him a fortune. Despite Maryam's schemes and abundant frequent-flier miles, Dan shuddered to think about what he'd just put on his credit card. It was an old corporate Amex, the bills went directly to him now, he could bankrupt himself and Amy both, without her knowledge until it was too late. How would he ever explain this to her? Maryam was wily. She knew how to skirt the Japanese bureaucracy, getting them both official orders in record time, a separate permit required for each town within the No-go Zone; they all were still heavily guarded, she'd said, but *she* could get them in. She made things happen. But in their weeks of planning, she'd never mentioned Amy, and he hadn't either. It was as if they were both pretending his wife, and kids for that matter, simply didn't exist.

It was night by the time they reached Fukushima Station. Dan knew where he was because it said FUKUSHIMA STATION in bright red neon English letters next to three big bright red Japanese characters slapped across the glassy modern and chrome building beside the tracks. Some of the other signs hanging on the terminal were also in English, which helped ground Dan; he was actually here! He couldn't believe it! Even after the long expedition that had started now over a day and a half ago and felt like a veritable lifetime, he was in fact at the gateway to a place that he had read about and pondered, worried for and twittered about, a cursed land.

It was a part of the Earth he had never dreamed he would see in person or even would ever want to. But the sign said it all. He *was* here, he did not have to take a selfie to prove it.

As they rolled in next to the platform, the train and station's lights illuminating ahead just a few short feet of Dan's future, the surrounding landscape looked similar to much of the Japan he'd already traversed, and was surprisingly and boringly intact. A graceful green mountain stood waiting ahead. Ungroomed brush sprouted alongside the tracks. Low-slung office buildings peeked out over the glass-and-metal station, cookie-cutter shapes, painted white, gray, and brown, an architecture that read as purposefully undistinguished as possible, like this was the outskirts of Scranton or part of those low monotonous stretches that extended from LAX, save an occasional splash of red. In juxtaposition, the sign itself, FUKUSHIMA STATION, he now noticed, was not exactly red, but a defiant blood orange. Poppy. He remembered a story he'd done in Afghanistan, long before Afghanistan *was* Afghanistan. The fields of opium red poppies. Like out of *The Wizard of Oz*. Once he had thought they were the most beautiful thing he'd ever seen. They were way darker than California poppies. Those were a sort of golden orange, Dan thought. Amy's favorite.

After they disembarked from the train, Maryam walked slightly ahead of Dan, dragging her two roller bags and adjusting her camera bag as she went. At one point, she stopped and politely let the other disembarking passengers pass them, and he waited, several steps behind her. Then they crossed over one of the elevated enclosed pedestrian walkways that got them to the other side of the tracks. They took the west exit out.

"I don't get it," said Dan. "The city looks intact."

"Fukushima City was never evacuated," said Maryam. "It's the capital of the prefecture. Evacuation orders started small in an expanding radius surrounding the nuclear power station. Some residents of this city didn't even know about the nuclear accident until ten or eleven days later. The authorities insisted it was safe, but they are still in the process of decontamination even as we speak. There are storage sites for the contaminated topsoil all over the city. I'll show you tomorrow."

"My God," said Dan. "All over the city?"

"You've seen my photos. They store them in schoolyards and in lots behind people's houses under blue plastic sheets."

"Let's just go home," said Dan, standing on the sidewalk. He was dead on his feet.

"Home?" said Maryam.

"You know what I mean. A hotel. Is there a taxi stand around here? Or do we take another goddamn bus? Or do we just pitch a tent in the contaminated topsoil in the center of the unevacuated city?"

"*Unevacuated*? That's not even a word, Dan. An unevacuated city is just a city, or perhaps a city in peril, or maybe even a city at ease . . ."

"Shut up," said Dan. "I hate it here. I want to go home. I'm not having any fun. You're not paying any attention to me!" He was aware that he sounded like a baby and for a moment hid his face in his hands. He rubbed his eyes; he was that tired.

"I will be with you," Maryam said. "You don't have to snivel." She pointed down the street. The Richmond Hotel. A tall white unremarkable building one could find anywhere on the planet. "A bargain. Sixty-nine American dollars a night. They have this marvelous breakfast buffet. *You* will love it. I picked it for *your* enjoyment. I *pay attention* to you. I *know* what you need. I just also happen to be alive."

"You spoiled, deprived child."

She took a deep breath, gathering back her patience.

"I'm sorry, Mar," said Dan. "I'm just, I don't know what, I'm spent, I guess."

She nodded. She'd accept his apology. She accepted him.

"It's where I stayed last time. They will remember."

Of course, they would remember. Who could possibly forget?

Dan followed her blindly across the street. He was so beat he could not believe his legs moved, but they did, seemingly of their own volition, they felt unattached to his body, which felt totally disassociated from his mind.

Maryam entered the hotel first, and again Dan toddled after her as she walked up to the front desk. A young woman in a black suit with a blue-and-white silk scarf poking out of the breast pocket was leaning over an open drawer. Her hair was in a sleek, slicked-back black knot at the base of her collar.

"*Kombawa,*" she said, without looking up. "Welcome to the Richmond Hotel, how may I help you?" She stood up straight and faced them; then she took a breath. She burst out laughing and bowed excitedly. "Maryam, kiuaku-san! *Hisashiburi.* I saw your reservation and was hoping you would arrive when I was on duty!"

Maryam bowed back, grinning, and said something in Japanese.

"Dan," said Maryam, "please meet my young friend Aiko Ikehara-sama." The receptionist bowed back, and now she laughed at Dan. Why was she laughing at him?

He bowed awkwardly in response, but he'd waited too long, as she had already turned her focus to her computer. Bowing, he thought, was a lot like the tip jar. All in the timing.

The lobby was white; the desk was dark wood. There were a few low-slung modular black leather sofas lining the perimeter of the reception area and surrounding an extremely large white rectangular, plastic coffee table. In the corner of the room there was a matching dark wood desk with three computer monitors on it. No paintings, plants, or wall art. Simple, Dan thought, and spare. Maryam's friend was the only sign of life, her scarf the only bit of color.

"What did you say to her?" asked Dan.

"That I've missed her and that we need two rooms."

"Two rooms," Dan repeated dazedly.

"I'm not going to fuck you, Dan," said Maryam. "I'm too knackered."

She knocked the air right out of him. But before he could even respond, the young woman presented them each with a key card. Maryam said something else in Japanese. Then she winked, and the two women laughed.

"What's so funny?" Dan said.

"I told her the bill is on you," said Maryam.

Finally, alone in his hotel room—the size of a walk-in closet in California—Dan sat down on the neatly made-up white double, gazed down at the dark brown carpet, took off his sneakers, and peeled off his socks. The skin on his feet was as wrinkled and damp as if he'd just come out of an extended warm bath. Ultrapale and pruney. His feet looked like they belonged to a dead person. He tried to wiggle his toes, but for one hot second, he forgot how. He forgot how to move his own extremities. Suddenly, the building shook. The shaking frightened him. An earthquake. Maryam had warned him, they come and go here all the time, she'd said. Still the minor tremor terrified him. Like an empty vessel, he filled with existential dread. It seemed to take liquid form and suctioned up through his toes and to the top of his throat, where it sloshed around noxiously, threatening to spill over and out of his mouth in pure, terrified vomit. You could die right now, Dan thought. How much beauty have you squandered?

Dan couldn't breathe then. He was drowning in the stuff of regret and stupidity and waste. A toxic stew. For a moment, he thought he might even collapse.

"Maryam," he eked out. "Maryam, please come back."

He looked around the empty room.

A long white desk was fitted against the floor-to-ceiling window. There was a lamp and a phone on either end. A brown leather rolling office chair was tucked in underneath it. The curtains that kept the night out, like everything else in the room, were brown and white. The white inner skirt was chiffon. Through it, he could see light bleed in from the street.

He was still on Earth. There was furniture. All the way here in Japan, there was electricity, things he knew.

"Maryam," he said, aloud again. "Please. I want you. I want me. I miss myself when you're not here."

She was his kindred spirit. He was simply lost without her. He couldn't stand her. He couldn't bear their separation. He felt like a teenager. Crazed and crazy. He did not know what to do with this kind of love. Dan folded himself over his knees and began to sob.

Later, Dan found himself snoozing on top of the bedding in the fetal position, still wearing his travel clothes, that same stupid green fleece. He'd cried himself to sleep the night before. Now, at last, there was the relief of daylight. It shone through the gauzy curtains like fairy dust. He looked at his watch. What he read there was latitude. He was seventeen hours ahead of his family. Those hours had revolutionized who he was, but they did not yet exist for them. There was still room to change his life.

. . .

It was 3:30 a.m. Kevin knew this because he was up and when he was up, which was always, he periodically checked his phone. Kevin couldn't sleep, he didn't like to sleep, he didn't like to dream, it wasn't worth it, his dreams were always bad. In them, sometimes he kept getting old real fast, like he had that bizarre aging disease, the kind he and the guys read about in tabloid magazines while killing time at the CVS across from Paly, in the Town & Country shopping mall during lunch period. Every so often there was some little kid who turned into an old man like overnight, and that's what Kevin dreamed happened to him. He dreamed he literally watched himself shrivel, and his teeth rotted in his mouth and crumbled into wet, gravelly shells that he had to scoop out with his fingers so he wouldn't choke, and then all his hair went white and it fell out and he looked like a cancer patient, like that poor freshman kid last year at school.

Or, he'd forgotten to take chemistry, the entire course, not only a semester but the whole year, but there he was at the final exam anyway and Kevin didn't understand one single solitary thing that was asked of him (even though in real life he'd aced AP chem). In fact, the letters on the exam paper weren't letters, at least letters whose shapes he recognized, and the numbers weren't numbers, but moved around like tiny insects, and if he failed his exam, a *final*, he wouldn't graduate. In this dream, if Kevin didn't graduate they would take away his scholarship to Stanford (the scholarship he didn't have yet, which made him feel even sicker when he woke up, sweaty with sheets twisted around his legs, because Kevin wanted that scholarship so bad).

There were more nightmares in his catalog, the one he hated the most was that he was a grown-up but he was still living with his parents, sometimes in his room, sometimes on the living room couch, sometimes in the garage, sometimes in the basement, and this part was really screwed up, it was so specific it made the dream feel really real; in this horrible dream he could hear his mom with her high heels walking across the hardwood floor above his head, doing stuff, rushing to get out, to start her long full important day, saving people's lives, clicking, clicking, clicking, while all he could do was just sit on his bed.

Also, in his dreams there was fucked-up sex stuff, stuff he didn't want to think about. Boys, girls. Boys and girls he knew. Boys and girls he loved, who didn't love him back. Boys and girls who actually had sex with each other but never with him. Jack said his mom said that in terms of sex everything was all right if it was consensual and you didn't hurt yourself or anyone else, but Kevin wasn't sure, and anyway Jack's mom wasn't his mom, and he wasn't sure he agreed with her even if the two moms were like besties. Both had older boys, and much younger twins. They had so much in common! they said, and they liked calling themselves Jack's and his second-mothers. Not-thinking about the sex stuff after one of his dreams was hard and he had to drive his fists into the top of his thighs to get the active not-thinking to kick in. But it was a great discipline. It helped him with the other not-thinking he had to do, just to get by. When he was conscious he still thought about sex, but he beat off to regular porn like normal people.

So, he chose to stay awake. Kevin didn't need sleep. He needed food, but not sleep. He was an athlete, so he needed to eat right. He was trying harder; he was trying not to be such a goofball; he was trying not to be a clown. For some reason, he always messed around with food, which made people laugh. Like his sisters, Josie and Suz, six-year-old twins—his parents waited for his mom to finish her training for that "second child" and, boy, did her training take a long time, four years of med school and seven years of neurosurgery. The twins were super-alike, they liked unicorns, they were summer ballerinas and winter figure skaters; they did everything together, and everything he did made them giggle. Probably in the world, they were the ones who liked him most.

He also made Lily laugh, Jack's girlfriend, which in the moments when he was trying hardest was all he wanted, her to look at him, not Jack, her laughter and her girlfriends', too. He made the girls laugh all the way from Texas the last time he and Jack split a burrito by shoving the whole thing into his mouth as Jack Instagrammed it. Kevin didn't want to do that anymore.

"Kevin, sweetie, don't keep doing this to yourself," Lily had said, he could see her beautiful face on Jack's phone, all scrunched up and, because she couldn't stop giggling, red from lack of air. "You can take little bites. We don't have to laugh. I'll still love you."

As if, he thought. Tell him.

And then, Bitch.

And then he took that evil thought right back.

Since then, he tried to eat açai bowls and rice bowls and dragon bowls—"Bowl Boy," Jack called him—but Jack was supportive and ate bowls, too, whenever they were together, which was all the time, except when Jack was with Lily, which was all the time, too, even when Jack slept. Jack slept, but not Kevin. No sleep for Kevin. He functioned fine with less than none. He had work to do, he always had work to do, he didn't mind doing work, he was good at it, his grades were awesome, he liked that. He opened his AP physics textbook. His phone pinged. It was Jack. Saved by the bell.

Dude, u up?

Hye ya, Kevin texted him back. *Hye ya* meant yes in Cantonese.

Happy Donuts? Jack wrote. *I'm feeling an apple fritter I'll pick u up*

?, Kevin wrote.

Dad's away got his keys Mom killed a whole bottle of wine at dinner LOL she's passed out C U in a few

Kevin rolled out of bed. He was already dressed. He did that to save time. He dressed after his shower before he went to bed at night. He had his Speedo on underneath his board shorts. They had water polo practice at 10:00 a.m., he and Jack. School started at 8:10, but Kevin hated changing and changing back in the locker room. He didn't like people seeing him naked. He had a six-pack and good shoulders from working out so much, but his dick was long and thin and it looked like there was something wrong with it to him, it kind of curved to the side like a banana when it got hard. And it got hard a lot. For no reason. Sometimes it even got hard when he looked at Jack. He couldn't risk it getting hard in the locker room. It wasn't big and full like the guys online.

He and Jack always played sports together. When they were little they played soccer, and biked and skateboarded around the Stanford campus. Swimming was their hands-down favorite; they both had their eye on water polo from the start. They used to go watch Stanford meets at the Avery Aquatic Center, right near the football stadium and the Sunken Diamond baseball field. Jack had a great eggbeater and long arms. When they were in middle school Jack used to practice sitting in a chair at lunch, in the cafeteria, he didn't give a shit, the right leg moving out in a circle as the left leg came in in a circle from the other direction. He looked like a retard, but the retarded moves paid off. He was a natural goalkeeper, born with his shoulders out of the water. But Kevin was fast, faster than anyone else at Paly. He did swim team in the spring and water polo in the fall, but water polo was his first love. He was a driver of the first order. No doubt, he could play in college. Even though it was only junior year, recruitment had already begun.

Kevin had collected his grades, stats, and videos and sent them with his résumé to coaches on both coasts. You had to be proactive in water polo because it wasn't a well-funded sport and it was supercompetitive with only a few scholarships per year for boys; girls had it easier. Also, you had to compete against international students, too. Some of them came from countries that actually valued water polo. Like Hungary, Croatia, Montenegro. Kevin wasn't exactly sure where Montenegro was, but he viewed it as a threat. There had been kids from Montenegro at his water polo camp last summer, but he'd been embarrassed to ask them. They kicked ass, those Montenegro kids. Kevin really wanted a scholarship. His parents could afford college for him and his two sisters, but he loved the thought of getting that scholarship anyway. He'd never gotten high, but the feeling he felt when he daydreamed about getting an email from Stanford that said welcome entering class of 2021 you have just received a water polo scholarship and walking his laptop over to his parents while they were sitting in the living room going over the bills or watching *Orange Is the New Black* and showing them the email, well he bet getting high felt exactly like that.

Kevin didn't get high because he was an athlete, and an athlete had to protect his lungs and his reflexes. All their coaches said that, and it was true. He got drunk a lot, but who didn't? USC was a five-peat champion and UC San Diego didn't suck, but it was D2. His folks wanted him to go to Stanford. His father had gone to the B-school, his father's parents had sent him all the way from Hong Kong to the States for college at MIT where he'd majored in math and he'd never looked back, and his mom was local, she grew up in Cupertino; she went to Stanford as an undergrad and graduated summa cum laude and Phi Beta Kappa and got her medical training at Stanford Hospital. She spent her days sawing open other people's skulls. They'd met at a singles blood drive at the Stanford Blood Center. How corny could you get? Buck/Cardinal was the best option, sure. But USC would be chill, the girls were cuter, and he'd be closer to the beach. He was more competitive than Jack for Stanford, because his grades were better and he was double-legacy; also, his parents were donors. Jack was a natural athlete, but in some ways Jack didn't care. That was what was so great about Jack and made him Kevin's best friend. Kevin cared about every detail of his life.

Outside his window, Kevin saw Jack's car lights down the street, he watched Jack dim them, then roll past his house with the engine off, so he wouldn't wake up Kevin's mother, or the girls. His dad would kill Kevin if he woke up the girls—they'd be up all night. Another reason to like Jack, he'd never get Kevin into trouble, even though he kind of courted trouble all the time. Kevin texted Jack: *B right down*

Then he loaded up his backpack with all his school stuff, just in case they hung out late enough to go straight to class, and he carried his sneakers and socks in his other hand. Good thing the staircase was carpeted. He went down slowly to avoid creaks, and then walked super-carefully across the hardwood floor in the entrance hall and cautiously opened the front door. It was dark out. The air was wet and smelled of damp leaves and cool earth. A different smell from warm earth. Hard to quantify.

Kevin entered the Volvo on the passenger's side. The wet, cold, gritty ground hurt his feet in a way that felt good. Jack was texting as Kevin slid in, Lily probably, even if it was around 5:00 a.m. in Texas, so Kevin quietly used his hands to wipe his bare feet clean of the pebbles and dirt over the road and then put on his socks and shoes, drawing his legs inside the car before closing the door. Jack kept typing with his thumbs. Jack's blond, greasy hair was in a man bun. Sometimes he said it itched his neck. Kevin wouldn't know. He'd always worn his hair clean and short.

"She up already?" Kevin asked. He strapped himself in with his seat belt.

"Yeah. Her mom went out to dinner with some married guy and she isn't home yet and Lily's freaked."

"Word," said Kevin. He and Jack said "word" ironically to just about anything, especially when they didn't know what else to say. They were making fun of people who used to say it seriously when *they* didn't know what to say. No one said "word" anymore but Jack and Kevin, which made it cool.

"Cindy, Lily's mom, she's still hoping she'll marry someone with money. This guy's loaded and he got her her job. He was crushed out on her in high school, but she was shallow. He's a ginger and had zits or something. She's still kicking herself that she married Lily's asshole dad and didn't give this guy a chance. Lily's afraid her mom will get hurt, again."

"Maybe she should go get breakfast with Grandma Rose," said Kevin.

"No, it's too early for that. Grandma Rose would have a heart attack and her teeth would fall out." Jack kind of stiffened. "How do you know about Grandma Rose?"

"What?" said Kevin. "Everyone who knows Lily knows about Grandma Rose. She's famous. Lily famous."

There was silence in the car.

"Cindy? Lily's mom? She's beautiful, right? Like Lily?" Kevin asked. He knew he was pushing it, but he wanted to.

Jack turned the key in the ignition and for a moment the car lit up. He looked at Kevin and Kevin looked back at him.

"Yeah, dude, she is," said Jack.

Then he put the car into drive and they took off.

Happy Donuts was in a freestanding maroon building on El Camino. It was open 24/7 and had great Wi-Fi, and the best part about it, besides the doughnuts and the widescreen, was the giant cream-filled papier-mâché doughnut that hung from the ceiling like a fancy chandelier. Kevin and Jack went there a lot after school and after meets and in the early-morning hours like this when Jack couldn't sleep. Usually, Jack could. But sometimes Lily kept him up too late and then it was sort of over for Jack. That's when he called on Kevin.

Now that they were inside, Jack perused the counters. He always liked to try something new. "Dude," he said, "I'm seriously thinking about the ham-and-cheese on a glazed doughnut and then the apple fritter."

"Your poison," said Kevin. "I'll have the Wild Berry Blast smoothie," he said to the Mexican guy behind the counter. The guy looked to be the same age as Kevin's father. "Please," said Kevin.

"Pussy," said Jack. But he smiled. "I'll have the ham-and-Swiss pressed on a glazed doughnut, and the apple fritter. And a vanilla with chocolate frosting and rainbow sprinkles for my friend here." He raised his shoulder at Kevin.

"Word," they both said in unison. Then they laughed. Jack said, "This one's on me." Kevin looked surprised. "I mean it's late and all, thanks for hanging out with me."

Kevin shrugged it off. "Sure," he said. "What are friends for."

They sat down at two wooden chairs at one of the long blue communal tables while the counter guy got their orders. There was a Stanford couple making out at another table in the corner by the windows, and some geek buried in his computer at theirs.

"So, dude, what's up?" Kevin said. "Where's Dad?"

"He went chasing after some job in Boston. I dunno, man. Seems dumb."

"Does that mean you might be moving?" asked Kevin.

"Nah, I don't think so. My mom doesn't think so, either. I mean, she's got some stake in that stupid start-up and we're all here. She said Dad's just got to get his confidence back."

Luckily at that moment their food came, on three paper plates with a fistful of brown paper napkins on a plastic tray. A straw for the smoothie, deep purple in its tall frosted-plastic smoothie glass, lay right next to it. The counterman looked tired, and his white apron was stained with Thai coffee, one of Happy Donuts' specialties, and berries and chocolate and other crud.

"Thank you," Jack said to the counterman.

"Yeah, thanks," said Kevin.

Then they both looked down at the food. Jack's was a gooey glazed panini.

"That looks sickening," said Kevin.

"I think it looks good," said Jack. He picked it up with a napkin, the grease instantly blooming out. He held it up to Kevin's mouth. "I triple-dog dare you," Jack said.

"Naw," said Kevin. "My body's my temple." He put his straw in his smoothie and took a big gulp and burped.

"Ha," said Jack.

Then Kevin took the whole chocolate-covered doughnut with rainbow sprinkles and shoved it into his mouth.

"You really are my brother," Jack said, laughing as the chocolate and sprinkles squirted out of Kevin's mouth. Kevin could feel it on his lips and chin. He used his fingers to push the rest of it back in. He hated himself right then.

Jack took a bite of his doughnut sandwich. "Mmm," said Jack. In three more bites, it was finished. Then he started in on his apple fritter.

Kevin drained his smoothie, vacuuming up the blueberry dregs. Then he belched again even louder. Even the geek at the end of the table looked up.

"Let's drive around," Jack said.

"Sure," said Kevin.

They drove around and around Palo Alto, through the Stanford campus, all those mission-style buildings with tan walls and red tile roofs, the globe lights punctuating the darkness, the emergency blue light telephones glowing like fake stars stuck on the walls at a high school dance, down Palm Drive, where a couple of crazy people were jogging wearing headlamps, and out onto University Avenue. The streets were empty. Then up Alma, past the Caltrain station, and then back up El Camino.

Once the sun started to rise, Jack said he better drive home. "My mom will have a heart attack if I'm not there when she gets up," he said.

"Okay," said Kevin. "Just, you know, drop me off at school first. I can hang out on the field and finish studying. I brought my books," he said, and he picked up his backpack like it was Exhibit A.

"Okay," said Jack, looking over at his backpack. There was a GO VIKINGS bumper sticker on it, same as Jack's. "But you know you're weird. I don't know how you can go day after day without sleeping, I really don't." He yawned, big-time.

Jack drove him the half mile to Paly. Ahead, across the field, the sky was beginning to get gray and then pinked from underneath as the sun rose. It kind of looked like a half-cooked shrimp. It was five thirty. Kevin knew because he checked his phone and sent a message. He had just enough time.

Jack parked by the baseball field.

"You okay?" asked Kevin.

"I got a lot on my mind," said Jack.

"I see that," said Kevin.

They were both quiet.

"I love Lily," Jack said. "I'm going to marry her."

Kevin looked at the rising sun. There was a weird hollowness in his chest where his heart should have been. He would never have what they had. He would always be lonely.

"You're lucky, dude," said Kevin.

"Thanks, man," said Jack. "Thanks for everything."

Then Kevin got out of the car and started to walk toward the field. He could hear Jack pull out behind him and drive away.

Kevin turned east and walked across the bike trail.

He wondered if Jack could hear the incoming 5:37 northbound Caltrain. He probably had just driven over the road that crossed the railway and was heading home. Kevin looked up at the sign in front of him next to the rails. THERE IS HELP it said, and there was a picture of two white hands clasping and a hotline number.

"I need help," Kevin said.

He stepped forward and lay down across the tracks with the backpack in his arms.

. . .

They made their way down Highway 6 behind a truck carrying radioactive topsoil. As Maryam had promised, the excavated earth was covered with a blue plastic tarp. Not exactly a bolstering sight. She drove, and Dan finally had a chance to ask her some questions; the more they talked, the more relaxed he became. Also, paradoxically, the more anxious and excited—it was hard to hold so many conflicting emotional truths in his hands at once. And yet that complexity appeared to be life with Maryam.

"I don't get it," he said. "You only met the guy once, but you love him?"

He thought, You've known me now for months.

He thought it, but he dared not say it.

"It is true that I met with Yoshi only briefly," Maryam admitted. "Some reporters I knew from Vice were producing a short video about his life, and I'd stopped by to visit the shoot on my way back from photographing my own project."

"Vice already shot him? So, what are we doing here?" Dan asked. He felt like such an idiot. She'd beckoned with her finger, *come with me,* and like a puppy, Dan obediently had followed.

His tone pissed her off. "It is now time for a follow-up photo essay, this is essential," said Maryam. "Yoshi's story and his life continue, the crisis is not over. Just because it's not been thrust in your face during the last five minutes doesn't mean it has lost its relevance."

"I know all that, but what's so great about him?" Dan persisted. He was getting antsy—*shpilkes*, his mother had called it. He stretched out his legs and arms. Maryam looked over at his elongated torso, then back at the road. Dan pulled down his polo shirt.

"Talk about resistance. He has been living all alone in the Red Zone since 2011. That's half a decade."

Dan knew what five years was. Five years ago, he was an editor and a writer with a job. Five years ago, his curly hair was brown. Five years ago, three kids, work, stress, whatever, he'd been overwhelmed, sure, but he had not hated his life. He had considered himself a fairly happy man. He'd been in love with his wife.

"Every six months Yoshi is tested by the Japanese Aerospace Exploration Agency and he has seventeen times the legal limit of radiation in his body. They are gobsmacked! Tell me why? Day in and day out, he eats the food he has grown; he drinks milk produced by the cattle he tends. He is the most radioactive person in Japan. Probably the world. He's been bathed in it."

Dan rolled up his window. For all Maryam's outrage, she, too, sounded surprised. Why? Why did any of this surprise her? Yoshi had stayed put. He kept living in Tomioka. His choice. *He* drank the milk; *he* ate the eggs. He was ordered to evacuate and he'd returned. He broke the law. Dan felt for him, sure. Most people don't want to leave their native soil. The world was full of refugees. Sixty-seven million was the last figure to register in Dan's head. This past year saw the highest number of displaced persons worldwide ever, including after the Second World War. The costs were enormous. His grandmother's four brothers and sisters paid a different kind of price when they'd refused to leave Vienna and ended up gassed in the camps during the Second World War. They could not have imagined the fate that awaited them. At the time, the Final Solution was an evil most people in their worst moments could not imagine.

Now torture, cruelty, and destruction were daily fare on Dan's Twitter feed. If Dan had learned one thing, evil was not rarefied, it was an equal-opportunity employer, it did not believe in exceptionalism and neither did Dan. But any way you sliced it, this guy, this guy Maryam *loved*, it was his decision to remain in Fukushima. Yoshi had not caused the ongoing nuclear accident, nor the shitty protective measures set in place to mitigate it. He had not lied to the people of his prefecture about the contamination following the tsunami like the Tepco guys. So he could not be blamed for his own initial exposure. But he'd returned to Tomioka knowingly, in frustration after evacuating, for his own reasons, saturating himself in radiation, causing harm to his internal organs, his cell structure, his DNA. Shouldn't that kind of stubbornness be what surprised Maryam? Or did she see kinship in the obduracy? Dan toyed with the idea of injecting some of this observation into their discussion, but then thought better of it.

He stole a sidelong glance at Maryam. Even in a momentary bit of repose, eyes on the road, mouth closed, her profile carried a look of intensity. Maryam had been alone most of her life, so perhaps this was how she kept herself company, getting worked up about the lives of others. When Dan thought about how forlorn she must have been as a child—a completely misunderstood little girl trapped in a boy's body, later without a mother, with a father fatally flawed, a man built without charity or insight—his heart broke. But it was hard to imagine adult Maryam lonely when almost everyone they encountered seemed to take a liking to her. Her life force was so strong; she was so full of enthusiasm; her face often glowed with exhilaration. Even those who merely stared, and there were many, weren't quite sure what they were staring at. She was a sizable woman, and she was gorgeous. Maybe the people who were riveted by her looks didn't totally understand her beauty—it was a strong masculine beauty, the broad shoulders, narrow hips—but evidently she was arresting to more than just him. Because everywhere they went together, people took notice.

Dan held some misbegotten macho pride in this, pride without association. It had been a long time since other men had stared at Amy in such a full-throated, hungry way. Not that she wasn't appealing: Amy was good-looking and in great shape; and when animated, charming and delightful! But these days she was always tired, and that diminishing combo of motherhood and work had somewhat erased her, the way it erased most women. Maryam's beauty commanded attention, even right now, driving their rent-a-car. Her black hair was loose and flowing, and in the moment, he imagined what it might feel like brushing against his face and chest. As he stared at her, in what was now undeniably a state of desire, it kind of freaked him out, how into her he was—when just five years prior she had still been male.

Dan tried to picture Maryam as a guy, in guy's clothes, with short hair, a beard, maybe. Knowing her now as he knew her, would he desire her then? He, she, were the same person. But the mind game he was playing with himself got Dan nowhere. One of the reasons Maryam was so attractive to him was that she *was* female, and because she was essentially female, she had necessitated this transition.

He looked at her hands curled around the wheel. She had managed to paint her nails red between last night and this morning, even though she had been so *knackered*. She wore jeans that fit her just right—she had great thighs, he noted they didn't spread when she sat, like Amy's did, no matter how much or how fast Amy ran—and a plain, white, close-fitting, scoop-necked T-shirt and a dusky rose-pink cashmere sweater that softened her breasts. Closed-toed shoes, ankle boots. Today, she'd left her jewelry back at the hotel. They were driving to a farm outside Tomioka City, so he guessed this was her farming attire. Her lipstick was as red as her nails. She'd lined her eyes with her trademark kohl. He wasn't used to women who wore a lot of makeup—Amy didn't, they lived in Northern Cal, and most of the women there had a fresh-faced look. Marilyn, Kevin's mom, sometimes wore eye shadow and had an understated elegance . . . The mothers at school wore lipstick to the various recitals or out to dinner. He wondered if Maryam had had the same physical grace when she'd been trapped in a male body. He liked to think she'd been a prisoner under a spell and had been set free not by a fairy godmother but by a series of brilliant physicians and therapists.

Right this moment, Maryam was who she was meant to be. Dan decided then and there that he would never know her pain and he would withstand the impulse to judge it. Perhaps he should practice the same resolve with her loverboy, Yoshi.

There was a lot of commuter traffic on Highway 6 that Thursday morning. It had increased when they left the Green Zone for the Orange Zone, when the cars and trucks began to pile up. This was a single-lane highway, and as they neared the coastline the assemblage of vehicles slowed down to a laborious crawl. It was one thing to be exposed to radiation for a story, it was another to be soaked in the stuff because of a traffic jam. Out his window Dan could see boats still stranded by the tsunami in the abandoned rice paddies. One boat, upon closer surveillance, turned out to be an upright piano lying on its side. What's wrong with this picture, Dan said to himself, remembering on autopilot the banal puzzles in the collection of ancient *Highlights* magazines in his childhood dentist's waiting room. How had the piano ended up here? What had happened to the house or school or temple or church it had been housed in? Where was the musician or student or teacher or child who hated learning to play it? At least sixteen thousand people had died in the tsunami alone. Five years out. Half a decade. The piano still stuck where it landed. Might this detritus be sitting out in these fields and paddies forever? The emotional consequences of all this upheaval seemed so vast. After Chernobyl, the average life expectancy of the survivors went down from age sixty-five to fifty-eight, not because of cancer, but stress, alcoholism, and suicide.

Over the Pacific yesterday Maryam had told some fellow passenger, maybe even him, that Tepco was building an ice wall of frozen dirt under the nuclear plant to prevent more groundwater leakage into the wounded reactors. When subsoil channels seeped into the plant they became highly radioactive. The idea was to prevent the now "hot" groundwater from flowing out into the Pacific. So far this phantasmagorical frosty plan was not exactly working for them. Every day radioactive water was still streaming into the sea.

A few more billion yen on that one. Like thirty-five. Which was— Dan did a quick calculus—over $300 million. This new cooling apparatus was also dependent on electricity, she'd said—electricity being the first thing to go during an earthquake, and of course, unusable during a tsunami. Dan shivered, remembering the temblors of the night before. Amy used to be a *General Hospital* fan. The freezing of Fukushima sounded like one of that soap opera's crazier story lines.

Maryam made a right turn and continued following their irradiated topsoil truck right up to a Red Zone checkpoint. How much of that contaminated dust was blowing into the car's vents right now? Two men in protective white suits wearing gas masks approached the car. Behind them was a blockade and some red Japanese writing. Maryam handed one guy the permit for entry.

"We should have suited up," Dan said.

"We have a Geiger counter, we won't stay that long," said Maryam. "It's no longer necessary for such a brief visit, I think. Besides, I'd feel awkward to be armed to the teeth while Yoshi greets us virtually naked on his beautiful farm. But there are gas masks in my satchel if you want one."

"You make it sound like the Garden of Eden," said Dan. "How about the Gates of Hell?"

"Believe me, this is no Eden," said Maryam. "And not hell, exactly, more like Roman ruins."

They were nodded along past the checkpoint by the first guy, while the second guy pressed some buttons and the barrier lifted to let them through. There were half a dozen cars in line behind them. But the barrier came back down as soon as they cleared its threshold, Dan could see it in his side mirror. Who were the officials protecting? He found the whole rigmarole patently ridiculous. They could have easily just navigated around the thing.

"A lot of people driving into town," said Dan. "I didn't expect that."

"They are driving *through*," said Maryam. "You'll see; the town is dead empty. No one lives there but Yoshi, and he has long vacated his own home—he found it just too painful without his family, although he does go back from time to time to make repairs and tidy up, I don't know who for."

"I didn't know he had a family," said Dan.

"Yes, his mother now lives outside the exclusion zone with her sister, I forget where, and his grown children are in Tokyo; I fear they worry. He separated from his wife long ago when the kids were small. She remarried and was living in Osaka for years before the earthquake."

Maryam slowed down to look at herself in the rearview mirror. She parted her lips and smiled. "Do I have lipstick on my teeth?" she asked. She turned to grin directly at Dan.

"All good," said Dan. Her teeth were strong and white.

"A lot of these cars and trucks are carrying decontamination workers." Maryam continued piloting down the city's main artery. "Most are middle-aged men, many homeless, without education or ties, subsisting hand-to-mouth. The fringe element of society. Besides collecting topsoil, they wipe off roofs and other surfaces and basically live like your American migrant workers, in barracks, toiling for low wages with no benefits for months at a time until they are considered too contaminated to continue this kind of labor. They are at the bottom of the service class. And even though they are retired after some arbitrary number of weeks, they are unmonitored and untested and sent out to the winds to land who knows where. Some just re-up, finding new contract work with another shady company. Some, even while employed, still sleep on the streets. They throw their used gloves and trash in convenience store garbage cans, and nobody is monitoring that waste's radioactivity either. The neighbors, however, are concerned about the dangerous nature of their rubbish, and I read on one of my blogs they have started a 'manners' campaign. Tomioka is no one's destination."

When the twins were born, Dan remembered, even after they had battened down the hatches with all their preparations, Amy had said that bringing them home from the hospital felt like the difference between knowing you are going to go fight in battle, and being in a battle and having people shoot at you. Everyone had told her she'd be tired; she'd had a baby before; she knew from tired, but twins were unfathomably hard. They were ridiculous. Tomioka was ridiculous. A ghost town. Stopped by a remote control pressed on pause. The town looked vaguely intact, a little jiggled, stirred up, Dan thought, but like a semifunctioning entity, although there was not a single living soul around. Neutron-bomby. The streets were completely deserted. Two cars flipped over by the earthquake met in a bumper-to-bumper kiss in the middle of the road, and Maryam had to navigate up on the sidewalk to avoid them. Tall brush was growing out of the cracks in the cement. Many of the storefronts and apartments were trashed. Some buildings had lost a front facing or side wall and you could see inside like a diorama: a table still set for dinner, while the room next door was flooded with rubble. In front of an apartment house a dollhouse lay smashed in the yard, as if it had been jealously heaved out a window by a demonic sibling.

Maryam stopped at a red light. A spotted dog meandered about the crosswalk. Since there were no competing sounds, Dan could hear it snuffling through the glass. Some bicycles lay on their sides, crowding the sidewalk. A house slumped into the street. Another stood tall. The light switched to green. Maryam drove onward.

"Why did you stop?" Dan asked, belatedly. That nonsensical bit of decorum just occurred to him. "I remember you did it also in your film."

"Did I? Habit?" she said. "Protocol? See that video store?"

She slowed down, Dan gazed out the window. Through the store-front's pane of glass, it looked like most of the stock had fallen from the shelves and lay untouched on the floor.

"You can take whatever you want, Dan. It's all still there. Any Japanese movies you missed in 2011? That is if you don't now just stream. There has been no passage of time here."

Next to the building there was a metal structure that looked like a robot, child-size, with what appeared to be solar panels on its square head and digitized numbers on its rectangular body. This one's torso read 2.07 in a vertical line. Then it read 2.08.

"What's that?" said Dan.

"It's a radiation sensor," said Maryam. "They're all over. They indicate the accumulated background radiation by millisievert. Perfect for one of your 'late night' talk show hosts."

"Why?" said Dan, feeling thick, but curious.

Maryam turned from the wheel to stare at him. "Because there is no one around to read the thing, silly," said Maryam.

She took a left. "I want to show you what life looks like stopped midsentence."

She drove toward a minimall. There were cherry blossoms lining the empty streets, breathtaking in their fulsome thick beauty. They wept pink snow.

"Do cherry blossoms smell?" Dan asked.

"If you bury your nose in them, yes, there is a faint scent of cherry," Maryam said. "It's plum blossoms that really have a strong perfume. 'Scent of plum blossoms,'" she recited, "'on the misty mountain path / a big rising sun.' That's Bashō, if you don't know."

She pulled into a parking lot in front of a grocery store. "Come on," she said. She got out.

Dan hesitated.

"Come on, Danny," said Maryam. "Don't be scared."

He got out of the car. It was a lovely spring day—one of the loveliest. The air felt good. Clean. He took a deep breath in through his nose. He thought he could detect the lightest scent of cherries. Maryam, ahead, she was always ahead of him, held open the market's glass door. They walked inside. There was packaged food all over the floor. The aisles were knee-deep. But the shelves were also stocked—chips in canisters, canned goods, Japanese crackers and cereals with bright funny cartoonish illustrations on them. "Are you hungry?" asked Maryam. "I bet some of this stuff is still good."

She turned down an aisle, and he followed her. The periodicals section held magazines and newspapers in the racks although the floor was slippery with glossies.

"No one's cleaned up," said Dan.

"No one's been back," said Maryam. "Let's check out the Laundromat next door."

They picked their way through the debris and once again went outside. The sky was blue. You could hear birds. Birds still live here, Dan thought. Maybe life was easier for the birds here without the people to bother them. Wildlife flourished in Chernobyl after the citizens had left.

In the Laundromat, clean laundry spilled out of some of the open dryers. Formerly wet laundry moldered behind the glass in the washing machines. There was a stray shoe on the floor. They sure left in a hurry, Dan thought. It was a little like Pompeii. A little like Vesuvius. Except none of this had been preserved in lava. How long, if ever, would it take to decompose? The bras and underwear on the linoleum floor, the children's socks, almost comical.

"I don't know why, but it's the laundry that gets me," said Maryam. "I hate laundry so much, you're never done, you always have more to do. Sometimes I strip naked just to have it all done at once. But here that eternal cycle is broken. It's so bloody intimate." There were tears in her eyes. The first time Dan had witnessed them. He reached out his hand and cupped her cheek and some spilled down through her black lashes as she closed her lids. When she opened them, their eyes caught. They had a moment, Dan was sure of it. She was speechless and so was he. Then . . .

"You are so smart *and* so nice," Maryam said. "Would that all people were just like you."

Dan experienced a wave of emotion. He had not known she felt that way.

Without thinking he took her hand and they walked out of the Laundromat and back to the car. He escorted her to the driver's side and opened the door for her. Then he walked around to the passenger's side and slid in. As he was buckling his seat belt, Maryam turned to him. They kissed. Softly, light, dryly. The kiss of two people who were vowing to be careful with one another.

Maryam started up the car and they drove off.

When they arrived at Yoshi's farm, he was feeding the ostriches. Maryam tooted the car horn as they approached so that they wouldn't frighten him or the animals. "I think it would be the quiet that would most get to me," she said. "But Yoshi seems to have gotten used to it."

"Does he know we're coming?" Dan asked.

"We emailed a bit, he and I, and a few of the friends he still keeps in touch with, but no Wi-Fi here. It was spotty, even before the earthquake. Once in a while, he'll drive to get Internet service. I hope he received my last few messages. He is not the world's best correspondent."

"He emails?" Dan said. "Does he Facebook?"

"His supporters set up a page for him, but it is full of a lot of rot and well-meaning twaddle, and also hot air. Fund-raising, most of it. For other causes! I have no idea if he even knows."

She pulled up next to the pen. Just some wire fencing and dirt and four or five giant birds next to an open shed. Dan had seen ostriches before—rich hippies he knew up in Marin kept them as pets, and local farmers sold their giant eggs at the Sunday farmers' market on California Avenue back in Palo Alto, but he'd never been tempted to buy one. There was something obscene about the egg's large shape, as if a baby could be cradled inside, which of course was how baby ostriches were born, but still. These birds were tall, taller than he was or Maryam for that matter. She was already out of the car.

"Yoshi," she called. A handsome middle-aged man came out of the shed, where he had been spreading what looked like grass. He had dark hair with graying temples and was wearing a white T-shirt and a charcoal gray pullover and a big smile. Well dressed for someone living all alone and farming, Dan thought.

"Maryam-sama," Yoshi said.

She said something in Japanese and he replied and burst out laughing.

"Well, I don't know whether to be flattered or insulted," said Maryam, Dan guessed to both of them, or maybe just to herself? She walked over to the fence and gave Yoshi a little bow and spoke with what Dan assumed to be a touch of sass. Then she pointed to Dan and waved him over.

"Dan," she said. "*Watashi no ashisutanto.*"

Dan came over, and each man bowed. Dan turned to Maryam. "Did you just call me your assistant?"

"Don't sweat the small stuff," said Maryam, laughing, and looking suddenly rosy. "He said I was prettier than he thought. He's only seen me in protective gear till now."

She is incorrigible, thought Dan. She can't help flirting. As if to prove his point, Maryam held her hand out across the fence to one of the ostriches. She let him sniff it or poke it or whatever a beaked bird does to get comfortable with a human being. The ostrich, with its fuzzy, buzzed, chemo head, nuzzled at her hand and then backed off. "It's okay, baby, we have all night," cooed Maryam.

Maryam rattled around her camera bag and took out both a video camera and a Sony α7RII. "Okay, Yoshi?"

He nodded. Yoshi unhooked the pen's fence, stepped out, and rehooked it again. He took out his lighter and lit up a cigarette. There was something dapper about him, Dan thought. Like a gangster in a movie.

"How are we going to do this?" Dan asked suddenly. "I don't speak Japanese, and he doesn't seem to speak English." Why hadn't he thought about any of this before?

Yoshi took a deep inhale on his cigarette. Politely waiting.

"We're telling the story in images, Dan," said Maryam. "You need enough only for an accompanying text. And I can translate." She laughed again. "Sort of."

"Okay, then," said Dan, skeptically, but also juicing up. He looked at the well-dressed farmer. Curiosity, as ever, taking hold. "What made you return to Tomioka, Yoshi?"

Maryam repeated this in Japanese.

"I had nowhere to go really," Yoshi said, and Maryam translated. "I mean, my daughter offered for me to live with her family, but I didn't want that. And I hated temporary housing. I felt like a prisoner. So, I decided to come back and check on the livestock. We had a dairy farm, and some cats and dogs. I missed my animals." He whistled between his teeth and a handsome black mutt came running. Then he bent down to scratch the dog's back. He stayed in a crouch, petting the dog as the animal licked his face, Maryam shooting away. "The other two dogs died, but this guy, he was still living."

"He's like Dr. Doolittle," Dan whispered.

"Don't act jealous," said Maryam.

"Isamu," said Yoshi.

"That's the dog's name," said Maryam.

"I mean, he was almost dead," said Yoshi, Maryam translating. "He was starving. We still had plenty of pet food in the cabinets, but of course he could not reach. So, I fed him. The whole neighborhood was this way, the dogs, the cats, the cattle. The house animals were locked up in the houses, the livestock in their pens, they could do nothing to fend for themselves. Some were roaming free, toppling garbage cans, breaking into things. I went from house to house, sometimes I forced in the front door, sometimes I crawled in through a window. If I had to, I smashed the glass. Many of the animals were already dead. I buried those. The others I fed. I gave them water. So many were famished, but they were also eager for affection, to be touched—especially the ones who'd lived their whole lives as pets. Only a few were crazed enough with hunger that they bared their teeth to attack. With those, I pushed food into the house and backed away, but I sang little songs as I went, the way you might with a small child, to show your best intentions. Let me take you to the barn."

As Maryam shot and translated, Dan took notes. He'd brought a pad and pencil; he also tape-recorded. He could get the tapes transcribed when he got back to Palo Alto. He'd hire a grad student at the university to check on Maryam's Japanese.

The barn was several yards away on the property. It was cool when they entered and smelled of hay, manure, and livestock. Flies buzzed overhead as Yoshi pointed first to the horse stalls. Several still housed skeletal carcasses and rotted hide.

"I tried to save the ones that were still alive by feeding them through baby bottles, but by that time anything locked in the pens had no chance."

He walked them over to gaze more closely at the skeletons. Dan saw both hide and bones half buried in the dirt, hooves, which seemed perhaps even slower to decompose. "We'd always kept a few horses for the kids to ride."

Dan asked why he had not removed the remains five years in; after all, he had buried the neighbors' animals; and Yoshi replied something in Japanese while flicking a piece of tobacco off a front tooth. "They were pets. Pets are like children. With these guys, the farm animals, he says they are evidence," said Maryam.

"If a tree falls in the forest," said Dan.

"What do you mean?" she said.

"There's no one else here," said Dan. "To see it."

"We're here and we see it," said Maryam. "We are bearing witness. We will make sure the rest of the world doesn't forget. Isn't that the heart of why we came? I mean, professionally?"

"With care some of the animals recovered, and now they seem to be flourishing," said Yoshi. "The cattle that had been abandoned in the pasture, I nursed back to health. Let's go see them."

They walked out of the barn and Dan looked out over the meadow. He estimated Yoshi had around fifty head.

"I milk them twice a day like I did before the earthquake. There are barn cats and kittens." He pointed toward the chicken coop. "Chickens, so I have eggs. I have been here so long now, some of the chicks I've raised have lived a lifetime and died a natural death. There's been a generation of rebirth. And there are more wild boar now than ever. With those, you have to be careful. They are prone to attack. I keep them away from the babies—calves, sheep, goats. The little ones I shelter inside the fences. The boar, they like them for lunch." He laughed. "For some of the animals it's a return to paradise. None are raised for slaughter. I take care of them and they love me. But then there are birds with cataracts in their eyes. There are tumors. Some of the cattle have these strange white spots . . ."

He continued pointing, but in another direction, toward the road that Maryam and Dan had come from. There was a tractor and a hay lift parked by the side of the road. Near the hay lift was a gray bunny.

"We had a rabbit born without ears. I took him into the house to live with me. He and the dog were like brothers; they'd sleep together in a bed I made of pillows and old sheets. Like a little nest.

"That bunny, he was also albino. He loved to sneak out, and one day I didn't catch him. He was a fast runner. One of the boars did. He was so white, a perfect target. I went inside my neighbor's house to borrow a gun, I was so mad, but then I thought, why? This is nature. There are other bunnies born to take his place. The boar was doing what God wanted him to do. To live his life."

"What does God want you to do?" asked Dan.

"The same," said Yoshi. "To live my life. That's what God wants us all to do."

He started walking toward the cattle. Dan and Maryam followed him.

"You said you went into your neighbor's home? What's it like here after so many years without your neighbors?" Dan asked.

"First I missed them, of course. The ones I liked, ha-ha. Now I'm used to it. Over time, everything has gotten easier. There's a rhythm to my days. I'll borrow, when I need it, some farm machinery, a tractor, from the farmers closest by. I take very good care of their things; I park them in their sheds and keep them well oiled. The guy next door, I take care of his animals. His fields. I plant and mow them. I grow food for the animals to eat."

Dan asked, "Do you think your neighbor would mind if he knew?"

Yoshi shrugged. "He has never come back," he said. "I don't think he will. See that pig? That's his. The ostriches are also his. If he wants them, he can take them."

"He must have loved the ostriches," said Dan. "They are so funny."

Yoshi smiled. "I never had ostriches myself. Look at their bellies, those long thin necks. They have a peaceful life."

"It's Walden Pond," Dan whispered to Maryam.

"Let's go visit the cattle," said Yoshi. He motioned for them to follow as he walked through the grazing field. "You can't eat them. They are too contaminated. So they can live a long unfettered life." A cow came up and nudged him gently with her muzzle. Yoshi petted it and it opened its mouth. He leaned over and inhaled deeply. "I love the smell of their breath. It's fermented. Look at her eyes."

"They are so beautiful," said Maryam.

"Dark like yours," said Yoshi. He leaned over and showed them the white spots on her flank. "See this? This is what I was talking about. There is another farmer who stayed nearby for a while; he was the first to see this in his livestock. He drove into the city with one of his cows to prove that radiation disease existed and was threatened with violence. A mob surrounded his truck. And not just the bureaucrats. Even the people wanted to run him out of town—they were afraid the sickness was catching. He ended up putting down all his animals. And then he moved away. I couldn't do that. I think, what can I do but make her comfortable? I put salve on the spots and hope for the best."

"This is a lot of work for one man," said Dan.

"The animals, they are like my friends," said Yoshi. "There is no loneliness worse than a loneliness being surrounded by other people." He paused. "The whole time I was growing up we had butterflies in our fields. I used to catch them in a net. I'd bring them to my mother. She loved them, but she always set them free. Now there are so much fewer butterflies in Tomioka. And the wings, they can be so oddly small . . . That makes me sad."

"You've been here five years," said Dan. "What about your own health?"

Yoshi took out another cigarette and lit up. "The doctors don't know what to do with me. I am so radioactive. There are some volunteers, old friends, a nephew. Every couple of weeks I meet them outside the zone and they bring me groceries that are uncontaminated. I do what I can. Plus, they buy me the shampoo I like." He smiled. "They say I will eventually get cancer." He shrugged. "I asked, 'When?' They say twenty to forty years." He laughed. "I'm almost sixty now. I'll be dead long before that." He inhaled again, and looked at his cigarette. "I promised my daughter, this summer, I'm going to try and quit smoking," said Yoshi.

"I love that plan," said Maryam.

Dan was out of questions after that.

Later that evening, back in Fukushima City and thoroughly exhausted, Dan and Maryam ate dinner at a hole-in-the-wall sushi place behind a bamboo curtain in the shopping and dining mall under the bullet train tracks at Fukushima station.

"It's not the world's most inventive food," said Maryam, when she suggested it. "But it's across the street from the hotel and it's fun. One of those conveyor belt sushi places like you see in Japantown up in the City."

After the strain of the day, the constant effort to communicate, the long ride back, the speechless show-and-grab form of ordering sounded very appealing to Dan.

Fun. That sounded appealing, too.

They'd left Yoshi alone on a farm in a radioactive no-man's zone to tend to his radioactive animals. It wasn't part of Dan's life plan to leave someone so vulnerable in such a hazardous spot, but number one, he was a journalist (you don't intervene or change a story you are reporting, he'd learned that much back in high school) and, two, Japan, outside the zone, was seemingly too difficult for Yoshi to navigate. Perhaps people were also too difficult, too disappointing. Yoshi was opting out, but still working. He was, it seemed to Dan, happier to live away from a world that built nuclear power plants on fault lines, in tsunami zones, and had no real functioning procedures to safeguard its populations, or knew what to do when their own meager plans failed horribly.

Yoshi chose to stay. Still, it felt criminal to leave him there.

"I am a journalist. It is my job to report. It isn't my job to try and save."

Dan had repeated these three lines to himself during the drive home, like a mantra.

Seated at the sushi bar next to an elderly, argumentative couple, Dan felt thankful that he didn't understand Japanese. He also figured he had received several decades of dental X-ray dosages of radiation already that day and one more in the form of eating sushi wasn't going to add to the damage. If it was, he was too tired and overwhelmed to care. Instead, he swore that he would never let the dentist take pictures again; it was the most resolve he could dredge up. Invisible, odorless, tasteless.

"Oooh, mackerel, yellowtail, giant oyster!" exclaimed Maryam as the conveyor belt displayed its wares in front of them, the sushi chef behind it, stocking the assembly line with his dishes, grinning and bowing at her zeal.

"That's the size of the tongue of my dress shoes," said Dan when she plunked a giant oyster in front of him and then one in front of herself. "I don't know if I can eat it."

"You can and you will," said Maryam, slurping the meat down, taking several seconds to dissolve it in her mouth. She took a swig of beer. "Wow! That's like eating the ocean."

Only you want to eat the ocean, Dan thought.

"Uni," she said, breathlessly. Four bright orange suns had been placed on the moving platform directly in front of them. Maryam had to dive a little to keep the plates from moving too swiftly away down the carousel. In an instant, she clattered a two-piece plate down on her small bamboo sushi tray and followed with another dish that she set down in front of Dan on his; the bright orange sea urchin embedded on sushi rice surrounded by warm seaweed paper knocking aside his as-yet-uneaten oyster.

"I wouldn't dare fuck this up with soy," said Maryam. "It is perfect as is. Try it, Dan. You'll see God."

Dan loved uni. It was one of his favorites. He picked the piece up with his hand, as all his compatriots at the sushi bar seemed to be doing, and bit in. Saline, sweet, creamy, a strong hint of umami. Indescribable deliciousness.

"I'm seeing him, I'm seeing him," Dan said.

It was as if he had been starving and hadn't known it.

He looked at her. "I'm seeing you," Dan said.

For a moment, she seemed to blush.

"Good, hunh?" Maryam said. "Delectable. There is nothing like sushi in Japan."

She recovered, but she kept her eyes downcast.

"No, yes. I mean, yes, this is delicious. But the whole day, Mar. That man. Those animals."

"I love Yoshi," said Maryam. She snagged a plate of octopus sashimi sailing by her.

"Why? Why do you love him so much?"

"For the same reasons you love me, Dan," she said. "He sees the unnoticed and concealed. What others want obliterated."

Dan thought for a moment. Was that why he loved her? It certainly was part of it. Her activism. But also, he had never met anyone else remotely like her. Mysterious and straight up. She made him do and say things he never thought possible. She was compassionate and full of empathy. She cared, she cared radically about the whole fucked-up crazy planet. The animals broke Yoshi's heart. The laundry broke her heart. Her broken heart restored Dan's heart. She'd put a heart back in his chest. There, it beat wildly.

"I do love you, Maryam," said Dan.

"I know," she said.

"And," he said.

"And," she said.

"Mar," he said.

"I love you, too," said Maryam.

As soon as Dan entered Maryam's room, he realized that it was twice as big as his was. He had a standard single and Maryam had a Hollywood twin—which was Japanese-train-station-hotelese for a suite. There was one queen-size bed and a sleeping sofa by the window. Probably for a small child, but Dan thought it just right for Maryam—a fainting couch for her to swoon on.

"Did your friend upgrade you?" Dan asked.

"I upgraded me," said Maryam, with a crafty smile. "It's all on your credit card."

Dan shook his head. Then he moved in closer, putting one arm around her waist and drawing her in near to him.

They were pretty much eye to eye, as her head was bent, and she seemed suddenly to be bashful or even a little bit frightened.

"Sweetheart, are you scared?" said Dan.

"A bit," said Maryam.

He softened his knees enough so that he could lean back and up under her bowed face to kiss her. Each eyelid, each cheek, the tip of her nose, and then her lips. Top, bottom. Both.

Soon she was kissing him back. Then they were on the bed. They rolled around for a while, getting used to each other.

Maryam tugged at Dan's polo shirt, and he pulled it off from behind his neck. He stroked the front of her pink cashmere sweater, across and between her breasts.

"So soft," said Dan. "Let me feel it against my chest." She moved in closer to him and snuggled.

"Can I take it off?" asked Dan, and she nodded, wordless, Maryam was wordless, and so Dan took off the pretty pink sweater and folded it carefully and laid it beside her on the other side of the bed. She sat up and he pulled off her white T-shirt. She was wearing a lacy white bra and he kissed her lips and reached with one hand behind her back, first to bring her in closer to him and then to unclasp it. (He'd perfected this move in high school, although it had been years since he'd trotted it out.)

"Is this okay?" Dan asked.

Maryam nodded her head yes. He slipped the bra off both of her arms, one at a time. He gently cupped her left breast. It was a beautiful breast. It felt real. He leaned down and kissed her nipple. It got hard. He'd wondered. Now he thought, what does this mean about me, that this all feels so natural and right? He'd never been with a man. He'd thought about it. He'd thought about almost everything. There was almost nothing he hadn't thought about. He'd never been with a man, but Maryam was a woman.

It was so sexy.

"Are my hands too cold?" Dan asked.

Maryam shook her head no. Slowly, one hand cradling her head, one hand behind her waist, he laid her back down on the bed and kissed both breasts. Then he moved down toward her tummy and kissed around her belly button. Then he unbuttoned her jeans, and unzipped them. He hesitated for a moment. He wasn't exactly sure what to expect.

As if she read his mind, she said, "My transformation is complete, Dan, if that is what you're worried about. We can do what we want, we're just going to have to use lube."

"I'm not worried," said Dan. "I'm curious. And I'm just sort of amazed at how I feel and how much I don't care. I don't care. In fact, I find it hot. It's you I want."

Then carefully, one leg and then the other, he tugged her jeans off her long brown legs.

"Would you look at that," said Maryam.

He looked where she was looking and saw his dick pressing hard against his jeans.

"No Viagra for you," she said.

"Hey, I'm not that old," said Dan.

"Take them off, Dan," Maryam said, in a husky whisper.

He obeyed her. Dan stood up, his feet on the carpet, and slipped his jeans down to his ankles. He stepped out of them and then he let his boxers fall to his knees and he stepped out of those, too.

"Wow," said Maryam.

"Wow what?" said Dan, smiling.

"You're my first circumcised penis," said Maryam.

A second, and they both burst out laughing.

Dan dived down on top of her. "Your first and your last," he said.

"From your mouth to the Gates of Heaven," she said.

He pulled back. "From your mouth to God's ears," he said. "My grandma always said that."

Maryam sat up on her elbows. "Well, my mother said it my way to me, and I've scoured the Internet on its origins. Somewhere someone wrote that the saying, which is Arabic in origin, mind you, probably entered the Jewish vernacular in southern Spain, Andalusia, and then it must have just been a verbal hop, skip, and jump to Yiddish. It seems to me it can be used to indicate our deepest wishes, as in 'yours will be my first and last circumcised penis for—we both hope—our love will be everlasting,' or it can be used lightly, with bite, as in 'if only,' or 'Insha'Allah'—"

Dan kissed her. Midsentence. Now he knew the secret to shut her up. He kissed her again and again, and again and again Maryam kissed him back.

.   .   .

Honey, we need to talk.

Her phone pinged, but it was a headache that woke her up. Amy felt as if her skull had been cleaved in two and was now being held together only by the skin of her face and scalp. She'd drunk far too much wine the night before. A whole bottle by herself at dinner with the boys, and then another glass or two when the kids went off to bed and she slunk alone upstairs to her bedroom. She remembered thinking: I need to pour myself some water and take a couple of Advil, but she had been too hammered to get up. This is what husbands are for, she remembered thinking. If Dan were here, he would have brought the rescue remedies to her. Instead, Amy had just lain on her bed, incapable of organized movement, watching the world spin. First, she had set her phone alarm on vibrate for an early-morning run, although apparently this headache beat that buzz to the punch—that or at some time in the night she'd had the sense to change the setting to an hour later. But she had not reckoned on that piercing ping. Her phone said 5:59 as she reached over to shut it off before the onset of dreaded vibrations.

The effort of grabbing the phone was too much and she had to roll onto her back. There were only a few times in her life when she'd awakened this poisoned, but she knew what was next in store for her: finding a way to slide off the bed and crawl to the bathroom, where she'd have to sit on the tub's lip and drink out of the faucet on the sink before finding the strength to stand. Once up, she'd need to take that Advil now and then crawl back across the floor, hoist herself again onto the bed, if that was in the realm of possibility, and lie still, paralyzed, until the ibuprofen and hydration began to do their magic. When that happened, she knew she could make her way downstairs and start the coffee.

All this measured activity would take courage. Flung on her back on her bed, Amy realized she still had her phone in her hand.

She could open her eyes. Maybe the news would scare her into action.

Amy opened her eyes and stared at her phone. She'd forgotten to charge it the night before and it was on low power, what remained of the gray-white bar on the right had turned to danger-danger warning red. Still there was enough juice for it to continue to torture her—the source of that horrendous ping, a text from Dan, who had been missing in action.

Honey, it read, *we need to talk.*

There was also an older text from Donny. From three in the morning. Thank God she'd slept through that one.

i.e. 8:30 sharp

Sharp? She'd like to stick something sharp up his anus.

Roger that, Amy typed with her thumbs. He was the last person in the world she wanted to see. She still hadn't gotten over how cruel he'd been to her with his stupid algorithms. Every time she looked at him at work she felt like she was going to puke.

As for that asshole, Dan, it took all the strength she could muster to write back:

You better believe it motherfucker. I haven't heard from you in three days! Where are you? Did you get the job? Why don't you answer my messages?

Then she dropped the phone off the bed and onto the plush carpeting. She could feel its thud on the roof of her mouth.

Now her heart was beating in her ears. She was so mad she could spit. Talk my ass, Amy thought. She rolled over to the edge of the bed and slid down onto the floor and slowly crawled her way across that same carpet to the bathroom. She sat on the lip of the tub and drank from the tap. Cool water sluiced down her throat and neutralized some of the acid in her stomach. She leaned on the porcelain and pulled herself up. She stared at her own face in the mirror of the medicine cabinet without recognition. Once I was a girl, she thought. (It sounded like the line from a poem.) A nice pretty girl. Where is that girl? Then she opened the cabinet and took out two Advil and swallowed them. The candy coating was sweet on her tongue. What's one more? she thought. She took another.

I am strong, I am invincible. (Amy remembered her mother singing that old Helen Reddy song under her breath as she was vacuuming the house, before Amy's older brother died—oh, my God, my brother died! Amy thought. Eric! My Eric! Why did that asshole Donny bring you back to life?—Mom wasn't so invincible after that. There wasn't much vacuuming done, either.) But right now, Amy was as tough as nails—she told herself this, using that exact cliché, brushing away thoughts of Eric and Donny and The Furrier, all—and she didn't need to go back to bed. She could brave a hot shower.

She took off the T-shirt that she'd slept in and stepped out of her panties and turned the water on in the tub as hot as she, or anyone else alive, could possibly stand. She stepped in as the water rushed out of the bottom nozzle, burning the soles of her feet and splashing her ankles, quickly flipped the little metal lever to shower. The hot, hot water felt so good on her face and neck. She put her hands together in a prayer right under the spray to conduct the heat as fast as she could into the rest of her body. Where the fuck was Dan? What did he want to talk about? Was he ready to file for bankruptcy? Running away from home? Did he not love her anymore? She started to cry, tear water joining shower water, her pores leaking poisons and alcohol and grief; she even peed under the shower's spray. She wanted to empty herself of everything. She picked up a bar of lavender soap and began to scrub. The little boys would need to be fed and dressed and walked to school. She was sure she'd also have to yell at Jack about something. She had a morning meeting to go to. She could kill Dan later in the day. She was "woman." There was important stuff she had to do first.

Downstairs, Amy drank her coffee black at the breakfast bar, with a side of dry sprouted toast, facing the twins huddled over their cereal. Not one to lie to her children, she said: "Shshsh, Mommy is hungover. She drank too much wine last night. Don't ever do what Mommy did, or you'll have a headache and want to throw up, too. Please be good boys and talk in a whisper. Now eat your Puffins and drink your juice."

The Things nodded at her solemnly. They were both so sweet. Their eyes were big and their hair was bigger. Each one had a different nighttime constellation of freckles on his nose, representing either side of the equator, she supposed, their own yin yang. Amy felt a wave of emotion, overcome in the moment with love for them. Thing One was in a blue-striped polo and Thing Two was in a red-striped polo and she hadn't even had to yell at them—the color trick made it easier for the teachers to differentiate on the fly. Even Squidward was behaving, without his morning run, because she'd let him go in the yard. (She'd deal with that mess whenever.) He was a warm sleek bedroll at her feet.

Jack came into the kitchen. "Hey, it's quiet in here," said Jack. "Somebody die?"

"Mom has a hangover," said Theo.

"That again," said Jack, patting Amy sympathetically on the back.

She was the luckiest woman alive. What nice boys she had. If Eric had lived he would have loved them, too. He would have gotten what was so great about them. She wondered if Donny could multiverse her into that slice of heaven.

She pulled Jack in for a little hug and without meaning to smelled the greasy topknot on his head.

"Oh, God, I'm going to vomit," said Amy. "Jack, when did you last wash your hair? You should take some hygiene lessons from Kevin."

"It's all good, Mom," said Jack. "I've got practice third period. I'll swim the stink out."

"Now, that's being a problem solver," said Amy, turning away. "Don't you want something to eat? How about a yogurt or a smoothie?"

Jack opened the fridge and pulled out three of the Things' Slurpee yogurts. "Got Go-Gurts," he said. "Hey, you look nice, Mom, how come?"

Amy looked down at her work pants and sweater set. "I'm not running today. Morning meeting. Going straight to the office after drop-off, but thanks, cutie. It means a lot."

"Sure," said Jack, one yogurt tube already emptied. He left it slack and gooey like a used condom on her cleanish counter. He picked up his backpack and tore a banana off the bunch in the fruit bowl. Then he ripped off another one for good measure. "See you guys." He headed out the door.

"Shower before you get in the pool," said Amy. "You don't want to spread your diseases."

The door closed behind him with a bang.

"Oh, God," said Amy. She rested her head in both hands.

"Poor Mama," said Theo.

"I love you boys," said Amy.

Outside school, Amy gave Theo a little shove toward the playground where the kids congregated before classes started. He'd been a bit clingy; maybe because she wasn't feeling well, or maybe because he missed Dan, or maybe because school for him was a minefield of disasters and he'd learned to be afraid. She would deal with this today. She'd offer to take Naresh out for coffee and talk to him about his kids' school seriously. With Dan out of work, maybe they'd qualify for financial aid. She would broach Lauren on the subject of borrowing money. Call their mortgage broker to see if there was any possibility of squeezing more out of the piggy bank they called their house. Whatever it took, Amy promised herself then and there to get her sweet kid out of his own private circle of misery. Later, but not now.

Instead, she kissed his soft curly head, which unlike his older brother's did not smell of Parmesan cheese because she herself still shampooed it every day; she untangled their fingers (they'd been holding hands) and pushed him into the fray.

"There's Blossom!" she said, loudly. Blossom heard her name and cried out: "Theo, come play!"

At the sound of Blossom's voice, Theo was shot out of a cannon, a red blur, chasing her or running after her, Amy couldn't tell which, but whatever it was, it was good.

Amy had to scan the yard then to find Miles to say good-bye. Miles had no problem separating. He was off in the corner as usual, playing Magic cards with his cronies.

Amy walked over. "Hi, boys," she said, but most of the kids didn't look up. Thomas Hannahan openly sneered.

"Oh, hey, Mom, bye," said Miles.

"Oh, hey, Miles, bye," said Amy. She kissed him on his Jew-fro, too, which he tolerated, the way he tolerated shots at the pediatrician's office. She had a thought, as she was walking away, and called out to him, "Maybe tonight after dinner you'll teach me how to play?"

"Sure, Mom." Miles waved her off. Thomas Hannahan stared at her like she was bat-shit crazy.

Amy hurried across the yard and up and out onto the sidewalk.

But a man in a blue sport coat with gold buttons waved her down. "Theo's Mom!" he called out to her.

"Yes," said Amy, her stomach dropping to her knees. "I'm Amy, Theo's mom."

"Well, I'm Chris Powell, Maximus's father, and something has to be done about your boy."

"Excuse me?" said Amy.

"He's a menace," said Chris.

Amy paused. Then she said, "I thought we cleared all this up several weeks ago, Mr. Powell. I checked in with your wife. Ms. Zhang said the boys are playing much better lately, that there's been improvement, I mean."

"Zhang's out of her mind," said Chris. "And your kid's deranged."

"Deranged?" said Amy. "Theo is not deranged. He is so not deranged."

"He's deranged and he needs to be disciplined. Which you and your husband seem unable or unwilling to do."

Amy took an involuntary step back. It was as if her body instinctively knew to keep away. "Are you kidding?" she said. "Theo is the sweetest child in the world. He doesn't torture other kids for kicks, the way Maximus does."

"Yeah? Well, my son doesn't break other people's property."

"What are you talking about?" asked Amy.

"Max's computer! Theo threw it across the room yesterday and broke it on purpose."

Amy was flabbergasted. "That doesn't sound like Theo, not in the slightest." She took a deep breath. Could Theo have done such a thing? She didn't think so, not even in anger. But still . . . She had a long day ahead of her. She didn't need this right now. She needed to be reasonable.

"Look, let's be reasonable," said Amy. "I have a long day ahead of me and I'm sure you do, too. I'm really sorry about your son's computer. I am. And I'm sorry if I snapped. It's been quite a morning already"—trying for levity, she pulled out her phone—"and it's only eight fifteen." The effort to power up turned the screen to black; the thing died in her hands. She shoved it back in her bag and forced out a smile. Chris Powell didn't smile back. "My husband's out of town," she said, trying to explain, reaching for sympathy. "I don't think Theo is capable of such a thing, but I'll ask him about it and then I'll get back to you and your wife tonight."

"You'll do more than that, you'll replace the computer."

"Sorry?" said Amy.

"It's a two-thousand-dollar fifteen-inch MacBook Pro and he needs it for school."

Amy took a deep breath. This was money they didn't have. "Chris, I can assure you that if Theo is responsible we will replace your computer, but I, as yet, have no reason to think he is. Have you spoken with Ms. Zhang? Did the teachers witness this?"

"I told you Zhang's an idiot. She said they were on a field trip yesterday."

"That's right, they were," Amy said. She remembered now, she'd forgotten to pack lunches and had to make a quick run to the Starbucks on the corner of El Camino to pick up two cottony bagels and two oxidizing fruit plates for the Things to hoover on the bus. Come to think of it, Theo must have survived the trip pretty well because neither he nor Miles nor Blossom's mother nor the school had bothered to report any differently. Maybe matters were indeed improving.

"All I know is Max came home with a broken computer and your son broke it." Chris Powell was turning red now, and sweat was dripping down his temples.

"Look," said Amy, "I'm late for work. Let me talk to Theo and the teachers and my husband and we'll call you later."

"You better call or I'll have my lawyer call," said Chris Powell.

"Your lawyer? They're in second grade," said Amy. "Are you out of your mind?"

"You're out of your mind!" said Chris Powell.

"You're sweating and spitting and screaming at me!" said Amy. "Some of your stupid spit is landing on my face!"

A group of parents had gathered, stopping to look. One nice guy, Bill Harrison, stepped up.

"Chris, cool down. Come on, you're both acting like the kids." He was trying to be funny. But none of this was funny.

"None of this is funny, Bill. This guy, this guy, he's insane. No wonder his kid is such a nasty bully," said Amy.

"Well, your kid's a weirdo. And so are you, lady!" Chris Powell said. He looked like he was going to haul off and hit her.

"Oh, my God, he's going to hit her," said a mother, Thelma Jeffers, who always wore running gear. Guess she doesn't have to work, Amy hiccuped momentarily out of her own darkening reality and thought spitefully, as Thelma ran off toward the school, calling out, "Excuse me, excuse me, we need help out here."

Bill Harrison said, "You both need to settle down. You're creating a spectacle. The children are watching."

Sure enough, as Amy turned around, just in time to see Thelma returning with Ms. Zhang in tow, a whole group of children, little children, including her Theo and Chris Powell's Maximus and Blossom Hernandez, whom she loved like the daughter she did not have, or maybe more like a niece, had gathered to watch her and Chris Powell scream at each other.

Theo's mouth was in an O, like a cartoon character.

Amy tried to pull herself together. "It's okay, kids, it's okay, honey, Chris and I were just having a conversation, and I guess we got a little wild, even grown-ups get wild sometimes, but it's all fine now."

"You lying insane bitch," said Chris Powell.

Poor Theo. At that moment, like a heat-seeking missile, he tore straight ahead, headfirst, for Maximus's father.

Thank God Bill Harrison was able to cut him off, with a firm grasp and an even firmer hug. "It's okay, buddy. It's okay. You don't want to do that. I got you now."

Theo squirmed in his arms, but Bill seemed to know instinctively what to do with him. If Amy put pressure on his body, crushing him against hers, sometimes the sensory stimulation was enough to get Theo to cool off. She wondered if Bill Harrison had a child with similar issues.

Amy should have married Bill Harrison. He seemed like an excellent father. Most likely he was employed. He would have answered her calls.

"Bill's right, Theo. Thank you, Bill. Everything's A-OK, sweetie. Mommy's fine." A few tears leaked out from Amy's eyes as she tried to smile.

Suddenly, there was a loud clapping of hands, one, two, three.

All the kids and parents, too, sprang to attention.

Ms. Zhang had arrived. "Students," she said. "School is starting, please go quietly to your classrooms."

Thelma was panting triumphantly by Ms. Zhang's side. But Zhang did not have a hair out of place. Today she wore tailored black pants and a short turquoise blue jacket.

"Mrs. Messinger, Mr. Powell, come with me."

That's not my fucking last name, Amy thought. I would never

change my name. Not for love or money. I have no respect for women who change their names! She wanted to scream all the venom out.

Instead, she followed Ms. Zhang back into the main school building.

When Amy finally walked into the i.e. office an hour and a half late, Donny was sitting at her desk, twirling around and around in her chair.

"I'm sorry," said Amy. "It couldn't be helped. Dan's away, some trouble at school." She took a breath, asking for understanding. "You know. Theo."

"This is unprofessional," said Donny. "Please don't ever bring your personal problems into work again."

She waited for him to break into his weasely grin, but the corners of his mouth did not change direction.

Are you fucking kidding me? thought Amy. I'm unprofessional? Who did you come to when you got jock itch? The semester you received an A minus? Sometimes you put the wrong Teva on the wrong foot and keep walking anyway and everyone is afraid to tell you except me. Fuck you, Donny. Fuck you, fuck you, fuck you.

All Amy could do in this horrible moment was nod her head, supposedly in agreement. She'd wasted enough words and emotions already this morning on someone who would never ever hear her. There was no point in repeating that useless exercise.

"You wanted to meet, let's meet," said Amy.

Donny got up and led the way into his office. He was in shorts, of course. The long basketball type. A T-shirt and a stupid hoodie. She hated his goddamn bandy hairy legs. In her head, she thought: no one is ever going to fuck you, Donny. You're going to die a virgin. But then she quickly took it back. He was just a kid. Lauren's kid. Amy didn't really believe her bad wishes could travel from her mind out into the universe, but she reeled them back in anyway; she wanted to make sure. Of course, she didn't want Donny to die a virgin. Even if he was acting like a total fucking jerk.

As she followed in Donny's wake, Naresh rolled his forefinger near his temple, signifying that Donny was a looney tunes, that he, Naresh, was on Team Amy. Amy smiled. The first true smile of the day.

"Want coffee?" asked Naresh. "I just made some."

"Yes, thank you," said Amy, gratefully.

"Milk no sugar," said Naresh, as a statement. *He* knew how she took her coffee. Amy's knees went weak with gratitude. Maybe she should marry him. "Donny?" asked Naresh.

"No," said Donny.

They walked into his office, behind the mirror, Donny first, Amy second.

"Close the door," said Donny.

"But Naresh . . ." said Amy.

Donny gave her a savage look.

"What the hell, Donny?" said Amy. "What's going on?"

"Close the door," said Donny.

Amy closed the door. Just when it clicked shut she saw Naresh through the one-way mirror arriving with a mug of her coffee in one hand and his in another. Two-fisted, he couldn't even knock. She opened it again, carefully, so he could take a step back in time and wouldn't scald himself.

"Thanks," she said.

"Stay cool," said Naresh, his voice low and conspiratorial. "Seems like Baby Bear hasn't had his soy mochaccino yet."

She nodded, and closed the door, finally bringing that fragrant milky coffee to her lips. After the morning she'd had, it tasted like a magical elixir. Another sip and she was starting to perk up.

"What's up?" said Amy. She sat down in the chair facing Donny's desk. He'd already sat down in his. His feet, in his Tevas (properly shod, thank goodness) were already up, lounging next to his keyboard. She could see that stupid leather thong that he sometimes wore on his hairy left ankle. Only Donny would wear it some days and not on others. She was a mother. She had children. She knew that once those things were tied on, you were supposed to wear them until they wore out and fell off, or you died—sort of like marriage and commitment.

"We're getting sued and someone wants to buy us," said Donny.

"Hunh?" said Amy. "What? Who's suing us? And why? We really haven't done anything yet."

"Just like you to ask for bad news first," said Donny. "You're like my mother." He withdrew his feet down to the floor in disgust. He seemed to prefer the desk as barrier to footstool.

Amy steeled. She wasn't going to fall for that one. She told herself to let it fly past her like water off a duck's bill, or back, or ass, whatever the saying was. Fucking Donny. Snot-nosed motherfucker.

"Tell me," said Amy.

"HiveFam filed suit in Santa Clara County Court."

HiveFam was an industry incubator. Adnan and Donny attended meetings there, sometimes lectures.

"For what?"

"The misappropriation of trade secrets, breach of contract, intentional interference with contractual relations, breach of the duty of loyalty, and injunctive relief."

"Oh, man," said Amy, shaking her head. She didn't know what most of it meant, but it sounded daunting.

Donny took a deep breath.

She was waiting for him to blame her. She was waiting for it to all be her fault.

"This is great news, Amy," said Donny. "They are taking us seriously. They seriously see us as competition."

He reached across the desk and took a long sip of *her* coffee.

"I'm not following you, Donny. We don't have money; we don't have money to fight back."

"Our will to fight is stronger. Nobody has stronger will than Team i.e."

i.e. was a playground of freaks and geeks. Mollycoddled West Coast pseudo–Ivy Leaguers. Cardinal wussies. Almost all of them were still on the campus meal plan. It wasn't like that when she went to Cal. They'd rolled their own burritos.

"It's a David-and-Goliath thing, they'll look like giants picking on midgets or, even better, little babies. Everyone loves an underdog. That be us. I already spoke to our lawyers. They think we'll prevail in court and they're ready for blood."

Amy relaxed back in her chair, relieved-ish, on the cusp of breathing regularly. "So, they are taking us on pro bono?"

"No way," said Donny. "They still cost eight hundred dollars an hour."

"Donny," said Amy.

"I know, that's also the problem we're going to face with Google."

"Google?"

"*They* want to buy us."

Donny was making her dizzy. He was also bringing back her headache. Amy rested her head in her hands. It weighed so much! They should subtract its weight when weighing you at the doctor's.

Looking down at the floor, she said, "Why? Why would anyone want to buy us? We haven't done anything yet."

"*You* haven't done anything yet. I created Furrier.com and Summer Fur. I sort of leaked the news to a hungry Googler I know who recently bailed out at Facebook."

"Furrier.com is a goddamn nightmare," said Amy. "It was like being on acid without knowing it."

"Language, Amy," said Donny. He began to spin around in his chair, 180s. "I've tweaked it," he said. "Or I'm going to. By the end of the day today or tomorrow, The Furrier and Summer Fur both will be in a whole other multiverse."

He did a 360.

Whee, thought Amy. She thought it loudly and her cerebellum began to burn. Why was he allowed to curse and she wasn't? Amy was so tired. She reached one hand out in front of her and took a sip of her now-cold Donny-cootie-infected coffee. It felt good slipping down her dry, dry throat.

"That's what I need you for. Stay put. Stay here. Don't go anywhere. As soon as I figure it out, you're going to try it on. Immediately. You are Subject X. Plus, you're my inspiration. And you make me feel comfy."

"Comfy? That's my job? Ugh, Donny," said Amy. "*You* make me feel like a prisoner."

"Yes," said Donny. "Effectively, from now on in, you are. And if I go out, you stay and wait, or you're coming, too. Wherever I go, you're coming with me. Except the bathroom."

"Runaway Bunny?" asked Amy. "What, I'm supposed to chase after you?"

"That's right," said Donny. He did another full 360 and back again. When he turned once more to face Amy head-on it was clear from his expression that he was now completely and officially unreachable.

She got up and left his office.

. . .

They spent the night together in one of the Dallas Museum Tower's model apartments, in a king-size bed with Frette linens, very modern, pale lilac sheets, a soft gray duvet and a mile of silver and purple pillows. Cindy had ordered them herself. She'd seen them in a magazine and it was a look she liked.

The boys were spoiled and the second marriage was bad. Poor Phillip. He had wanted her since high school. High school! Which was a long time ago now—twenty-four years and counting. For some reason this night, unlike all the other nights of all the other years, Cindy had been powerless to say no to him. How could she say no to someone who'd loved her practically her entire life? Especially when she felt so relentlessly unlovable, her latest "relationship" (euphemism) like all the others, having just fizzled out?

Cindy and Phillip had been friends since the ninth grade. There was history there. He remembered her at her finest hour, when her strawberry-blond hair hung down her back to her waist, when she'd made all A's, when she'd scored a full ride to Rice, even though her daddy had died junior year of a surprise heart attack and her mother was aching to move back home to Durham. Cindy was a cheerleader. Student body VP. Homecoming queen. Nothing nor nobody was going to stop her from realizing her dreams. Her daddy would have wanted it that way, and when she thought about him hard enough she could feel his presence, reassuring, like an arm around her shoulders. Back then, Cindy could have had anyone. Back then, she had not picked Phillip.

When she initially returned to Dallas, marriage kaput, with Lily, her reluctant teenage daughter, in tow—at first to live with her ex-mother-in-law Rose, because, guess what, busted broke with nowhere to go, Rose, guilt-ridden over the human dung pile she'd given birth to, was the only port in the storm—Cindy had pretty much started dating right away. Her marriage had been so over for so long, her husband totally and resolutely gone, like, vanished! and with him the marital assets, plus money they didn't have and somehow *she* owed; she'd been ready to move on.

A bunch of Cindy's old girlfriends, as an act of sisterhood, a few divorced, too, a few wishing that they were and beginning to plan their own next moves, had gathered what they could of the old gang together at Five Sixty, the Wolfgang Puck place in the Reunion Tower, to middle-age-man-shop. Lois Benedictus thought it might be fun. "A Reunion at Reunion Tower," she wrote, and since this was on a group chat, and she'd used the dancing girl emoji a whole bunch of times, plus *that* glass of red wine 🍷—she'd always been a sweetie, Lois—no one could raise their rejuvenated eyebrows and poison the fun. (That was a thing in the Big D, eyebrow grooming. Regrowth serum and semipermanent shading and microblading. In the Bay Area, it had been pretty much au naturel for the moms at school or an elegant tweeze and trim for those raised to look their best, like Cindy.) That inaugural night out had been one for the record books. Cindy remembered ending up at 3:00 a.m. at the Lizard Lounge, dancing barefoot in a puddle of beer because Ted "Hand Job" Handy thought it would be fun to go back in time to a place they'd enjoyed when they were all still young and fancy free (and he was still getting hand jobs from the rally girls under the bleachers!!!); she'd never located her silver sandals that night and had to drive home with sticky feet.

Three more marriages had broken up since then, and two of the girls had hooked up with two of the boys from high school. One couple, who had also been a couple back in the day, was now even planning *their* wedding—Melissa had asked Cindy to be an attendant, because it was Cindy's move home that had brought her and Kurt back together (and blown up two families, Cindy thought, but did not dare say out loud). The group, with various additions and subtractions, had been meeting about once a season, ever since, for the last two years. Friday nights. Happy hour. Reunion Tower. "Same bat time, same bat planet." (Lois was still the chief communicator and she sent out cute reminder emails each Monday before, although as Cindy gently kidded her, not everyone had watched old *Batman* reruns as a kid.)

Last night Cindy got off the elevator at 6:25 in her new Camilyn Beth cocktail dress, the *Fiona,* lime green, body hugging, and sleeveless with a "luxurious ruffle at the hem." It had set her back $290, but the green was great for her eyes and the shape was great for her butt, and the ruffle made it fine for work with the block heels she'd bought on sale at Nordstrom at North Park Center for a date with the guy who'd just blown her off by text.

this isn't working, he wrote.

you're not working, she wrote back.

He was an unemployed jazz musician, UNT grad ten years her junior who delighted in calling her "cougar-bae," and had been sponging off her the last two months.

When the elevator door opened, Phillip was standing in the landing as if he'd been waiting in that exact spot for her to arrive all these years. Like he was born for this moment. The room had floor-to-ceiling windows and a revolving bar, and even though she was a regular now, the first thing Cindy said was, "Oh." The panorama never failed to startle. Also, she was still a little afraid of heights, and took a tiny step back, but Phillip, in a blue sport coat with gold buttons and khakis, Italian loafers, clean-shaven, his rust-brown hair going white at the temples and cut short, drew her in by her arm and gave her cheek a kiss and said, "Now, Cin, don't be scared," and after that she just wasn't.

He'd led her to the group, twenty-five in all (the gathering had grown over time as word spread), some from the debate team and some from football, a bunch of the girls had done cheers alongside her, and they had held her up in a pyramid from which she would do a backflip and land in a crosshatching of four other girls' arms. If that didn't bond you for life, what did?

She sat down at a table with her back to the view—the rotation plus elevation got her woozy before the first cosmo was plunked down—and started gabbing right away with Melissa about the wedding reception and what to do with her three kids and Kurt's two when they moved into that big new place in Preston Hollow. Phillip bought her drinks and kept an eye out for her, making sure she got some of the shared appetizers—Cindy favored the pork belly bao buns with house pickle and sweet beans, and the tamarind ribs with black bean dust off the Izakaya menu, but the ribs were a big hit with the boys as well, so Phillip set aside a whole serving just for her. He kept checking in on her the way she'd always wanted her ex to do, which he'd never done, by the way, even when he was still crazy about her.

Phillip checked in, but he never hovered; he allowed for enough space between them so they both were free to have fun with the crowd. But he'd still flash a look at Cindy from time to time, and it felt a little like the way it seemed when her parents had company over for drinks when she was a kid, how whenever her mother would bring a cigarette to her lips (they both smoked back then), her daddy would be there in a flash with his lighter. It was one of his smoother moves, her mother always said, with a secret smile.

All night long, they were in and out of other conversations,

Cindy and Phillip—Pete Carville had twin girls Lily's age and they were in her homeroom at Ranch View, nice girls, a bit giggly, which Lily liked, and the smart one, Jaynee, was also gearing up for the International Baccalaureate program next year, which Cindy made a point to tell Pete made her extra-especially glad that their daughters were friends; and Suzi Rathbone's bank was talking about transferring her to London.

"Take me with you." Cindy laughed.

Phillip said to Suzi, "No way, they need her in the office." Then he turned to Cindy and said: "You know Bobby thinks the world of you."

Bobby was Phillip's friend at the Dallas Police and Fire Pension System who had helped Cindy get her job.

Phillip turned to Cindy and said, "If you go to London, you'll have to eat Marmite."

"What's that?" asked Cindy.

"It's like British peanut butter," said Suzi, bobbing her reddish ponytail. "But it's real salty."

"It's boiled brewer's yeast," said Phillip. "Boiled and fermented. Tastes like old shoes."

Not for the first time did she notice that his whitening sideburns gave him more gravitas than he'd had as a younger man, and that the dermabrasion resurfacing had done a lot to even out his skin. (Melissa told Cindy after Phillip confided in Kurt about the procedure. "He's trying to leave the pain of his teenage years behind," said Melissa.)

"I'm just worried about Brexit," said Suzi.

"I'm worried about Trumpaggedon," said Cindy.

"Then don't go," said Phillip to Suzi, but he was looking at Cindy. They all thought the time Cindy had spent on the Left Coast had made her a little soft and nutty. (She'd voted twice for Obama.

But she wasn't sure she could bring herself to vote for Hillary. She might just sit this one out.) "You all can work for me."

"And just what would I do for you, Phillip?" said Suzi. "I'm a finance modeler."

"Doesn't matter. We can always use a smart, beautiful woman to class up the office. Especially if it keeps you two lovely ladies home here in Dallas."

They laughed and laughed and they talked all night. Phillip even made sure that the table was full of coconut onion rings and duck confit egg rolls so nobody got too drunk. Mostly the girls drank fruity cocktails and the boys drank beers like old times. It was good to be back at home, where the boys were still gentlemen and the girls liked to dress up. Cindy had been out of Rose's house for almost a year now. She and Lily had their own apartment; they rented a condo at Meadowbrook ranch, which was a forty-five-minute commute from the Museum Tower, where she worked, but she'd leased herself a silver Mercedes roadster, so she didn't mind the drive. The complex was near the high school, which was great for her daughter; there was a bus, sure, but it was also easy for Lily to catch a ride from a neighbor's kid, and it even had a little pool. There was also a small fitness center there—sometimes Cindy would get on the bike or lift weights and use the machines, and watch the news or Spanish telenovelas on the one flat screen if she wanted something mindless, but she was saving up for a gym membership; she wanted to take spin classes again—it helped when a teacher yelled things out—and have the use of a steam room. There was something about that little shed crammed with equipment that felt slightly crummy, the damp gym carpet, the mushroomy corners, the husbands who hung out a bit too long as she did her crunches on the worn-down mat; she could see them watching her in the mirror.

Cindy was definitely looking for a step up, but she liked her job.

It was to make the Museum Tower tenants happy, and she liked making people happy; it made her feel good, although the building was even now half-empty. The architect still couldn't figure out how to control the sun's glare reflecting off all those glass windows, and she'd guessed it kept some folks away from buying. Art lovers. The ones the building was designed for. The vacant public areas— lounges and lobbies and lawns, a fire pit—kind of scared her, they reminded her that if things didn't turn around soon she could be downsized. Also, when she thought about the police and firefighter retirees, she felt queasy. If their money was in the building and the apartments didn't sell out, what would happen to all of them? The city?

Suzi had whispered to her once that Dallas itself could go bank-rupt, and Suzi was a banker, so she knew about financial stuff, whereas Cindy was still kind of clueless.

So, Cindy worked extra-hard. Word of mouth and all that. She wanted the tenants to love living there. Cindy organized their wine tastings and book club parties; like a hotel concierge, she procured tickets for their church groups to go to the opera. What she loved best was being in control of the model apartments, rotating the de-signers and curating the looks. A little like playing dollhouse. Here she could dream her dreams three-dimensionally. It was the only time she'd ever had control of any environment. At the Museum Tower, Cindy could make a room look exactly the way she wanted it to look. (The condo where she and Lily lived came with rented furniture, and in California they'd never had money to fix the place up.) Her job was a lot like being a rich man's wife.

Last night, as Cindy glanced around the bar at all her old friends, she didn't care that the guys maybe were a bit tubbier than they used to be just five years ago, the last time she and her ex and Lily had come home together to visit Rose for Christmas, and that the girls had more fine lines and almost all seemed to still color their hair through traditional foil highlights—no balayage. They looked good. The girls were fit and in fighting condition and youthful if not exactly young, and anyway it was nice to be with people who loved you because they'd always loved you, not for what you did or for what you had or if you mountain-biked on the weekends or ran marathons or you invented something and your husband made tons of money. It was nice to be loved for who you were.

Even though this last guy had been a louse, Cindy had dated quite a few guys since she'd come back to Dallas; they just hadn't worked out. But they were sweeter than the hotshots in the Bay Area; none of that Tinder crap had worked out, either. Although not even one of the Texans was as sweet as Phillip. None knew her so long. None had been to both of her weddings.

"How come you didn't invite me to your first wedding?" Cindy asked him pointedly at around eight thirty, when some of the gang went home to their families and there was more room at her table and he'd finally sat down next to her. "I invited you to both of mine." She laughed.

The first time she'd married, her ex was at the end of high school. Her mother got that one annulled real quick. The second time she married him was out in Durham, after college, and Phillip and the gang had traveled all that way to stand by her. It was in a church, with a big white dress, and seven bridesmaids. That was the one that was supposed to stick.

When Phillip finally sat down, she'd been drinking Hitachino Nest Japanese Classic Ale after her first few cosmopolitans had gotten her lit and kept sending her to the ladies' room to pee. But then she'd eaten her ribs and a bunch of the other snacks Phillip had ordered for them, and now she was steadier, just tipsy enough to feel flirty and bold.

"Well, now, Cindy," said Phillip, and he leaned in and looked at her with his warm brown eyes, like the inside of M&M's when they got melty. "I was afraid that if you were there in the audience at the ceremony and the reverend said, 'Anyone present know why these two should not be joined together in holy matrimony,' I wouldn't have been able to hold my peace."

She'd laughed then. She threw back her head and showed off her throat.

"What about the second time around, Philly?" Cindy said. "You and Melinda? How's that working out for you?"

"I won't lie to you," Phillip said, slowly. "The marriage's gone bad, Cin. The boys are spoiled. If I were to tell the truth"—he looked her in the eyes again, those damn brown eyes of his, plain and kind, weirdly gooey—"and I could never *not* tell the truth to you. I knew it was a mistake at the start."

"Oh, Philly," Cindy said, and she patted his hand. She legitimately felt bad for him. "Then why the hell did you go through with it?"

He curled his fingers around hers, before she could withdraw her own hand and hide it in her lap.

"Melinda was pregnant. I wanted kids." He picked up her beer with his other hand. "Do you mind if I have some? Cotton mouth," said Phillip.

"No, sure," said Cindy. "Take it, take it all. I've had enough. Take it, hon."

He took a deep sip out of her glass, which was still frosty. She loved when they served beer in frozen mugs.

"I understand wanting a family," said Cindy. "Nobody wanted a baby girl more than I did. Lily's the reason I stayed so long, you know, in my previous situation."

She picked up the glass now and took a sip herself.

"Love that baby girl," said Cindy.

"You should, a pretty girl like that. She looks just like you."

Lily was pretty. Cindy took pride in her prettiness. She was happy for the comparison. She liked it when people said that Lily resembled her.

"I can understand getting married to have a family," Cindy repeated herself.

"Well, that sure is nice of you," said Phillip. "So maybe you can understand this part, too."

It was a statement, but he said it like a question.

Cindy nodded. She was ready to be understanding. Plus, she was curious.

"The girl I'd loved all those years wasn't ever available," he said, looking into her eyes seriously now. "I'd given up on hope."

That's when she'd texted Lily: *Phillip and I are gonna go grab some dinner*

That next morning, Cindy also gave up on hope. She woke in the model apartment next to Phillip, in the great big king-size bed, with the fancy sheets she'd chosen herself, looking out the floor-to-ceiling window at the entire Dallas Arts District and watched the day break and the lights start to go on in all the surrounding buildings. While the sun rose, streaking the horizon orange and pink, she wondered how long it would take for it to go up high into the sky, high enough to shine its thick beam of white-hot sunlight right onto the very window she was looking out of, and what would make that light bend and boomerang back down onto the Nasher Art Museum across the way and through those special skylights, and begin to burn the fragile and now hurting, maybe even ruined, art inside. It was a million-dollar view.

Phillip was sleeping with his back to her. She could see some hairs on his shoulders, the muddy mix of acne scars and freckles beneath them. She now knew that below the soft lilac duvet, sandwiched between the world's softest sheets, top and bottom, Phillip's skin was white like a baby's right where his trunks should have been. If they'd only gone down to the lobby mezzanine last night, he could have worn some (there was a dresser full of extras in the locker room), and she the high-neck tankini that she kept at the office because she loved to take a refreshing dip once in a while, and they could have camped out by the eighty-foot pool, swum, lounged in the hot tub, and dozed on the chaise longues. Right now, in fact, as the sun rose higher and higher, they could be enjoying the Museum Tower's exceptional amenities like hand-squeezed orange juice and coffee brought by waiter service, instead of being upstairs in bed having done what they'd done. Last night, Cindy learned a lot of things, like below the outline of his trunks, Phillip was as freckled and pocked as he was above the waist, kind of like a Twinkie, what was down there in the middle—which was still snowy and unmarred from the sun—seemed young and pure and innocent. Except it wasn't.

Finally, after all those years of him wanting her, Cindy had slept with him. But instead of waking up full of hope, realizing that they were truly meant to be, and looking forward to confiding in all their mutual friends that she'd had her own private "aha" moment the minute she'd stepped off that elevator at Five Sixty, with Phillip waiting there for her and all, and him saying, "Now, Cin, don't be scared"; instead of daydreaming about how she'd go out for coffee with Melissa as they strategized the melding now of *her* and Phillip's two families; she knew better.

It hadn't exactly been a revenge fuck, but it had been close to it. Cindy had been his mountain to climb, and he'd climbed it, all right. He'd gotten directly on top of her and pushed in and pulled her hair and covered her mouth with his hand when she'd gasped, and then he'd fucked the shit out of her. "I always wanted to fuck the shit out of you," he said. "Now, shut up and let me do it."

She shut up then. And she shut her eyes. In her head, she was hiking out by Tomales Bay, her ex at her side, carrying little baby Lily in the forest-green baby backpack that some of their friends back home had sent as a baby gift. The water was blue and the sky was gray. Later they would stop for oysters at one of the stands and picnic tables that lined the Peninsula. You could shuck them yourself and drink great cheap Chardonnay that you'd picked up at the grocery store. Her ex had the most beautiful eyes. Her daughter had inherited them. He was a fucking rat-bastard prick, but he'd never done anything like Phillip just had.

Cindy looked at Phillip's shoulders, they were moving gently with his breath. He was still sleeping. She carefully swung her legs over the side of the bed, found her dress on the floor, and slipped it over her head. She got down on her knees on the rug and looked for her panties, but she found only her shoes. She held them in her hands as she padded softly around the room, taking her purse off the bedside table—her side—and looking around the floor and where the drapes met it, the chrome and lavender velvet love seat by the window. She couldn't find her underpants. Quiet as a cat, she walked out to the foyer, glad that each apartment had its own elevator access, and rang. The elevator door opened, and she entered it.

It was still early. Most of the penthouses had not sold yet. So, Cindy used the passkey she always kept in her purse and pressed the button to PH, another model apartment that she'd helped design. This one was traditional, and it was stereotypically gorgeous, but traditional wasn't Cindy's thing, which is why she'd picked the modern one for last night. Stepping out of the elevator, she headed straight for the bathroom. She hung her dress off the gold-plated hook she'd picked out. She stepped into the marble shower and unwrapped the fancy decorative soap that no one was ever expected to use. The hot water felt good on her face and neck and she let it run down her hair, even though it would necessitate another blowout. She rubbed the soap rough and hard under her arms and between her legs.

The shower took fifteen minutes. Cindy used the fluffy white towels to wrap up her hair and powder-puff the landing strip of her bush. She opened her purse, pulled out her lipstick, and even though her hands were trembling, she was able to apply it to her lips and cheeks for blush. She took out her comb and combed out her still-wet hair. Slicked back that way, it looked shiny and straight by design, like she'd gelled it on purpose. Then she slipped the dress back on—she was forty-two, and sixteen and a half years ago she'd had a baby, but her boobs were still high enough that she could wear whatever she wanted and did not need a bra. She tidied up the bathroom—except for the soap, no one could possibly notice, so she rewrapped it in its elegant wrapper and put it in her purse. Then she slipped her feet into her pretty new shoes and exited the bathroom.

In the entry foyer, she pressed for the elevator and held her breath, but luck prevailed, the elevator and the concierge's desk were both empty. She walked straight down the hall to her office. There was a wrap she kept on the back of her desk chair; sometimes with the AC cranked it felt like a meat locker in there. It was a pink pashmina, and she draped it around her so that if anyone entered the office and she were sitting behind her desk they wouldn't notice that she was wearing the same dress as the day before. Then she turned on her computer and started answering emails.

Phillip had not written to her. Maybe he was still asleep. Maybe he had already gone home and crawled back into bed with Melinda. Maybe, like she had, Phillip had gone straight to work. With any luck, he had died in a car accident.

Lily had texted several million times. *where r uuuuu?*

Cindy wrote back: *stayed out so late i went straight to work*

She fleetingly thought about calling, but by now Lily was on her way to school, and they weren't allowed to use their phones during the day or they'd get suspended. Besides, what would she say?

Business first, thought Cindy. She loaded up Excel. She had a budget to write.

After a while, Cindy noticed that her hands were still trembling, even as she typed. Lack of sleep, she said to herself. I must be hungry. She picked up her phone and called the Tenants Lounge.

"Joe," she said, "Cindy here. Any goodies left over up there this morning?" There were always more croissants and mini jam jars than customers.

He said, "Sure, Cindy, and we've got some fruit and coffee, too, would you like me to bring you up a tray?"

"Well, aren't you a gentleman," she said.

She made sure she was on the phone to nobody when fifteen minutes later he knocked on her glass door. She waved him in with a big smile, then made a castanet-like chatterbox hand signal so he'd realize she couldn't talk.

Joe was cute and foreign, the other workers called him José, but he'd asked her to call him Joe, so that's what Cindy called him, and would continue to do so until he told her otherwise. He put the tray on her desk with a big smile—he'd made it so pretty! A carefully folded napkin and even a little rose in a little bud vase on the tray, like she was one of the tenants. Cindy gave him a big smile, mouthed "Thank you!" and blew him a kiss. Now, wasn't this nice man one of the people Donald Trump wanted to send away? He was a single dad, two boys, and she was a single mom. Every once in a blue moon they had a real conversation. But today was not one of those days.

After Joe left, Cindy hung up the receiver, sick to death of that dial tone. She could still hear its echo in her ears as she put a couple of sugars in her coffee and a lot of cream. It tasted sweet and comforting that way, and the cup warmed her hands, and then she went back to work.

Around eleven thirty she called Housekeeping. Unless he'd had a heart attack, by now Phillip was definitely out and about.

"I have a high roller on the fence so I let him do a sleepover in model apt two. Yep, the Moderno. Will def need servicing. Thank you."

For a moment, she wondered about her panties, but screw that, he could have ordered in a Russian prostitute, for all anyone cared, she was sure if the walls could talk . . . Housekeeping had seen it all before, anyway.

She decided to drive home, grab lunch, and change.

She left her office with the wrap still on, waved to the concierge, who was tending to Mrs. Allen, one of the biggest pain-in-the-ass tenants, and mouthed to him "bye-bye," then took the stairs down to the parking garage. There was no one around and the staircase was un-air-conditioned, like the garage, and the wrap was making her sweat, so she unwound it and carried it over her arm.

Then she walked over to her designated spot and got into her car. Everything was easier after that, even the little wave she waved at the parking attendant she hadn't noticed leaning on a pillar as she passed him on her way out. There were a million and one reasons why she could still be in the same dress as yesterday, she thought. Probably he hadn't even noticed anyway. She tried to remember if she'd seen him the day before but came up empty. She knew this kid, he was a nice kid, he went to college at night. He was too polite and southern to ask her later, anyway. He'd been brought up right.

Lily was sitting outside the condo on the front cement stairs near the grass and trees that landscaped each redbrick unit as Cindy walked up from the carport. Lily was in pajama pants and one of her boyfriend's water polo team sweatshirts. She had her cat on her lap and her phone in her hand.

As Cindy walked closer, she could see that her girl had been crying. A lot. God have mercy on her, but Cindy's first thought was, What now?

"Lily, honey, why aren't you dressed? Why aren't you in school? I hope you haven't been out here all morning."

She stood over her daughter as the tears started running freshly down Lily's cheeks. Cindy sat down next to her. "Honey, baby, talk to me."

Lily looked up at her in anger. "Talk to you? Talk to you? I've been calling and texting you forever!"

"I told you Phillip and I were grabbing dinner."

"Dinner? It's after lunch!"

"It is? I didn't realize it was that late. There was plenty of traffic . . . Now, why the hell aren't you in school?"

"I didn't know what happened to you. You never came home! I was scared to death. I was worried about you."

Cindy leaned over; she moved the silky hair behind Lily's ear. "I emailed you in the morning, baby," and in an instant Lily's arms were around her neck and she was breathing wetly into Cindy's shoulder.

"You're going to get boogers on my new dress," Cindy said. But she said it sweetly, like a good mother. Like one who didn't care about a silly thing like a new $290 dress. She reached into her purse and pulled out a pack of Kleenex.

"Now blow your nose like a good girl," she said.

And Lily did.

"I'm sorry I scared you. But it's not like I haven't stayed out nights before. I'm a single woman, I'm allowed to date."

"He's married, Ma."

"I know that, hon. We just all had so much fun, we stayed up to watch the sun rise. Then since I was still jazzed, I thought I'd go into work and catch up on some stuff and then I took a shower in the spa to wake myself up, but these new shoes pinch, so I came home to change. It never occurred to me I'd find you here waiting. I thought you'd just go on to school."

I have diarrhea of the mouth, Cindy thought.

Lily started weeping again.

"Sweetie, something else is wrong. I can feel it." The girl immediately looked down. Cindy reached out her hand and took Lily firmly by the chin and gently tilted her face back up so that they met eye to eye.

That's when Lily told her about Kevin. How Jack and Kevin had been out all night and Jack had dropped him off at school, but Kevin hadn't gone to school. Jack didn't find out until third period when he showed up at water polo practice. She meant, Jack knew another Paly kid had jumped in front of a train, but he hadn't known that this time the kid was Kevin, until he got to the pool house.

"What?" said Cindy.

"Yes," said Lily, nodding her head. Her eyes pleading: *now do you understand???*

"Kevin," said Cindy. "The Chinese boy?"

"Asian-American, Ma," said Lily. "He was born here." She sounded exasperated. "You know Kevin Choi. He's Jack's best friend."

"Oh, my God," said Cindy. She put her head in her hands. "That poor mother."

Lily started to cry again, and Cindy draped an arm around her shoulder.

"What's with those kids in Palo Alto? It's like it's contagious. I'm so glad we moved away from there."

"Oh, Mama, there's more," said Lily. She said it like a wail.

"Okay," said Cindy.

"I can't," said Lily.

"You can't what?" said Cindy. "What? What more can there be? Lily, honey, I've been up all night."

Lily handed her mother her phone. As soon as she did, Lily picked up her stupid cat and snuggled him close to her mouth, her pale pink lips brushing his white fur. That cat was the most docile creature on God's green earth.

Cindy picked up the phone. "What am I supposed to do with this? You want me to read the text?"

Lily nodded into the fur. If it were any other day or time, Cindy would have made a joke about the white fur looking like a beard, Mrs. LilyRose Claus, but right then it made no sense. No sense at all. She looked down at the phone. There was a text from Kevin.

i couldn't tell him

"'I couldn't tell him,'" Cindy read out loud. "What couldn't he tell who? When did he send this to you?"

Lily spoke into her cat. It was as if she were a cat ventriloquist, the words coming out of the white cat's white-whiskered mouth. "He sent it this morning. I was waiting in your bed for you to come home. I didn't answer it. I wanted you. I didn't know he was going to lie down in front of a train."

"He lay down in front of a train?" Cindy shook her head, still incredulous. "These parents put too much pressure on these kids." Lily's body was shaking like a leaf. "Honey, calm down. You're scaring me. Who's him? Who couldn't he tell?" Cindy was feeling panicky now herself. "Lily? You mean, Jack? Kevin couldn't tell Jack?"

Lily nodded. Tears slipped down her face so fast, the part Cindy could see, the tops of her rosy cheeks, were all wet. No tracks, just a clear, sugary glaze. The cat's fur beneath Lily's cheekbones was also changing hues. From white to dark gray from the waterworks.

"What?" said Cindy. "Lily, this is like pulling teeth. What couldn't he tell him? What?"

"That he was in love with us."

"Us?"

She nodded. "He was in love with us both."

Cindy closed her eyes and shook her head. These kids were idiots. There was no such thing as love and they were too young to know what it was anyway.

"What about you, Lily?"

"I love Jack, Mama. I'm going to marry Jack."

Cindy looked at Lily. Straight in the eyes.

"Did you tell him that?"

"Of course, Mama. I mean I said yes." She smiled shyly. "He sort of asked. Jack knows I'm going to marry him." She looked like she was holding her breath. Waiting for her mother's response. Hoping.

"'He sort of asked,'" Cindy repeated her daughter's phrasing. She remembered when her own ex "sort of asked." And then did ask. And then asked again. But this Jack had a future. He was a nice, cute boy; he was a good student, going to college. Her ex was a bum. Long on charm, short on everything else worth anything. This Jack came from a good family. The parents cared about her daughter, they fed her nights that Cindy was out. Jack lived in College Terrace, Palo Alto, for God's sake. By now his ratty old house was worth at least a couple million dollars. His parents were still married. He clearly was in love with Lily, Cindy had seen it with her own eyes. This boy was a catch. Worth holding on to.

The last thing she wanted was for Lily to end up alone like she was.

"All right," said Cindy.

The alleviation of Lily's fears, even for a split second, was visible on her face.

"Did you tell Kevin, Lily?" Cindy asked.

Dewy tears weighted down Lily's flower petal lashes.

Just the mention of that boy's name, Cindy thought. She's never going to get over this. She doesn't even know enough yet to know she's never going to get over this. "Did you tell Kevin that Jack was the one you love?"

"Yes, Mama. But . . ."

The silence between them was like a pulse of something cold and awful, chilling Cindy's heart and flooding her veins.

It's worse than I thought, Cindy said to herself, lips pressed together and shaking her head. Please God, she doesn't love him back. Please God, it's not her fault the dumb kid killed himself.

For the rest of my daughter's life she's going to have to carry this utter stupidity on her back, the guilt and shame of it, and walk bent over by the burden.

"But?" said Cindy, in her own mother's voice. "But what?"

Lily shrank deeper into the cat. She was disappearing into the cloud of his white coat.

"Kevin and I talked, Mama. We talked a lot. We talked about things I never, I mean he didn't care if I was nice or not. I could be mean and he thought I was funny or just mean, I guess. He didn't judge, and he didn't care if the things I said were smarter . . . You know, Jack thinks I'm sweet, he thinks I'm perfect."

"Well, you practically are," said Cindy. And then it dawned on her. "LilyRose Leighton Kelly, did you sleep with that boy?"

Lily looked up at her mother, away from the cat's darkened fur. Her eyes were so blue. Her face was so wet. For a moment, all Cindy could think of was Lily as a little girl, naked in the bath, her blond hair slicked back, her eyes so blue they hurt to look at. They looked just like that now.

"Lily!"

Lily nodded yes. "I mean sort of. Only on the phone."

"On the phone?"

"I sent him pictures."

Cindy slapped her across the face.

The slap knocked the tears right out of Lily. The slap rocked Cindy to her feet. She stood up. "Pictures?" said Cindy. "Are you insane?" She started to pace on the little cement walkway. "Pictures can't be erased, Lily! Pictures can live forever! Pictures can ruin your future. They can ruin everything.

"Why?" said Cindy. She was talking to Lily but she was looking across the sky at the day moon, round and cratered and low, sitting on the horizon. Her daddy used to call it "the children's moon," because he said little girls were too young to stay up at night to see the real thing, so God gave them this one to gaze on. Her mother still called it the "jejune moon," rocking on the porch swing in that assisted-living facility back in Durham, because that's what her own granny had called it, something to do with its lack of luminosity, its weakness, Cindy supposed. How pale that watery silver satellite seemed, haunting them from the wrong side of Earth.

"Why? Why would you ever do something so unintelligent?" said Cindy.

Lily looked down. "He asked me to."

"He asked you to?"

"Yes," said Lily. "Yes, Mama," and she was that little naked girl in the tub again. Only now her shoulders were shaking, her whole body was shaking, out of control, so Cindy sat down again on the steps next to her.

"Hush now," said Cindy. But Lily's body kept shaking, her knees were jumping like she was in the doctor's office and the nurse was testing her reflexes with that tiny rubber hammer. Her teeth were chattering. It seemed to Cindy Lily's whole body was shuddering and rattling. In between her sobs, Lily appeared to have trouble catching her breath.

Cindy put both her arms around her. She pulled Lily in close. She tried to steady her daughter. "Do you think he showed them to anyone?"

"Kevin isn't like that," said Lily. "Besides, it was Snapchat. He promised me no screenshots."

Cindy knew about boys and their promises. "You trusted him on that?"

Lily stopped crying long enough to roll her eyes. "If he screenshotted it, Snapchat would have notified me."

"What about that phone? Do you think he had it on him when, you know, when the train came?"

"Oh, my God, Mama," said Lily. But when she saw Cindy's face it must have scared her, because she said, "Yes. He'd just texted me, and I know Kevin, he keeps that phone in his right front pocket."

Cindy sighed. She whispered fiercely in her daughter's ear. "You must never tell Jack," said Cindy.

"I won't," said Lily into her mother's chest, where her tears were soaking Cindy's new lime-green silk dress, now. Ruining it. "I won't."

"You must never tell anyone else. Promise me. Your hand on a stack of Bibles, Lily. This is just between us. Let's hope the authorities don't find that phone."

"I won't, I promise, Mama," said Lily.

It was hard for her to form the words, with her teeth going like that wind-up chattering-teeth toy that assholes like Phillip kept on their desks, but Cindy could feel some of the anxiety and tension flow out of her daughter's body and into her own. Cindy would carry this load for her. She could feel the beginnings of her daughter's relief along with the beginnings of her grief. And she could feel Lily's fear and pain enter Cindy's own bloodstream, another tributary poisoning her. That is what mothers were for.

"Now, you told me Jack's daddy is away, right?"

"Yes, Mama, that's why Jack had the car. His mother, well, she drank a whole bottle of wine last night. She's been so worried, Dan hasn't called home, she conked out early. And Jack's been worried about her and about him, too, the dad . . . Do you think he could be having an affair, Mama? Or a nervous breakdown? Or maybe he's just dead somewhere?"

"He's not dead," said Cindy.

"How do you know?" said Lily.

"I just know. Infidelity. I can smell it."

Lily's eyes were so big. She nodded in agreement. "I think so, too, Mama."

"This is *his* fault," said Cindy.

"How?" said Lily.

"If he hadn't gone away, Amy wouldn't have been messing in the liquor cabinet, and Jack wouldn't have been out all night, and Kevin would have gotten some sleep, and today would have been just another day."

"You think it's that easy?" said Lily.

"Sleep is like medicine," said Cindy. "People who get a good night's sleep don't lie down in front of trains first thing in the morning."

Lily slowly nodded.

"Do you hear what I'm saying?" Cindy said.

"Yes," said Lily.

"That much and that much alone you can share with Jack," said Cindy.

"I love you, Mama," said Lily. She wrapped her arms around her mother.

"I love you, too, baby girl," said Cindy. "More than anything in this world. You are my life, baby." Cindy rocked her back and forth, both arms around her now, like Lily had just been born.

"You sent that picture because Kevin asked you to," said Cindy. "But you didn't have to. Right? You don't have to do things just because men ask."

"Yes, Mama," said Lily.

"Next time you say no."

Cindy gave her daughter another squeeze and then she let go. She stood up and pulled her chin in toward her chest to examine the stain on the front of her shift.

"Better rush on down to the mall and get this to the dry cleaners," said Cindy.

She started climbing the cement stairs. Halfway up the first flight, she stopped and turned to look at Lily.

"You know you are more than just your pussy."

"Yes, Mama," said Lily.

. . .

It was a good thing Naresh followed Amy when she exited the building after leaving Donny's office. She'd walked straight out the door, without her handbag or her jacket or her phone, and down the outside staircase. All she could think to do was flee.

She heard him holler from two stories up and half a block away, as she took the turn left on California Avenue.

"Amy," he yelled from the i.e. landing. "Wait up!"

As she stopped walking to do just that, wait up for Naresh, Amy flashed back to her brother Eric. He'd been on her mind ever since Donny had fucked with her head. Like Naresh, Eric always went after her when she ran away in fear or in anger. No one else had ever done so, not even Dan, who often just chose to let her stew. Even though there was seven years between them, Eric liked to say that he and she were "psychic twins." Their other brother was psychotic. The middle child. A violent, sadistic bully. Whenever possible, they skipped over him as best they could. Although Eric was never Michael's target. He was too old and cool for that. Eric was the only one who'd ever seemed to intimidate him.

Eric died when Amy was still in high school. Not like he did in Donny World. He was backpacking alone through Europe, trying to mend a broken heart. That bitch, Elodie, his high school girlfriend, she'd floated in and out of his life for years. Years! College, summer, and then later in San Francisco, when they were young adults trying to create visions for their lives, she'd sleep over one night, then vanish the next, date a friend of his, try to worm her way back inside. She couldn't seem to live with him or without him. She'd crook a finger and beckon, and Eric always ran back to her. Maybe he would have tired of all that mysterious Elodie bullshit if he had lived? Maybe the two of them would have gotten it together finally, married, had kids? There was no way to know. Except, Donny would say, The Furrier. But for some reason that was not what Amy wanted to find out. She'd learned to accept that Eric was gone.

Although now that Amy had been party to Donny's crazy algorithms—like a Universal Studios ride in reverse, like a Universal Studios ride with a full stomach, in reverse, on acid—maybe the reason she accepted Eric's death was that it seemed now that Eric would probably have died anyway, just later in his life while *rock climbing*. He wasn't a rock climber when Amy knew him, but maybe he just hadn't lived long enough to have been introduced to the person who would have turned him on to rock climbing. Maybe that person was a woman, a woman he met in his own multiverse, who would have cured him of the evil Elodie once and for all, birthed his children, and climbed rocks with him on weekends. Donny World had done nothing to make clear to her why the hell Eric had gone rock climbing anyway. If he ever did go. If *that* dreadful multiverse even existed. If it was better or worse than this one.

A part of Amy always blamed Elodie—if she hadn't kept jerking Eric around, he wouldn't have been halfway across the world when he was; and if he wasn't halfway across the world when he was, he wouldn't have been murdered.

Amy had bumped into Elodie at an airport years after Eric's death, years she'd spent fantasizing about just such an encounter, and all the clever and acidic things she'd planned to say to her. The timing had been inopportune, and the cutting remarks Amy had rehearsed again and again in her head scattered away like crystal beads let loose from a necklace Elodie herself might have worn back in the day, haute hippie and expensive, multifaceted; Amy couldn't scramble fast enough to gather and string her sentences back together. She was juggling the twins, and Dan was up ahead, with Jack riding astride a luggage cart, aiming for their gate, when Thing Two ran straight into Elodie's exceedingly tall and handsome husband, a green-eyed black man with dreadlocks snaking down his long, broad back. The guy said, "Whoa, little dude" as Amy's kid plowed right into him, and Elodie turned around at the sound of his voice. For a second they were all locked in a tableau, staring as Thing Two overreacted, classically, by squalling and crying and rolling on the floor. No one owned the term "temper tantrum" like little Theo.

Elodie was even more beautiful now that she was older, Amy had noticed in the moment with a lightning-like fury, Elodie's increased loveliness like a match to Amy's angry live gas jet. The soft, slow curve of Elodie's younger face had melted away over time to reveal pronounced cheekbones and a jaw that was strong and set, and she wore her now-dark blond hair long and fluid in one of those perfect messy ponytails. She was holding the hand of what appeared to be her daughter, a pre-Raphaelite blondie herself, with long, loose curls and golden-brown skin, wearing a spotless white linen trapeze dress—she looked like a little angel. What Amy would have given, especially back then, to have one of *those* in her house of boys.

"Oh, Amy," Elodie had said, and she'd hugged Amy before Amy could step away or even try to calm Thing Two down. "I think about you all the time," Elodie went on, wetly, she was crying now into Amy's ear, while holding on to her for dear life. "I think about Eric every day," she whispered. "I've never gotten over it." Then she pulled away.

"Darrell, honey, this is an old friend, Amy *Reed*."

"Hi, Amy," said Darrell, warmly, and seemingly oblivious to the emphasis his wife put on Amy's last name, or her tears. Or maybe Elodie was the type of grown woman who cried all the time—one could have predicted that—so that hottie-hubby Darrell simply was just used to her, and he stuck out his hand. On his wrist were a series of striking sculptural silver bracelets.

When Amy had googled both husband and wife later that night, she read that they were a design team of very expensive houseware—

sold privately from their website, or exclusively at Barneys. Worse, they lived in Bali, in an open-air house, many of the rooms lacking walls to the outside. The weather there was so balmy, who the hell needed walls, Amy thought. Instead, they had waterproofed screens that their servants could roll down at night to keep out the chill or rain. A piece about the house, the porcelain and silver they designed, happy gorgeous *them,* had appeared in *Vogue,* but when did Amy have time to read *Vogue?* When did she have time to read anything? Butterflies the size of a human hand flew in and out of Elodie and Darrell's living room. (There was a close-up of one on Vogue.com; it had alighted on the hubby's bejeweled wrist, bright blue, yellow, and black, like a tropical neon fish, and the photo itself was shot by Annie Leibovitz.) Elodie and Mr. Elodie had started their own school—he must have come from a pile of money—for *indigenous* children as well as ex-pats' brats.

They were probably on their way back to Bali when Amy ran into them, at San Francisco International, most likely after visiting Elodie's alive and healthy and helpful parents. But all this was a combo of conjecture, envy, and Internet stalking; Elodie's tearful confession and her spouse's quick handshake had been the end of the conversation, because Thing Two had run off just then— screaming—and was instantly lost in a crowd of potential child molesters. Thing One was pulling on her arm to run after him. Most embarrassingly, Dan was bellowing at her from up ahead, "Goddamn it, Amy. We're going to miss the fucking flight." And that was the end of Elodie, who still seemed to carry Eric around in her heart, as Amy ran off to follow her family. Ironically, they were on their way to Disneyland. The Magic Kingdom. Happy Land! To this day she didn't understand what anyone saw in the place. Giant turkey legs and spinning teacups. Kids throwing up. Long lines for the rides, the concession stands, the souvenir stores. Although she'd been grateful for the endless wait for the women's room. It was the most peaceful she had felt in months, Amy blessedly alone in a winding row of strangers, separated from her family finally by gender, her excuse inviolate: she needed to change her tampon.

The rainy night Eric died in Amy's real life, or at least in this multiverse, he was camped out in a train station in Italy, when he rose from his sleeping bag to defend a woman, a stranger, whose boyfriend or husband or pimp was brandishing a knife and swinging her around by the hair and threatening to cut her throat. A bystander (they were told all this via the American embassy sometime later), a Polish man, said to the police in broken Italian that when Eric tried to step in between the couple, the boyfriend stabbed Eric in the leg, apparently severing the femoral artery. The woman and the man ran out of the station hand in hand, laughing, as Eric rapidly bled out.

Hand in hand and laughing.

Was it nervous laughter? Amy wondered. Or the outlaw glee of getting away with something? Was it because Eric somehow knit them back together with the sticky thread of his spilled blood? Whenever these thoughts persisted, initially all the time, and then periodically over the years, when at odd moments like now they once again caught her by the throat—Naresh jogging slowly toward her, stopping to talk to Esmeralda Sanchez, late again, dismounting from her bike—she'd tried to shake them out of her head. Who cared, really? Her brother had died for nothing.

Amy had been in those Italian train stations. If it was raining outside, as the authorities reported, then Eric had bled to death on cold, wet, filthy stone, alone except for this well-meaning Polish gentleman, another hapless Good Samaritan like Eric himself,

who'd foolishly pressed down on the wound with that dirty sleeping bag rather than applying it as a tourniquet, forcing the blood
out faster. Although even a tourniquet probably could not have
saved him, a doctor friend had reassured her father at the time (as
if the surety of his child's death were any kind of comfort) once the
full reports came back from the embassy. It seemed young Eric was
simply destined to die.

After that, when Amy grew up enough to escape her family
home, she kept widening the gap between holidays and visits. Her
parents were useless to her, and it was only prudent to move Michael out of her life as best she could. His anger regarding Eric's
death was volcanic. He blamed all of his failures (and what part of
his life was not a failure? No relationships lasted, he could not hold
a job) not only on the loss, but also on their parents' response to
the loss, which was numbness and prostration. As for their folks,
they'd always been either in denial about Michael or terrorized by
him. They probably should not have had children at all.

The last time Amy had seen her surviving brother was when
the Things were still toddlers and she'd paid for two sitters for
her three kids with money they didn't have and she'd driven seven
and a half hours up to Humboldt, where Michael's photographs
had been part of a group show against violence. In a panic, she'd
thought, All I have left is this one brother.

What a laugh. Michael the activist! The do-gooder. He'd taken
a Christmas card photo of Jack playing Splashball, which was like
water polo Little League, and blown it up for the exhibition. (So
now he's an appropriation artist, Dan had said in a sideways effort
to soothe, before threatening that if she ever exposed the kids to
Michael again, he would divorce her.) Jack was so little back then,
maybe six or seven; in the picture, he was wearing a soft helmet
and he was sitting in the pool on a purple Styrofoam noodle, with

the world's biggest grin on his face. It was a beautiful photo of a beautiful kid. He'd always been a looker. Michael had superimposed an image of a bullet whooshing toward Jack's happy head. That was it, for Amy. No amount of wishful thinking would ever change who he was.

Naresh reminded Amy of Eric. She'd never realized it before. They both had been attuned to her. Tears came to her eyes as Naresh finished scolding Esmeralda for her lateness, and jogged up to meet her. He took one look at Amy's face and said: "That bad?"

Amy nodded, brushing the tears away. Eric, Dan, Chris Powell, Donny? She didn't even know exactly why she was crying. "This day sucks and it isn't even lunchtime."

Naresh looked at his watch. "Why not? Why not call it lunch? Come on, I'll sport."

"Well, if you're sporting," said Amy, aiming for lightness.

"Your choice. Subway or Mediterranean Wraps?"

"Mediterranean Wraps, be still my heart," said Amy. They continued walking toward the storefront.

Amy sat outside on the terrace while Naresh fetched his shawarma platter and her lentil soup from inside. It was a gorgeous day in Palo Alto, where it was reliably gorgeous. She'd lived in this neck of the woods for most of her life now and she was used to it, but she also knew enough to feel grateful. There must be an expression for that, for the pleasure you expect, maybe take for granted, but still appreciate anyway. A quotidian exaltation? A red-tailed hawk ascending over the Stanford Dish. The silvery shadow of the moon on naked skin through an open window. Her children at night safely dreaming in their beds. The day was bright enough for sunglasses—Amy's were back at her desk—but the air was so cool that the wind was a constant caress and the sun felt so, so good. She closed her eyes and let it warm her and flood her bloodstream with vitamin

D and damage her skin and give her wrinkles. She'd earned those wrinkles this morning.

"Here you go," said Naresh.

Amy opened her eyes. Before her was a recyclable brown paper bowl of steaming lentil soup, a brown paper napkin, a brown compressed-paper spoon, and a brown paper bag full of pita chips. Also, although she hadn't asked for it, he'd brought her black tea and *white* rice. No one in Palo Alto ate unadulterated white rice unless it was with their sushi. Naresh was already digging into his shawarma platter. There were two cups of water on the tray where his lunch still sat. He hadn't even bothered to deplane it. He was scooping up the lamb and hummus before his bony butt hit the seat—he must have been starving. Naresh reminded her not just of her brother Eric but also sometimes of Jack. There was a specific pleasure in watching a male adolescent eat, and Naresh still ate that way, endlessly inhaling massive quantities of food with loud and apparent gusto, and he was still super-skinny even though he must by now be in his late thirties. How old would Eric be? He'd missed his whole life really. Work, love, kids. She did not want to do the math.

Amy sipped her soup. It tasted like rocky hot brown crayon water, which over multiple visits she'd kind of grown to like. The lentils still held firm.

Without looking up, Naresh said: "Thing Two? Dan or Donny?"

Amy said: "All of the above."

He nodded. "Eat the rice," he said. "Drink the tea, it's sweet."

She took a spoonful of the plain white rice, basmati, dry as tiny packing Styrofoam peanuts, fit for a dollhouse. She sipped her tea. It *was* sweet. And maybe there was some cardamom in it. What was Mediterranean about it? Still, it tasted good. Then she told Naresh about drop-off. The dreaded Maximus and his evil father. Theo. How she was failing him.

It took a while, constructing and presenting the narrative, adding color, hyperbole, jokes. The dry rice and the sweet tea gave her energy. How had Naresh known she was hungover? It felt good to let her hands fly in the air as she talked, to sip her stone soup now in between breaths, to be allowed to ramble. She was gratifyingly aware that Naresh was listening to her, really listening, as he shoveled away his hummus and his salad, all her pita chips, and then motioned toward the remains of her soup with eyebrows raised, as she had seemingly lost interest, she was so delighted by conversing, expressing herself, getting the chance to speak. She nodded yes, of course, he could have the remains of her soup, he could have anything he wanted if he just kept listening, and she continued, sufficiently warmed up, and let the real news of the day slip; her husband had texted her: *Honey, we need to talk*. Which was a sickening kind of warning, anyone on earth could tell you that much, right? It was a red neon sign. What the fuck did they need to talk about?

Naresh pushed the now empty bowl aside.

"First things first," said Naresh.

"My marriage?" said Amy.

"Before your marriage," said Naresh. "You have to keep your eye on the kid."

He was right, thought Amy, even though when he said it, it felt a little like a punch to the stomach. It felt like a punch to the stomach in a way that somehow felt kind of good. It woke her up. The truth may hurt, but at least it's true.

"You're right," said Amy.

"Escondido's too hard on him," said Naresh. "It's the wrong school, the wrong place. Too much noise, too much distraction, he can't learn there, they are not teaching the way he learns."

He leaned back in his chair. "Durjoy was the same," said Naresh. "Then, after six months at Waldorf, one day at breakfast he said to

Nancy, 'My life is getting better.'" Naresh's eyes filled with tears. "Out of the blue. We didn't even know it was that bad." He wiped his eyes with the back of his hand. "It kills me now that we didn't know."

"So you're saying Waldorf?" said Amy.

"Maybe," said Naresh. "Or maybe somewhere else. You are going to have to look, Amy. You're going to have to open your eyes and ask questions. Maybe you'll have to sue the state, or sell your house, or move."

"That's easy for you to say," said Amy, with a little laugh. "Nancy is a venture capitalist."

Naresh smiled. "And I work for a narcissistic despotic two-year-old. Kim Jong-un junior. It doesn't matter, Amy. You just have to do it. Nance and I are here to help you."

His phone tweeted. The first bar of "The Ride of the Valkyries."

"Donny," said Amy.

Naresh read off his screen: "Where the f is Amy?"

"I'm right here," said Amy. "Why the hell is he texting you?"

"You forgot your phone?" said Naresh.

"I forgot my phone," said Amy. "It's on my desk."

Back at i.e., Donny was in the middle of a protracted paroxysm of neuroses. Apparently, he'd been pacing, Fitbit in hand, trying to make his fifteen thousand steps early and get it out of the way. (Zuckerberg did this sometimes at meetings when he was afraid he would come up short, Donny had previously explained to Amy.) He was also manically chewing Twizzlers, in an attempt to calm himself. The inside of his lips was lipstick red.

"My office," he said when Amy and Naresh walked in the open door.

"Good luck," Naresh said as Amy followed Donny behind the mirrors into the inner sanctum.

"Could you charge my phone?" said Amy, over her shoulder.

"Sure," said Naresh.

"What's up?" Amy closed the office door behind her. "Where's the fire, Donny?"

"I think I cracked it," said Donny. "Sit at my desk. Put on the VR headset." He pointed to a familiar-looking apparatus near his computer.

"What?" said Amy. "Something that pedestrian? So you scrapped the old-fashioned hair dryer concept?"

"Too cumbersome," said Donny. "Please effing sit."

She said, "You know I hate this, right? I hate it, Donny. It's like nostalgia, only a billion times worse. It's like being boiled alive in oil."

She hated it, but she was still curious. It was awful, but there was still something there calling her back. She'd tried to put it out of her mind since the last time, but she'd been thinking about it just the same.

She sat down in his chair.

"This go-around will be better," said Donny. "I promise."

He started to put the headphones on her. But she put up her hand.

"Where's the weed?"

Donny sighed. Clearly, he hadn't wanted to share. But he took an ashtray out of his desk drawer and a joint crumpled out of his shorts' pocket and he lit up. "Not too much, Aim," said Donny, the smoke still in his lungs. "This shit is strong."

Amy took a deep inhale. She put on the VR headset. She let Donny put on her headphones. Then she toked twice before passing him the joint.

.   .   .

He was a motherfucker, but Amy loved him. He slept with other women, but she loved him. She was pregnant and she loved him. Her ankle was broken and she called him from the hospital, come get me and take me home. When he arrived at the ER, he shook hands with the guy who brought her in. It seemed like a touchingly grown-up thing to do.

Thanks, man, said Amy's boyfriend.

Dan, said the bicyclist.

Thanks, Dan-man, said her boyfriend, and he hunkered down to look at her broken foot in its cast, and then he hugged both her knees.

Baby, what did you do to yourself? he said. He seemed really upset and concerned.

Actually, I ran her over, said the man named Dan.

Her boyfriend looked up. He was the best-looking guy in the world. Those dark gray eyes. No one else had eyes that were that color, a shade lighter than black. Plus, no one was sweeter than he was when he wanted to be.

It was my fault, said Amy. I ran into him.

Why? said the boyfriend.

Destiny, said Dan.

Destiny, said the boyfriend.

She's pregnant, said Dan. She's afraid to tell you. She says you cheat on her all the time. You're a serial cheater and you come home smelling of other women's vaginas.

What the fuck? said the boyfriend. Who is this guy?

We spent a lot of time together waiting at the first aid station in the park for an ambulance to come, said Dan. It took forever. She told me a lot of things.

You're pregnant? said the boyfriend. Wow, that's amazing! We're going to have a baby? You and me?

He was back kneeling again, on the filthy Formica waiting room floor at Bellevue, only this time he was kissing Amy's knees, both of them, including above the cast on the left side.

We'll have a little blond girl, he said.

But neither of us have blond hair, said Amy, crying now.

I told you, you should tell him, said Dan.

Of course, you should tell me, the boyfriend said. This is exactly what we needed. A reason, a reason to make it official. A reason for me to man up.

To grow up, said Dan. It's not about being a man.

Get lost, said the boyfriend. Amy, tell this guy to get lost.

Get lost, Dan, said Amy sweetly. But thank you so much! Thank you so much for helping me!! She was crying again.

Okay, said Dan. Here's my card. If you ever need a friend, he said, looking meaningfully at the boyfriend. The card said his name and beneath it "writer guy."

What's that supposed to mean? said the boyfriend as Dan walked out of their lives, seemingly forever.

C'mon, he said, handing her the new crutches. I'll spring for a cab, it's time to take you home.

When they got to the building, he helped her up the four flights of stairs. When they got into the apartment he helped hoist her up into the loft bed, lifting the now heavy ankle for her. Then he brought her iced tea with lemon—he made sun tea every day on their kitchen table, the light snaking in from the air shaft through their open window. Alley cats came in sometimes, too, to play with Elle. Then he handed Amy the phone on the long extension cord.

Time to call everyone, he said. Invite them to the wedding. Just our friends, I mean, he said. Fuck the families. Your brother, Michael, man, that dude gives me the creeps.

He shuddered.

Are you kidding? said Amy.

Nope, not kidding, he said.

Where? she said. When?

Just like that they were deciding everything. It was so much fun to plan. City Hall with his roommate from prep school, Hal, playing the best man part, and Lauren, in attendance. Then a big dance party on the roof of their building. He even called City Hall to make the appointments, to get the license, and then for the two of them to get hitched.

He was annoying that way. He said "get hitched" and "howdy," even though he came from Main Line Philly. He was full of pretentions. Smart, sexy, weak, trading on his good looks and charm. There was family money. He wanted to be an actor. Honestly, she didn't see that working out, not because he wasn't talented, he was, but because that road was so hard and he didn't seem made for hard. When she'd pictured a future for them together she pictured him teaching poetry or history or guitar, being an environmental activist, maybe even starting his own theater company, but at the moment, who he was in his soul and who he would grow up to be wasn't yet totally evident. But the baby, their baby, that seemed to give him direction. Definition. A reason to move forward. She knew he'd love that baby. She knew in her heart he would be a good father.

She pretended not to notice how irritating he was.

The next couple of weeks were insane! He had to help her up and down the ladder just to go to the bathroom. Lauren took over the party planning because (a) it was easy, cake and beer, and if they were still hungry they could order pizzas, and (b) her ankle wasn't broken. She could do the legwork. Lauren even picked up a cute little retro white minidress from one of the boutiques on Ninth Street that looked great on Amy and went out to Bay Ridge to get her a veil from Kleinfeld. Lauren was so generous; it was worth suffering through all her disapproval.

I owe you, said Amy.

You do, said Lauren. Someday, and that day may never come, I'll call upon you to do a service for me.

It took Amy half a second to realize she was quoting Don Corleone from The Godfather.

At the time, both girls laughed.

The day they got the license, they went alone to City Hall, Amy on her crutches and him cute in his cutoffs and pink man-tailored shirt and huaraches. They took the Second Avenue bus. It was hot as hell and her foot itched inside her cast. She was lucky she was a girl and she could wear airy Mexican dresses that floated over her head and hung down to above the knee. Even putting on underwear was a chore. Sometimes he helped her pull them on. Sometimes his helping her led to sex, which was pretty fun, even when it was so motherfucking hot out.

After they got the license, they hobbled up to Little Italy and toasted with iced cappuccinos and chocolate-covered cannolis in one of the only old authentic Italian places to survive, the ceiling fans working so hard they sounded like they might spin out of control and take somebody's head off.

He told the waitress, a young girl, younger than Amy, maybe even a teenager, that they were getting married and that they had just gotten their wedding license, and the waitress brought them a piece of cheese-cake on the house. She also slipped him her phone number, which Amy saw, and made him tear up, laughing together on the corner. How am I going to live a lifetime this way? Amy thought, but she pushed the thought out of her mind, when he sprang for a cab home; his grand-mother had sent him a rather big check after he'd called her. He was feeling flush. He was always welcome in the family business, Grandma said. They owned real estate in Denver and in Aspen. Grandma was sweet on him, too. Amy liked this idea. She loved the Rockies. She liked the idea of him having a job.

In the days before the wedding they were so busy and so tired and it was so hot up there in their apartment—the heat from the street rose, and also beat down through the roof from their ceiling—it was hard to sleep. Plus, she still had to work, which was a nightmare. Every morning he'd help her crutch her way to the bus and then go back upstairs to bed. Two days before they were supposed to go before the judge, in the middle of the night, she needed to pee. In her efforts to be a good wife in advance, and because he was sleeping so angelically—he looked like a Caravaggio when he was sleeping, that odd mixture of cherubic and alluring—she tried to get down the ladder by herself, but slipped. Amy swung out from the rungs and then swung in again, wrenching her arm and bruising herself pretty badly along her right side, before she fell to the floor in a laundry-like clump.

Fuck, said Amy, and she cried into her own arms. She had not wanted to wake him up. She spent the rest of the night on the futon couch below the bed and wondered why she had not thought of this before. How stupid could she be? Why couldn't she see the nose on her own face? From then on in, that is where she would sleep until the cast came off, or they moved out to Colorado, fingers crossed.

On the day of the wedding, Lauren came over to help her dress. She wore a brand-new white satin lingerie set, tap pants, and bra under her mini, which thankfully covered the bruise down her side—it spanned from her ribs to her hip—and Lauren helped her get the undershorts over the cast. She helped Amy slip the dress over her head and piled her long, dark hair loosely on top of her head with lily of the valley flowers cascading down with her curls. Lauren even did her makeup. And she brought with her a matching bouquet of lilies for Amy to carry. They are so beautiful, Amy said, sniffing deeply. If it's a girl, I'm going to name her Lily. Calla Lily.

That's a pretty name, said Lauren.

You're my best friend for life, said Amy.

You're mine, said Lauren.

They air-hugged so they wouldn't mess up Amy's dress.

Amy's boyfriend was wearing a tuxedo jacket he had bought on Broadway at a thrift store called Reminiscence. He looked surprisingly dashing in it, and Amy couldn't help loving him as he helped her down the stairs of their building, and then they all took a bus to City Hall. The passengers were staring because of the veil, until Lauren yelled, They're getting married, and then the passengers burst out in applause. Hal, the roommate from prep school, met them up in the judge's chambers with four plastic champagne flutes and a bottle of Asti Spumante. The four of them were giddy with excitement. Like something new and great was about to happen, which Amy thought was true—something new and great was about to happen! This time for her.

The ceremony was short, the two witnesses kept goofing around and taking pictures, and Amy flash-forwarded for a moment and thought: I bet they sleep together tonight. Everyone was in a good mood.

Then they all went out to that old Ukrainian place, Veselka, for brunch, Amy still in her wedding dress and veil, and the boyfriend in his tuxedo jacket. Kasha and eggs. Sour coffee. Challah French toast. Table syrup, read Hal, when he picked up the squeeze bottle. That means no maple trees were involved or harmed. Lauren smiled big at that, and then Lauren and Hal played footsie under the table. When the check came, they split it. Now we don't have to get you a wedding present, Hal said. Amy wasn't sure if he was serious or not, but she was so happy, it was funny either way.

Back at the apartment, Lauren and Hal took over. They went up to the roof to string lights and to show the keg rental guys where to set up. Some other friends brought dips and chips and finger foods, falafel from the neighborhood, black-and-white cookies from Moishe's, and a big white three-tiered wedding cake from the Puerto Rican bakery on Avenue B. The guys moved the boyfriend's stereo and speakers onto the roof, while he and Amy cuddled on the futon couch and basked in their young married love.

I'm basking in my young married love, Amy thought. She literally thought those words and then she laughed out loud. Soon I will be living in the Rockies. I will have a blond daughter named Calla Lily and we will be a family and get a dog and everything will finally be right.

More of their guests started arriving, including this girl Tessa, whom he had slept with over the summer, and another of his old girlfriends, Isadora, who had gone to Cal with them and one time had broken them up. They'd stop and poke their heads into the apartment to say congrats and grab chairs or pillows before heading up to the roof, but he only had eyes for Amy. He was literally "doting" on her—he didn't leave her side. Maybe marriage, vows, and all that, commitment, would make a difference. Some of the girls, including Isadora, gave Amy a cold, hard look, but she tried to shake it off. I wonder how many of these girls he's slept with? Amy thought. She made an effort to purge the negative brain waves right out of her head: this is my wedding day. The music was blaring so loud, Amy could hear it down the stairs and in the apartment and on the futon. "Uncle John's Band." The Grateful Dead. That had been his and Isadora's song. Had that bitch put it on?

The boyfriend said, It's time we made our Mr. and Mrs. Entrance.

What tune do you want us to play for the first dance slash hobble? Lauren asked. I'll tell the boys.

"They Love Each Other," said the boyfriend, now her husband.

Okay, she said, and she left the apartment and headed up to the roof.

Ready? said her husband, and he extended his hand to Amy to help her stand up. She swung up on one foot.

Ready, she said. Except I need to pee.

So, she hopped on that same foot, holding on to him, until she got to the bathroom. She went into the bathroom and closed the door. She looked in the mirror, and thought, I'm beautiful. I'm beautiful and I'm the bride and I'm married and I'm in love. Her eyes sparkled with hap-piness and her cheeks were pink. Her hair had tumbled down and now it was petal strewn and wavy from the heat.

She hopped over to the toilet and straddled it. She lifted and gathered her dress, and pulled down her tap pants. She sat on the wooden seat and looked down between her knees. Her white satin underwear was dark and meaty with blood.

. . .

"Jesus Christ," said Donny. "What the fuck are you doing in here, Naresh?"

Amy pulled off the goggles. She pulled off her headphones. Her heart was going a mile a minute. Her heart was beating in her throat. Apparently, Naresh had just burst into Donny's office.

"I'm sorry," said Naresh. "I'm so sorry, Amy, but I finally remem-bered to plug in your phone . . ."

Amy stared at him like he was welcoming her to this earth. She felt wet and new and uncomprehending.

"It's been ringing like crazy. Plus, you've got about a million texts. Something's wrong," he said. "Something's wrong."

Amy reached out her hand and Naresh handed the phone to her.

She tapped into voice mail and put it to her ear.

"Oh, my God," said Amy. "It's my son."

"Which one?" said Naresh.

But she was scrolling now. Reading her texts. Her emails.

"Oh, my God," said Amy.

"I'll drive you," said Naresh.

"What?" said Donny. "We're in the middle of something im-portant."

"Give me your hand," said Naresh. "I'll help you stand up."

Amy looked at him. She looked at Donny. She handed Donny the goggles and the headphones. She gave Naresh her hand.

"Let's go," said Naresh. He helped her up and they rushed out of Donny's office.

"You can't leave," said Donny. Then, when he saw Amy's face: "Shut the goddamn door."

So Amy did, just in time to see him put the goggles on.

In Naresh's car, on the way to the high school, Amy's fingers flew across her phone.

I'm on my way, she texted. *Tell him his mom is coming*

She tapped on Dan's icon and it rang and rang and then went to voice mail. She screamed: "Pick up the phone!"

She wrote: *I don't care where the fuck you are or who you're with you better come home Jack is in trouble*

She started to write *Kevin threw himself in front of a train* but then she deleted it. Let him worry about what it was.

She wrote: *thank you, Lily, for reaching out I've got this now we'll all facetime you later. Glad to know you're with your mom.*

She wrote: *Dear Ms. Zhang, thank you for your note. I can't come to school right away, there has been a tragedy at the high school and my older boy needs me. Please find Theo a quiet space in the library to cool down.*

She wrote: *Marilyn, there are no words. Our darling, beautiful Kevin! Please, please let us help you all. The boys are like brothers.* Then she deleted the word *are* and replaced it with *were* and then replaced it again with *are.*

"That poor kid," said Naresh. "Do you have any idea why?"

"No," said Amy. "He's a great kid, Kevin. Brilliant, super-sweet, an athlete, an A-plus student. An A-plus-plus student. The parents are heaven. His mother and I are so close. We always joked that we were coparenting. They have twin little girls a couple of years younger than our twins. The girls can't stand our twins. They're like these perfect little princesses . . ."

Amy took a deep breath. She sighed it out.

"All those water polo bake sales and auctions, the picnics, the car pools, the meets. He grew up in my house and Jack in his. Oh, poor Jack."

"Have they got the breathing under control?" Naresh asked.

He turned onto El Camino.

She looked at her phone.

What are you talking about? You're scaring me.

She pressed redial: straight to voice mail. She screamed: "I know you're there! You're texting me, you stupid asshole! Coward!!!! Pick up the fucking phone!"

She wrote: *Kevin jumped in front of the commuter rail after Jack dropped him off at school He's dead Jack's in the nurse's office He's had trouble breathing. An anxiety attack Naresh is driving me there now Come home!!*

She read: *I am sorry about the tragedy at the high school. The trouble is not with Theo. The trouble is with Miles. He is sitting in my office awaiting pickup. I can explain it when you or your husband get here.*

She wrote: *Miles is in Zhang's office. I don't care where you are. YOU HAVE TO PICK HIM UP!!!!!*

She read: *Amy please come. The pain is unbearable. I feel like my skin is melting. I don't know what to do with the little kids. They don't even know yet. Nellie took them to the playground to get them out of the house. How will we tell them? Wei is at the police station with his brother. My parents are on their way over, but I'm virtually alone here. Please come.*

"Oh, my God, Naresh, Marilyn is alone. She wants me to come. Her husband is at the police station. I don't know what to do. I don't know where to go first. Dan won't even pick up the phone!"

"I'll drop you off at the school. Jack first," said Naresh. "Is there someone else to call about Marilyn? Maybe I can go over there? I think we've met before? At your Fourth of July party? Pretty, right? A little coiffed?"

She read: *it's not that easy. i can't pick up miles.*

She wrote: *i don't care who you're fucking or what drugs you're on but you better pick up miles, I have to pick up jack and poor marilyn is all alone. Grow a pair dan, you mother fucking asshole.*

She read, *I don't want to alarm you Mrs. Messinger, but Jack's getting hypotoxic from all the hyperventilating. His hand has cramped up and he can't open it. We've called the EMTs. We're afraid he'll lose consciousness. Please hurry.*

I'm on my way, wrote Amy.

I'm on my way, wrote Amy.

I'm on my way, wrote Amy as Naresh pulled up in front of the high school. She was out the car door even before he came to a full stop.

She hopped up on the curb and started quickly across the grass, sidestepping groups of children gathered in clusters. Some of them she knew and some of them she didn't, some were hugging and some were crying and some appeared to be talking to teachers. There were police at the school, but Amy didn't stop.

She ran.

PART THREE

A FTER FRENETICALLY WORKING THE TRANSIT search engines from Maryam's hotel room, and some even more frustrating forays on the phone—those damned interactive voice responses— Dan was looking at two straight days of travel. (He'd screamed a series of expletives into the receiver: *You fucking bitch, I want to speak to a fucking person!* Did you ever notice that they're all female operating systems?" Maryam whispered into his shoulder; she'd curled up beside him on the bed, to console him. "All part of a misogynistic global tech collusion.")

Once again, Dan was spending money that he did not have, but finally there was a semblance of a plan as to how to get back to Palo Alto.

It was only a twenty-eight-hour time differential from his original departure date, but his sense of urgency was on overdrive after Amy and the school nurse had put him on speaker in the Paly infirmary out of complete and utter desperation. In between the mellow bass notes of his own (he'd hoped) soothing phrasing—*take it easy, kid, take it easy*—Dan could hear the agonizing contrapuntal sounds of his boy Jack frantically fighting for breath.

Through the chaos of it all, tears were streaming down Dan's face, Maryam, alarmed but not flummoxed, intermittently kissed and stroked his back, and got up to get him tissues and water. He had proven himself totally useless in his efforts to settle Jack down, although his voice, the last vestige of his parental powers, remained preternaturally calm.

EMS arrived on the other end and Dan could pick up the gist of the male technician's own practiced narration ("Hey, buddy, now we're going to get you a little air") as they strapped an oxygen mask on

Jack and shot him full of Ativan, until Dan, absent and ineffectual (was this same phrase later to be engraved upon his tombstone?), was summarily disconnected. That's when he made his plans, threw his clothes into his bag, had a quick fight with Maryam, and went to the Fukushima train station to wait for the next train, whenever it might come.

Now he was instead waiting for the bus, at the very same station, the Yokohama Tohoku overnight bus, the Suite, which would take him directly to Tokyo. The flight was longer from Tokyo, by forty-five minutes and $1,300, but at least he'd be on his way, because he'd already missed the Sunrise Seto/Izumo, Japan's last surviving night train, which anyway required advance reservations.

"I understand you are upset, Dan, but the travel time save is truly negligible. You might as well come back with me and get some sleep. You're going to need your strength for Jack's sake and that poor boy's family." Maryam, in her nightie and bathrobe and slippers, had followed him across the street from the hotel to the train station.

"He couldn't breathe! My son couldn't breathe! And I wasn't there to help him."

"He heard your voice. The EMTs gave him oxygen. They gave him Ativan, hopefully that will give Jack a bit of relief. The doctors at the hospital are trained to talk to him."

"I wish I was with him," Dan said. "He must feel so alone."

"His mother is with him and she'll bring him home. He's safe. He is loved. She is there."

Dan shook his head. "You don't understand," he said. "You don't have children."

Maryam stiffened. It was cool out, she was barely dressed, and she was shivering. From anger or from the cold?

"In another world, I might have liked to have been a mother," said Maryam.

"I'm sorry," said Dan. "That was thoughtless."

"And in this world, like you, I am a former child," said Maryam. "And in this world, like you, I am still a person."

"I know that, Mar," said Dan.

"I really hate that shit, Dan, as if we all have to be identical to understand the texture and taste of what are bedrock human feelings. One might think that you did not believe in the divinely human and universal qualities of compassion, sympathy; the ability to empathize is a gift we are all born with. It has to be beaten out of us, and regularly it is. But it has not been beaten out of me."

Here she took a deep breath. Tears stood in her eyes.

"My heart breaks for your son. And I can see and feel how you long to be with him."

Dan ran his hands through his hair.

"Thank you. I appreciate that. I really do. And I didn't mean you aren't capable of feeling what I feel. Not at all. It's just I'm upset! A boy I know, a boy I love—more importantly, a boy my boy loves—is dead. He took his own life. At seventeen! A seventeen-year-old lies down in front of a fucking commuter train and guess what? He's not the first. He's not the last, either, I bet. There must have been at least ten kids just like him in Palo Alto the past six, seven years.

"We've had all these training sessions and all these specialists and the media has been all over the place, and now not only is it another kid, it's my kid's best friend. Suicide by train! So please, Maryam, try to understand. Ativan isn't going to help Jack with that, it'll just turn him into an addict. And I am in Japan with you, not home with him. Not helping him. Not helping my wife. Not helping Kevin's family."

"You are right," said Mar. "You are here with me. You are here with me *working*. Reporting a story. A story that needs to be told, a story that the world has forgotten. To their peril, Dan. And if you have forgotten, you are on your way home, to your son, to your wife, to that boy's family. You are doing what needs to be done. I understand that. I want you to do that! I just thought you could be more reasonable—if you wait here or in the security of the hotel in my arms? If the bus is slower than the train but you get on it first, what does it matter? It doesn't get you home that much quicker. I wanted you to rest."

She shook her head. She gathered herself.

"But apparently, you are too upset. I erred. This is not the time for reason."

She reached out her hand. She smoothed back his hair.

"I am so sorry, darling," said Maryam. "I know what it is to love someone who is in so much pain they cannot think of you, they can only think of how to stop it. For better or for worse in that final moment, Kevin needed his pain to end. This is what you must impart to Jack. What Kevin did was not about Jack, or Kevin's parents, or anyone else who loved him, it was about Kevin."

Dan looked at her. Kevin had his whole life ahead of him. He could have gotten over this hurdle, this bump. Plenty of kids went through rough patches. They needed help. Kevin needed help. The irony of course was that there were a million people eager to help him. His parents loved him. All the Reed-Messingers loved him. He was popular at school.

Dan and Maryam, they barely knew each other. They were so different from one another. Still they had found each other. A miracle. As he looked at her, angry, baffled, besotted, it began to dawn on him, just a little, what she was referring to.

"Your mother," he said.

"My mother," said Maryam. "She took her own life. For a long time I was very angry at her. Worse, I felt that she didn't love me, I thought if she'd loved me she wouldn't have left me. At times, I thought it was the truth about who I was, who I am, that made her leave. But that is not what it was, Dan. Her life was ceaseless agony; I know that now. It took courage for her to last as long as she did. It took a mother's love and courage to last that long."

Dan looked at Maryam. He thought about the struggle that had taken her to become the woman she was now, and he thought about Amy, and what she might say if the two women were ever to meet. Because for Amy, being a woman, a wife, a mother, in many ways robbed her of her sovereignty, and for Maryam being a woman set her free.

He reached out his arms and he embraced her, and they held each other, giving and receiving comfort, a constant loop of energy, deeper and more satisfying and less complex than any conversation. Fuck the singularity, Dan was grateful for his body. Holding Maryam like this, he did not know where he ended and she began again.

"But look at me now," said Maryam. Stepping back, her hands running up and down her sides, in her nightie, in her robe. Her long black hair tousled and wild from a night of sleep and sex.

"I had to fight hard, I had many years of agony, I lost my mother, I had this serious medical condition, *I was in the wrong body, Dan,* until my treatment, I could think of nothing else, but now I have a glorious life. This, too, can be true for Jack; it can be true for Kevin's family."

"I'm not so sure," said Dan. "I'm not sure attachment works that way."

"Attachment? Your definition, please?" said Maryam.

"Need, entanglement, intimacy, reliance, what stands between us and the abyss, the way an infant requires a parent, the way caring for a child makes one feel whole, the way partners share responsibilities, one taking over when the other one can't. Habit. Habituation. One's view of oneself. Who we are in the world."

"Well, then," said Maryam sadly, "that does not bode well for us. Because I love you, Dan. But I am not attached to you. I can never again afford to be."

The bus pulled up. It had bright pink trim, and when the door opened he could see that the seats were also bright pink and sort of compartmentalized. Some of the passengers had bright pink awnings hanging over their heads, he guessed to block the overhead light so they could sleep. It was as if he were entering a vehicle that would soon take him to a theme park. Very Hello Kitty.

Maryam stepped back, reached down, and handed Dan his bag. She leaned over and lightly kissed him on the lips.

"I'm sorry I have to go," said Dan. "I love you, too. And I'm afraid that I am also attached to you."

"Don't be sorry," said Maryam. "It's not your fault. None of this is your fault, really, except cheating on your wife and lying to her. Besides, it's good to talk. Talking is almost always good. Now have a safe flight, *habib albi*. I will finish reporting and email you the pictures and my notes. You will fashion it into a story and then we will get it in print or throw it up online. I'm thinking atlantic.com? *Longreads*? *Mother Jones*?"

"*Habib albi?*"

"Love of my heart," said Maryam. She gave him a little push then, and Dan stumbled two steps back, and then turned around and climbed up onto the bus.

By the time he took his pink seat, and looked out the window, Maryam had her arms wrapped tightly in front of her and was trotting toward the hotel, away from him. She didn't swivel to wave.

Dan settled back in his seat and took out his phone and began to text his sins to his wife, beginning with his confessions and jump-starting his self-flagellation and contrition from thousands of miles away in the safe confines of a Japanese bus. It was cowardly, he knew, but he was a coward.

The house was quiet when Dan got home. He entered through the back door, took off his shoes and put down his bag, and walked into the kitchen. Squidward was napping in his crate, the door wide open. A creature of habit, thought Dan. He was reminded of his grandfather's story, one told to him by his own father, because Dan's grandfather had died before he was born. As a young man, before he emigrated from Russia, Dan's grandfather had worked at a grain mill. Eight horses were harnessed to the mill and all day long they walked in a circle around and around the mill, turning it, grinding the wheat down to flour. On Sundays, the horses were given the day off along with their owners, and were set free in the surrounding pasture to graze and run. But they just ambled back to the mill and took their spots in their circle and walked around and around untethered. Work was all those poor creatures knew.

Dan walked quietly past him and into the family room. Miles was sitting on the couch reading a book. *His Dark Materials* by Philip Pullman. Dan had never read it.

"Hey, bud," said Dan.

Miles looked up. "Hey, Dad," said Miles.

"Whatcha reading?" said Dan. "Any good?"

"I like the part when the two universes link up," said Miles.

"What are you doing home?" said Dan.

"What are *you* doing home?" said Miles. "We thought you moved out."

"Did your mother say that?" said Dan.

"Nope," said Miles. "It just seemed obvious. Especially on Tuesday when you never picked me up. Ms. Zhang had to drive me here. It was embarrassing. Her car was full of Mentos candy wrappers, but she didn't offer me any."

"I didn't move out," said Dan. "I just went away for a few days."

"You were in Japan."

"Yes. Who told you that? Never mind. Why aren't you in school?"

"I'm suspended," said Miles.

"Zhang drove you home?"

"Yep," said Miles. "Everybody forgot about me."

"What about Theo?"

"He had a playdate with Blossom."

"Where's he now?"

"At school. And then he has another playdate with Blossom. I told you, *I* got suspended. He didn't. I don't want to talk anymore. I want to read."

Dan didn't know what to say. He wanted to know why Miles got suspended but he didn't. He'd never heard Miles say anything like that before, that he wanted to continue reading, and Dan didn't want to mess with it. Books were a better babysitter than video games.

"One more thing, bud, where's your mom?"

"She and Jack are getting ready for the funeral. It's private. I'm too young to go."

"So she's leaving you home alone?"

"Beats me," said Miles. "Now please shut your pie hole, Dad."

"Okay," said Dan. "I'll shut my pie hole."

Then he left the room and went upstairs.

The door to their bedroom was open. Amy came out of the bathroom just as Dan entered; she was putting on her gold watch bangle bracelet. It was a gift he had given her for her birthday about ten years ago and she wore it only on special occasions. She had a black shift dress on, drop-waist, bare shoulders. Amy had beautiful shoulders. Her hair was swept in a French twist. She glanced up from her watch and faced him. She was wearing no makeup, which made her look pale and young and soulful and luminous. Beneath her eyes were purple satin circles, bruised by tears.

"What are you doing here?" she said.

"I live here," said Dan. "This is my home."

"Um, I really don't think so," said Amy.

She walked across the room to her dresser and opened one of her top drawers. She pulled out a brand-new pair of black stockings still in their white cardboard envelope. She sat down on the unmade bed, ripped open the packaging, and rolled one of the legs up into a little black roll, like a nylon bagel. She pointed her foot and slipped it inside, and guided the hose up over her knee and then repeated the same on the other side. She had runner's legs, strong and striated, the calves curvy like the legs of a grand piano, thick thighs. She stood and turned away from him and pulled the remaining tights up under the skirt of her dress and over her panties. She smoothed her outfit out. Her hands were shaking the whole time and she looked like she'd lost five pounds in the handful of days that he'd been gone.

"Where's Jack?" said Dan.

"I think he's still taking his shower."

"I'm going to do the same," said Dan. "What time is the service?"

"It's in a half an hour," said Amy.

"Where?"

"Mem Chu," said Amy.

"Mem Chu?" said Dan. The campus church was enormous. It was as ornate as they came. "Built with a Victorian aversion to blank space." He'd heard that somewhere, but where in the hash in his head had it come from? "A Victorian aversion to blank space." Was it on a tour? The goddamn website? Wikipedia? Dan needed a docent of his own mind. The building's shape was cruciform and full of foliate carvings with detailed mosaics inside. The stained-glass windows were ravishing.

"How did they get Mem Chu?"

"They both went there, Dan, remember?" Amy said, clearly exasperated. "Marilyn works at Stanford Hospital. They were married there. And they have no other church, no affiliation, they're heathens, like us. Her chief of staff arranged for the space."

"Miles said it was a private ceremony," said Dan. He sat on the bed and started to take off his shoes and socks.

"You've spoken to Miles?" said Amy, the timbre of her voice rising higher. "Now you take *his* calls?"

"I saw him downstairs," said Dan.

He was winging it. He had no idea what to do or say to her. He'd texted her about all he could stand to tell her from the bus that night, he had not gone to Boston, he'd gone to Japan with a Knight fellow for a story, he'd been afraid to tell her about it because of the cost, but it was an exciting story, one he couldn't wait to talk to her about. But in the headiness of the endeavor his professional relationship with this Knight fellow had crossed inappropriate boundaries, it was a one-night discrepancy in their long marriage, but because they had always been honest with one another before, he wanted to come clean.

Do you love her? Amy had texted him.

He'd hesitated and wrote back: *I can't say that I don't.*

He was chickenshit, an asshole, Amy wrote back, and once she let him know Jack was safely home from the ER, she'd ghosted him. No matter how many texts or emails he sent in transit, she did not respond. She'd learned this technique, he suspected, from Dan himself. He'd treated her the same awful way most of the last week, the days of his affirmation and her abandonment.

Dan stood up. Now he was back where he'd started. If he closed his eyes he felt like he could transport himself into a world where none of this had happened, not Japan, not Maryam, not Kevin. It could be like any other time spent in his house in his bedroom with his wife. He headed toward the bathroom.

"I'm going to take a quick shower and then we can drive over together."

"Are you kidding?" said Amy, her voice about to break. In a minute, she'd be screaming. She'd have a heavy object in her hands and she'd be bashing his brains in.

Just then Jack walked into their bedroom. He was wearing Dan's blue suit, but the arms were too short for him and his wrists hung out. He was holding Dan's turquoise Armani tie in his hands, a tie Amy had bought for Dan for some awards ceremony back when his work sometimes won one. Jack's hair was freshly washed and looked about two shades lighter, and it was tied back in a neat ponytail. His face was clean-shaven but nicked. There were some angry red scrapes on his throat.

Better buy him an electric razor, Dan thought.

"Dad?" said Jack. He looked at Dan like he couldn't believe his eyes.

That look nearly killed Dan.

"Jack," said Dan. "Honey. I'm so sorry, I'm so sorry, son."

In that minute Jack flew into his arms, just like he used to do when he was a little boy and Dan came home from work, back when Dan had an office to go to.

Jack cried into his father's shoulder. Dan wrapped his arms around him and patted him up and down his back, kissed his wet head, his wet cheeks.

"I'm so sorry I wasn't here to help you. I came home as quickly as I could. I love you so much, Jack. I couldn't love you more than I do."

Jack tried to pull away. "Um, Dad, you smell pretty ripe," Jack said.

Dan laughed and stood back. He wiped the tears from his eyes. "Now, that's the pot calling the kettle black."

"You better take a shower, Dad," said Jack. "I promised Marilyn I'd sit up front with them, next to Josie and Suz."

"Okay," said Dan. "I'll take the fastest shower of my life." Dan started to walk to the bathroom.

"Use soap," said Jack, mimicking his father. Then he turned to Amy. She'd been staring at them the whole time, thoughts clearly forming and re-forming. "Mom, who invented ties anyway? Can you help?"

As always, she turned to help him.

Dan entered the bathroom and closed the door.

As it happened, Donny was coming over to stay with Miles.

Of course, Amy wouldn't leave him home alone—that was Dan's job.

Dan gave Amy a look when Donny came in through the back door, but Amy said, "Donny owes me," and "Miles loves Donny."

"Well, I like Donny," said Miles, calling out from the other room. "I *love* you and Magic cards," he yelled to Amy.

"I effed up big-time with Amy," said Donny. "I want to make it up to her."

"You, too?" said Dan, trying to be funny, but nobody laughed.

"You effed up," said Amy to Donny. "But you also set me free."

"I want to talk to you later about that," said Donny.

"Oh, goody," said Amy, but she nodded.

"Come on," said Jack. "There's only family and, like, us. Coach. The team. The Chois' babysitters. We gotta go."

"I'm sorry Kevin threw himself in front of a train," Miles yelled from the family room.

Jack startled, and then yelled: "Thanks, Thing One."

"Don't call me that," yelled Miles.

"Walk, but don't lose, the dog," Amy said to Donny. His head had already disappeared inside their refrigerator, so Dan wasn't sure if he heard her.

"All right, we're off," said Dan. The shower had done him a world of good and even though he dreaded the next couple of hours, he had a second wind. He was wearing his other suit, which was black and fit him better. He only had two these days. He didn't need a suit for custom publishing. He didn't need a suit to freelance. He couldn't believe Jack's arms were longer than his. He was probably taller now, too. Maybe Jack could take him in a fight. So much had happened in the short time Dan had been away. Jack was bigger; Amy was smaller. His house was no longer his house, according to the woman who used to be his wife. It was as if he'd fallen down a rabbit hole and entered a planet that only looked like the one he'd left behind.

They took the car to visitor's parking and then hustled over to Stanford Memorial Church. The facade was both Romanesque and Byzantine, rococo even; it was certainly over-the-top, but awfully pretty, made of sandstone, with a dusty bloodred roof of terra-cotta tiles. Because of all that clay, the church always looked Spanish or Mexican to Dan, California-mission style, but various Googles and tours had told him different. Out front there were three arched doorways with three bronze doors, now closed, decorated with angels. Dan pulled open the heavy center door and let Jack and Amy enter; Jack suddenly a baby giraffe, all spindly legs and height, little balance.

"Beam me up, Scotty," Jack whispered in Dan's ear. "Dad, I don't know if I can do this."

"You can, honey," Dan said. "Mom and I are here."

Dan put his hand on Jack's shoulder as they stood in the heavily mosaicked entrance hall beneath the organ balcony. He wanted to steady him, to reassure him, even as the action itself felt hollow. Maybe they could find some comfort here, Dan wondered, although he had never found comfort himself in a house of worship. That said, Dan had always loved this church; it was lavish with its gemstone colors and opulent textures, so unlike the awkward midcentury, flimsy synagogues of suburban New Jersey that he had grown up on. All that pine and cement and brick, weird angles. Ahead of them at the nave they could see the chancel, with its three luscious stained-glass windows and an upper porthole of circular white light. It shot down in a single, thick beam the way shafts of light sometimes do in the woods and often in Renaissance paintings. Amy called it the "light of God" when they encountered that bolt of incandescence while hiking, but he'd never heard anyone else refer to it that way. It looked like a stake of illumination cutting through ignorance, Dan supposed; it was a metaphorical architectural device. Bathed in all that radiance was the sanctuary, where truth and goodness were supposed to lie.

It took a moment for Dan's eyes to focus, the daylight he'd just escaped was dazzling and the church itself dark, except for what was streaming through the central glass aperture so brightly. And those windows, which were almost blinding in their kaleidoscopic hues. Up ahead in the first two rows of pews, mourners clumped together, except for those who seemed to want moats around them. Suddenly down the dark aisles there was a streak of pink running. Suz! Barreling straight into Jack's arms.

"Jackie," she cried.

Jack lifted her up and held her tight, her pink skirt billowing out from beneath his embrace.

"Do you like my new dress?" she said.

"You look like cotton candy," said Jack as he carefully set her down.

Suz, like her identical twin, Josie, was petite and pretty, with black bangs and black eyes. She wore her hair in a minky ponytail and she was young enough that her tummy still stuck out, like a baby Degas ballerina.

She grabbed Jack's hand and tugged.

"Come with me," Suz said, so Jack followed her bravely down the church aisle to the belly of grief—those two occupied pews—and all the abject pain that would greet him at the end of it.

"Oh, God," said Amy. She was shaking her head, at Suz, Dan supposed, at Jack, at the agony of the day and the days to follow, the agony that right now seemed without end and would, Dan knew, forever riddle the fabric of their lives. How frightening it all was to her. It scared the shit out of him, too, that was for sure.

Prior to this moment, Dan had never dared to seriously contemplate anything close to this disaster happening to the people he cared for. The city of Palo Alto had been dealing with teenage suicide as a community for years now. But he didn't think it would happen to them.

Dan wondered why most people never weighed the cost of love before they wagered on it. Even when he'd married Amy, he hadn't contemplated her dying. He certainly never allowed himself to think about the possibility with any of his three boys. He hadn't thought about it when he'd taken the leap and gone to Japan with Maryam, and extended his heart to her. Hubris of youth? Idiocy? Denial? The latter two, because no matter how much Dan may have lied to himself, he knew now that he was not immune, and that he was certainly not young any longer.

He turned to Amy. She'd been his best friend for the last twenty-something years. He longed to tell her about his thoughts. He wanted her to help him untangle them.

But Amy looked like she might faint then, so Dan instinctively held out a hand to steady her. She shook her head no. She didn't want his help. Her gesture indicated what he feared, that he was useless to her now. And he no longer had the right, he supposed, to ask her for hers. Amy's compassion and understanding were gifts, like so many others, Dan had squandered out of greed.

"Prepare yourself for immeasurable pain," said Amy, with a hint of moral superiority and bitterness—two tones he'd never heard from her before. She said, "I've been with them all nonstop the last few days."

Dan had heard that bitter and morally superior tone from his own mother when his father left them; and again, and again, out of her mouth, forever after.

As Amy walked away from him down the dark aisle toward the light of the sanctuary he could see her legs and the waistbands of her underwear and of her panty hose through her skirt. No slip. Who would have thought she needed one? It was a trick of the light that lent her black dress transparency. Even though she was unaware of it, that tiny imperfection added further somehow to her degradation, and, in spite of the fact that he was its primary source, he cringed for her.

Amy sidestepped her way across the second pew to kiss Coach and a few of the boys, some Dan recognized by sight and some by name, but all of whom seemed to know his wife and looked sheepishly glad for her hug or her tousling of their hair, the way they would have back in the days of Splashball tournaments. No one ever cheered them on louder than Amy. She'd called it "releasing her vocal urges" and "primal screaming."

After making her way through the pew, she walked down the opposite aisle and then alongside the front row to where Marilyn sat. When Marilyn stood up to greet Amy, a little cry escaped Marilyn's throat—Dan could hear it in the back of the church, more, he felt it in his knees and wrists—and she fell into Amy's arms.

Dan had always liked Marilyn. She was smart and crisp and funny. There were times when she kind of intimidated him—she had such a big, scary job; she laid open people's craniums and then danced scalpels and lasers across their brains—but she was so warm and lively that that feeling always lapsed when the cocktail or picnic or sidelines talk turned away from medicine. She was also frankly lovely to look at and dressed impeccably, even on summer weekends, capris and crisp linen shells and cardigans lightly tied across her slim shoulders, all in bright, cheerful colors. Seeing her now, her hair pulled back in a simple ponytail, in dark blue pants and a dark blue turtleneck, shaking within the encirclement of his wife's hugs and her own suddenly size-too-large clothing, was enough to make Dan want to run away from home again. As he turned on his heel as if to go, one of Wei's brothers entered the church.

"Dan," said the brother. "Sam." He put out his hand to shake. "We met on Fourth of July." He had that same Hong Kong British accent as Wei did.

"Of course," said Dan. "You're Kevin's uncle." He put out his hand, too, and then almost by accident he pulled Sam into a clinch. For which man's sake, Dan wasn't exactly sure.

At the shock of Dan's touch, Sam started to sob, and Dan patted his back until Sam gained control of himself.

"I'm sorry," said Sam. He reached into his suit pocket for a handkerchief. "That kid," Sam said. "What the hell was he thinking? My poor brother and his wife, what are they supposed to do now? I could kill that kid myself."

Sam sucked in his breath. Taken aback by the brutality of his own words, he bowed his head to his chest and pleaded, "God forgive me. I don't even know what I am saying."

"Please," said Dan. "There is nothing to be forgiven for. You're only human. I've had the exact same thoughts, too," even though he hadn't.

Sam nodded and then chucked Dan's elbow before he started walking down the aisle. A few paces back, Dan followed him.

Jack was already seated in the front pew by then, with Suz on his lap and Josie, in a similar pale green ballerina dress, sitting to his right. Next to them were Marilyn's parents, looking ancient, and Marilyn's sister Julie and her husband—Dan forgot his name. Amy was on Marilyn's right side and had her arms around Marilyn, who was sobbing uncontrollably. Wei, on the far side of them, sat by himself, looking off to nothing. He was very handsome, though suddenly weak-chinned, Dan thought, as if the strength in his face had melted in the clerestory light.

"Excuse me," said Sam. "I'm going to go sit beside my brother."

"Sure," said Dan. "Of course."

Sam backed up a couple of pews to an empty one and made his way across to the right aisle and then down again to slide in next to Wei. Dan noticed him put his palm on his brother's thigh for a moment, then Sam leaned back against the wood. Of the two, he had the stronger profile.

The church was full of empty spaces, but no place fit Dan exactly. He decided to pick an aisle seat two rows behind the water polo players.

On both sides of the church, Paly kids started to walk somberly down the aisles. Dan noticed them because the mourners' heads in front of him had begun to turn, so he turned, too, in that automatic way that one might follow the tides of the crowd at a BART station looking down the tracks. The kids were dressed in white tailored shirts and black slacks and skirts, three of them were male, one girl was African American, one of the boys white, and the rest Asian and Southeast Asian. They began to sing as they walked, and Dan noticed that the high school choir teacher, Joseph Ming, standing by the pulpit, was quietly conducting them. Ming was across from the coffin.

God, thought Dan, could Kevin truly be in that coffin? All that dark, polished wood, the flowers, the brass handles glinting in the sun. When would the lid spring open and Kevin triumphantly jump out again? Why wasn't this a joke, a prank, a game? Or was his body so mangled by that train that he'd had to be cremated? The coffin empty but for a tiny bag of ashes . . .

Dan's own father had been reduced to a tiny bag of ashes, ashes that looked more like kitty litter to Dan than cinders, or even gravel, when he'd taken handfuls of the stuff out of the bag and thrown them into the surf at the Jersey Shore after his dad's funeral was over. The Messingers had a pretend coffin then, too. Dan's grandfather's tallith had been draped over the plain, practically empty, pine box. No one wanted a tiny bag of ashes to represent his father during the service, and a funerary urn—Dan's sister Molly's suggestion—had felt too dramatic and oddly comedic at the same time, like something out of that old show *Dark Shadows*. He'd said this to her over the phone, and both the siblings had laughed.

Dan immediately recognized the song the choir was singing. It was one of his favorites; Wei's, too. They'd long ago bonded over Bob Dylan. "Knocking on Heaven's Door." The kids' voices were high and sweet as they slowly made their way up to the chancel. There had been organ music before, but Dan didn't remember the organist stopping, and it took him another hiccup in time to realize the kids were singing a cappella.

When they reached the front of the church, the group of kids on the right climbed those steps to the pulpit and the others climbed the steps on the left. They continued singing with tears streaming down their faces.

When they finished, and all was quiet, the children bowed their heads and Mr. Ming walked stage right and stood next to half of them.

At that point, the Very Reverend Erika Stanton approached the pulpit. How did Dan know her name? Maybe he'd read the program that was suddenly sitting in his hands. Who had passed it on to him? Or had it been lying on the next seat, and somehow migrated up into his lap?

On the cover was a photo of Kevin grinning. He was a handsome kid, and that grin went on for miles. He was wearing a Paly hoodie and his hair looked wet, so the team must have just won something when the photo was shot. Underneath the picture was his full name, Kevin Bingwen Choi, and below that, Dan assumed, his name again in Chinese characters. There was the date of his birth and the date of his death. Then in printed script: *All of life is a dream waking, all of death is a going home.*

Dan opened the paper pamphlet and wondered idly how they

had possibly gotten this whole production choreographed and up and running in just the time he'd been away. That's when he read or reread the afternoon's lineup. Paly Choir, led by Mr. Ming. Followed by the Very Reverend Erika Stanton—what was that "Very" for, anyway? Dan would have to look it up later, his phone now holstered, silenced to vibrate, but ready to be drawn in an instant in his pants' pocket. Followed by the Paly Choir singing Leonard Cohen's "Hallelujah," not one of Dan's personal favorites, but, he guessed, a conventionally appropriate choice. A eulogy by Wei Choi.

Wow, the guy has balls, more balls than I would have, under the circumstances. Better him than me, Dan thought.

At that moment, he felt so guilty about his flip response, and so relieved that the pageant unveiling before him was all about Wei's boy, not his, that he had the impulse to punch himself in the gut, just to do something to punish himself; and to save himself from divine retribution for his own selfishness.

It's all about me, Dan thought, it should be about them, in case the God-he-did-not-believe-in was peeking into his thoughts at that exact moment, recognizing his self-awareness, and would take pity.

Coach was up next. Then Jack.

Dan felt icy-cold water flood his guts and his bowels tighten. Jack was going to speak after Coach. How could Amy agree to this? In so many ways Jack was still just a little boy. Then Dan read the next name: Suzannah Choi. Suz? In front of all these people? She was truly a baby! Was this good for her? Later, would standing up for her brother that way scar her? Or would it forever be an element of pride? Surely Amy had thought this through with Marilyn. Dan always trusted Amy's judgment when it came to the kids—perhaps she knew better than he did, but the notion of this series of events all unfolding before him made him squirm. The Very Reverend would follow Suz, and deliver the closing remarks.

In fact, the future was now, as the Very Reverend was already talking. She seemed kind, pretty; her face round and freckly; her hair red, wavy, and shoulder length. She wore bangs and a warm countenance. She looked about ten years younger than Dan, and she was talking about how sad this was, how tragic, to lose such a young man, a boy of integrity and spirit. She admitted that she didn't know Kevin, only what she'd learned about him through his beloved family and friends, so she would let them talk, here in the house of God, a God who loved us all equally, a God who had loved Kevin so much more equally that he'd been eager to bring him home.

Dan wasn't sure she'd said any, or all, of this consoling and platitudinous bullshit, it was possible he'd just imagined it; it was possible he'd just conjured up the language from those old four thirty movies he used to watch as a latchkey kid when he got back from school in the afternoons. He couldn't concentrate on the Very Reverend or her words, just the fact that she stood there speaking simply and from the heart about a boy she had not known, but he did, which made him feel disgusted and moved both. This was a boy who'd slept in Dan's home, and brought head lice with him into Dan's home, and infected Jack and the Things to boot—even Amy had to have her hair treated by Lice Enders—costing the Messingers over five hundred dollars for all of them to be deloused. (Marilyn had offered to cover the cost, but it felt too degrading to accept payment from her.) At the time, Amy had joked that the "critter distribution" was proof positive of Dan's absentee fathering (he'd been working around the clock back in those days), as he was the only one in the family left unscathed. The boy that the Very Reverend was now talking about was a boy who had eaten Dan out of house and home almost daily, a boy whom he'd taken for granted like all the other boys he knew, his own included, boys he'd left behind when he ran off to Japan to chase a woman and/or to save himself, a boy who'd found a permanent place in his heart without Dan's truly knowing it until now, while this kind, brilliant imbecile of a woman intoned on.

The membranes between the world and the incessant chatter of Dan's mind had been broken, one rushing tributary of information flooding into the other.

The children sang "Hallelujah." He forgot why he hated that song so much. It was stirring now when they sang it. Maybe it was because Dan associated it with the soundtracks of the movie *Shrek* and the TV series *The West Wing*?

Wei got up to speak. He was well dressed and neat. He told funny stories and people laughed out loud and cried, too. He spoke of his pride in his child, a scholar and an athlete. A good-looking boy, a good boy, the light of his life.

He said, "Several days ago, my beloved son Kevin made a mistake. A tragic mistake, to be sure, but that's all that it was. An impulse. A momentary lapse. He left no note, there were no signs, nothing was wrong. I keep wondering, what propelled him to do what he's done? Was it a desire to feel everything? I have desires like that myself sometimes."

He paused. Dan wondered if Wei, a contained guy, had ever been so publicly exposed before. He'd always seemed like a man who didn't want to feel a lot of things. It felt oddly prurient to hear him talk of his own longing.

"We need to forgive him this mistake," Wei said. "None of us are perfect. I'm not perfect, you're not perfect. We all make mistakes."

It got quiet. He just stood there. For several moments too long.

Marilyn stood, too, and called out gently: "Wei!" She appeared to wake him. He waved her away. Like he was swatting at an insect.

"I'm all right," said Wei.

Still, he didn't move.

Finally, Sam climbed up the stairs and took his brother's arm and walked him off the stage.

Or something like that. Dan couldn't even be sure he was recording what was going on or if he was inventing it, if he was dreaming the day into place or if it was happening in another space and time.

Coach was up next. He spoke about Kevin's love of the game, about his "elegance" in the water. He said, "I've never used that word before about the sport, but Kevin was like a dancer in the pool. Man, I never saw a kid like that. I was sure he was going to get that scholarship to Stanford. Well, he's here now."

He turned to the coffin: "Congratulations, Kev."

Dan felt the urge to stifle a laugh.

As if Coach had heard him, he turned back to the congregation. He looked embarrassed. "But this isn't how I thought he'd get here."

Coach walked away from the altar.

Jack stood. He started to make his way down the wide front pew but then pivoted, remembering to give his mother his phone. Dan assumed he wanted Lily to watch him perform. Dan imagined he could not execute this hideous task without her moral support.

Hideous. He thought the word, solidly and out loud in his mind. *Soul.* He said the word *soul* to himself so that it rang in the hollows of his head like a church bell.

He thought: My God, they have found true love! As thoughts went, this one shouted inside him. True, he thought. Love. He coughed to cover up. He watched as Amy held the phone out ahead of her. Was it "rude" to film a eulogy? Who cared? Was it a "mistake"? When had lying down in front of a train ever been termed a "mistake" before? Words had lost their meaning and taken wing and were flying around and around the church, blind as bats.

At the pulpit Jack said: "Kevin was a lifelong friend."

As if either of them had lived a life yet, Dan thought.

Jack said: "He was my best friend since I was small. My brother from another mother."

Dan looked involuntarily at Marilyn. Her head was resting on Amy's shoulder.

Jack told locker room stories and victory stories. He made everyone laugh about how persnickety and "metrosexual" Kevin was—the bathing suits beneath his jeans, the color-coded notebooks.

"But it all went out the window when he ate. You should have seen that boy inhale a doughnut."

The whole room broke out laughing.

Jack said: "No one loved doughnuts more than Kevin."

He said: "I really wish I had made him stay in the car with me that morning. I wish I had refused to drop him off at school. I don't know why he did what he did. I don't have a clue. If you're wondering—and I would wonder, I know I would wonder—he didn't tell me anything. He seemed fine. He seemed like normal. I guess it's like Wei said, he made a mistake. I don't know. He just didn't seem unhappy.

"We always did everything together. I knew we'd probably go to separate colleges and maybe we'd even compete against each other, but in my head, we were always going to be on the same team. We would still be going through it all together. I'm not sure I know how to get older without Kevin."

Jack abruptly walked away from the altar, and down the stairs, his chin wobbling as he struggled to set his jaw.

Marilyn stood up when he reached the pew and hugged him and whispered something in his ear, and when Jack flinched, she patted his back and he straightened his shoulders. Then Jack sat down next to his own mother. He took the phone from her hand and bowed his head. Dan was sure he was talking to Lily, or at least looking into her big blue eyes.

Wei was up on the pulpit, again, this time holding Suz's hand.

She said, "I have written an acrostic poem for my brother. Kevin. *K* is for the kindness he always showed me. *E* is for the earwax he'd chase me around the house with on his finger. *V* was for the valentine he made me every year. *I* was for, isn't it amazing you were ever here. *N* is for nincompoop, because only a nincompoop dies before graduation."

She turned to the crowd and curtsied. For a moment, no one knew what to do, but someone laughed and someone else applauded.

Wei picked her up then.

"How long does Kevin stay dead, Daddy?"

Wei bowed his head. "I'll explain when we get home." They walked down the steps, Suz in his arms, gently patting his hair.

It was a scene out of a TV movie. The whole room was sobbing. The Very Reverend said some more shit, but who the hell was listening? Not Dan. He refused to hear another generous, empty word. Then Mr. Ming took center stage to conduct the choir's final song. Not a moment too soon, Dan thought. He looked at his program. "American Tune." He wept before the children's voices broke the air. And then the sound they made, it permeated the air like sweet perfume.

Paul Simon. Dan had worshipped him like a god. The service was over. Dan couldn't wait to get the hell out of there.

.   .   .

Back at the house, Miles was enjoying his book, *His Dark Materials,* in the playroom. The story had opened above him like a big umbrella the afternoon Ms. Zhang brought him home from school to an empty house and left him there with nothing to do but prowl the bookshelf, and today already he had been sitting in its shade for hours, his dreams entangling in the unfolding narrative. He had already read up to the middle of the second installment and it was a book meant for grown-ups.

The problem in the book was a lot like the problem that plagued Miles in real life: like Miles, the boy in the book, Will, did not know how to get from one universe to another. Will's problem got solved in the story by a magic knife; in the book, it was called a "subtle knife," and he used it to cut a hole between the different worlds. Once that happened, Will was free! He could travel between them. For a kid like Miles, that would be the equivalent of human heaven, because for a kid like Miles, one world was never enough. He wanted to drink from both glasses, the hot chocolate in one and the lemonade in the other. He wanted to be a bad boy in school and also a perfect child at home. He wanted his father to live in their house again, with all of them; and he wanted to be alone forever with his mom. A knife and a hole made it easy for Will, the character in the book in Miles's lap. It was not so easy for Miles, the flesh-and-blood boy in Palo Alto, with two needy and imperfect overshadowing brothers; Miles, who had to make do with card games and video games and his own imagination, plus *this* book, to get him to where he wanted to go; even if that was only in make-believe. It was Miles's life's goal to turn that kind of made-up travel into something real, something that he could in fact truly do, not just on a screen but in his body. So, reading this book was kind of like a mind-vacation; during the moments his head was buried in its pages it eased his profound need—his abject yearning.

But that hard-fought-for tranquility didn't last nearly long enough because Donny had quickly gotten bored in the kitchen and came in and sat next to Miles, on the couch, pestering him as a means of entertainment, like another brother—the last thing in the world Miles needed. Donny was wearing his board shorts and a Cardinal FEAR THE TREE sweatshirt—Stanford's mascot was a tree; Miles thought that choice was lame and pathetic—and swung his hairy legs over the overstuffed arm. Donny swung his feet in his Tevas near Miles's face. They stank. No one could possibly keep reading with Donny crunching away on Pirate Booty from one hand and slurping one of the last of the Slurpee yogurts in the other, in a cloud of stink, like Pig-Pen, the Charlie Brown character.

"Quit it, Donny," said Miles. "I want to read my book."

"What's it about?" said Donny.

"You must have read it," said Miles.

"I've read them all," said Donny.

"Then why are you asking?" said Miles.

"I don't know," said Donny. "I've got nothing to do."

"I like the parallel worlds," said Miles, exasperated.

"I like the parallel worlds," said Donny.

Miles shook his head. Donny wasn't going to give up and his reading spell was broken now anyway. He put the book down.

"So what do you want to do?" Miles asked Donny.

"Dunno," said Donny. "Any new video games?"

Miles walked over to the PlayStation 4 sitting on the TV cabinet. He rifled through the games that were kept in a basket (and on the shelf and on the floor), then held up one of his favorites; he had gotten it this past year for Christmas. "Know this guy, Donny? Uncharted Four?"

"No," said Donny. "Is it any fun? Should I buy it?"

"I like it," said Miles. "It's landmark," he said, proud of the term; he'd heard it from an older boy, Kevin actually, "and if you like interactive, it's worth the money. A lot of shoot-outs. Great details. Naughty Dog, those guys can't be beat, really."

"Hmm, they produced it, right?" said Donny.

For a supposed genius, Donny was pretty dopey.

"That reminds me," Donny said. "'Naughty dog.'"

Hunh, thought Miles. Are you retarded, Donny? Then, "You mean Squidward?" he asked.

His mom told him to always be polite to those less fortunate, and Donny was simply less fortunate. He was like a kiddie-man. A big baby without his diaper. So, Miles supposed he should be kind to him. But his mom was also always talking about what a retard Donny was, too. So maybe Miles needn't go too far out of his way.

"Yer ma said we should take him for a walk."

"If Mom said," said Miles. "Otherwise, he'll poop in the house and she'll have another seizure."

"Another one?"

"It's been rough around here the last couple of days," said Miles. "Kevin got hit by a train. Dad ran away. You know I got suspended. But nobody seems to care much."

"Feeling overlooked, Thing One?"

"Sure," said Miles. "But I also like it that way."

Donny looked surprised.

"Why?" he said.

"Because I get away with more," said Miles. "And all that attention doesn't seem to be doing either of my brothers any good."

"Ahh, the wise middle child."

"We're twins, Donny."

"But Two is the baby. You know I'm right," said Donny. "Anyway, you came out first, your mom told me. So, come on, let's round up Mollusk-boy, but you have to show me how."

"How?" said Miles. "Are you kidding? You go outside. You walk around the neighborhood. Are you really my mom's boss?"

And then he shouted: "Squidward!"

Poom! The dog came screeching around the corner, nails clacking against the hardwood floor, before his paws slid against the area rug, bunching it up and splaying his legs until he rebounded and leaped over to Miles, jumping up and licking him on the face. The dog's tongue was big and wet, like a palm leaf after it rained on Palm Drive. Also, flattish and gross. It tickled and was sick-making. He almost knocked Miles over with it.

"Down boy, down." Miles giggled, shoving Squidward aside, wiping his face with his forearm, Squidward always bouncing back.

"Hey, you guys have the same color hair," said Donny. "You and the dog. You're both the color of a penny."

"Who cares," said Miles. "Get his leash off the hook in the kitchen. C'mon, Donny, help out."

Donny went into the kitchen and as soon as he picked up the leash, Squidward took off. He had supersonic hearing for that leash. "The old leash trick," Dad called it. Miles knew it would work like a charm.

Outside, there was a question whether to walk to campus past Miles's school, or the other way toward California Avenue. Miles wasn't sure he wanted all the kids to see him suspended or not. There was some status in being suspended, but it was also humiliating. *Humiliating* was a new word for Miles. He'd heard his mom say it, over and over again, the past few days on the phone to her friend, Donny's mother. He liked the sound of it. It kind of rolled in his mouth and melted like pancakes made with lots of butter. It also occurred to him that the other kids might be resentful of him getting to stay home from school.

Actually, that idea he got from Donny, who wanted to walk the dog to Lake Lagunita on campus, and play Frisbee or toss a ball. Donny had never had a dog and had never played Frisbee or tossed a ball to even a borrowed dog before, and he said he was keen on having the experience. "All the kids will see us wild and free and they will wish they were as cool as you. Trust me," said Donny.

Miles shrugged. Whatever.

So, they walked down Stanford Avenue, Squidward straining against the leash, on the other side from Escondido Elementary School. It was no big whoop really (Miles's dad used to say that a lot, "No big whoop," but it had been a while since he'd said it and every-thing seemed like a real big whoop lately, anyway) because recess and lunch were both over, so if anyone saw him they'd be looking out the window in class instead of paying attention and they'd be getting into trouble on their own, making them no better than Miles. Then they turned down Bowdoin and made their way through campus.

Lake Lag was an artificial lake that these days—almost all of Miles's life—was always dry. So really, it was more like a sunken meadow. Except this spring with all the late snow and snowmelt, "all the global warming jazz," Miles's dad said, it had filled with about three feet of water. His dad had taken him and Thing Two on a nature walk there this winter, and they'd seen tiger salamanders breeding in the muck. They weren't allowed to pick them up—tiger salamanders are an endangered species, Dad said, and the univer-sity had spent $100,000 building them tunnels under the highway so they wouldn't all get flattened during migration.

Now Squidward was nosing at the water. Soon he'd be splashing and swimming. There was no stopping him, so Miles didn't try. He was the realist in the family. Why waste your time on something that would never possibly happen? Miles only bet on sure deals, even if they seemed out of this world to grown-ups.

Donny sat down on the grass. He'd chased Squidward to the water's edge—he was afraid of getting fined for the dog being off leash and in "the puddle," which is what he said his dorm-mates called Lake Lag, and now he was tired.

"Fuck it," said Donny.

"Yeah," said Miles. Although he had no idea what Donny was talking about—they let Squidward off the leash all the time. You couldn't keep a dog like Squidward on the leash for very long anyway. It was impractical. He sat down next to Donny.

"So tell me why you like Magic cards," said Donny.

"You like Magic cards," said Miles.

"I do," said Donny. "It seems like you and I have a bunch of things in common. Philip Pullman, parallel worlds. Do you know about multiverse theory?"

Miles rolled his eyes. "Everyone knows about that, Donny. Are you trying to make me look stupid like Jack does?"

"No," said Donny. "Not at all. It wouldn't even occur to me. I'm an only child. But I'm pretty interested in multiverses myself these days."

"You are?" said Miles. "I thought you were reinventing Snapchat or something like that, Mom said."

"That's what she said?" said Donny, looking a little offended. And then willing to brush it off, "Come on, tell me why you like Magic cards."

Miles let out a deep, annoyed breath. "Okay," he said, purposely sounding like he was answering a question in school: "The reason

I like Magic cards is since every player has a deck, and every deck gets reshuffled every bout, two people can play and play and play again. Each time you duel, your cards might line up in a different way, making the options of battle pretty close to infinity, but not beyond, giving you another shot at a positive outcome. That's what I like about Magic cards." Then he couldn't help himself: "Presentation over, Donny."

But Donny didn't seem to care if he irritated Miles or not. "So that's why you were suspended?" asked Donny. "Because you bet on the game and won money?"

Miles nodded. He'd won lots and lots of money. He had $150 in his pocket when Zhang busted him. Mom had heard an earful about that. But no one else knew about the money he had between the box spring and his mattress at home. His mom never changed the sheet between them. He hadn't counted in a while, but he guessed he had about three thousand dollars, considering all the trading he'd done online.

"You make a lot?" asked Donny.

Miles thought for a moment. "You promise not to tell?" he said.

Donny nodded, looking serious. He held out his pinkie. "I pinkie-swear," said Donny, and the two boys shook.

"Well," said Miles, "there is what Dad calls a 'secondary market.' You can buy the cards you exactly want—but Dad won't let me 'purchase my luck' that way. Also, you can trade. Trading being my specialty."

"So you make your money trading cards?" said Donny.

"Yep," said Miles. "I just traded a Death Rite Shaman for a Black Lotus alpha. There are only eleven thousand Black Lotus alphas in print. On eBay, a card like that sold for twenty-seven thousand, three hundred and two dollars last year."

"That kid must have been a moron," said Donny.

"He's a second-grader. Caveat emptor," said Miles, standing. "Do you want to play Frisbee now?"

"I don't know how," said Donny.

"I'll teach you," said Miles.

"Where's the dog?" said Donny, looking around the lake.

"He'll come back," said Miles. "He always does. Come on," he said, and led Donny back to the large field of grass.

Donny had been telling the truth when he told Miles he did not know how to play Frisbee. He would bring the disc in toward his chest the way Miles had shown him, but when he let loose, that fast slingshot from bent elbow to straight arm, it was anyone's guess which way the Frisbee was going. Sometimes it flew horizontally ahead and Miles had a chance at catching it, although Donny usually threw too low. Other times it winged right or left, a few times he'd held on too long and it flew out from Donny's hand and behind him. That's when Miles started running in a circle around Donny. He figured, law of averages, if he was running in a circle he had a better chance of catching those unpredictable free throws than if he was standing still.

This was fun for a while until it wasn't. Miles was a good runner, but eventually he lost his breath. Plus, Donny always just stood in one place, and Miles was the one who had to chase after the thing. If Squidward was around he could have done the chasing for them, but Squidward wasn't. This time when the disc hit the ground it rolled on its side like a wheel for a while before it spun slowly to the ground. Miles stopped running and walked over to it. He sat down on the ground.

"What up?" said Donny. "I thought we were having a good time?"

"I'm tired," said Miles. "It's been a long week." He sounded just like his dad.

Donny walked over. He sat down next to him.

"Are you bumming about the suspension?"

"Yes and no," said Miles. He was running his fingers through the long grass now. "I'm glad not to be in school, but number one, I don't want anyone to take my cards away from me, and number two, I want to keep on making money."

"What do you plan to do with all that money?" Donny asked.

"If you really want to know, I'm saving up for a multiverse machine," said Miles. "I figure that by the time I'm in high school there will be some pretty sweet ones on the market."

"I told you we were alike," Donny said.

"We are *so* not alike," said Miles.

Donny ignored him. "You want to go forward or backward?" asked Donny. "To before you got suspended?"

"No," said Miles. "I don't care about the past. If it got better because of something I did back then, how will that help me now? If it got worse because of what play I made or risk I took, what do I even care? If I can't go there, it didn't happen to me; it would just be like watching TV. And the future doesn't matter yet. It would only matter if I could do something about it now so that when I got there it got better. If I can't, what's the difference? I want to be able to go side to side."

"What do you mean?" asked Donny.

Miles looked at him suspiciously. "Like you care."

"I do," said Donny. "I seriously care, and I'm interested."

"Well, you know in Magic cards the multiverses are sort of equal. You can hop back and forth between them. All of reality is sort of like a fan, it springs from one source or player or spell or whatever, but then you can bounce around a lot back and forth. Grown-ups seem to think that this one, the "in real life" one, is the most important because that's where we live. But I don't. I think every moment on the fan is of equal importance, if you can get there. You know how they say 'value' in math? I think every moment has the same value. I don't think now, or this playing field, matters more than any of the others. I think we can work to change that, because, well, it's dumb. And it keeps me from the things I want to do."

He paused and looked at the clear blue sky. "Every day I pray I can go there. I pray that I can go there and come back. By the time I'm in high school someone will have invented a way for me to do just that. Then I won't have to waste time praying anymore. I'll just be where I am."

He stood up. "Come on, Donny," he said. "We should be getting home. The funeral must be over."

Donny stood up, too. "What about the dog?" said Donny.

"In one of my sideways multiverses, Squidward is already home," said Miles. "In another, he's probably roadkill."

They started to walk across the field toward Miles's house.

Back on Bowdoin Street, the talk circled again to Kevin.

"If he was my kid," said Miles, "I'd just freeze him. His head, you know, if they can't afford to cryo his whole body, or even just his DNA, from his bones or hair. The technology is almost there, we could almost bring him back, right this minute. With cloning and the singularity, I mean, I wouldn't hurry to give away his room to one of the girls."

"You've got good instincts," said Donny.

"Thanks," said Miles, puffing up a bit. Even if Donny was a

dummy, he was supposed to be a genius, and Miles liked to be praised. "When my machine gets built, his parents can hop around, see what it's like with him here or there, if he didn't jump in front of the train or not, I mean. What if Kevin grew up to be an evil genius or something? Maybe at that point they'd like to hop right back here."

They were in front of Miles's house now.

"That's interesting," said Donny. "Do you think people would pay to take these kinds of multiverse shuttles?"

"Sure," said Miles. "Wouldn't you? They pay me a lot now for Magic cards, and they're just pieces of paper. My parents pay for bottled water. My mom pays to take her own money out of an ATM. Why wouldn't they pay for a service that is the real deal?"

He turned around and started walking in the carport.

"Hey. Where are you going?" said Donny.

"Inside," said Miles.

"Can I come, too?" said Donny. "I want to keep talking."

"Sure," said Miles. "But I've got to go to the bathroom."

"That's all right," said Donny. "I'll wait outside in the hall. Besides, I promised your mom I'd look after you."

"Right," said Miles. He climbed up the back stairs. The door was unlocked and he held it open for Donny.

"Miles," said Donny.

"What?" said Miles.

"You should come work for me," said Donny.

"After I pee," said Miles. He entered the house, Donny following.

. . .

Dan wasn't sure why after funerals all anyone ever wanted to do was eat, because he himself was usually nauseated. He remembered after his father's service, the groaning tables of appetizing foods set up by the neighbors, waiting for them back at the house; bagels and lox and herring (his cousin Louis saying: "There's *herring*," to his wife, as if the slimy fish in cream sauce finally made this a party worth attending), platters of roast beef and tongue and pastrami sandwiches, and the salads: whitefish and cucumber and tuna and macaroni and potato—all that disgusting mayonnaise making his stomach turn. He could still see in his mind's eye his relatives stuffing their faces while his stepmother sat on a wooden box and cried and laughed with her mouth full of babka, a delicious Russian chocolate coffee cake, that used to be one of his favorites. He couldn't bring himself to taste it that day and he had never eaten it again since.

When his roommate from college died in a hang-gliding accident at thirty-five, Dan flew to the wake in Chicago and drank whiskey and eyed the corned beef on the sandwich platter warily; a different culture and religion, sure, although the ingredients were similar, cured brisket, and smoked salmon sandwiches, this time on brown bread. He hadn't taken a bite but spent all night with three of his old buddies getting drunk. At 2:00 a.m., the cute midwestern hotel concierge called up to the room they'd retreated to, and said: "I'm sorry your friend died, but could you guys please stop singing 'Danny Boy'? There have been complaints from the rooms above and below you." Dan's roommate's name had been Dan, too; and once he and the fellas started passing joints around after all that drinking, they couldn't stop singing it. Dan's roommate Dan had been too young to die, and at the time his death had flattened Dan, but he wasn't a baby like Kevin.

Now, sitting in the Chois' backyard, Dan watched with a certain kind of awe as Amy and some of the other boys' mothers rolled out the food on the Chois' big outdoor dining table, which was covered with a white cloth on their redwood deck. He was surprised to see that the feast was Chinese. But there was Amy directing the deliverymen, who were laying out platters of roast pig, chicken, duck, something that looked like a vegetable-tofu stew, and rice. On an auxiliary table was fruit, tea, beer, and wine, and then all different pastries the guests must have magically brought or sent: cookie and brownie platters, coffee cakes, pies. Tall incense sticks were burning and placed around the deck, their gray brume curling up into the sky.

"Holy moly," said Dan to Jack.

Jack said, "The smoke is a signal to Kevin's ancestors to help him on his journey to heaven. Marilyn's parents had a fit yesterday because the service wasn't going to be 'Chinese,' so she threw them a bone for the reception, Mom told me. But they are still going to have hot dogs and hamburgers for the kids."

"That's thoughtful," said Dan.

"Mom's idea," Jack said.

Dan looked out over the yard. Already Josie and Suz were playing tag with their friends. Adults milled around, some drinking tea, some drinking beer out of the bottle or wine out of plastic tumblers. Round little picnic tables that must have been rented just for the day were spread out over the lawn. There were plastic chairs, with cheery red-and-white-checked plastic cushions on them, most likely from the same rental company. Dan wondered if Amy had had a hand in this, too.

He put his palm on Jack's shoulder. "You were amazing in there, son," he said. "You showed such strength and grace. I could never have done that when I was your age." Dan paused, and thought. "I don't think I could even do that now."

"Thanks, Dad," said Jack.

"Was that Lily you were talking to on the phone?" Dan said.

Jack nodded. "I don't think I could have done it without her. She gives me courage."

"That's good," said Dan. "Do you want something to eat? You must be starving. Do you want me to fix you a plate?"

Jack shook his head. He looked pale and tired. "I don't know. I don't feel so good. It's hard to think about eating now. I'm surprised there's food. And drinking. Mom warned me, but I'm still surprised."

"Do you want to sit down?"

"I don't know. It feels like a party, Dad. It feels like a party."

Dan looked out at the crowd. The children playing, the adults clustered in circles, eating, talking, drinking. Some were even laughing.

"People here are hungry. They're thirsty. They need a break from all the sadness. It doesn't mean they don't love Kevin. It doesn't mean they are not sad."

"I know," said Jack. "I just want to go home."

"Okay," said Dan. "Then let's go home."

Jack looked at Dan. His eyes so wide. "Can I? I mean, Mom? Marilyn?"

"Sure, you can. I'll explain it to your mother," said Dan. "And then I'll go with you."

"You'll go with me?" Jack asked.

"You betcha," said Dan. "Let me just tell Mom."

"Okay," said Jack. "Lily and I will wait for you in front of the house." He reached into his pocket for his phone.

"Sounds good," Dan said.

He found Amy inside the kitchen. She had a big box of Saran Wrap out and she was covering a bunch of serving dishes. She kept unrolling that thin plastic, ripping it off the metal teeth of the container, and stretching it clear and tight again around the rim of whatever she had in front of her. There was a lot of repetitive motion involved, and Dan was reminded of the guys who made those giant iridescent bubbles in Golden Gate Park.

"People brought too much," said Amy. "They brought the wrong things. Carnitas and deli plates. There's stuffed ziti here. Someone left homemade quiches on the front steps uncovered—Nellie, you know, their sitter? She almost stepped on one answering the door. If I wrap and freeze, the Chois and their guests can eat it all later in the week."

"Sounds smart," said Dan.

Amy raised her eyebrows.

"I mean it, Aim, you're doing so much to help, you're amazing. I wouldn't know what to do. I *don't* know what to do. I'm sure Marilyn appreciates it."

"Marilyn is in hell," said Amy, coldly. "If it weren't for the girls . . ." Her voice trailed off.

"I'm taking the Lifeguard home," said Dan, using her private nickname for Jack. "He's worn out. He's exhausted."

She hesitated for half a moment, about to protest, and then thought better of it. "You're absolutely right. This is way too much for him, way too much for anyone." She waved Dan off. "Go on, go ahead. I'll stay on here. That's enough. You boys go home."

"Thank you," said Dan.

Then he dug in his pocket and took out the car keys. "Here," he said. "You take the car. We'll walk." He put them on the counter.

Amy looked at them for a moment. She bit her bottom lip. Then she turned back to the Saran Wrap. She ripped off a sheet and pulled it taut over a homemade lasagna in a burnt orange casserole dish. Some of the red sauce and oil splashed against the top of the clear plastic film; it seemed so violent. Dan had to turn his eyes away so that he wouldn't vomit.

Dan couldn't bear the idea of going back out into the yard, of shaking Wei's hand again or hugging Marilyn, of watching the once hot food coagulate in the big silver trays on the serving table. Instead he walked to the front door through the dining room, which had piles of paperwork on it. Was that the work that comes with death? Dan wondered. Forms to sign? Checks to write? Or had Wei or Marilyn brought the stacks and disarray from their offices the night before Kevin died, because they'd planned on catching up with some stuff at home and never had a chance to look at it again? Was this "before" or "after" paperwork?

The hallway was tidy and so was the living room. There were flowers on the coffee table and on the end tables. There were flowers on the hall table, and under the stairs there were shoes, Wei's running shoes, Kevin's flip-flops, the little girls' plastic clogs—what were they called? Crocs. They were bright pink and orange and they had tiny little charms embedded in them. Dan opened the front door.

Jack was leaning on their car across the street.

"I gave Mom the keys," Dan said. "I thought we'd walk. Okay by you?"

"Sure," said Jack.

Dan crossed the street and they headed down the sidewalk.

"Do you want Lily to join us?" Dan said.

"She went for an early dinner with her mom," said Jack. "It's later there, and they were starving. Her mom watched the whole thing with her. Cindy said I was awesome." There was a hint of pride in his voice.

"You were," said Dan. He put his arm on Jack's shoulder as they walked. "Cindy likes you, hunh?"

"Yeah, I guess," said Jack. "What's not to like, right?" He grinned weakly at Dan, looking for his approval, Dan supposed. It was a phrase Dan used a lot. What's not to like.

"Nothing. You're a great kid," Dan said.

"That's what Marilyn said," Jack said.

They turned the corner. The sidewalk was slick with rotting persimmon paste; the skins had busted open a while ago and people and dogs had trodden on them. The muddy mold that grew on the fruit's intestinal slime gave off a specific composite odor, the sweet scent of putridity.

"Let's cross," said Dan. There were no cars in the street anyway, so they walked in the middle for a while before stepping up onto the opposing sidewalk. The first house on this side had a lemon tree in the front yard. Sunny yellow and prettier than the persimmons even in their prime, Dan thought. They would look lovely collected in a bright blue bowl.

"When did she say that?" Dan asked.

"Marilyn?" said Jack. He pulled his ponytail holder out of his hair with his right hand. He shook his head like a wet dog and those long dirty-blond locks rolled down his shoulders. They were still damp from being gathered up after his shower and were browner at the edges. "When I finished speaking." He rolled the ponytail holder up onto his right wrist, next to a light gray twisted rubber bracelet, three strands, one that read HOPE, the others COURAGE and FAITH.

"That bracelet in honor of Kevin?" Dan asked. "You know the school expressly frowns on stuff like that."

"I know. Teddy made them for the team. The school is a bunch of morons, Dad."

"They're afraid of copycat . . ."

"I'm not going to kill myself because I think a bunch of dumb kids are then going to wear some ugly rubber bracelet."

"Okay," said Dan.

"We just wanted to do something for today. I'll take it off Monday."

"Okay," said Dan. Then, remembering where they had been in the conversation . . . "So she was thanking you, Marilyn, I mean, when she called you over?" Dan said. "After you finished speaking?"

"Yeah," said Jack.

"Is that what she whispered in your ear?" Dan asked. He was thinking of Jack's little flinch and the squaring of his shoulders.

"Yeah," said Jack. "And then she said, 'Now you have to live for the both of you.'"

"What?" said Dan. He stopped walking.

"Yeah, Dad, that's what she said," said Jack. He stopped, too, he looked bewildered. "The thing is, I don't even know how to live for one of us. I mean me."

"Well, it's not true," said Dan. "She shouldn't have said that. I mean I know we can't . . . I mean she's beside herself. She's to be forgiven. But it's so not true." He took Jack's shoulders in his hands.

"You don't have to live for Kevin and you can't anyway. You never have to live for anyone else. You have to live for you, Jack. That's all. Do you understand? Not me, not your mother, not Lily, not anyone."

"Yeah, Dad," said Jack.

"All right, then," said Dan. They started walking again.

"Dad," said Jack. "Why did you go to Japan?"

Now it was Dan's turn to flinch. "Because I was selfish," said Dan.

"The way you're telling me now to be," said Jack.

"There's a difference between selfish and selfless," said Dan. "You can't allow yourself to be sacrificed on that boy's funeral pyre."

"Do you wish you didn't go?" said Jack.

"I don't know," said Dan.

"If you didn't go, maybe Mom wouldn't have gotten so drunk at dinner, and I wouldn't have taken your car in the middle of the night, and I wouldn't have dropped Kevin off at school, just a few minutes before the Caltrain."

"You're going to blame that on me?" Dan said.

"Maybe," said Jack, not looking at his father. "Maybe if you were where you were supposed to be and I was where I was supposed to be, Kevin would be where he is supposed to be right now."

"It's not your fault," said Dan. "And it's certainly not mine."

"I think maybe it is," Jack said. "Lily thinks so. Cindy, too."

"Look, I know you all feel bad, and everyone wants to find a reason, but that's just ludicrous," said Dan.

"I don't think so," said Jack. His voice began to rise. "You cheated on Mom, didn't you?"

"None of your business," said Dan.

"She's my mother. She is my business," said Jack.

"I didn't go to Japan," Dan said. "I made that part up. I was asked to go to Japan and I thought about going to Japan and I wanted to go to Japan but I went to Boston instead. I did what was best for our family. I made the choice not to go. In life, we have choices. I went for a job I didn't get."

"Dad," said Jack, clearly incredulous.

"I didn't go," Dan said.

They stopped walking and looked at each other for a while. Dan noticed he was panting even though he was standing still.

Because even as he knew in his panic he was dissembling, being craven, and childish, and ridiculous, he tried to cover up. "Is it still my fault? Kevin's death? If I went to Boston like I said I would, would Kevin not be dead?"

"Do you love Mom?"

"Of course I love her. She's your mother."

"Are you leaving her? Are you leaving us?"

"I don't want to. We're a family. I went for a story, Jack."

"A story."

"Yes. A story. I'm a reporter, remember? And it's a big one. An important one. It's about radiation leaking out of the crippled nuclear reactors in Fukushima Prefec—"

"You're not a reporter, Dad. It's been years since you've been a reporter. Who hired you anyway?"

"Well, I met someone. She needed a partner, and we did it on spec. Everyone is ignoring this thing, sometimes in today's world you need to sell a story after you write it or present a sizzle reel—"

"You met someone? Are you kidding? You think I'm two years old?"

"I met a crackerjack journalist, a Knight Fellow—do you know how hard it is to become a Knight Fellow?—and she's smart and alive and she's doing the work of the world. And, well, we connected. We had a Vulcan Mind Meld, you know?" Dan tried to draw him in. But Jack wasn't taking the bait. He stared at his father like he was a crazy man.

Dan persevered. "She cares about the things I care about. She made me feel alive. So, you know, when she asked me to go with her, I thought, why not? All I do is lie on my bed every day staring at my computer, looking for work and not finding any, and here was work coming and knocking right on my door."

"So you lied and went behind our backs. Didn't you think about us? Didn't you think about how we might feel?"

"I've been having an existential crisis," said Dan, feeling naked and inept. "For months now, years even. How could you possibly know at your age what it's like to be my age and be out of work and feeling like your life is over but you still have to live it every day? I had to make changes. Changes don't come without costs or heartache."

Jack shook his head. All that dirty-blond tangled hair. He really did look like a lifeguard. Or a golden retriever puppy with giant paws.

"I never knew you were an asshole until now, Dad," Jack said.

"Don't talk to me that way. I'm your father. I'm trying to acknowledge the pain that sometimes comes along with risk."

"What you're really saying is that it was worth hurting us for you to *maybe* feel better. Where's your costs and heartache?"

"Believe me, I'm feeling some serious heartache right now," said Dan.

"You're an asshole, Dad," Jack said, this time with certitude.

In Dan's imagination, he slapped his son right then. His grieving wounded teenage baby man of a son. Right across his smirking ugly mug.

But on terra firma, Dan did nothing.

They walked the rest of the way home in silence, Jack a few steps ahead of his father. When they got to the house, they entered through the carport, Jack letting the back door swing in Dan's face instead of holding it open the way he'd been trained to do. Dan stopped it from hitting him squarely on the nose with the heel of his hand.

"Hello," Dan called out as he made his way past the laundry room and into the kitchen. "Anyone home?"

"We're in here," yelled Miles.

Where? thought Dan. But he didn't feel like yelling.

Instead he walked through the kitchen and out through the

dining room, past the living room and into the family room, where Donny and Miles were playing PlayStation 4.

"How was the funeral, Dad?" Miles said, eyes locked on the screen while he played and Dan stood in the doorway.

"Awful," Dan said. "I'm fried."

"Why don't you kick back," Donny said. "Miles and I are playing a game." He was furiously pressing the buttons on his controller.

"You sure you don't have to get to the office, Donny?" said Dan.

"I'm sure," Donny said. "Go take a nap, Dan."

"Yeah, take a nap, Dad," said Miles.

"Okay," said Dan. "I will."

He started to walk toward the staircase. He turned back. "Did Jack say anything to you?"

"Jack who?" said Miles.

"Your brother," said Dan.

"Is he back, too?" said Miles.

Dan walked up the stairs. The door to Jack's room was closed. He almost knocked, but then changed his mind. There was no way they were going to get to a better place right now. The door to the master bedroom was open, so he entered it.

As soon as he sat on the bed, Dan was hit with a tsunami of exhaustion. He'd been traveling for days, without sleep, without end. He'd been around the world and back. He'd exited the atmosphere of his life and entered another and was enlarged, and then returned, changed, and small. He felt like a lost and forgotten cosmonaut, revolving endlessly in an unbreakable orbit. Everything he'd done had been a mistake. Everything he'd touched had gone wrong. This last bit with Jack, that took the prize. When hard-pressed, he'd told half-truths, fantasies, and out-and-out lies. Jack was right. He was an asshole. Would the kid ever trust him again? The trouble with being a parent was that even with the enormity of all that mind-bending paternal love, Dan still couldn't be bigger than he was. You'd think it would stretch you, Dan thought, but it doesn't, at least not far enough. He was the world's worst father.

Dan reached into his pants pocket and brought out his phone. He pressed his thumb to the home button. The phone woke up.

There was a mammoth text from Maryam, he kept rolling back the screen as her gray block of characters scrolled on:

Dan, I sent you my compiled Yoshi notes via email. I stayed up all night transcribing. They are fantastic. I also sent you the preliminary photo series. The pics are heartbreaking and also beautiful. Exquisite. When I finished, I had lunch with an old contact. He put me onto the most amazing story. I think we should sell these as a series! I don't know if I ever told you but for a while I was a competitive surfer. As a teenager I summered in North Cornwall. My friend told me that at Tairatoyoma beach, 50km from the nuclear plant, the surfers have returned. There are thousands of bags of contaminated sand stored on the beach, and the radioactive water pours forth from the crippled plant continuously and yet nothing overawes the human spirit. One guy I interviewed said: "Who knows what this is going to do to us? Who knows what's going to happen ever anyway? I'm alive now and it feels great." What a metaphor for life. I'm going to suit up and go out with them tomorrow. More importantly, how is your family? Darling Jack? Remember, these things take time, but there is healing ahead. When there is love, there is hope. I send you kisses upon kisses upon kisses. As ever, M.

Dan read and reread the message. He was so tired he was seeing double.

He typed: *You are crazy.*

He erased it. He typed: *Don't be a fool! It's too dangerous!*

He erased that, too. Nothing was going to stop Maryam from going into the water. Nothing, not even his family had stopped him, and he possessed one-eighth of her courage, and used to be a man of honor who had sense; a man who didn't knowingly go out and hurt the people he loved.

He clicked on his email. She had sent him forty-five pages of notes and several series of photos. The last one was of a somewhat younger Maryam in a wet suit standing next to a surfboard; she was waving happily at him, even from the past.

Dan was tired, but he brushed the tired out of his eyes with his hands. He decided he was past tired.

He walked over to his desk. His laptop was still sitting on it. He picked it up and brought it back to his bed. He kicked off his shoes. He took off his suit pants and hung them over his desk chair. He did the same with his shirt and tie and jacket. He went into his drawers and took out a T-shirt. He took out a pair of gray sweatpants. He put on his clothes and walked over to his overnight bag and took out his notebook and a pen. Then he went back to his bed. He put his laptop on his lap. He began to read Maryam's notes. After a while, he opened a new Word doc. He read from her notes and then from his notepad, and then, returning to his own document, Dan began to type.

·   ·   ·

By the time the reception was over, Amy had filled up six Hefty bags of garbage, packed both the bottom freezer and the auxiliary freezer out in the garage with enough meals to feed an army, and supervised the flipping of burgers and dogs by enlisting Wei's younger brother, Sam, who had agreed to do the honors at the grill. Amy had always liked Sam, and he seemed to appreciate having a job to do—Jack's teammates had inhaled the food as fast as he could cook it, and even little Josie had come back for seconds, mustard dribbling a line of gold all the way down the front of her pretty tea-green dress. Sam smiled for what was probably the first time that day and grabbed his heart with a couple of staggering steps backward, when Amy fetched him a cold beer and held out the frosty bottle.

After she had run out of obvious chores to do (and even the unobvious, like replenishing toilet paper rolls in the bathrooms and folding the top square into a little triangle), Amy had checked in on Marilyn, rescuing her friend from her own mother and ancient aunt who were clearly tormenting her. Tears were streaming down Marilyn's face.

"I told you he didn't look right at the anniversary party; he was too pressured, Mari," Amy overheard the mom say.

"Nonsense," said the aunt, "this generation doesn't have enough to do. They are all too spoiled."

Marilyn looked like she might collapse at any moment, so Amy grabbed Marilyn by the elbow, and said: "Excuse me, I need Marilyn in the kitchen," pulling her inside, whispering in her ear, "Ugh, I hate them," pouring them both a tumbler of scotch on the rocks and taking her out the front door for a walk around the block.

"I'm so sorry," said Amy. "How could they talk to you like that?"

Marilyn shook her head and dabbed at her eyes and runny nose with the cocktail napkin Amy had handed to her.

"The things people say. 'He's in a better place.' A better place? Better than here with me and Wei? 'I don't know how you can stand it, if it was my child I'd kill myself,' as if they love theirs more than I love mine? As if I still didn't have two little girls at home to take care of?"

"Oh," said Amy. "Oh, honey, people are idiots. Don't listen to people."

But Marilyn was on a tear. She continued to mimic: "'Didn't you or Wei notice he was depressed?' For God's sakes, if I thought he was depressed, I would have taken him to a psychiatrist! I'm a doctor. I'm a doctor," said Marilyn, sobbing.

"He didn't look depressed, sweetie. I didn't see it. Wei didn't see it. Jack didn't see it. None of us saw it. The people who ask you, they're just scared. They want to have something to look out for, but there was nothing to look out for with Kevin. There was no, I don't know what you call it, smoking gun? You're the doctor. Symptoms?"

"You didn't see it, either?" said Marilyn, with hopeless hope. And then, when Amy nodded, "I'm sorry, you just said that. You say it all the time . . ."

"You can ask me a thousand times. You can ask me for however long it takes. The rest of our lives," Amy said. "I will always tell you, Kevin seemed fine. He seemed better than fine, he seemed great. He was a great kid and he was doing great."

"Then why did he do this?" sobbed Marilyn.

"I don't know," said Amy.

"Last week, he wanted to talk to me about something, I don't even know what, and I said, 'Later, Kev, I have to do the laundry,'" said Marilyn. She was really crying now. "Why did I do the laundry? Who gives a shit about dirty clothes? I shouldn't have done the laundry. I'd have my boy right here, right now."

Amy said, "You did the laundry because it was dirty." This time letting her just cry. Since Kevin died, sometimes she hugged, or patted, or tried to jolly Marilyn out of it, other times she didn't.

Amy wasn't exactly quite sure why she responded one way or another at any given moment. Instinct? Maybe she gave Marilyn what she needed at the time? Or had she, Amy, entered a horrible new state? Was she becoming accustomed to her friend's emotional tidal waves?

"The laundry didn't kill him," Amy said. "We don't know why he did what he did. Maybe Wei's right. Maybe it was the imp of the perverse, or some freak panic, or I don't know, an ecstatic moment . . . But one thing I do know, he knew he was loved. That boy was bathed in love. Every single day. I'm a witness, I saw it. That I can tell you till the cows come home."

Marilyn nodded weakly. Then she said: "I never heard you talk about cows before." They both smiled a little as Marilyn brushed the tears from her cheeks with her fingertips. The waterfall slowing. The tears coming and going all day in surges.

"I never did," said Amy. "I never said one word about cows before in my life. It's my first time." She handed her drink over to Marilyn. "Hold this for a second?"

Marilyn nodded yes.

Amy reached into her purse and brought out a pack of cigarettes and a lighter.

"Want your own?"

"No," said Marilyn, softly. "Let's share like always."

"It's a girl trick," Amy had said when they first started smoking together this way, on the sly, in the parking lot behind the boys' Little Fishes day camp. "Like eating tiny slivers of chocolate cake, rather than taking a whole piece," said Marilyn, nodding in agreement. "Or scarfing all your boyfriend's fries. You can't get fat, because you didn't order them," said Amy.

They'd bonded that day. They both were mothers of boy swimmers, and weirdly they both had much younger identical twins—

although Suz and Josie were more classically alike than Miles and Theo, who looked the same but acted fraternal. What were the odds? Amy and Marilyn instantly understood the other's difficulties. And then neither one of them cared for the group of swim mothers who always went for fro-yo together during practice, and ran the bake sales, and fought over what to do with the money that they could have just as easily donated—the ladies were loaded and the kids didn't need the sugar. Even by then, Marilyn and Amy were already sick to death of the constant schlepping to the pool that would prove to be the common thread of the next eleven years of their lives—one volunteering to drive the boys to one meet, and then the other to another, until they finally realized they preferred going together, so they could at least talk to each other in the front seat and slip out for a glass of wine or a cigarette while the boys did their thing in the cold water.

Amy lit the cigarette now and took a drag. She handed it to Marilyn, who took one, too.

For a while, they mostly walked without speaking. Then at some point, Marilyn slipped her hand into the crook of Amy's elbow.

"If people are not knifing me in the gut every five minutes with their platitudes and their stupid questions, they're giving me that horrible face." Marilyn made a face of mock sympathy. "It's both pity and aversion," said Marilyn, "with a soupçon of 'I'm so glad it's happening to you, not me,' right around that patronizing fake smile. And except for the idiots and the narcissists, and the sadists like my mother, everyone else is being *too* nice to me. I can't stand it. Even Jody Bledsoe." Marilyn took another drag on the cigarette. "And she's a cunt of the first order."

"Don't worry, they'll get bitchy again," said Amy. "I bet you Jody's being a bitch right now somewhere." Then she reached out for the cigarette. "Hey, quit hogging that thing."

Marilyn smiled and passed it to Amy.

"You are like another sister," said Marilyn. She rested her beautiful head on Amy's shoulder. It felt so good there, it was all Amy could do not to kiss her soft black hair. Instead she took another drag and blew the smoke away in the other direction.

Marilyn's gratitude was a gift. What would the day be like if Amy could not have serviced her friends this way? Could she have borne it? They graced her with their needs. Like Wei's brother, Sam, Amy had craved a job to do to mitigate her own fears and pain.

"How long has Sam been divorced?" asked Amy. She took a drag from the cigarette.

Marilyn looked over at her. "Why? Are you interested?" She took the cigarette out of Amy's hand and inhaled, too.

Was she? He was certainly handsome enough. Her own husband was sleeping with another woman—the one thing she couldn't abide—and when she'd asked him if he loved this person, he'd replied by text message: *I can't say that I don't.* She'd discussed some of this the past few days with Marilyn, in between bouts of crying and planning the funeral, taking calls and fending them off, and making the Choi girls breakfast and lunch, telling the various sitters what park to take them to, giving them money to go to the movies.

"I'm determined to stay neutral," Marilyn said, "but on the Fourth of July Sam told Wei he thought you were cute. Plus, Dan's an asshole, in a textbook midlife crisis-y way. Teexxxxtbook." She drew out the word. "But I'm neutral," Marilyn said. She passed the cigarette back to Amy.

Marilyn's mother was waiting on the front steps when Amy and Marilyn turned the corner. She was a diminutive woman, even in grief, where Marilyn was lithe and elegant, her mother was short and dowdy. However, standing on the steps that way, too tiny for the world, but mighty enough to come out to search for her shattered child, Marilyn's mom suddenly looked a whole lot more like Marilyn; or Marilyn had somehow shrunk and, now more wraithlike, looked a lot more like her mom.

Marilyn nodded at the cigarette and said: "It's officially yours. She doesn't know that I smoke." She rolled her eyes.

When she spotted them, Marilyn's mother commenced waving frantically; she must have been worried.

"She looks worried," said Amy. "Maybe she realized she said the wrong thing."

"She always has," said Marilyn. "She's always been mean. Why change now when I need her?" She paused and downed the rest of her drink. "I think it's time for me to go back inside."

"Okay," Amy said, and handed Marilyn her own highball glass, which she had somehow emptied, although she had no recollection of drinking that much in that short a time. "Will you be okay?"

Marilyn started to nod, and then she started crying again, the crying came and went so quietly, by this point in the day it came in sighs. "No," she said, "I'll never be okay. But thank you, Amy. And thank Jack for me. For us."

Amy kissed her friend's wet cheek and stepped back, giving Marilyn's mother a little wave.

"You know what kills me," Marilyn said as she began to walk away. "I don't think he ever had sex." She climbed the steps, and her mother opened the door, and they both retreated into the house.

Amy was alone outside.

There was no reason for her to go back into the kitchen or the yard. No reason to dive back into the murk and fury of another family's anguish. So, what now? What should she do?

Go for a run? Running always made her feel better. But to run Amy needed to go home, get the dog, and change. Dan was at home. She couldn't deal with Dan. Jack was at home. Her sweet boy. But his pain overwhelmed her. Maybe it was okay to let Dan do some of the parenting now that he was back, and she could take a tiny break? Miles was at home. He was easy, Miles. Usually he was the easiest of all, but right now, facing the results of her own neglect and her surprise at *his* getting into trouble, too, she wasn't ready to face this kid, either. Thank God, Theo was with Blossom. Theo even on a good day could have tipped her over the edge. Begonia would keep him that night as well if Amy wanted, that's what she'd said on the phone: "Theo *es mi hijo*. We can keep him as long as you want." What would the world be like without other mothers? How could any of them have survived?

The car was across the street where Dan had parked it. It was a little crooked, the end jutting out just enough into the street to bug her. The last thing she wanted was to open the door and go inside. She felt like right now if she were to enter that car, the air inside would smell like a mouth and she would never get out of it again. So, she walked right past it and headed down the block.

The Chois lived in one of Amy's favorite neighborhoods in Palo Alto. She had always coveted their house and their location, but as Dan reminded her, Wei was in finance and Marilyn was a brain surgeon. It was out of their league. Dan was an unemployed journo and she was what? A PR girl? Now a tech den mother? Back in the day she had wanted to work in film or maybe magazines. Those dreams had gotten her into public relations.

The Chois lived in a beautiful old mission-style house in Professorville where it met Evergreen Park. The houses were larger than they were in College Terrace, where Amy lived, although there were some old-fashioned bungalows here, too, plus some modern types, and a few stately two-story Colonials that looked as if they'd been shipped out from back east. The sidewalks were leafier, and the yards more verdant, and often there were citrus trees. It was more gracious than it was where she lived with her boys; there the houses were closer together and the interstitial spaces narrower, more cement in the alleys and carports, less green.

Kevin was dead.

Even after the last few days had forced her in such an intimate way to face that gruesome fact, she still couldn't really believe it. That dear, sweet, vibrant, living boy was dead. Her own son had gone from inconsolable to easily comforted and then back again. At times, he raised his hand to step up to the plate, like today at the service; at other times he was a human puddle, crying in her arms. She knew from her own experience that time would take care of some of this; and she also knew that a loss this deep was everlasting. The only peace to be had at this moment was in leaving the Choi house and, also, not going home to hers.

Amy turned down Cowper. It was a nice, broad, leafy street and it went on forever. There would be no more decisions to make, she could just turn back when she hit the stores and restaurants on California Avenue. Her feet hurt in her shoes, black pumps with a kitten heel. She took them off and stood on the cool cement. Her panty hose made her feel like her pelvis was choking. She looked up and down the block and saw no one—which was not unusual for this time of day in the middle of the week. The kids were probably at afterschool or already doing their homework, the parents who worked were commuting, the ones who weren't were contemplating the endless puzzle of dinner; it's the worst part of having kids, Dan always said, trying to figure out what to feed them.

With the coast clear, Amy reached up the skirt of her dress and pulled her panty hose down, then stepped out of each leg and out of the little sock-foot at the end of them. Now her feet were on the crunchy pavement. She balled up the panty hose and started to walk, panty hose in one hand, shoes dangling in the other. The corner house still had its recycling and garbage bins out by the curb. She deposited the panty hose in the trash and kept walking. She vowed never to wear panty hose again. The cooling late-afternoon air felt nice on her legs.

Dan was sleeping with another woman. Dan had lied to her and told her he'd gone job hunting. He'd spent money they didn't have. He'd gone to Japan to write a story. He'd said he'd gone to Japan, after he'd said he'd gone to Boston, but for all Amy knew he was shacked up in San Francisco or had gone wine tasting with this person in Sonoma. Who was she? How had he met her? Was she younger, prettier, richer, smarter, funnier, kinder, more interesting than Amy? Better in bed? Was this just a midlife crisis, as Marilyn said? Or was he leaving her? Who even wanted him? He was a lying, cheating, unemployed slob, and he'd left her all alone at the absolute worst time in all their years together. She felt like a single mother. Wasn't that what she'd been afraid of becoming all along? The only responsible one?

Amy looked back down Cowper, she had just come that way. What if after leaving the reception she had actually gotten into the car and driven home? Might she have burst into tears and then hit a neighborhood dog by accident, while reaching into the glove compartment for a Kleenex?

What if she'd walked the other way, toward home and campus, like Dan and Jack presumably did? Could she have run into Naresh skipping out on work and taking his kids out to the playground? Would they have sat down on a bench, while his boys took to the swings, and had yet another thought-provoking and soothing conversation?

Amy loved Naresh.

Or maybe if she'd walked toward home she would have run into some nosy parent from the high school, right by the Starbucks on the corner, like Jody Bledsoe; someone who wanted to be reassured that Kevin had really been on drugs—which he hadn't—so that she could separate his fate from that of her own beloved son's?

What if Amy had chosen not to walk, but had taken the car and not burst into tears and not hit a dog, but had driven around and around, the way that Jack said he and Kevin had done so aimlessly that fateful morning? What if in all that directionless driving, at one point she'd looked at the dashboard and saw her tank was close to empty, and then she'd pulled into the gas station on campus just as, after all these many years, her old boyfriend had pulled up at the other pump?

Is that what Donny meant with all his multiverse theories? Would Furrier.com allow her to know the outcome of all these decisions if they were ever to be made? Or were Amy's petty problems to be delegated by Donny and his minions to the forthcoming crisis-light social media service Summer Fur?

Maybe in the multiverse where Amy floated around in her car all day, so as not to go home, and decided to get gas on campus (which was more expensive and something she never, ever did anyway), he was here on business. Just like that, after twenty-five years or so, except for grainy LinkedIn photos, she got to finally see his older, softened face. It was lined and dusted by a silvery close-shaved beard, but he still had his hair and he still had his smile. Or maybe in another multiverse he was taking his living daughter (she'd seen that kid's Facebook page and she was a cutie) on a college tour of Stanford. *Their* daughter had never been born. Amy thought she'd aborted her, but if Donny's algorithms meant anything it turns out she might have miscarried her anyway, even if she'd married him and tried to make things work. (Why didn't I try? thought Amy. If I'd tried back then, would that pain be anything like the multilayered one I'm experiencing right now?)

And, wow, in that same multiverse, he said: "Don't you look great?"

He said: "You're still beautiful," making Amy's stupid knees grow weak and this horrible day somewhat better.

Amy doesn't think that! She doesn't think that! She knocks on a wooden fence, she spits over her shoulder three times, she erases her own memory, a psychic do-over, she chooses early Alzheimer's or cancerous death over that now-forgotten, instantly obliterated, totally immature and egoistic thought.

"How long has it been?" he says. "At least twenty, twenty-five years. There's so much I've wanted to say to you, there's so much I've wanted to know. My daughter's got an interview after her tour. And an info session. Do we want to get a coffee?"

Or maybe in another multiverse Amy sees this guy, this guy she doesn't even know anymore, she sees him pull up to the pump and get out of the car and stretch, and his T-shirt rides up, and she sees an unwanted sliver of his hairy belly, and knowing it is best to let sleeping dogs lie, she'll pull out again without getting gas; she has read *The Age of Innocence* by Edith Wharton, she knows it's too late for anything but awkwardness and sorrow, relief and regret, so maybe as she backs away from the pump she almost runs over the evil Maximus's evil father, Chris Powell. Chris has taken a leak inside the bathroom in the station's minimart. He's bought a candy bar from a vending machine and, without looking either way, while stuffing his ugly, nasty face, he walks right into the path of her car and she stops in time, no roadkill Chris, but he still chases her car out of the lot, screaming again about his lawyer.

Or perhaps instead of going for gas on campus, Amy decides

she'll get her gas at the station near the entrance to 101, and after filling her tank so high she almost floods it, Amy thinks, gotta burn some of that up, why the hell not, and turns onto the freeway.

She drives and drives. After a while, a good long while, hours maybe, or even a couple of days, she decides it is high time she visited Lauren back in Scarsdale. Dan can deal with the boys. Dan can deal with the dog. Dan can deal with Jack's misery and Thing Two's not-reading and Thing One's money-laundering and his own fat-faced fat-bellied unemployment and infidelity. She can take 101 North to the Bay Bridge and 80. She can drive and drive and drive three thousand miles and land herself at Lauren's front door. Lauren will take one look at her and fix her a cocktail, that's for sure, a vodka martini, three olives, the way she likes it, when she arrives.

Or when Amy turns onto 101, before she gets to the bridge, she can exit into San Francisco, and she can risk life and limb and her driver's license by texting Sam Choi, one hand on the wheel and the other on her phone, asking him to meet up in the city for dinner. He says yes of course. He thinks she's *cute*. He needs something else to contemplate aside from his dead nephew and his shattered brother, and when the check comes, he will insist and Amy will let him pay.

She thinks about how Sam looked when he clutched his hands to his heart when she'd handed him that beer. She imagines how grateful he'd be if she fucked his fucking brains out.

Amy stopped walking. Her feet were hurting from the hard, gravelly sidewalk. She put her shoes down and rubbed each sole clean with her hand before slipping first the left, then the right shoe back on. She reached into her purse for her cell phone. She pressed CALL

BACK on the last number to call her. When he answered, she said: "I'm going to the Nut House. Meet me there when you can."

Amy turned off her phone, dropped it in her purse, and kept on walking to California Avenue.

.   .   .

Donny loved the Nut House. He'd gone there the first time, orientation week freshman year, when his RAs coerced most of the floor—that is, the truly smart kids who came to college with fake IDs fully loaded—to join them in a classic Palo Alto night out. It was a real dive, the RAs said, with pride, a perfect "old man's bar," where truck drivers and construction workers and grad students and service-industry folk all drank cheek to jowl with tech giants and coding stars. Bobbins, the humongous football-playing RA who lived on Donny's hall, said: "Might even be some creepy-crawly hookers prowling if we're lucky." But what got Donny instantly on his computer creating his own fake ID was when an RA named Sheila said: "Zuck even hangs out there sometimes."

Donny and his cronies had been going to Antonio's Nut House ever since, although never, not once, had Zuckerberg been there when he was. Donny had seen him at Palo Alto Sol, but he was there with his wife, so Zuck had not looked that approachable. Donny thought it would be easier to talk to him in a bar and was for a long while disappointed.

But as the weeks and months passed without a sighting, Donny didn't care so much, because there was enough at that crazy pub to entertain him. Playing to theme, a squirrel plaque hung over the front door, and a giant gorilla statue, dispensing free roasted peanuts, lived in a cage in a corner. The floor was covered with their shells—everyone just threw the empties on the black linoleum; it looked like no one had swept it in the four decades it had been in business. An electronic news ticker displayed cracked jokes behind the bar. The twining lights spelled out: SO A DYSLEXIC WALKS INTO A BRA . . . BOOZE IS THE ANSWER. NOW I CAN'T REMEMBER THE QUESTION . . . WELCOME TO ANTONIO'S NUT HOUSE!! GET A DRINK AND GRAB YOUR NUTS!

Donny liked the noise, which could get thunderous when the place was packed, and the neon lights that were hung around the rooms were bright and shiny. Sometimes when he entered the bar, he felt like a metal ball just shot into the game in an old-fashioned pinball machine. Bam! Zam! Whap! Whoop! It was a great joy-ride. Plus, bras hung from the ceiling. Donny didn't often get to see bras IRL.

An old guy once told them how the bra business got started, while he and Adnan attempted to play pool. "I saw the whole thing," the guy said. "I was sitting next to this young lady at the bar. Maybe it itched or something, because she got busy with her hands under her shirt, and then, holy shit, she slid that thing out one armhole, it was one of those lacey white ones and she flung it up in the air where it got stuck. It's still up there." Beer bottle in hand, the guy acted out the entire hard-to-imagine feat as he narrated. When he mimed the final skyward gesture, he ended up pouring beer on almost everyone in the pool room. Donny and Adnan had nearly peed in their pants, they'd laughed so hard.

But bras weren't the only thing that hung from the ceiling at the Nut House. For fifteen bucks, you could paint your own tile and hang it up there, too, which Donny did on his nineteenth birthday; he painted the first line of code he'd ever written, and a lot of the squares were kind of art house versions of bathroom graffiti: private jokes, sports boasts, crude drawings. The windows were covered with sloppy hand-painted signage listing the available food items:

hamburgers, dogs, fish and chips, burritos, popcorn, nachos, chili fries. Whiteboard and handmade posters, announcing the daily specials, helped block the natural light (they were virtually the same as the menu). Happy hour prices all the time. You could get a G&T for three bucks and a margarita for $3.50. Donny liked the super chicken burritos, but Adnan said the food was rancid, and whenever they came for beers, Adnan would run back across the street to use their office bathroom because the men's room was so effing filthy. Not Donny. There was a sign in there that made it worth flirting with giardia: PLEASE DON'T PUT YOUR CIGARETTES OUT IN THE URINAL. IT MAKES THEM SOGGY AND HARD TO LIGHT. He'd Instagrammed that several times, until his mom begged him to stop. That and foosball and two pool tables? What more could a freshman want? For Donny's first year and a half at Stanford, the Nut House was collegiate nerd-boy nirvana, the perfect place to hang out in pink, polished, pricey Palo Alto.

This was the heaven in which he'd lived until one mean, rough, and ragged waitress entered his life, with her dyed red hair, and too-tight wifebeater, and heroin-chic skinny black jeans; Donny and Adnan decided to call her Old Red behind her back, even though she wasn't much older than they were. One night, after serving Donny about a million times, in the middle of sophomore year, for no reason at all, she confiscated his fake ID.

When Donny said, "Hey, no fair," she said, "Stanford University students are our worst customers, rude and cheap," and she walked away. She wouldn't even acknowledge Donny's presence when he followed her and tried to talk reason. She threatened to turn the bouncers on him if he persisted and gave him the silent treatment the rest of the night.

Other times when Donny patronized the place, like during the middle of the day when the coders at work were making him crazy, the waiters would serve him margaritas and beer, whatever he wanted. But whenever that evil witch was on duty the best Donny could hope for was a Diet Coke. In those days, if Adnan were with him, Adnan would order two shots and slip one into Donny's drink out of pity and the largess that comes with superiority. Old Red seemed to have no problem with Adnan.

Then when Donny turned twenty-one, just a few weeks ago, and returned with his New York State driver's license, legal and ready to play, Old Red looked at it and then at him, back and forth, and back and forth, and said: "Your schnoz looks bigger in the picture."

She looked at it again.

"Nope," she said. "It's bullshit." Reading off the card: "Donald. Donald fucking duck. What do you think, I'm stupid? Get outta here."

"Good one," said Donny.

She refused to return the ID until Donny offered her stock options. He gave her ten shares of i.e. Now, whenever he entered the bar, Old Red called out: "Hey, Ding Dong," as a sign of affection. She even poured him a beer, always before he asked for one, even when sometimes he would have preferred a mixed drink. The last time, the beer was warm.

"If you like cold beer, go to the bar next door," she said.

Old Red was a bit of a minefield. So Donny felt a little trepidation walking inside, but it was a cool, late afternoon on a weekday, no one was at the food counter, and there was a single guy with tattoos pouring drinks. No sign of the Red Devil anywhere. It was dark inside and it took a moment for his eyes to fully adjust. Donny walked over to the bar.

"A margarita, please," said Donny.

"Sure thing," said the bartender.

Donny looked around the room while the guy did his magic. She was sitting at a wooden table up front in the shadows by a window. The paint let in little light. She was staring right at him.

"Amy?" said Donny.

"You walked by me," said Amy.

"My bad," said Donny. "I didn't see you."

"The boys okay?" asked Amy.

"The boys?" asked Donny. When she nodded, he said, "Oh, yeah, Miles, he's fine. Dan came in looking a little tired, so we sent him to bed. That was right, right?"

She ignored him. "Jack?"

"He went straight up to his room. Can't blame him. Poor guy."

"Just get us some peanuts," said Amy.

So Donny walked over to the gorilla in the cage and scooped out a plastic basket of nuts. He brought it over to her table.

"Do you want another drink?" asked Donny.

"Yes, please," said Amy, draining the one in front of her. She held up the margarita glass. "Hit me again." He took it from her, but not before he noted that she looked like hell. Her eyes tearstained and puffy, her underarms sweat-soaked, her hair loose now and in a zigzag part.

"Sucks, Amy," said Donny.

"What?" said Amy. "You mean Kevin? You've said that before."

"No," said Donny. "I mean yes. I mean yes totally, the kid, for Jack. Dan."

He stopped speaking as Amy flinched.

"My drink, Donny," said Amy.

"Back in a flash," said Donny.

He took the glass with him and went back to the bartender. "How about another?" he said. "In fact, how about a pitcher?"

The bartender looked at him. He looked across the room at Amy. "That your old lady?" he said.

"You mean my mother?" said Donny. "No. She's my . . ." For a moment there, he was at a loss for words. "Just bring over the pitcher when it's ready, okay?"

"Sure thing," said the bartender. "She's a real MILF, that lady who's not your mother." He winked—that is, if he didn't have something in his eye.

Donny looked across the room at Amy. She looked a lot better from far away. His mom was always talking about how hot Amy was back in the day. He figured his mom was just jealous, because Amy got to hang out with him all the time, but right now, in the dark at the other end of the Nut House, he kind of saw it.

He went back to the table and sat down across from her. Amy was cracking peanuts and piling up the shells.

"Excuse me," she said. "I was so busy at Marilyn's, I forgot to eat."

She brushed the shells together with the side of her hand and shoved them off onto the floor.

"I got us a pitcher," said Donny. "He's making it. Here," he said, pushing his glass toward her. "Drink mine, until it comes."

Amy reached for the margarita and took a sip.

"Wow," she said. "You must really feel guilty about something. I've never seen you share anything before."

It was true, thought Donny. He had never been much for sharing. He'd failed sharing in preschool.

"So cough it up," said Amy. "What's all the guilt and generosity for?"

"I did not understand the gravity of the situation."

Amy looked puzzled. Her head turned to one side.

"When Naresh burst in the office. When I told you not to go. I didn't understand everything you were up against."

Amy nodded. "You mean that everyone under the sun needed me at that same exact hideous moment?"

The bartender brought over their pitcher and another glass. He smiled at Amy. One of his front teeth was missing. He said, "Anything else I can get for you, pretty lady?"

"Thank you, no," said Amy.

It struck Donny that, wrung out and tired, she looked less like a Palo Alto housewife and had the skanky look guys like the bartender liked. When the dude continued to hover, she turned her focus back to Donny.

"So you're expressing regret for being such a selfish little douche bag when the whole world was raining shit down on my head? Is that what you're saying?"

Donny shook his head no, slowly.

"No?" said Amy. Then to the bartender. "Would you mind?"

"Yeah, sure, sorry," said the bartender as he backed away.

"Even he can say he's sorry," said Amy to Donny. "Say you're sorry for telling me to stay put when I needed to help my children."

"No," said Donny. "I mean I guess I'm sorry for all that, too, but that's not what I meant."

"You said you owed me an apology," said Amy.

"After you left? I kind of binge-watched your multiverses."

Amy looked at him. She reached for the pitcher. She refilled her glass.

"Hey, I haven't even had a chance to pour my first one," said Donny.

She poured him one, too.

"Donny, do you know how wrong that is? You binge-watched my multiverses? That's *my* information. That's like reading someone's diary. That's the biggest violation of privacy I can think of. I could have you arrested. I could sue you."

"Well, you sort of can't, because Furrier.com isn't regulated, it isn't even really a thing just yet, and anyway you were a willing subject. Actually, you came to me. You kind of begged me, Amy. I'm just saying."

"Oh, my God," said Amy. She rested her head in her hands. "Could any of this get any worse?"

"Well," said Donny. "Actually it could. I mean, in several of your multiverses, it gets a whole lot worse."

"What?" said Amy, looking up. "What happens to me?"

Donny sighed deeply. He took a big sip of his margarita. There was not enough salt around the glass rim but it would do.

"I'm not sure I should tell you," said Donny. "I mean, in some of the multiverses you might be a little better off, I mean, in one you live in a lot less shitty house, but in others, it's pretty fucking bad. As a friend, I'm telling you, you might be best off staying where you are."

"Friend? You're my friend?" said Amy.

"Trust me, I'm just looking out for your best interests."

"What happens in my other lives, Donny?"

"Same life, other variations," corrected Donny.

"You tell me. You tell me right now! Do I stay married to that other guy? Do I meet someone else? What happens to me?"

"You have children with other people and you love them and shit happens. But I'm not sure this does you any good to see or know unless I can take you there. And I'm ashamed to say it, I just don't have the technology yet. I mean, I'll get there. I know I'll get there. But I'm wondering about the Furrier. I mean, I think people will want to watch it; I mean, even I wanted to watch it, and it was your multiverses, Amy. I mean, I was at that computer for about eighteen hours, I forgot to eat, I didn't go home to sleep; I even shat in my pants and I didn't realize it."

"You shat in your pants watching different iterations of my life?"

"Just a little. Look, what I'm saying is it's addictive. It's way addictive. I mean, it's crack, but it's *really crack*. We could make a lot of money but we don't want everyone shitting in their pants. Especially over other people's stuff, you know? I mean, we could get in trouble. That's where Miles comes in."

"Miles comes in?"

"He's brilliant."

"Miles? My Miles?"

"He's a fresh new voice."

"He's eight years old."

"That's right. That's why he can think outside the box, and me, I'm just too inured and jaded."

Amy rolled her red eyes.

"Miles is the one who taught me that the real money will be in actually being able to go there. To multiverse-hop. To shop for the best variation or take what we find in one place and transplant it to another, having our cake and eating it. You know, escaping illness and accidents and herpes, as long as we possibly can."

"Are you saying i.e. can cure death, Donny?"

"That's not my purview. I mean, none of what I'm talking about is going to keep you from dying eventually. I mean, you're still going to die, you're going to die infinite times."

"Whew," said Amy. "That's a relief."

"I'll leave curing death to Peter Thiel to solve. He's a lot older than me so he's hungrier, you know what I'm saying? For that meal, at least. I'm a Happy Meal kind of guy myself."

His left leg was starting to fall asleep and he stamped it on the floor next to him.

"My leg fell asleep," said Donny. "Anyway, *you* called me. You asked me to meet you?"

Tears started to slip from her eyes.

"Don't cry, Amy. Please don't cry," said Donny. "Do you want me to get us another round?" Even though there was still plenty of that yellow-and-green moonshine left in that plastic pitcher. It would be better to look at the toothless bartender than to face Amy's tears.

"You know, when I saw all the stuff you were going through, I felt you. Deep feels, Amy. I mean, I felt what you felt. I never felt what another person felt before." Donny sensed his own cheeks getting hot. That had never happened before, either. "Tell me why you called?"

Amy brushed the tears from her face with her left fist.

"I wanted to be sure, I wanted to be sure that . . ." said Amy. "I mean, in any of these multiverses, do I try harder, and am I ever more careful, do I ever not fall down from the loft bed? Does the baby ever not die? I miss that baby. I've missed her my whole life."

"Nah," said Donny. "Not that baby. I mean, yes, that baby never gets born, Amy. You keep missing her. In all your lives. I'm sorry. I'm sorry I ever brought her up. I mean, you don't always fall down from the loft bed, but you never carry her to term. My guess is that it just wasn't a viable pregnancy, you know. I mean, there are other multiverses where that marriage plays out, you do try harder, in one you guys are really happy, I mean, eventually. In some you're unhappily married, you get divorced, or you just drive each other crazy."

"Do we have other children? Do we have other children together?"

"Yes, just not that one. I mean, there's other good stuff; in one you're a movie producer, not a big deal, kind of Roger Corman-y, but you make some money. In one you stay friends with Dan after you break your ankle. In fact, in one you two get kind of cozy, you even have an affair with him, even though you stay with the other guy. I mean, that part happened really late at night and I think I was floating in and out of consciousness. I mean, weirdly, though Dan is, I think, in all your multiverses, at least the ones I saw, I mean, there are infinite multiverses, I just saw the tip of the iceberg, but he was in all the ones I saw, even one where you just sit down next to him on the subway. They all had Dan in them or ended with Dan, even when you married the other guy. Or a couple of guys you don't even know about, that you haven't met here. I think there was a woman, too, maybe when you were really bitter?"

"Dan?"

"Yeah. A lot of times he's your husband, or he's your lover, or your friend, or, like I said, he tries to pick you up. He's like Waldo or something. Your multiverses are chock-full of Dan, Amy."

"Fuck Dan. What about my boys?"

"No boys."

"No boys?"

"No boys, without Dan. Not these boys anyway. Well, even you can figure that out, no? I mean, no Dan means no Things, no Jack. I mean, maybe boys with someone else? I'm a little not clear on that. I got pretty dehydrated."

"You shat your pants."

"A little bit, Amy. C'mon."

"What about girls? Did I ever have a daughter?"

"Not with Dan. I guess all his little swimmers are XY, at least with you, I don't know what happens in his multiverses, but at least in the ones of yours I found online, his sperm are all of the male persuasion. The fast ones."

"So I never had a daughter?"

"Yes, in one you have a daughter. Yes, in one you stay married to the dude downtown. Yes, in one you are happy," said Donny.

"All in the same one?" said Amy.

"Yes."

"I want to see her."

"Are you sure?"

"I need to see her."

"It's not the same daughter. I mean, the one that you lost so many times. I mean, it got kind of heartbreaking, watching you lose her over and over again. In none of the multiverses I watched, at least, does *that* baby ever get born."

"I know. But I need to see her," said Amy. "My daughter." *Daughter.* She said the word like it was a prayer. She picked up her bag. She slid her feet back into her shoes. She stood up.

Donny was still sitting down.

"Let's go," said Amy.

"Go where?" asked Donny.

"Back to the office."

"Why?"

"What do you mean 'why'?" Amy was totally fed up. "So you can get me high and make me put on those horrifying headphones and goggles. So you can torture me."

"Unnecessary," said Donny. He whipped out his phone from his front pants pocket.

"You can do the Furrier by phone already?" said Amy. "No way. You've progressed that quickly? Don't tell me you've already got an app for it."

He could tell she couldn't help herself, but that she was in fact impressed.

For a second, Donny thought about allowing her to remain impressed. But then his better side took hold.

"Nah," said Donny. "No app yet. I just took a screenshot. I knew this moment was coming."

He held up his phone. Amy took it in her hand.

He watched her light up. He watched Amy smile.

In his whole life, Donny had never seen anyone look that radiant.

Maybe there was a way to monetize *this*. He made a mental note to discuss it with Adnan and Miles.

.   .   .

It was already dark outside when Amy walked home, there was a chill in the air, and a handful of stars were thrown scattershot across the sky. Donny had asked her for a ride back to the dorm, but she couldn't bring herself to hike all the way back to the Choi house. She'd go tomorrow, she thought.

Donny ended up taking an Uber and Amy walked by herself down California Avenue with a right onto Cornell. From the street, she could see lights on in every room in the front of her house, a little diorama of suburban life. Dan was upstairs at his desk on his computer. He never pulled the curtains. As if nothing had happened! Miles was in the family room, reading a book. There was a little glow behind the shades in Jack's room. She opened the mailbox at the foot of the driveway; it was packed with catalogs surrounding letters, so she yanked them out in a little paper log and put it under one arm. She headed through the carport and walked around back, where all was blessedly dark and unilluminated, and entered the house. In the kitchen, she put the mail down on the breakfast bar, a domino fall of bills and debts. All the money they owed. God give me strength, thought Amy. She wasn't ready, but she had no choice.

She went into the family room.

"Milo," she said. "Honey, how are you doing?"

That cloud of red hair; that darling, sweet, freckled face. "Mama," said Miles, looking up. He smiled at her. "I love my book."

"I love my boy," said Amy. "I hope it wasn't too hard being stuck with Donny all day."

"It was okay," said Miles. "But we kind of lost the dog. We took him on a walk to Lake Lag."

"He'll come back when he's hungry," said Amy. "He always does."

"That's what I said," said Miles.

"Smart kid," said Amy.

"Can I finish my chapter?" said Miles. "Before dinner?"

"Yes," said Amy, because she hadn't even thought of dinner. She wanted to go for a run. She hadn't run all week.

"I'm going to run first," said Amy.

"Good," said Miles. He returned to his pages.

Next she walked up the stairs and knocked on Jack's door.

"Jack, honey, can I come in?"

"Sure, Mom," Jack said.

He was lying on his bed in the semidark, in shorts and a T-shirt. Dan's suit and shirt and tie were balled up in a corner of the floor. His laptop was open.

"Are you talking to Lily?"

"Yeah, Mom." He turned the screen to face her. In Texas, Lily was curled up on her bed with her white cat, her hair in braids, in sweats and a lacy tank top. She looked exhausted.

"Hi, Amy," said Lily. "We're just cuddling. It was such an emotional day." She seemed a little nervous, or guilty, like she'd just got caught at something. She seemed sad.

Poor girl, Amy thought. Maybe "cuddling" was Lilyese for cybersex? Amy said, "That's good that you're cuddling," not exactly sure if Lily really meant her and Jack, or her and the cat, or whatever. Amy just wanted to be reassuring. "I'm so glad you two have each other," said Amy.

"Thanks, Mom," said Jack. "I feel about a thousand years old."

She leaned over and gave him a hug. "I am so proud of you, Jack.

What you did took so much love and so much bravery. You were a great friend today, to Kevin and to his family."

"Thanks, Mom."

"Would you like me to leave you guys alone?" asked Amy.

"Thanks, Mom," said Jack. "That would be great."

Amy blew a kiss to Lily and said to Jack, "I'm going for a run, honey. I haven't given a thought to dinner."

"I'm not really hungry, anyway," said Jack. "Thing One can always have a sandwich." He gave her a look. "Dad's still here. Is he staying with us?"

"I know," said Amy. "And I don't know."

"Go for your run," said Jack. "You'll feel better."

"That's what I'm going to do," said Amy. She left the room and gently closed the door behind her. Then she walked back down the stairs.

Her thought had been to go through the kitchen and see if there was a frozen pizza or two to share, but instead she veered right into the laundry room, and after stripping off her dress and her good underwear, she searched around in the dryer and found some clean running tights and a sports bra and put them on. There were no freshly laundered tops in the dryer—it was mostly sheets and towels and socks; she pulled out two that sort of matched. Then she fished one of Jack's dirty T-shirts out of the laundry pile and pulled it on over her head. It smelled like him, like a crowded Metro in Paris in August where she and Dan had gone for a last hurrah before he was born, like the human equivalent of skunk. How could I live without that boy, she thought, I could never live without any of them. Poor Marilyn! It was unendurable. Amy knew Marilyn loved her children just as much as she did.

For one long moment, Amy counted her blessings.

Then she tied her hair into a ponytail with a rubber band she found conveniently on the floor.

She walked back outside and put on her sneakers where she'd left them on the steps so many days before, a life and a half ago. She hadn't run since Dan supposedly went to Boston, and her shoes had been moldering outside all that time.

She did a little ballet stretch, using the handrail as a barre, and then bounced up and down on her toes, listening to her ankles crack, trying to psych herself up. The stars had begun to sparkle against the darkening evening sky.

"Amy," Dan said. "We need to talk."

She turned around, and there he was. Her husband. He had been her husband for twenty-something years. He was standing in the doorway.

Somehow this struck her as funny. She started to laugh.

"What's so funny?" said Dan. He closed the door behind him and stood at the top of the steps, looking down at her.

"Nothing." Amy laughed. "Only you, Dan, you. You want to talk. What's there to talk about? You lied to me and the kids and you ran away with another woman. I don't think there's anything to talk about. I think you should pack your things and get in your car and go."

"I don't want to go," said Dan.

"You don't have a choice," said Amy. "I'm throwing you out of the house."

"It's my house, too," said Dan.

"Not anymore," said Amy. "You gave up that right."

"I did not," said Dan. "I made a mistake and I want to make it up to you."

"That's a joke," said Amy, but she wasn't laughing now. In fact, she was dead serious. "Pack your things and go." She repeated herself.

"I won't," said Dan. "I have nowhere to go to."

"Go to your girlfriend's house."

"No," said Dan. "Besides, I don't see my car."

Amy looked at the carport. For a minute, she'd forgotten that she'd forgotten the car.

"I left it at the Chois'."

"Have you been there all this time?"

"None of your business, Dan. You don't tell me where you go; I don't tell you where I go."

She started to jog in place, warming up her calves and thighs. She wanted to run. She wanted to run as far away as she could from him. She would leave this world if she had to, just to get away from him.

Dan said:

"I didn't go to Japan, I went to Boston."

"I needed to get away."

"I needed to find a job."

"I hiked the Appalachian Trail."

"I didn't mean to fall in love."

"I wanted to fall in love."

"She's got me up and moving. She makes me feel alive."

Amy was dizzy with his multiple realities; she was trying to escape all of them.

In one, she said: "That's interesting, because I am up and moving, and I basically keep you alive."

"I love you," said Dan. *"I've always loved you."*

She thought he said that, or maybe she just could not follow the conversation. She simply could not keep track of all his decisions and declarations, his truths and lies, all the alternatives and alterations.

While Dan talked, Amy could hear him and see him, but she couldn't record what she heard and saw. It was as if what she heard and saw passed right through her.

She wanted to run. She wanted to run, run, run into the bluest night. If she let him in she would have to stay and listen, so she let the words fly by, but still she stood there dreaming.

"I love her, not you," Dan said.

"I don't think I ever loved you," Dan said.

"You're my best friend, I need you to help me figure it out. No one understands me like you do."

"It was a fling; it didn't mean anything."

"It was just sex."

"We're a family. I want to preserve our family."

"I've been depressed. I've been out of work. A man needs to have work to feel vital and alive."

"We should both think of the children."

"I think the children should come first."

"I'm torn between my love for her and my love for the children."

What about me? screamed Amy. What about me? Aren't you torn by your love for me? she screamed at him in the seclusion of her mind.

"I went with her to Japan," Dan said, *"but nothing inappropriate happened between us."*

"I think we're onto something big with this story," Dan said.

Maybe he said that. Who knew? Who cared?

"I would never risk my marriage."

"I'm a happily married man."

"Our marriage is over."

"I am attached to you."

"I am motherfucking attached to you."

There were tears now, this time. Whatever planet they were on. Whatever universe. Her husband of twenty-something years was crying in his beer.

They were separated by a million miles.

But then Dan reached out his hand. He said, "Amy, come back inside. I love you. I love the kids. I'm sorry I hurt you. If I could take it back I probably would. Even though in a way it was good for me. Even if in a way it was also good for us. But I want to make this work. More than I've ever wanted anything in my life. You're my wife. I love you. Please. Please. Come with me."

His hand was outstretched. Amy could see it from the other side.

Out of the solid wall of night, Squidward erupted, dashing past her in a blur of fiery fur and muscle. Where had he been all this time? He circled through the carport, and like a bolt of lightning streaked down the block. Instantly, he was a dark shadow on the corner, his eyes glinting an unholy red under the haze of the street-light, waiting for her, for Amy, to join him.

She could smell the eucalyptus.

This is what I have instead of heroin, Amy thought. I can run.

She looked up at Dan. She looked at his hand.

His face was flushed with hope.

"I hate you, Dan," said Amy.

His head snapped to the side, as if she had reached out and slapped him. Still his hand stayed outstretched, waiting for her.

"But, apparently," said Amy, "I have also loved you infinitely."

The words hung in the air between them.

"Me, too," said Dan.

She climbed up the steps, and although she didn't take his hand, she opened the door for him. And then Amy followed her husband back inside their house.

AUTHOR'S NOTE

MY FEARS about and obsession with the Internet have no bounds. Like my character Dan Messinger, I often find myself looking up a tiny fact online and reemerging into the world hours later, enraged, enraptured, sometimes spent, and in need of an intellectual shower, dizzy with information. This book is a work of fiction, but it was heavily researched—a Gordian knot of fact and fantasy. One of the blessings of my job as fiction chair at the MFA program at the New School is access to brilliant young writers, some of whom have worked with me as research assistants over the years and some of whom just fed me great information. Many thanks to Ben Hurst, Jaclyn Alexander, Stephanie Danler, Rebekah Bergman, Alan W. Holt, Catherine Bloomer, Kris-Anne Madaus (who taught me the term "balayage," among a thousand other things), Michaelene Meinhardt, and Yasmin Zaher.

When I started this novel, even I didn't know what I was writing about, except that I was haunted by the tragedies that befell the people of Fukushima, Japan, after the earthquake, tsunami, and nuclear meltdown in 2011. My students fed me a steady diet of research from dead-tree publications and a million and one Internet sites (some more reliable than others). Rebekah Bergman interviewed Norman Kleiman of Columbia University's School of Public Health, who answered some of our questions regarding radiation exposure. Thank you, Dr. Kleiman. Thank you (but no thank you) to Tepco, the Japanese utility company overseeing the cleanup at Fukushima, whose website was useful to me even if their efforts on the ground have been lacking. Thank you, Al Jazeera and Eric Lafforgue, for your photo-essay "Fukushima's Surfers Riding on Radioactive Waves." Thank you, the *Mercury News*, the *San Francisco Chronicle*, the *Stanford Daily*, the *Japan Times*, *Mother Jones*, the *Guardian*, the *New York Times*, and the *Washington Post* (particularly for an article written by Ariana Cha, "Tech Titans Defying Death"). Thank you, Google. Thank you, Trip Advisor. A shout-out to Yelp. Quora! Wikipedia and the hive mind! Conspiracy theorists! Thank you, Renegade Writer. Dan Boeckman. The Museum of Fine Arts in Boston. Google Earth. I tried wherever possible within the narrative of this story to integrate and cite my sources.

Thirty-some years of visiting the Stanford campus, where my husband grew up, and a long-ago tour of Google Mountain View (thank you, Leslie Leland) gave birth to my fascination with Silicon Valley culture. I am indebted to Walter Isaacson and his biography of Steve Jobs. As a fiction writer, there are all these crazy, streaming, invented narratives that are forever playing out inside my head. Max Tegmark's book *Our Mathematical Universe: My Quest for the Ultimate Nature of Reality* finally gave me a name for this that didn't imply madness: multiverse theory. It also gave me the governing idea for this book. *Chaos Monkeys: Obscene Fortune and Random Failure in Silicon Valley* by Antonio García Martínez was also a terrific tech-industry resource. Hannah Rosin's article "The Suicide Clusters at Palo Alto High Schools" in the *Atlantic* helped me to understand the sad contagion that colored my niece's and nephews' experiences growing up in Palo Alto. I spent many hours searching blogs, high school newspapers, and community newsletters for information regarding the emotional cost of the loss of these young lives.

My character Yoshi Hibayashi was inspired by a video produced by *Vice* on Naoto Matsumura, a man who returned to his home in the no-go zone in Japan to take care of his abandoned animals and stayed; just like my character does. But to be clear, Yoshi is fictive;

Naoto Matsumura is not. Similarly, I had a profound artistic crush on a photographer who took analogous photos and videos to the ones my character Maryam did in an exhibition that preceded her trip to Japan. Again, Maryam is purely fictive and is not meant to represent anyone living or dead in any manner.

I am very grateful to the Aspen Institute, specifically Aspen Words, its director Adrienne Brodeur, and the Catto Shaw Foundation for providing me with a monthlong residence in Woody Creek, Colorado. I don't think I've ever been more productive than during that glorious stay. Isa Catto and Daniel Shaw, I will never forget your hospitality and kindness.

This book was profoundly shaped by the intelligence, wit, meticulousness, patience, and care of my editor Jennifer Barth. Anyone who says, "Nobody line-edits anymore" has not met the divine Jennifer. Sloan Harris has been my literary agent for over twenty years; more, he is my friend, confidant, coach, truth-teller, and has stood steadfastly by my side through so much. I have tears in my eyes while writing this.

I am ever grateful to the cast and crew at the New School for their support and friendship. Thank you, lifelong friend and photographer Denise Bosco, for the gentleness of your lens and the generosity of your spirit. My civilian (i.e., not writers) mental health team: Joan Aguado, Eve Evans, Melissa Katz, Steve Lipman, and Natalie K. Fisher. There are no words to thank you for your support all these many years.

Finally, to the West Coast Handys, in *all* their iterations, thank you for making California my second home. As for the East Coast Handys, my squad: in-house editor, Bruce, and our children, Zoe and Isaac. You fill my days with light and love. I'm so honored that you continue to put up with me.

ABOUT THE AUTHOR

HELEN SCHULMAN writes fiction, nonfiction, and screenplays. Her most recent novel, *This Beautiful Life,* was a *New York Times* bestseller. She is a professor of writing and the fiction chair at the MFA program at the New School. She lives in New York City with her family.

ML 11/2018